DARK STATE

JASON TRAPP BOOK 1

JACK SLATER

NOTE

Please also note that this book, *Dark State*, contains scenes of a violent nature, and deals with themes of terrorism that sometimes entangle innocent victims. If this doesn't sound like something you'd enjoy, maybe it would be best to choose a different book!

I hope you enjoy the book!
Jack Slater.

1

The California Zephyr Amtrak line is often described as the most beautiful rail journey in all of North America. The route runs from Emeryville, California to Chicago, Illinois, and takes over fifty hours to complete.

The two men boarded the Zephyr in Provo, Utah at 4:35 a.m., using tickets booked under assumed names and paid for using prepaid credit cards. They were of Middle Eastern extraction and carried no form of identification, save fake drivers licenses that would stand up to a moderate amount of scrutiny. The licenses bore the seals of different states – Virginia and Nevada, a detail which investigators would puzzle over for months, but which meant nothing.

They did not acknowledge each other at the station. They could not have if they wanted to, for they had never met, nor seen so much as a photograph of the man with whom they would go down in history. It was basic operational security, and both men knew it was for the best. And besides, what they were to accomplish did not require idle conversation, just steely resolve.

They had arrived in Provo by different means. The taller of

the two men had purchased a used car from Craigslist in Phoenix, Arizona, and paid cash. It was not registered under his name – real or otherwise. The shorter, and younger, man had made his way there by Greyhound bus from Las Vegas, after discarding his worldly possessions in a trashcan outside the station.

Each had rented a motel room for a night, paid for in crumpled, non-sequential bills, and freshened up before heading out. They dressed smartly in case they were stopped for any reason by local cops, and had believable cover stories that were more than skin deep. Both spoke more than passable English, accented of course, but were comfortable with American idioms. Their beards were shaved.

The younger man was booked into an ice climbing "experience" the next day, along with a wife who didn't exist; the elder had lift tickets and equipment reserved for a day on the slopes at Sundance ski resort only fifteen miles away. As it happened, neither was stopped, asked a question, or even spoke a word that night, beyond ordering dinner at nondescript local diners.

One visited Lakeside Storage, the other Provo Central Storage, where each accessed a unit that had been rented months before by more men they had never met. Inside they found hard luggage cases – both used, so as not to stand out, and in different colors. Everything they would need was in those bags. Nothing had been left to chance.

As they stood in line, waiting for their tickets to be checked, surrounded by yawning travellers—vacationers and businessmen look much the same that early in the morning—they understood the righteousness of what they would do that day. The message that they would send to the entire world. Both were nervous. It would be unnatural not to be. After all, they would die that day. Glorious deaths, to be sure, and they would be rewarded with eternal Paradise, but they would die nonetheless – and no man goes into the darkness without feeling at least a hint of trepidation.

"Ticket, sir."

The younger man, his head filled with visions of the future, took a second to respond, and the Amtrak employee thrust out his hand impatiently.

"Sir, I need to see your ticket."

"Of course, of course," the man replied in accented English as he hurriedly reached into his nondescript bomber jacket.

As he did, his eyes passed over a woman, a mother, with her young daughter and several pieces of luggage. The child had blond hair and beautiful blue eyes, but so early in the morning she was struggling to keep them open. She was holding a little white teddy bear.

"Come on, Anna," the mother urged. "Stay awake a little longer, and then you can fall asleep on the train. Just not yet, okay honey?"

"Okay, Mommy," the little girl replied. "I will."

The sight of the mother and child, dressed for a holiday, or to visit grandparents, might have warmed the man's heart, if he had been there for any other reason. But he wasn't, and it did not. If anything, it was a reminder of what he had lost: a wife and a child just like this little girl, stolen from him in the night by an American bomb.

There wasn't enough left of either to fill a burial shroud. With his family gone but unburied, the man's grief fermented into rage. Rage drove him to violence.

And violence had brought him here.

What investigators would not learn until some weeks later was that the man was Iraqi. His real name was Raheem. He was in his early thirties, and this was not his first encounter with bureaucratic American efficiency.

Raheem was first apprehended in 2006 by military police working alongside the 503rd 'First Rock' Infantry Regiment outside of Ramadi, the capital of Iraq's Al Anbar province, after an unseen, unheard Predator drone circling overhead identified him as a suspected insurgent. Lucky for him, military intelligence refused to okay a kinetic strike, and ordered that he be brought in for questioning instead.

As he was discovered in the middle of the night beside an unburied Improvised Explosive Device – a converted M107 high explosive, 155 mm artillery shell – Raheem was lucky not to simply have been shot and buried in an unmarked grave.

An extrajudicial killing would, of course, be illegal. Forbidden by both the Rules of Engagement and the Uniform Code of Military Justice. But in Al Anbar province in 2006, the 503rd was losing good men every day to IED attacks, and the general feeling in the ranks was that the only good militant was a dead one. So, that day, Raheem was very lucky indeed that it was the MPs who apprehended him, and not the fine men of the First Rock.

America would never know it, never learn that history could have been changed by an act most would consider reprehensible – and yet which, more than a decade later, could have saved so many lives.

"That's fine, sir. You've got a Superliner suite, car number seven. Next."

Raheem shook off the unaccustomed wave of memories, and noticed he was holding up the line. He chided himself silently, knowing he had only one job: to remain unnoticed. He had his mission, one that Allah willing he would complete. And Allah no doubt willed it so. He had provided everything so far through his servant, from passports to weapons to instructions to be on this very train at this very time. All so that Raheem could be remembered for generations as the man who struck the first blow in the final crippling of the Great Satan, America.

THE TWO MEN lay in their cabins, at opposite ends of the ten-car train, for over seven hours. Neither could sleep, their brains suffused with adrenaline, cortisol flooding their veins. Their heartrates were elevated, and the younger man was sweating slightly. The rhythmic *clack-clack-clack* of the locomotive's wheels did not disturb either as they silently prayed.

They did not perform the *rak'ah*, the prescribed movements and words typically performed by Muslims, just in case someone entered their cabin. The doors were locked, of course, but they knew it was better to be safe than sorry. After their work today, Allah would forgive any transgressions against his faith.

As the train pulled out of Glenwood Springs, Colorado, Raheem pulled a cell phone out of his jacket pocket. He inserted the sim card and battery and turned it on. He did not know if anyone would call, but he had his instructions. Outside the cabin window, the small town disappeared into the distance and the rugged beauty of the mountains returned.

His instructions were simple: if the train departed on time then he was to conduct their operation as planned, at 30 minutes past the hour. If, for any reason, it did not, then 10 minutes after the train finally left Glenwood Springs, they were to begin. If he received no telephone call, then he was to destroy both the phone and sim card and throw both out of the window.

"*Allahu akbar*," he whispered under his breath, reaching up to the empty top bunk of his cabin. He flicked open the battered hard travel case, revealing its contents: a brand-new Brügger & Thomet MP9 Maschinenpistole with a shoulder sling and folding stock, two G19 handguns, a set of combat webbing complete with holsters for both pistols, more loaded magazines than he could count, and half a dozen green-painted

M67 fragmentation grenades. The weapons – grenades notwithstanding – had been recently test-fired, cleaned and oiled. They were ready.

As was he.

The phone rang. A jolt of adrenaline flooded the Iraqi's brain. Why would his handler phone now? To call off the operation?

Ignore it, he thought, dreaming of the rewards waiting for him in Paradise. *Your duty is to Allah, not to him.*

But Raheem answered the call. Though they had never met he owed this servant of Allah too much, and trusted his judgment implicitly.

The voice on the other end of the line sounded the same as always: flat and tinny from the software being used to disguise his identity. "Raheem?"

The man's reply was short and curt. "Yes."

"You are ready?"

"I am."

"Good. Everything is in place. I wanted to check that you are prepared to do what must be done."

Raheem's response was harsh and angry. "You doubt my faith?"

The flat voice paused for a long second. "I do not. Go with Allah, my brother. The whole world will be watching."

The line clicked dead, and Raheem discarded the phone.

With seventeen minutes left on the timer on his Casio wristwatch, Raheem made his final preparations. He shrugged on the desert-colored Army surplus combat webbing and loaded the pouches around his waist with ammunition.

In total, by the time he was done, Raheem was loaded up with almost 500 rounds, six fragmentation grenades, and filled with a sense of cool, calm determination.

As the General Electric P42 locomotive pulled its ten-car train out of Glenwood Springs, Raheem raised the blinds that covered the windows, and took one last look at the peaceful snow-dusted hillside outside, zipping past so fast it was almost a blur.

The alarm on Raheem's wrist beeped. The one-time Iraqi militant grasped his MP9 to his chest, exhaled deeply, and stepped out of his cabin to face his destiny.

2

Jason Trapp sat in a café in Boston's Chinatown district, watching the world go past the steamed-up windows and wondering if he would ever feel a part of it again. It was eight in the morning, on February first, and he had been there for the best part of an hour, observing the street – watching for anything and anyone that didn't fit. So far, he was all out. As far as he could tell, the street was clear. No one was watching, no one was waiting. Not for him, or anyone else.

Trapp knew there was no reason that he should have picked up a tail. After all, the world, and more importantly his former employers in Langley, thought that he was dead.

He liked being a dead man. There was a freedom to it. He had spent the last twenty years in the service of his country, shuttling from war zone to war zone, solving America's problems with the barrel of a gun. That kind of work does things to a man. Changes him. Makes him jumpy.

The kind of jumpy that had him sitting opposite the street from his objective, pretending not to study every person passing by for a hint of a weapon, or the subtle tell in their walk that hinted at military training. It was an old habit, and it died hard.

It was better that way, Trapp thought, since the alternative was ending six feet under the ground. He'd screwed up six months ago and almost lost everything. It had taken that long to recover, at least from his physical wounds. The mental scars would take longer to heal.

Absently, Trapp fingered the faded scar that ran the circumference of his neck like the mark of a noose. It was the reason for his call sign: Hangman. It was a name fit for a dead man, he thought. The man who'd given him that name was gone, too. And that was why he was here.

The scar was faded now, the line a gentle white against his weathered, tanned skin, not the raw red it had once been. It was marked at intervals with thicker cuts, like beads on a necklace. The scar was far older than the ones he'd acquired in Yemen; the mark of a desperate childhood. Trapp caught what he was doing and grimaced. It was an ugly habit, one he'd quit years ago.

But it was back.

He attracted the waitress' attention and motioned her over. As far as he could tell, the coast was clear, and sitting here wallowing in the past wasn't doing him a damn bit of good. He had a job to do, a man to see, and a conscience to clear. In that order.

"Can I get you something?" she asked. She was Chinese, at least by birth, but spoke unaccented English.

"Just the check."

Trapp left cash and didn't stick around to pick up the change. He didn't tip either enough or too little to give the girl any reason to remember him. Just another anonymous face in the sea of tourists she served every day.

Mostly, Trapp looked like any other man. His face wore a rough, dark stubble that could be shaved off or grown out at will, and often was. He was tall, at least six three, and topped with dark brown hair that was tousled and overgrown, intentionally disguising his rugged good looks. His sizeable, muscular frame was similarly lost in the bulk of a jacket that was two sizes too large.

The only outward clue that he wasn't like other men could be found in his left eye. The right was a cold battleship gray, cold in the gloom and glittering in the light. But the left was different: split in two, black as night on one side, the same icy gray on the other.

It was a benign medical condition that affected one in ten thousand, and Trapp had never bothered to learn its name. In a way, his eye resembled the Rio Negro in Brazil; the black river which meets another without their waters ever mixing.

The locals in that area believe the Rio Negro births shapeshifters. Perhaps Trapp was one, just born in the wrong place at the wrong time. A wraith in the night.

He stood up, shifting the chair back with a heavy, dark boot, and left the café. The Beretta 9 mm felt comforting where it sat in the groove of his lower back. He was wearing a Yankees cap pulled low over his face, dark jeans and a sheepskin lined black leather jacket that he'd picked up in a Goodwill a few blocks over. The leather was soft and supple and wouldn't stick if he needed to draw his weapon.

Trapp's unusual eyes scanned right and left, falling on face after face as he stepped into the streets of Chinatown. Except for the Beretta, he was only carrying a small wad of cash, a safety deposit box card, and an envelope. The last item felt heaviest.

He walked across the street, stopping at a small bodega. It was run by an elderly Chinese man, wrapped up warm enough against the biting cold of the winter morning that Trapp thought he'd survive a climb up Everest. He stepped into the shop, making sure his face was obscured from the security camera above the entrance. It probably wasn't functional, he thought, and even if it was it almost certainly didn't have a high enough resolution to pose him any problems in the future. But Trapp was a careful man who knew that his enemies only had to get lucky once.

He grabbed a nondescript black rucksack off a hook against the wall and turned to the cashier.

"How much?"

The man looked up from his cell phone. Judging by the tinny sounds emanating from the slim black device he was watching some Mandarin talk show. Trapp almost grinned. He didn't carry a cell phone. Didn't have anyone looking to contact him. Especially not these days. But if even this old guy had one, Trapp figured he was about the only person left who didn't.

"Ten dollar," the old man said, in thickly accented English. Then he squinted. "No – that one, fifteen dollar."

Trapp peeled a bill out of his jacket's inner pocket. His fingers grazed against the envelope as he did, and he winced.

"Got change for a Jackson?"

The man nodded, bending his arthritic body to retrieve a five-dollar bill from the register.

"Hey, you need a bag for that?"

"I just bought one."

Trapp stepped out of the bodega with the empty rucksack slung over his shoulder. His eyes flickered right and left once again, fastidious as always with his countersurveillance routine. He knew there were a million ways someone could track him, and there was only so much he could do if someone was observing him through Boston PD's camera network, or had rented an apartment a few floors up, and was even now gazing down at him through the lens of a DSLR.

But he thought it was unlikely. He had a pretty good sense for when he was being watched, and that instinct wasn't telling him anything, not right now.

Trapp walked across the street and entered the building he'd been observing for the last hour. The sign on the door read *Orchid Federal Savings Bank*. The bank only had a few branches up and down the East Coast, and was mainly used by Chinese immigrants. It was old world – they didn't ask very many questions, and that's the way Trapp liked it.

"Hello, sir," a smiling woman called out. "Can I help you?"

He walked up to the counter, as always careful to make sure his face was hidden.

"I'd like to open my safety deposit box," he said. "And I've got a letter of authorization here from my –" He paused, and a trained observer would have picked up a flicker of emotion on his face. "– my friend. I need to pick something up from his as well."

"Of course, sir," the bank teller said. According to the name on her tag, she was called Mei. It was a nice name, Trapp thought. "Can I see your card? I'll need to see the letter as well."

"Sure thing."

As Trapp slid the two documents over the counter, he thought about how the contents of the envelope had come into his possession. A special operator's career could, if they were lucky, be a long one. After all, they were the best of the best. Given millions of dollars of training, flown on well-maintained helicopters by dedicated special forces aviators. Over the course of a long career, the US of A might invest twenty million dollars in training a tier one operator. If the government was good at anything, it was making sure an investment like that didn't go to waste.

On the flipside, in organizations like the three-letter agency that once employed Trapp, operators were treated as deniable. If anything went wrong on a mission, if they were careless enough to allow themselves to be captured, if their existence merely became embarrassing to the US government, a man like Trapp might find himself cut off behind enemy lines.

No exfiltration plan. No pension. Don't pass go. Don't collect a million dollars. Just disappear.

That was the reason that Trapp had rented the safety deposit box in the first place. He'd done it almost ten years ago now. He had others elsewhere, but this was the primary. His backstop. If everything went to shit, the contents of this particular box would buy him enough time to breathe.

At least, that was the theory.

"Thank you, Mr. Flynn," Mei said, tapping something into her computer terminal as she looked at the assumed name on the card. "I'll just be a second."

"Take your time."

Once every six months, Trapp purchased a burner phone with cash. Using its Internet connection he navigated to a specific webpage – its address just a random collection of alphanumeric characters. Once there he entered a code and reset a timer. Somewhere, a letter just like the one Mei was currently reading would sit for another six months, and maybe another six after that.

As long as he reset the timer.

For Trapp to have received the envelope now lying on the counter in front of him meant that someone was dead. But he knew that already. He had been there when it happened. Had been unable to do anything to prevent it.

"Okay, you can follow me, sir. Everything looks good here. Have you got the keys?"

Trapp nodded, pulling his T-shirt collar down a couple of inches to reveal a stainless steel necklace, like a soldier's dog tag chain, hanging around his neck.

"Perfect. Then follow me."

Trapp did as he was told. The bank had certainly seen better days, but Trapp liked the fact that they weren't wasting his money front of house. He trailed the bank teller down a flight of stairs into the basement and turned away as requested while she punched a code into the vault door. It clicked open.

"You know which boxes you're looking for?" Mei asked.

"Yeah."

"Great. I'll wait outside. Just yell if you need something."

Trapp didn't say another word as Mei pulled the heavy vault door open. Behind it lay hundreds of safety deposit boxes, chrome locks accenting polished stainless steel. The air smelled of stale disinfectant, like it always did. He walked confidently over to his own, which he hadn't accessed in a couple of years, lifting the chain from around his neck as he moved. He inserted the key, twisted, and waited for the click to signal the mechanism had unlocked.

The moment it did he opened the door and pulled the box out, setting it on a stainless steel table that stood in the middle of the room. He lifted the lid and was pleased but unsurprised to see the contents exactly as he'd left them. He swung the rucksack off his shoulders, unzipped it, and began filling it with stacks of hundred-dollar bills, each about an inch thick. They were worth ten thousand dollars each, and by the time he was done stacking them, the rucksack held a little over $1.1 million.

And then there was nothing left but brushed steel. Trapp just stood there, dreading what came next. The only memorial service the best man he'd ever known was likely to get. And Trapp was here to zero out his life savings.

"Just get on with it," he said, his voice husky in the deathly quiet of the bank vault. A nuclear bomb could go off overhead, and Trapp doubted if he'd even notice.

"Sir – did you say something? Are you done?" Mei called out.

"Give me a couple of minutes."

The necklace clinked in Trapp's fingers as he pulled the key from his own box, heavier than it had any right to feel. He chewed his lip, then chided himself once more for procrastinating and unlocked the second. He knew that there wouldn't be anything as melodramatic as an 'if you're reading this, then I'm already dead' letter. That wasn't Ryan's style. Besides, a courier had delivered that message with the authorization document a few days before, just not in so many words.

Just as he had done with his own, Trapp set the second safety deposit box on the steel table. It was weightier than his own, but only fractionally so.

The first thing he noticed upon unlocking and opening it was the pistol, along with half a dozen neatly stacked magazines. Despite his somber mood, a slight grin forced itself to the corners of his lips. Trapp shook his head.

Ryan, you paranoid bastard.

He considered pocketing the weapon, but even for a man of Trapp's not inconsiderable bulk the Desert Eagle was a hell of a weapon. A forty-four caliber, the pistol packed a punch that could tear a fist-sized hole out of a man's side. In Trapp's view, it was overkill. But Ryan Price always did have a flair for the dramatic.

Maybe that was what had drawn the two men together; opposites attracting like fire and ice. Trapp the shy, awkward teen, no family left, and broken by the tragedy in his past. Price the exact opposite: a tall, blond kid from the streets of Boston, son of a bartender, mouth as loud as his hair.

Trapp set the weapon aside before continuing. Just as his own had been, Price's box was stacked with cash. Dollars, of course. Euros too, thick folds of five hundred denomination notes. Fewer of them than the stacks of hundred-dollar bills, but more valuable. And all of it taken from black budgets and slush funds, from suitcases of cash delivered in the night to warlords in conflict zones across the globe. A little here. A little there. The CIA knew exactly what its operators were doing and turned a blind eye.

It was part of the bargain, if never stated aloud – 'if we

disavow you, you're toast. So you'd better be prepared. We won't stand in your way if you don't get too greedy'.

Trapp started filling the remaining space in the rucksack with Price's cash. It didn't take long. Combined with his own take he'd have enough to retire on a beach somewhere, drink beer and scuba dive until the end of his days. Maybe take up deep-sea fishing. Buy a charter boat. Take tourists out. The full works.

As he was almost done, something fell out from the jacketed cash. A Polaroid photo, judging by the shape, though it had fallen face down.

"The hell?" he muttered.

Trapp picked up the photo and flipped it around. The memory hit him like a truck. Him and Ryan, taken at a Company barbecue maybe three years before. Sun flickering through the trees at the Farm. They were both younger then. Less worn. He remembered it being taken, and the scent of meat sizzling over the coals. Remembered *who* had taken it.

Mike Mitchell. The deputy director of the CIA's Special Activities Division. A friend, once. And the man that now Trapp suspected of betraying him. His jaw tightened, and his heart beat a little faster as he contemplated once more what had to be done. He would be called a traitor. But that wasn't the truth. They had been sold out, and Ryan had died for it. What lay ahead wasn't murder, it was justice.

"I'm done," Trapp called out after sliding the two safety deposit boxes back into their respective slots. He doubted he would be back. But the leases were paid up for another twenty years, so unless the place got robbed, he didn't have to worry about anyone stumbling across the fake IDs, or the Desert Eagle.

Trapp walked out of the vault, rucksack heavier on his shoulder now. He noticed Mei's eyes on him, on the bulge in the bag. Knew what she was thinking. Maybe a younger version of himself would have taken her with him. Gone to that beach. Whiled away his days drinking and screwing until they were both worn out, or dead, or both.

But this money wasn't Trapp's. Not really. And in his world, the world of shadows, wraiths and shapeshifters, there was no currency more valuable than a man's honor. So it was time to pay a debt.

3

G lenwood Springs has a population of 9,962 residents. Its police department employs just seven full-time officers and several part-time administrative staff. The most common cause for a local citizen to contact the department is due to a misdial, which the previous month had occurred 62 times.

Garfield County, however, does maintain a Special Weapons and Tactics unit. While they frequently send representatives to the US National SWAT Competition, they are not particularly well-trained, and do not perform well when compared with their peers. With a limited budget, in statistically one of the safest counties in the entire continental United States, this is no great surprise.

Sadly for the 422 passengers aboard Amtrak train number Six on the California Zephyr line, no response time could be good enough to save them from the onslaught that lay ahead.

At precisely 12:28 p.m., Mountain Daylight Time, a small explosive charge detonated on a signal box about 10 miles down the track. Within seconds, a warning message blared in the Amtrak Control Center in Chicago. Seconds after that, the driver of Amtrak train number Six was informed that there was a technical issue further up the line, and that until more information could be established, he was to halt the train immediately.

He did so. It was the last thing he ever did.

Raheem's partner shot out the lock on the door that separated the locomotive with the rest of the train, stepped through, and fired three rounds into the driver's chest before spinning around and heading back down into the main body of the train. The man was dead before the locomotive stopped rolling.

Raheem shivered as he heard the sound of gunfire. It reminded him of years spent fighting in the desert. First against the Americans, who had defiled his country. Then against the Iranian-backed *Shiite* militiamen who had attempted to take control of its burning wreckage.

"*Allahu akbar*," he whispered once again.

God is the greatest. It was a statement so obvious, it did not need saying. And yet he said it anyway. Because it was the truth. God was the greatest, and he, Raheem, was his most faithful servant. His reward would come not in this life, but the next.

Shrieks of horror punctuated the carriages. "Oh my God," a high-pitched voice screamed. "Frank, Frank, did you hear that? It sounded like –"

After stepping out into an empty hallway, he proceeded up the train, weapon braced at his shoulder, handguns holstered against his chest. His MP9 barked twice as a man stepped into the corridor. Perhaps his name was Frank. Raheem would never know, as the man's now lifeless body slid to the floor, arterial blood spraying from his neck and painting the walls of the hallway a bright red.

"One," Raheem muttered.

More shrieks now. Animal howls of terror as man became beast. Some would freeze, Raheem knew. They would be the easiest to kill, and he would do so, sending them to Allah himself to judge. And they would be found wanting.

Raheem's MP9 clattered almost continuously as he stepped through the train carriage, the shot selector on the side of the weapon set to fire three-round bursts. The short-barrelled machine pistol was perfect for the cramped environment of the train. Unlike a rifle, it didn't catch against any impediments. Raheem held it close to his body, where no hero could reach out and attempt to take it from him.

"Please," the blond woman from the platform screamed, her beautiful daughter nowhere in sight, "I have a –"

"Two."

The Iraqi suspected she was about to say that she had a child, that he should spare her life, oh please, just spare the child's life, but he never found out, because he put a tightly-aimed burst of lead through her body, at least two of the rounds exiting the ribcage and punching through the seat in front of her and sending up a spray of white cushion stuffing like a flurry of snow.

"Run!"

Raheem shot the man in the head while his lips were still moving, the screamed command not yet dead before he was. He paused for a second after doing so, watching the fine spray of red mist, fragments of skull and brain that briefly filled the air before falling back to earth. It was a damn good shot.

Or it would have been, if he'd been aiming for the man's forehead instead of his chest. Then he shot the man's wife, and she slumped over his body. It was almost poetic. In sickness and in health. To love and to cherish.

"Four."

Till death do us part.

Out of the corner of his eye, he saw that he had missed a young man, maybe nineteen years old, built like a linebacker, wearing a red baseball cap pulled backwards over his head.

The kid must have been cowering behind the seat as he first stepped through the coach, but now he wanted to be a hero. He lunged toward Raheem's weapon, attempting to pull it from the terrorist's hands.

"Fuck," Raheem muttered in flawless Arabic, taking a step back to avoid the kid's outstretched fingers.

He figured he probably didn't need to bother speaking English anymore. Judging by the trail of death he had wreaked through the carriage already, and the sound of gunfire and abject terror coming from the other end of the train, the ruse was most definitely up.

He took a step back, letting the MP9 thud against his chest and hang loose against the strap that was wrapped around his torso. As the kid charged toward him, scrunched up with fear and rage, not knowing he was about to die, Raheem clenched his fist, twisted his body, and smacked him in the temple. The boy was half stunned before he knew what was happening, and Raheem took full advantage of the situation.

He reached down, grasped his black MP9, careful not to touch the barrel, which would now be easily hot enough to blister his skin, and with all his strength he brought the stock of the weapon down on the back of the boy's skull. It connected with a sickening thud, and his victim crumpled.

"Five," Raheem said with undisguised pleasure, as for good measure he took a step back, brought the stock of the MP9 to his shoulder and fired a single round into the kid's now limp body.

He looked up and saw faces of horror staring back at him. It was like the world had stopped for a second to watch the little vignette of terror.

"*Allahu akbar,*" he said, conversationally. God is great.

Raheem fired three-round bursts until the magazine was empty. He could taste pennies at the back of his tongue, the air was so thick with blood. Now the infidels began to run, clambering over seats and tables and the bodies that littered the floor like an obstacle course.

It just made it easier for him. Aim and fire. Aim and fire. The empty magazine dropped to the floor, and within a second Raheem had replaced it. The fat, lazy Americans fell one after another, just like the cartridge cases spat relentlessly from the side of the MP9 cradled in his hands.

He had spent months in training camps, from the deserts of Libya to freezing mountain passes in Syria. Back then, mostly, he'd been taught to fire the Kalashnikov AK-47. It was, in his opinion, a superior weapon. It never jammed, could fire whether it was wet or dirty or hadn't been cleaned in months. It was chambered with a heavier round. But this gun would do, too. Any weapon used to kill an American, the pathetic spawn of the Great Satan, was a good one.

Raheem emptied another magazine, and then another as he stepped through into the second of the train's coaches. Behind him, men, women and children lay dead or dying, some gurgling as blood filled their lungs, others crying out for mothers, brothers, fathers, sisters, lovers. To the Iraqi, it was like the sound of an angelic choir.

In front of the terrorist – for that was what he was – the coach was more empty than the last. Those who could had run. The others, the freezers, were no threat. He had time.

He reached down to the webbing around his waist and selected a fragmentation grenade. The M67 grenade, designed as a replacement to the M26 grenades used during the Vietnam War, had been sold as part of an arms deal to supply the Mexican Marine Corps. The batch that this particular grenade came from had found its way into the hands of the cartels some years before.

How it had made its way back across the border, perhaps no one would ever know. Raheem certainly didn't. But if he *had* known its history, he would have found satisfaction in the knowledge that the Great Satan's greed in selling weapons all across the globe had come back to haunt it.

"There is no God but Allah, and Mohammed is his messenger," Raheem murmured as he pulled the grenade's safety lever.

He tossed it as far down into the previous carriage as he could, crouched out of the way, and counted.

Four, five...

Six.

The grenade exploded, filling the carriage behind him with shards of steel from its casing. The fragments ripped through windows, seats, tables, and the bodies of the wounded and the dead. Three survivors, who had pressed themselves against the floor of the train when the gunfire broke out and covered themselves in dark clothing so as not to be noticed, were ripped apart, after the grenade fell just a couple of yards away from where they hid.

As the sound of the explosion faded away, Raheem experienced a sensation of complete calm. Of bliss. As though his entire life had been leading up to this moment, as if this was the task for which he had been born. Of all the battles that the Iraqi had fought, against the infidel soldiers of the Great Satan, against the Iranians, this was the greatest.

And God would reward him.

He gripped his weapon. Ejected another empty magazine. Looked to his waist, noticed with surprise that he was out of magazines, and discarded the weapon entirely.

Raheem drew the first of his Glock pistols and caressed it with a lover's touch. He strode forward once more and murdered every infidel who stood in his path.

4

rapp was seated in a dive bar on Prince Street in Boston near the waterfront, nursing a beer. It was barely a quarter to one in the afternoon, and it wasn't his first. He was there because he had a debt to pay, owed to a man he'd never met.

Or at least, a man he'd never introduced himself to.

The room was decorated with American flags, and had an M1903 Springfield rifle mounted over the bar, along with a variety of other military memorabilia. Trapp knew the rifle had belonged to the man's grandfather, who had carried it in the trenches at Belleau Wood, near the River Marne in the First World War. Could still see the mark of a bullet that had scarred the wooden stock, saving its owner's life. Or that was how the story went, and Trapp should know: he'd heard it often enough.

The man was called Joshua. Joshua Price. And for almost the first time in his life, Trapp was having trouble working up the courage to introduce himself.

Joshua Price was a friendly man, as far as he could tell from this distance. Like his brother, he stood well over six foot tall, with light blond hair and shocking blue eyes. He wasn't a twin, but it was a close enough resemblance to make Trapp shiver with recognition. It was the eyes, Trapp thought, before he was whisked two decades into the past.

The bunched electrical cord whistles through the air like a whip. It cracks against the little boy's back, leaving red, angry welts in places, deep, bloody scores in others. The boy's body strains against his restraints, rope biting into his wrists. His frame is weak, more like a boy of five than nine. His mother cowers in the corner, her palms pressed against an already swelling eye socket. She is a broken woman. The boy understands that already – she will clutch him to her breast when her husband is finished, wipe away tears and soothe his wounds.

But she will not stop him.

He doesn't blame his mother, not even as his body sags against the stained bed, exhausted from the pain, or as tears leak from his eyes. He knows better than to cry out loud. It will not help, only blast more air into the furnace of his father's rage. This is how his mother was broken. But the boy vows that it will not be the same for him.

The salty tears cut pale gorges through his filthy cheeks and puddle on the bed. The cord cuts through the air once more, and the little boy can't help it this time. He screams with pain, and then the blackness takes him.

HE WAKES, his bedsheet tangled into a rope, and clutched between fingers turned white with pressure. The dream's clutches release him, but adrenaline still surges through his veins. His heart thunders in his chest.

He's not a boy anymore, but not a man either. Just sixteen, a few weeks from his birthday. A figure looms over his bed like a scarecrow in the darkness. The figure's eyes are a piercing shade of blue, even in the murky gloom of the army barracks. He's looking down with an unaccustomed emotion – one the young man doesn't immediately recognize.

Concern.

"What's your name?" the scarecrow asks, speaking in a low whisper.

The teen's sheets are soaked wet with sweat. He steals a look down before answering, checking whether he has soiled them. Not this time. He sags back against the bed with relief. A trickle of sweat dances down his temple, cool against his skin.

Trapp doesn't know whether to answer, or how. He knows he is the odd one out in a place like this. His back is already marked with a lifetime of scars, his frame thin and pale. He's younger than most of the recruits, but he is hard where they are soft.

He is a survivor.

"Who's asking?" he replies. His voice is gruff, but still boyish.

"Price," the man replies, leaning forward with his hand outstretched. A shaft of moonlight briefly passes across his face. "Ryan Price."

Price isn't much older than Trapp himself. Eighteen, perhaps a year older. He's a little taller than Trapp, but with a broad, well-fed frame, where Trapp's own is narrow and starved. He looks like a surfer, like he strolled into basic training straight from Long Beach.

Trapp studies the man for a few seconds, his heart racing. He is wary – not used to kindness. He loosens his grip on the bedsheet and accepts the man's hand. It is warm and dry, where his own is cold and clammy.

"Trapp," he whispers. "Jason Trapp."

Price beckons Trapp to follow him, a grin on his face. They sneak out of the barracks, each knowing if they are caught, they'll be on KP duty for weeks. But Trapp has to be out of the darkness, so he follows Price to the center of the parade ground, where they lie on their backs looking up at the stars. The air is cool, but the sound of crickets chirping in the background reminds them the heat of the day will soon be upon them.

"So what's your story?" Price asks, his accent tinged with a Boston brogue.

Trapp doesn't know how to answer. No one has ever asked him a question like that before.

"Why?"

"You're different," Price replies. "The rest of us, we're just kids. But not you."

Trapp is silent for a long time. He closes his eyes, and sees a police sergeant's concerned face staring back at him, red and blue lights playing across the man's brow. Trapp knows what he looks like to this man.

Beaten.

Broken.

Abused.

His mother is dead, her battered body lying at the bottom of the stairs, a trickle of blood beginning to escape her ear. Her body is shattered, but her face is at peace. Trapp doesn't regret what he had to do, but he knows he's going away for a very long time.

And then the police sergeant tells him a story that will set him free. Says he must never reveal the truth. It would be a heavy burden resting on a grown man's shoulders, let alone a scared, lonely teen.

Trapp opens his eyes. He stares up at the sky and decides to tell Price the truth.

"I killed my dad," Trapp admits. Angry tears sting the corners of his eyes. He's ashamed; he's never shown emotion before. It was always a route to more pain. He's never felt more like a child.

When Price replies, he speaks with no judgment, just a curiosity, tinged with sadness.

"Why?"

Trapp lifts his T-shirt, revealing the cuts that mark his body. His fingers trace the angry red scar that runs the width of his neck. Price reaches out, his face torn wide with horror, his finger grazing a welt on Trapp's side.

"*Because of this,*" Trapp whispers. "*And because he killed my mom.*"

"Hey buddy, you want to order anything?" Joshua Price asked, coming over and startling Trapp back to the present. The shock of the man's sudden presence was almost physical. It was as though Ryan himself was standing right in front of him, and not his brother.

"Kitchen's closing up. I'm short on staff today. You know how it is, Warriors come to town and big surprise, everyone calls in sick."

"I'm good," Trapp replied, his voice thick with pain. Was he imagining it, or was there a hint of sadness in Joshua's eyes? Was he still grieving, as Trapp was, in his own way? It had only been six months. Just a blink of an eye.

Price shrugged. "No problem, man. You want another beer?"

"Sure."

Trapp glanced down, checking that the black duffel bag was still at the bottom of his stool. It contained just over two and a half million dollars, in a variety of currencies. He'd kept a hundred grand for himself, and the passport. Enough to leave the country and start fresh somewhere else. He didn't want the rest. Maybe it could buy him a little peace.

Of course, that would rely on Trapp plucking up the chutzpah to strike up a real conversation. Right now, he was a mute. Introducing himself meant explaining who he was, and why he was there. And that meant reliving that night in Yemen, and the friend he had lost.

So right now, it could wait. Maybe another beer would help.

There was a lot to like about Price's bar. It was anonymous. Loud. A place a man could lose himself, and not have to think about the things he had seen, the things he had done, or the people he had lost.

And, naturally, it sold beer.

Trapp drained the dregs from the bottle he had been clasping for the past twenty minutes – warm, not that he cared, and accepted its replacement gratefully. He sent the empty sliding down the wooden bar.

"Hey Josh," a man from the back of the bar yelled. Trapp couldn't help but listen in; two decades of instincts were hard to ignore, especially when the yeller referenced the man he was here to see. "Change the channel. You – shit man, we *all* gotta see this. Put the news on. Any channel. It'll be on all of 'em."

"What you talking about, Jimmy? I turn the game off, people in here are gonna riot."

All around the bar, cell phones began to chime and buzz and rattle. In spite of himself, Trapp looked around, at the faces of surprise, then confusion, then horror as people stared down at the shining screens of their phones, or else held them to their ears. One woman began to sob, great, heaving, choking cries that tore through the suddenly deathly quiet bar.

"Just do it, Josh," the man said in a tone of horror that rang true. "Trust me."

Josh grumbled, but did as he was told. He reached back to a control panel behind the bar, fiddled with something, and suddenly the massive, widescreen TVs that decorated every wall in the sports bar began to flick through the channels – reality TV, HBO, all the crap that fills five hundred cable channels from dawn to dusk. It settled on ATN News. The two anchors looked ashen.

"Hey dude, what the hell are you doing?" A drunk man yelled from the back of the bar. He was quickly cut off by whoever was with him. By now, the bar was silent. In spite of himself, in spite of the alcohol coursing through his system, Trapp was now alert.

"– And of course, we're still getting reports. As we just said, what you are about to see is live. We don't know where it's coming from. Less than nine minutes ago, an anonymous email hit our tip line, containing only a link to a stream which we are putting up for you now."

The TV screen filled with an aerial shot of an Amtrak train, standing motionless on the tracks. The video danced a little, became blurry, and then resolved.

"This is Amtrak train number six, which travels between Chicago and Emeryville. Right now it's about ten miles out of Glenwood Springs, Colorado, and ATN has received information that there's been some kind of – some kind of terrorist incident on board. What you're seeing on your screen appears to be footage from overhead, a helicopter, maybe, or –"

"– or a drone, Tom –"

"– that's right. Our analysts are telling me that due to the altitude of the shot that it's most likely to be a drone. As we just told you, we don't know where this footage is coming from, and if you are a viewer with a sensitive disposition, or if you have children in the room, then we advise you to look away now."

Trapp was engrossed now. As he watched, the TV went to split screen.

"The video you are about to watch was posted on Twitter just moments ago. It's 19 seconds long, and it's from *inside* the train."

The anchor was clearly vamping. Trapp figured that they didn't know any more than he did. He watched as a fuzzy, blurred image came up on the screen, and then as the video began to play. As the anchor had suggested, it was clearly taken from inside the train. Bodies lay everywhere, and blood painted the windows and walls and floor. Scorch marks and damage from the shrapnel fragments that had ripped through the coach made it look as though there had been a terrible accident. But this butchery had been intentional.

"Jesus fucking Christ –"

Trapp didn't know if he had said the words, whether it was someone in the bar around him, or hell, whether it was the

ATN anchor himself. But they fit. What he was watching was carnage – the kind of thing he had seen dozens, maybe hundreds of times through a long career, in more countries than he could count.

But he'd never seen it in the US before. Certainly not on a train in the middle of the Colorado country, amidst snow-kissed mountaintops and the surging Colorado River.

"Oh my God," someone gasped behind him as the camera panned around, now showing the scene outside of the train. There was no sound, but Trapp watched as two men sprinted away from the tracks. Both were armed. They were hurrying toward a third man, who was cradling a rifle of his own, standing next to what looked like three motorbikes. Dirt bikes, probably. Trapp half-nodded with appreciation. In that terrain, it was as good a move as any.

As Trapp stared in horror, every fiber of his being wishing he could be on-scene, so that he could do something instead of sitting here impotently, clutching a beer, he saw the third shooter raising his rifle to his shoulder, dropping to one knee and firing a burst toward the train – toward the camera. The footage cut out, and the overhead shot returned to fill the screen.

"According to the metadata on the file," the male news anchor said, sounding distracted, as though he was reading the words for the first time, "this video was shot about ten minutes ago. It appears to depict the shooters – the terrorists – fleeing the scene of this terrible attack. We can only hope that the person who shot the footage is still..."

He paused, and didn't finish the sentence.

"Let's bring in ATN's security analyst, Kyle Walters," the other anchor interjected. "Kyle, what can you tell us?"

Trapp didn't care what Kyle, Kyle Walters, had to say. The images told their own story. The attack had been planned and executed brilliantly. It looked like two shooters, at least two shooters, had waited until the train was in an isolated area, and then attacked the defenseless passengers with rifle, handgun fire and maybe even explosives.

And most interestingly of all – because it was merely *interesting*, now that Jason's brain had processed and compartmentalized the sensations of overwhelming horror that he had experienced only a few seconds before – were the clear signs of coordination and planning that had gone into this attack.

Trapp ran through it in his mind. The train was stopped. Either the shooters had killed the driver, forced him to bring the train to a halt, or they had somehow knocked out the track signals.

If he was a betting man, he would have gone with the latter option. It made sense. It was how he would've done things in their shoes. The terrorists had given themselves both time to complete their mission, and space – they had halted the train far enough away from any population center to know they would most likely not be interrupted by the authorities before their murderous rampage was complete.

But the most interesting hallmark of the operation, the one that pointed both to the clear signs of planning that lay behind it, and the inevitable conclusion that the track signals had in fact been knocked out, was that the train had come to a halt in a predictable location – a location at which the shooters had support, getaway vehicles, the whole works. They'd known exactly where this was going to go down. Had planned the whole thing. Had somehow arranged for the act of terror to be *livestreamed* around the globe.

Onscreen, the security analyst was still talking.

"And Tom, it looks like the authorities are starting to arrive on-scene. What I would expect to see, in a situation like this, is a full-spectrum response from federal, state and local authorities."

The sound of the man's inane chattering faded away as

Trapp watched ambulances, police cars, even a couple of small fire trucks driving down the tracks, and converging on the train from either side. The convoy wasn't just made up of rescue vehicles, either, but civilian pickup trucks too; it looked like anything in Glenwood Springs that could drive had headed directly for the scene.

Trapp clenched his fists together, then cracked his knuckles. Without intending to, he ran through a mental checklist of the actions he would take if he was on site. Secure the area, first. Ensure there were no more shooters. Get some aerial support. The attackers were heading away from the scene, and in this kind of terrain, if someone didn't start tracking them fast, it would be too late.

On the TV, tiny figures ran toward the train. By now, survivors were starting to stream away from the tracks. The resolution wasn't good enough for Trapp to see the blood that no doubt coated them, but he could tell by the way they were walking, stumbling, some dragging injured limbs, that they were in shock.

But something wasn't right here. He could feel it at the back of his spine. A sense of danger – not to him, but simply the finely honed instincts of a trained killer screaming out that something was *wrong*.

He watched as it played out on screen, only a second later.

"Oh, Jesus, no…"

5

Nadine Carter – though she hated the name, and insisted that people call her Dani – was one of the Federal Bureau of Investigation's fastest rising stars. Thirty-four years old, with shimmering black hair tied back in a no-nonsense ponytail, and startling emerald eyes, she had never intended to enter law enforcement. With an uncanny intelligence, and a degree from MIT's world-renowned computer science program, every top recruiter in Silicon Valley was after her for months.

But Dani was the daughter of a retired US Marine Corps gunnery sergeant who had served with distinction in Beirut, Lebanon, where he found and married the love of his life. She benefited from both her father's unusual height and a year-round natural tan, courtesy of a mother she had never met.

But she'd also inherited an understanding of the value of hard work, service, and sacrifice. Those values had been drilled into her from birth – and Dani took to them like a duck to water. Perhaps it was the loss of her mother that eventually swayed her into following in her father's footsteps, not by entering the military, but by joining the FBI. She'd turned down the offer of mid six-figures in favor of a government salary. And she hadn't regretted that decision once.

Today of all days, the memory of a face she had only ever seen in photographs, and the vivid portraits painted by her father's loving stories, hit her hard. She paused for a second to master her emotions, then knocked on the door of a glass-walled conference room hidden somewhere in the bowels of the J Edgar Hoover Building, the headquarters of the FBI.

The room's sole occupant was the special agent in charge of the Washington DC field office, Rick Olsen. He was squashed into a chair that didn't come close to being sufficient for his six-foot-four-inch frame. He'd played college football until a mistimed tackle had put him in the hospital for two weeks, leaving him with two fused vertebrae and a permanent scowl. He looked up from his papers, at just about the only agent under his jurisdiction who could lift the grimace usually plastered across his face.

He beckoned her in. "Dani, you're a sight for sore eyes. Sit down."

"Yes, sir."

"I wanted to see you before the ceremony. You've done good, kid. Real good. Caught the director's eye. He's going to be here today."

Dani's eyebrows kinked up with surprise. After all, there was no particular reason that the Director of the FBI, should even know her name. She was just a lowly agent, toiling away in the DC field office. Sure, she'd cracked her fair share of cases, but the Bureau had thousands of agents. What was so special about her?

"He is?"

"Yep." Olsen grinned. "Wanted to pin the medal on you himself."

Dani almost frowned at the reminder of the reason she was even there today. The FBI Medal for Meritorious Achievement.

It was a hell of a mouthful, and also, she knew, a hell of an achievement. And yet, it didn't feel that way.

"What's wrong?" the SAC asked, point-blank. He wasn't a man who missed very much. And he wasn't one to hide his feelings, either. "You look like someone just took a dump in your cornflakes."

"No, sir. It's just –"

"You don't want the damn thing."

Dani's forehead creased with surprise. She wondered how Olsen knew. She had only half-admitted it to herself. "How did you guess?"

"Because no one does. Medals, pah. They aren't for us, you know that, Carter?"

"No?"

"They're for your family. They're to give your old man something to talk about when he visits his barber. Something for your mom –" Olsen grimaced. "Crap, Dani. I'm sorry. Last thing you needed was me putting my foot in my mouth like that."

"Don't worry about it."

The truth was, the fact her mother wouldn't be here today wasn't the reason for Dani's unease. She had long ago come to terms with the loss of her parent – as much as any child can. The pain of absence was no longer the sharp stiletto it had been through her teens, but more of a background ache.

"That's not the reason. The last case..." She paused, working out how to express her concerns. "We set those kids up," Dani admitted, the words coming out in a rush now as she let loose a torrent of feelings. "They were just a couple of pissed-off Syrian refugees. Keyboard warriors. And now they're doing thirty to life in a SuperMax somewhere because of me. An hour of sunshine a day, and they're as likely to get stabbed by some Aryan Brotherhood psycho as ever make it out alive. And I'm getting a medal for it."

Dani tucked a stray strand of hair behind her ear, remembering how damn long it had taken to whip the dark strands into any kind of shape. She grimaced with irritation, and her voice came out softer. "It just doesn't feel right. This isn't why I joined the Bureau. We don't even know where the intelligence comes from, but we're supposed to trust these guys are existential threats? I don't buy it."

The case had been assigned to her about six months before. Just one of a stack on her desk, forwarded directly from a classified program at the National Security Agency. They were a couple of disaffected Syrian kids. Refugees from the civil war still rumbling on over there. They talked a big game, when they were safe behind a keyboard on some extremist forum, but Dani knew that's all it was: talk. It was just a phase, and one they would grow out of. She'd recommended as much in her report. Considered the case closed.

But the higher-ups didn't agree. Not the SAC, but the bureaucrats in this very building. It was budget season in Washington DC, and every terrorist taken down, no matter how flimsy the case, no matter how unlikely they were to actually commit a crime, was ammunition to use in some budget meeting. More dollars meant more resources meant more agents meant more criminals behind bars.

The question of whether they had actually posed a threat was considered superfluous.

"I don't like it any more than you do," Olsen sighed, leaning back against his chair, and attempting to squeeze his enormous frame into a position that offered even a hint of comfort.

"So why do we do it?"

"It's how the game is played, Carter. At least, it is these days. The beancounters run the Bureau now. It's a numbers game, even if we have to arm the terrorists ourselves, and drive them down to the target, talking them into it the entire way."

"It just feels shit, sir," Dani said.

"I hear ya. Listen, one of the perks of the director pinning that hunk of metal on your chest is you won't have to take any more cases like that."

"No?"

"It's one of the perks of being a rising star, Carter. Now you're on the director's radar, you'll have your pick of the crop." He leaned back, rolling kinks out of his neck as he did so. "Anyway, enough of this. Your dad will be here, right?"

"Sure will." Dani grinned. She glanced down at the slim leather watch strap on her left wrist. "In fact, sir, if you'll excuse me, I just need to finish up a bit of paperwork before he shows up."

Olsen grinned, waving her away. "Go. You've made him proud, kid. I'll see you at the ceremony."

6

The KX 450 motorbike has a liquid-cooled four stroke engine, a digital ignition system, a hydraulic clutch, a top speed over flat ground of 123 mph, and retails for more than $11,000. This particular model was equipped with studded snow tires, perfect for the rock-hard, snow-covered ground of Colorado in early February.

The three bikes had been stolen from a Kawasaki dealership just outside of Salt Lake City two weeks earlier and transported in the back of a pickup truck to Glenwood Springs under a tarpaulin before being ridden out into the meeting spot, one by one, by a Syrian man called Farad.

The dirt bikes were best in class – ordinarily ridden by motocross competitors, though they didn't need to be anything special. After the rendezvous, the trio of terrorists drove just half a mile through rough ground before ditching the bikes underneath the cover of a copse of frozen pine trees.

"My brothers," Farad said, turning around and embracing two men he had never met as the echoing, coughing sound of the dirt bikes faded into the distance, bouncing off the faraway mountainsides before dying for good. "What you have done today will be remembered for generations."

Raheem nodded. He noticed, absentmindedly, that his hand was trembling. He didn't know whether it was from the cold, or a delayed reaction from the glorious actions he had just taken in the name of Allah, the most merciful.

"Thank you, my brother. You have them?"

Farad nodded and gestured to a low mound on the ground a couple of yards away. It was dusted with snow and pine needles, and if it had not been pointed out to him, Raheem would have missed it. The new man strode over, grasped a corner of canvas, and shook the material clean.

Underneath, laid out neatly, was an arsenal. Three brand-new AR-15 rifles, a selection of grenades and loaded magazines, and three thick black vests. They were, as Raheem correctly guessed, lined with 4 mm steel ball bearings and packed with plastic explosive. Once detonated, they would kill anyone within a fifteen-meter radius, and grievously wound anyone else unlucky enough to escape the kill zone. Unlike the iron-sighted weapon he had discarded in the target-rich environment of the train, these rifles were equipped with optical scopes. He had no doubt that the weapons would be perfectly sighted.

"You have done well, *shaqiq*." Brother.

Farad nodded his thanks. "My work is not done yet, my friend," he said, bending over and grasping one of the vests. He picked it up, turned back to Raheem and gestured. "May I?"

Raheem grunted. The cold was biting at his face now. He knew he would not have to bear it for very much longer. It reminded him of his time fighting against Assad in Syria. Bitterly cold, endless nights trekking through the mountains, with just a Kalashnikov at his side. Hard times, yes, but the best days of his life. Soon enough, it would be over, and he would be with the Prophet.

And it was all because of a man he had never met. A man who had made all this possible. Who had sent funds, procured documents, arranged a route across the Mexican border and a safe house once he had arrived. Raheem owed this man everything, and he didn't even know his name.

Farad stepped up toward him, and gently slid the explosive vest over the Iraqi's shoulders. He pointed out the detonator switch, and then helped Raheem's silent partner don his own vest.

The three men quickly gathered and checked their weapons, rearming themselves. Raheem noticed that Farad was shivering, and given that the man was wrapped up in thick, warm winter clothing, he surmised it was due to apprehension over what lay ahead.

"You are ready, my brother," he said, embracing the Syrian. "I am proud to die alongside a man such as you. I will see you in Paradise."

The three men abandoned the bikes and crept back toward the crippled train. They split up, moving to preassigned fire points, and waited for the first responders to arrive. Their instructions were clear: wait long enough for the whole world to become aware of what had happened in Colorado.

Wait until the infidels were watching, and then strike.

WITHIN JUST TEN minutes of receiving word of the attack, first responders began to arrive on the scene. Better trained men might have set a perimeter, but this was Glenwood Springs, and it was not a place that had ever expected to be the focus of such carnage.

Stan Greening, the chief of police, had a grand title for a man who ran a department of just seven officers, but was brave nonetheless. He drove as fast as he could down the tracks in his cruiser, a shotgun on the seat beside him, his Smith & Wesson 9 mm service weapon sitting on his hip. He hadn't fired either weapon in months. He brought the cruiser to a halt and rushed toward the train, ready to do whatever he could to help. His subconscious noted the out-of-place hum of the drone hovering overhead, even if he didn't recognize it for what it was.

"My God," he groaned, a chill running through his entire body as he saw blood splattered on the cracked, bullet-ridden windows of the train. Slumped half-out of the nearest door was a body – a woman who had made it this far before her heart stopped pumping.

"Help," a child whimpered from somewhere close. Stan looked around and saw a boy of no more than seven years, clad only in a blood-spattered shirt. "Mister, have you seen my mommy?"

Stan wordlessly shook his head, barely able to process what he was seeing. "Kid," he croaked. He cleared his voice. "Are you hurt?"

The boy's eyes were glassy. He shook his head, and began to tremble. Whether it was from the cold or the shock, Stan didn't know. The veteran police officer – veteran of no bloody shootouts, little more than the odd confrontation with a drunk driving farmer – was slow to react, but he was a good, kind-hearted man. He shrugged his thick department-issued winter jacket off and placed it around the boy's shoulders.

Perhaps it was the white shirt underneath that drew Raheem's attention. Perhaps it was no reason at all. But several minutes later, after the flow of first responders and concerned citizens arriving on-scene began to slow to a trickle, Stan Greening was the first to die.

As the sound of gunfire cracked out in the frozen valley and police officers, nurses, schoolteachers and first-aiders began to fall under a hail of lead, the Chief's skull split like a ripe water-melon, and his body fell to the ground with a heavy thump.

The child whimpered and began to cry.

7

T rapp gripped the wooden bar, his fingers white with tension as, almost in slow motion, he watched his worst fears play out in front of him.

The police officers were the first to die. The academic side of his brain admired the cold logic of that simple fact. The shooters were well-trained. Anyone could kill civilians in a crowd – well, perhaps not anyone, but any fanatic suitably equipped with the weapons of war. Killing at that distance required skill. And picking off the men who were capable of shooting back first suggested that the shooters were both intelligent and experienced.

"Get to cover," he muttered under his breath, too late. Almost before the words escaped his mouth, the last of the men in blue jackets fell to the hail of gunfire.

"What sick fuck is filming this?" someone said. Trapp thought it was Joshua Price, the guy he'd come to see, but he wasn't certain. It didn't matter.

It wasn't his job to care, not anymore. He had spent his entire life protecting people who would never know what he had done. After all, that wasn't why men like him did the things they did. He had paid his dues. Given and sweated and bled more for his country than any man in a hundred mile radius.

And yet he did care. More than that, a cauldron of anger bubbled in his stomach at the scenes of devastation being beamed out to every home in America, right on cue for the lunchtime news bulletins.

Part of him wanted to scream that ATN, Fox, and every last money-hungry news company in the country should refuse to broadcast images like this. It was what these terrorists wanted, so why give it to them?

After 9/11, a community of conspiracy theorists had grown up around the idea, fed by endless YouTube videos and half-baked Internet blogs, that the planes that hit the twin towers were not planes after all, but missiles. That the footage was faked. Jet fuel couldn't melt steel beams. It was nonsense of course, but it was a product of the time. Just after the turn of the millennium, almost no one carried video recorders. They had been bulky things, back then, either recording on tape, or onto tiny digital drives with file sizes too large to transmit.

These days, everyone carried a thirty megapixel camera in their pockets, and a device powerful enough to broadcast video to anyone on the planet. If September 11 had happened today, the second plane would have been captured on film by hundreds, thousands, perhaps hundreds of thousands of different people.

There would be no denying it then.

Amtrak Six, as this attack would soon come to be known, was the first of a new wave of terrorist attacks. Intentionally live streamed around the world. Not just mindless violence, but intentionally directed, exquisitely produced propaganda.

Trapp did not know it, did not in fact have a personal email address, but at the very same moment as a link to the live streamed footage from the drone was emailed to the ATN tip line, it was also delivered to hundreds of millions of email inboxes across the globe.

Seconds later, horrified viewers began to share the live video on social media. On Facebook, Twitter, Snapchat, the link spread like wildfire. In every office, bedroom and diner across the nation, viewers watched the worst terrorist attack on US soil since 9/11 play out in high definition.

Trapp took a swig from the beer bottle in front of him. He had almost forgotten it was there, but now he was glad of it. He looked away from the screen. He had seen enough.

And that was when he heard it.

The unmistakable crackle of gunfire. Trapp blinked, sensations dulled in part by the alcohol, but mainly by three months living in Boston as a civilian. Drinking more days than not. Barely bothering to exercise. Surviving, not living. He glanced back up at the screen, but even as he did so he knew he needn't bother.

The sound had come from closer. Much closer.

"Jesus, Josh," a drunk yelled from the back of the bar, the gravity of the occasion completely passing the man by. "Turn it down, will ya? Almost deafened me back here."

Trapp stood up, glancing around the bar for something he could use as a weapon. Then something occurred to him. He clicked his fingers, attracting Joshua Price's attention. The man looked white as a sheet, like he couldn't believe what was happening around him. Trapp couldn't blame him. This wasn't supposed to be happening, not in a place like this.

"Have you got a weapon back there?" Trapp snapped. "Behind the bar?"

"A what –?"

The gunfire sounded again, but this time closer, louder, and someone screamed toward the back of the crowd. It was a chilling sound, a primal one, born of pure terror. They knew it now, all of them – or they would in just seconds. Whatever the hell was going on today, the violence wasn't just confined to some snowy flyover state, it was here. Boston, Massachusetts, a stone's throw from TD Garden, where right now twenty thousand basketball fans were watching the Celtics take on the Warriors.

It was a perfect target.

"I'm a cop," Trapp lied, leaning over the bar and grabbing Josh's T-shirt. He knew he had to move fast, and he needed the man's cooperation.

"You hear that?" He continued, jerking his thumb in the general direction of the bar's entrance. "They're here. So I'll ask you again, you got something I can use back there?"

Price nodded, first hesitantly, then vigorously. "Yeah, maybe. I mean, I don't know. The rifle up there doesn't work. I have a baseball bat. It's for –"

"I don't care what it's for," Trapp growled. "Get it."

A fucking baseball bat. Jesus. He was about to go toe to toe with heavily armed terrorists armed with nothing more than a fucking baseball bat. He wanted to say that he'd gone into battle facing worse odds, but this wasn't the fucking movies. He couldn't kill a man with a paperclip. This was real life.

Josh bent over, scrambled behind the bar, and then thrust a dented aluminum bat into Trapp's grasping hands.

The former CIA officer accepted it, spun on his heel and began sprinting out of the bar. Then he stopped dead and turned back to Price, gesturing in the black duffel bag which contained almost everything he owned.

"That's yours. Your brother was a good man, Josh. I wish he'd been here, not me."

And then he left, dozens of pairs of shocked eyes on him – and none more so than the man behind the bar.

Trapp ran unhesitatingly toward the sound of gunfire. You couldn't train a man to do that. Well, you can try, and the army does. But the truth of the matter is that most men in most armies across the planet would rather shit their pants than go into combat. Survival is a natural human instinct, and men who can willingly short-circuit that impulse are few and far between.

Trapp was one of them, although he didn't see it in those terms. His job was simple: get the mission done. Today was no different, though no one was giving him orders. Today the mission was exactly the same as it had always been: keep America safe.

As he ran toward TD Garden, dodging screaming, terrified civilians flooding in his direction, part of Trapp's mind wondered whether he was doing the right thing. He wasn't as young as he had been. His left knee ached every morning, and he still hadn't had that operation on his shoulder that the Agency had promised him for so long. The wounds he'd suffered in Yemen had only just healed. Maybe he should leave this for someone else. Someone younger.

But he ignored that part of him, as he always had. After all, it wasn't like he had a choice. There wasn't anyone else. Only him.

Trapp closed the two blocks between the bar and the arena in record time. It was quieter here. In terms of people, anyway. In the distance, a car horn blared. He figured that those who could run had, and those who couldn't were trapped inside the arena.

Still moving fast, he spotted flashing lights about twenty yards ahead, and saw a police cruiser, its windshield riddled with gunfire, passenger door open. In the driver's seat, an officer was slumped against the wheel, holding down the horn, which sounded out his mournful last rites. Trapp didn't have time to grieve for the man. He closed the distance between him and the cruiser, glanced around for a shooter, but saw nothing.

"Shit, man," he sighed, tossing the baseball bat to the ground. It bounced with a clink, then again, then rattled as it rolled to a stop against a nearby curb. "You deserved better."

Trapp hated looting the dead, but this time he didn't have a choice. He rarely did, when it came to relieving a body of its weapons and ammunition – because when you're that desperate for ammo, shit has most definitely hit the fan.

It felt wrong, somehow, as though a man's gun should be tied to him in death, just as it was in life. He knew that was nonsense, but it was a superstition, and old habits are hard to break.

Nevertheless, he felt better having a weapon in his grasp that could actually shoot back. He checked the magazine, then clicked it back in. The pistol was a Glock model 22, .40 cal, with a fifteen round magazine. The cop had two more clipped to his belt, and Trapp took those gratefully, too. He glanced at the ignition, checking for a keychain, knowing there would most likely be a shotgun in the trunk.

"Crap," he whispered. Boston PD had plumped for keyless ignition, and the fob was nowhere to be found. That meant no shotgun. It was just him and the peashooter in his hands.

Trapp didn't dwell on his luck. He never did. When something was a problem, he either found a solution or ignored it entirely. This time, he chose the latter option. He paused for a second and took stock of the situation.

He was at the far end of Canal Street, about half a block away from TD Garden, and he had a weapon, along with about forty-five rounds of ammunition. Enough for a few minutes of combat, if he was sparing. To add to the bad news, he didn't know whether he was up against two shooters, or twenty. From the limited amount of gunfire he had heard so far, he suspected the former, not the latter, but he couldn't be sure.

Get moving. You're not getting any younger out here, and people are dying in there.

"Get down," someone yelled. It was a man's voice, but high-pitched, the vocal cords twisted tight with a toxic mix of adrenaline and fear, and maybe a dash of pain.

"Drop the weapon, or I'll shoot!"

8

Dani Carter stepped out of the elevator into the lobby of the Hoover Building a few minutes after her meeting with her boss. The whole way down, she had bounced from foot to foot as a bout of uncharacteristic nerves ate away at her.

She had never been showy, growing up. So while she was more than happy to go toe to toe with a hardened terrorist cell, the thought of standing at the front of a room packed with experienced FBI agents, and more importantly her own father, filled her with dread.

Carter shook off the sensation and stepped through the gates that regulated access from the lobby to the rest of the Hoover Building. The lobby was large, with several sofas laid out for visiting guests, large flat-screen televisions constantly tuned to rolling twenty-four hour news channels, and a huge FBI crest on the far marble wall.

Her subconscious picked up on a strange atmosphere in the large room as she nodded to the armed agent at his duty post by the gate. He wore a dark navy windbreaker, zipped to the neck, with the letters 'FBI' on the back. Dani knew that underneath he was concealing a bulletproof vest rated to take a 5.56 mm round at a distance of under ten yards. The man's face was drained of blood.

Dani immediately recognized her father, even from the rear. He was near the entrance, and stood up, watching one of the television screens. She couldn't see the topic of interest, not from this distance. Her dad was mostly bald by now, and had his fingers interlocked, holding the back of his head. His posture was strangely slouched, which stuck out like a sore thumb. She'd never seen him like that before. The old Marine was usually ramrod straight. As she walked up to him, she heard his voice, almost in a whisper. It was dull with shock.

"My God..."

The expression on Dani's face was quizzical as she reached out and tapped Mitch Carter on the shoulder.

"Dad. You made it."

A surge of pride overcame her as her father turned to look at her. Pride that was immediately squelched out of existence the moment she saw the look of horror on his face. His eyes were black with a mixture of shock and rage – something Dani had never seen before on her father's usually jovial appearance.

"Have you seen?"

"Seen what?" Dani asked.

But as she did so, her eyes were drawn inexorably to the television screen her father was standing in front of. To the scenes of devastation in Colorado. She watched as a man fell to the ground, monitored by a clinical overhead camera feed, his body blossoming red against the snowy ground.

Dani froze with shock, but just for a second. Her brain kicked into high gear. She didn't need to be a member of Mensa to know that the medal ceremony would be canceled today. Every agent in the Bureau would be working triple shifts for weeks to run down the monsters responsible for this attack.

And she would be working alongside them – as soon as her dad got to safety.

"Dad," she said, turning to her father. He was good in a crisis. "I need you to go home. I'll call you when I get a chance. Don't fly. Rent a car, just in case."

Mitch Carter looked at his daughter, that familiar look of pride battling with the unaccustomed role reversal. She could tell that he thought he should be the one telling her what to do, and not the other way round. Times had changed. His little girl had grown up.

He nodded curtly. Took a step toward her. Gave her a tight hug, and whispered in her ear, "You got it, kiddo. Stay safe, okay?"

Dani savored her father's touch, holding onto the hug a second longer than she would have normally. He was all she had in the world. She couldn't bear the thought of anything happening to him. Though he was older, now, the retired Marine was still full of life, and fitter than many men half his age. Dani was thankful for it every day. She had already lost one parent. She wasn't ready to lose both.

Finally, she let go, taking a deep breath and steadying herself for what was to come. She had a job to do.

The next few seconds happened in slow motion. But Dani Carter would remember them for the rest of her life.

Behind her dad, behind the television, a man stepped into the lobby of the Hoover Building. Even from this distance, Dani could tell he was sweating. Profusely. Her eyes were drawn to him almost as though by magnetism. Her subconscious screamed at her that something was wrong.

She took a step forward, and then another, circling the television, all thoughts of her father forced from her mind, and her hand on the gun at her hip. The man at the entrance looked left, then right. He was dressed in a long, dark coat, his hands thrust into its pockets and wasn't fat, exactly, but thick, somehow.

No, not thick...

Dani's veins ran cold, the sense of shock sudden and immediate. The man was wearing a suicide vest. She knew it, as well as she knew her own name. She had to act fast. She stole a glance around, and noticed her father looking at her strangely – but no one else in the room appeared to have responded. They were all staring at the TV screens, even the two armed agents in the lobby who were supposed to be monitoring the metal detector.

Distracted.

Dani grimaced, motioning her fingers to the ground as she looked at her father. He looked back, uncomprehending, and then a light of understanding blossomed behind his eyes. Dani couldn't look at him any longer. She wanted to scream. Wanted to run to him and protect him, or maybe it was the other way round. But she couldn't.

And she couldn't think about her father. Not now.

Dani did her best to look casual as she unholstered her gun and moved toward the glass entrance of the FBI building's lobby, briefly shielding herself behind a concrete stanchion. Her eyes were locked on her target now, studying him intently.

She'd been right. He was perspiring, heavily, and his chest was rising and falling fast, as though he was on the very edge of panic. He scanned the room once again, not seeming to notice as an unarmed security guard approached him.

Dani took a chance. She drew her gun, took aim, and yelled. "Down!"

The sound exploded in the room like a gunshot. Every eye was drawn to her now, not that she knew it. She was focused on the only eyes that counted – the ones that belonged to the Middle Eastern man in the long coat, now drawn unerringly to her own.

"Get your hands up," Dani shouted. "Out of your pockets. Now!"

A look of shock registered on the man's face. And then, horribly, a sight that Dani would remember for the rest of her life, a macabre smile stretched across his thin lips. He took his hands out of his pockets, and Dani tracked them every inch.

"You're too late," the man said, as his right hand departed his jacket pocket. And as he released the switch he was holding underneath his right thumb.

Dani fired, and an instant later a small red dot punctured the man's forehead. But he was right. She was too late. Even before the terrorist's neurological impulses cut out, before his knees had a chance to collapse and send his body slumping to the ground, the lobby of the Hoover Building exploded in fire.

9

Trapp froze, mainly because it was good practice not to move unexpectedly when someone is holding a gun on you. That was how you ended up with a hole in your back, and Trapp had seen too many friends die, or else end up in a wheelchair, to harbor any desire to have the same thing happen to him.

"I said drop the weapon," the man repeated, his voice trembling. "Slowly. No sudden movements."

Trapp mentally figured him to be in his mid-twenties. Armed, which either meant he was a wannabe hero, or a cop. And if he was a cop, Trapp realized, along with a sinking feeling in his stomach, that meant he was probably the partner of the dead officer in the cruiser next to him. If the man's partner was dead, then a surge of adrenaline and cortisol would be flooding his system, heightening his emotions and reducing his propensity for rational behavior.

And that was bad news.

"Listen to me, officer, I'm with the state police," Trapp lied, hoping that he remembered correctly, and that Massachusetts did in fact have a state police department, and not

Rangers, like the Texans, or his day was about to go sideways fast.

"Drop the weapon!"

There was a noticeable tendril of fear in the man's voice now. Trapp couldn't blame him. His partner was dead, along with God only knew how many ordinary Bostonians. The streets he had been sworn to guard had been turned into a war zone. And now a strange man was stealing his partner's service weapon.

"I'm going to put the weapon down," Trapp said. "You hear that, officer? I'm about to move. I'm going to crouch down, and place this pistol on the asphalt. Don't shoot me, okay?"

"Do it."

Trapp did exactly as he had described. Once the weapon was on the ground, he nudged it with his foot – made it look as though he was kicking it away, but in reality left it at least somewhat within reach. If he had to dive for the pistol, he was probably already dead, depending on how much range time Boston's finest got every year, but he felt more comfortable with the pistol two feet away than ten. He turned around slowly, and met the officer's eyes.

"Tell me what happened here, officer," Trapp said, his voice low and commanding. In stressful situations, he knew, people responded to confidence. It stirred something inside them – a need to feel safe. "What am I going up against?"

"What are you going –?" the man repeated dumbly, a fountain of dark blood blossoming at his side. "What are you talking about? In fact, quit talking at all. Get down on the ground, and don't –"

Trapp swore internally. He didn't have time for this. None of them had time for this. "Officer," he said through gritted teeth. "Do you hear that?"

"Hear what?"

The fucking gunfire, he wanted to scream. But he bit his

tongue. "What's your name, kid? I know you're scared. Are you hit?"

"Yeah," the man whispered, and Trapp knew he had his man. He met the kid's eye, and communicated a look of sheer compassion.

"I know you are. And I know you just want to do what's right. But believe me, kid, if I don't get over there soon"—he jabbed his thumb over his shoulder, and vaguely in the direction of the basketball arena—"it's going to be too late. You want that on your conscience?"

The police officer shook his head dumbly.

"I didn't think so. What's your name, officer?"

"Mikey, you can call me Mikey."

"Good," Trapp said reassuringly. He watched as the officer's hands trembled around his service weapon, then as the man's arms lowered, until the weapon was pointing at the ground. "Tell me what happened here, Mikey."

"They—they came out of nowhere," the man said. "Two men. Armed with rifles."

"What did they look like"

The cop shook his head. "Everything happened too fast," he whispered, slumping down on his ass.

Trapp patted the man on his shoulder, then retrieved his weapon, along with the spare magazines he had been in the process of taking when he was interrupted.

"You did good, kid. Keep pressure on that wound. I gotta go."

The gunfire in the background was crackling more slowly now. Not in full, automatic bursts, but more considered, as though the shooters were taking time to pick out well-aimed shots. Trapp knew that even though this distraction had eaten up less than a minute, people had died in that time, and he had been unable to save them.

The cop reached out, handing Trapp two more magazines. "It's all I've got, take it."

"Keep pressure on that wound."

Trapp stuffed the extra ammunition in his pockets, and took off at a dead run. He wasn't quite as fit as he had been six months earlier, before Yemen, but he was fitter than most. He could still handle a five mile run at a six-minute mile pace and bust out a couple of hundred press ups when he was done without breaking sweat.

Well, maybe the breaking sweat part was a lie, but the rest of it was God's honest truth.

A hundred yards later, Trapp entered the basketball arena through a set of glass doors, barely panting. The scene was eerily quiet. He held the pistol in a double-handed grip and started scanning the lobby. Popcorn tubs and big gulp drinks splattered the floor, and sports merchandise lay everywhere, abandoned in the crowd's panicked rush to escape.

Trapp's eyes fixed on a tiny baseball cap, made for a kid no older than three. Jesus. What kind of monster would attack a place like this? No matter what the attackers had been through, no matter what they had seen, no matter what America had probably done to them, Trapp would never believe that anything could justify a scene like this.

In his world, men fought men. A battlefield was a fair fight. A basketball game sure as shit wasn't.

Trapp came across the first dead body once he entered the stairwell that led up to the bleachers. The woman, blond, about thirty years old, would have died instantly. The bullet entered her chest directly at the heart. There was little blood spatter. The heart had stopped pumping instantly, and without the pressure caused by the muscle contracting, there was nothing to cause the violent explosion of crimson liquid so beloved of Hollywood directors.

Trapp took the concrete stairs slowly, knowing that he had

to resist the temptation to charge into the arena, all guns blazing. That was a sure path to ending up dead. And if he died,
then so would more innocent people.

No matter what the government had done to him, no matter
what it had taken from him, Trapp was still a wolf in a world of
sheep. Or maybe he was a sheepdog. It was time to keep his
pack safe.

His hands did not tremble as they held the weapon. It had
been months since he done any range time, but years of
training had ingrained in him a deadly accuracy. He wouldn't
miss. He took the time to master his breathing, and control the
adrenaline that was now surging in his veins. The energy was
necessary, but it could easily get him killed.

Trapp entered the arena about halfway up the bleachers.
Every few seconds a fresh gunshot rang out, marked by a
scream or the gurgling of blood. He heard whimpering as terrified parents tried desperately to hush the babies they had
brought into this world.

As he pressed his body against the concrete wall, he saw a
young boy's large, brown eyes peeking back at him. They were
wide with shock. The boy's father lay on top of him, painted
red, his chest still.

Christ.

The sight brought Trapp back to his own childhood, the
memory of his mother's broken body flashing across his mind.
But he didn't have time to process. He needed to act, or more
innocents would die.

Trapp pressed his finger against his lips and looked directly
in the kid's eyes. There was little recognition. Trapp figured the
boy's mind had shut down. It was probably for the best, at least
in the short term. He had no doubt that the kid would never
forget this day. He would wake up screaming for the rest of his
life. Trapp had experienced enough of his own childhood
trauma to be certain of that.

But even that sad scenario was only possible if Trapp managed to save him. To save all of them. They would never remember this day. But it was better than the alternative.

Trapp inched forward, years of practice meaning his boots made no more sound against the concrete floor than if he was barefoot. He crouched low, scanning the arena for the shooters he knew were there. His heart pounded, but his breathing remained steady as he moved forward.

The first terrorist came into view. He was on the court, reloading what looked like an AR 15.

Trapp ran through what he knew. There were two shooters – at least two shooters, he corrected himself. He couldn't allow himself to get tunnel vision. Not now. They were probably both armed the same, and as far as Trapp could tell, the terrorist wasn't wearing an explosive vest.

That was good.

Of course, it was not the whole story. The terrorists might have brought explosives with them. The whole place might already be rigged to blow. But Trapp knew it didn't matter. This wasn't a hostage situation. He couldn't wait for the FBI to get there, roll out their famed negotiating strategy, trade half a dozen kids for a pizza, another half dozen for a bus and a suitcase of cash.

No. This situation was more like the Bataclan terrorist attacks in Paris back in 2015. The police had hesitated back then. Didn't want to go in. Followed protocol.

And dozens of innocents had died.

Trapp would not, *could not* let that happen again. Not on his watch. Not while he had breath in his lungs, or a gun in his hands.

A scream split the basketball arena, puncturing the relative calm of the gunshot and whimpering. "Please, please – I don't want to die. Please!"

A single gunshot sounded out, silencing the woman in an

instant. A cacophony of cries of fear broke out, and quickly died away. And then a chilling laugh. The other shooter. It gave Trapp what he needed. The man's position.

Trapp was still in the exit of the stairwell, looking down at the shooter on the court from an angle at which the shooter could not see him. The other shooter, the source of the laughter, was above him somewhere in the bleachers. Trapp could picture it now. The man was walking along, executing anyone he came across.

And then he saw it. Just a basketball, a couple of yards away from him, probably purchased from a merchandise stand downstairs, and dropped in a frantic rush to escape. To anyone else, it would have meant nothing.

But not to Trapp.

A plan quickly formed in his head. He inched forward, stretching, stretching, before he touched the basketball and quickly rolled it back toward him. He picked it up, transferred the Glock to his left and weighted it in his right. He could make it.

Trapp crouched, mastering his breathing, pushing back down on the natural spike of panic that threatened to overwhelm him. It happened the same every time, no matter how many times he went into battle. That fear would never go away. But as always, he controlled it. Used it to push him on. He had to do this.

No matter what it cost.

In one swift motion, Trapp drew his arm back, the basketball in the center of his palm, uncurled from his crouching position into a standing one and hurled the basketball as hard as he could down onto the court. The ball traveled in a perfect arc over the bleachers and landed with a loud boing in the center of the court, before flying back up and bouncing over the shooter's head. The man turned, surprised, his eyes tracking the ball. His back to Trapp.

Trapp made his move.

He closed both hands around the pistol grip, aimed at the shooter down below him, and fired three rounds. *Bang. Bang. Bang.* The distance was nearly forty yards, too far for most recreational shooters, but not Trapp. Before even checking to see whether the man was dead, he sprinted forward. He knew either way the shots would have bought him some time.

He turned, searching for the second target. He saw him. A swarthy man, dressed in a thick North Face winter coat that was now open to the chest. He wasn't wearing a vest. His eyes tracked his dead accomplice, now open wide with horror.

Payback's a bitch, Trapp thought with venom. He pulled the trigger twice. Both times, aiming for center mass. Then one last time at the man's head.

Each bullet hit its intended target. As the terrorist fell, his finger pulled back on the rifle's trigger, but the chamber was empty. The sound echoed around the basketball arena, and then he fell to the ground.

Dead.

10

Since throwing his hat into the 2020 presidential race as a five hundred to one outsider, President Charles Nash had lived a charmed life. He was the first Republican to win the state of New York since Ronald Reagan in 1984. The first presidential candidate of either party to win more than 60% of the popular vote since Nixon, all the way back in 1972.

A Republican who even liberals could hold their noses and vote for, a man whose charm, confidence and self assurance had managed to unite the nation around one common goal – to return America to her former glory. And for Nash, it was personal. America's decline hadn't just hurt him, but his family too. Perhaps that was how he'd ended up here, behind the Resolute desk of the Oval Office. For other men, attaining the presidency was the goal of a lifetime. For Nash it was merely an escape.

Nash was sitting in the Oval Office, supposedly catching up on paperwork – but really snatching a few minutes of personal time between waves of meetings which never seemed to end. Right now, he needed a break. He dropped his pen on the desk and stood up, absently checking his pockets for a pack of cigarettes. It was a habit he'd picked up on Parris Island as a raw recruit, and it was one he had managed to drop for years.

Until the campaign, with its endless nights of stress away from home, away from a wife who was pulling away, and a son who was long since gone. So now Nash smoked once again. He would probably quit for a second time, especially as his chief of staff kept telling him it didn't poll well with the soccer mom demographic.

But that could wait.

The President stepped outside, onto the Oval Office patio, and tapped the pack of cigarettes. A Secret Service agent lifted his hand to his mouth, and reported his position to the control center. The constant monitoring was something Nash wasn't yet accustomed to. He wondered if they called in whenever he was taking a shit.

A US Marine sergeant was standing post right outside the White House in blue dress, and snapped to attention as Nash placed a cigarette between his lips. The President looked at the clean-cut, ramrod-straight NCO, and wondered what he thought about standing there all day. The kid reminded him of his own son—the way George had been before Iraq, and the painkillers, the lying and the stealing.

A pained expression crossed the President's face, and he hid it by cupping his fingers around the cigarette and scraping the flint. The tip glowed as he took a deep drag, savoring the way the smoke burned his lungs.

"You smoke, son?"

"Not on duty, Mr. President," came the reply.

Nash grinned. "Not worth an ass-chewing from Gunny, right?"

"You got it, sir," the Marine said, without ever once deviating from his eyes-front posture. Nash was impressed.

"I guess I could order you to smoke with me." The President grinned. "But someone would probably leak it to the papers."

"Not me, sir."

"I believe that. What's your name, Sergeant?"

"Roy, sir. Roy Murphy."

Nash puffed on the cigarette for a few seconds, exhaling a thick cloud of smoke into the cold February air.

"Tell me, Roy, why did you enlist?"

"No bullshit –" the Marine started, before catching himself and turning red. "I mean – honestly, Mr. President?"

Nash nodded. "You don't need to watch your mouth around me, Roy. I started out just like you."

"It was a job, sir. Don't get me wrong, I like it – best one I ever had. But I'm a farm boy. Ain't nothing for me back home, not anymore. Not since the conglomerates moved in. No way for a small farm to survive."

Nash grimaced. It was a story he had heard thousands of times over the course of his election campaign. America was hurting. Sometimes he wondered how big a task he had taken on. He'd been powerless to save his own son. What made him think he could do any better for the entire country?

"That's why I'm here, son," he finally said. "I want to make America what she once was."

"That's why I voted for you, Mr. President."

Nash was about to turn and thank the Marine, when something entirely unexpected happened. The door from the Oval Office crashed open, and several suited Secret Service agents barreled through, their weapons drawn.

At the exact same time, the Marine sergeant took two paces forward, to the edge of the patio, and dropped to one knee. He brought his rifle to his shoulder and scanned the White House Gardens for any sign of an incoming threat. His crisply pressed dress uniform made him look like a man out of his time.

"The hell is going on?" Nash said.

"You need to come with us, sir," the nearest agent said, quickly closing the distance between the door and his principal, and shielding Nash with his own body. The agents of his protective detail formed a close circle around him, two of them grabbing him by the shoulders and hustling him out of the Oval Office.

"Gaslamp is secure," an agent reported.

"What's going on?" Nash repeated. But no one spoke. At least, not to him.

The Secret Service agents carried the President in a chokehold as they hustled him through the corridors with silent, focused efficiency. They had their weapons drawn in the hallways of the White House itself, and Nash was certain that if an unlucky visitor happened to get in the way, they would be mown down without so much as a second thought.

The agents didn't stop until Nash was a hundred feet underground, safely ensconced in a surprisingly nondescript conference room situated in the 'PEOC' – the Presidential Emergency Operations Center. The PEOC, a $376 million complex situated underneath the North Lawn, had replaced a smaller bunker with the same name underneath the East Wing of the White House just two years earlier.

Nash hadn't even been given the grand tour yet, though he had sat through a thorough briefing. The place was supposedly built to withstand a direct strike from a two hundred kiloton nuclear warhead, and was filled with sufficient supplies to feed the entire White House staff for over three months.

Nash felt claustrophobic already. His thoughts drifted to his wife. She'd stayed at the family home in upstate New York when he moved into the White House. Their marriage was as good as dead, Nash knew that. Now it was just a matter of optics. Timing. A thirty-year marriage dissolved in a press release and a statement from the White House briefing room.

"Will somebody," he thundered, somewhat flustered from the helter-skelter rush through the White House's surprisingly narrow corridors, "tell me what the hell is going on!"

His chief of staff, Emma Martinez, a no-nonsense woman who had made her political bones in the underbelly of the Chicago machine without ever getting caught up in a scandal, entered the conference room. She was conversing in hushed tones with an aide that Nash didn't recognize.

"Sir, you need to see this," Martinez said, not standing on ceremony.

That was what had first impressed Nash about her – she treated every man, woman and child exactly the same, no matter the situation. She had managed his presidential campaign with frightening efficiency, and after two weeks of helping Nash lead the free world, nothing had changed.

Nash nodded, his irritation immediately forgotten.

"My wife?"

"Secure, sir," she affirmed. "I just got word."

Nash breathed a sigh of silent relief. No matter what had happened between them, Holly was still his wife, and the mother of his child. He cared for her deeply, even if she couldn't love him back.

"This is Ryan Stone, the Director of the National Counterterrorism Center," Martinez said, gesturing at a surprisingly slight African-American man in his late fifties, who had somehow appeared on the opposite side of the conference table. Nash didn't know where all these people appeared from. So many senior people, experts in their fields, all just waiting for the White House to call on the off-chance he needed to pepper them with questions. It didn't exactly seem an efficient use of resources.

"Sir." Stone nodded. Despite his diminutive size, Nash sensed a feeling of calm assurance in the man. He liked it.

"Let's cut to the chase, Stone," Nash said. "I'm figuring by the way my detail just acted that something serious just happened?"

"Yes sir," the director affirmed, picking up a small black

remote control from the center of the conference room table. "About twenty minutes ago, a train was attacked by three terrorist operatives in Colorado, somewhere just outside of a town called Glenwood Springs."

"Casualties?" the president asked.

Hell, this didn't feel real. Two years ago he'd been a first-term senator, with no greater ambitions than getting re-elected. Now, somehow, he found himself sitting in a nuclear bunker underneath the White House, interrogating a man with ten times his experience.

"We don't know for sure, sir."

"Cut the sir, call me Charles," Nash said. "Give me an estimate."

"Yes, uh, sir," Stone said diplomatically. "According to our best guess, at least four hundred people had seat or cabin reservations. We can expect at least one hundred, and perhaps twice that to have boarded the train with a ticket, but no reservation. We are expecting a high mortality rate."

"My God," Nash muttered, realizing for the first time that he was still standing. He sank back into a leather-backed conference room chair, and watched as the rest of the conference room's occupants followed his lead.

"Yes, sir," Stone agreed. "Judging by the aerial footage, very few –"

"Aerial footage?"

"Yes sir," the director agreed, still using that damn honorific. He tapped a button on the remote in his hand, and an LCD screen on the wall began to flicker to life.

"How did we get surveillance assets there so quickly?" Nash asked, quickly dropping back into the lingo he half-remembered from his days in the Marine Corps almost exactly thirty years before.

"We didn't, sir," Stone replied, an ashen look on his face. He gestured at the television, which now displayed ATN, albeit with no sound. "Whoever carried out the attack had a drone on site. A small explosive charge onboard the device detonated shortly after the last shooter was taken down."

"Hell," Nash muttered. His eyes were drawn to a scene of carnage the likes of which he had never seen before.

"Are you telling me that ATN has better information than the entire fucking US intelligence establishment?"

Stone grimaced at an aide before replying. "Yes, sir. Right now the only boots on the ground are locals. We're getting a torrent of information, but it's fragmentary at best, mainly pulled from 911 calls, and frankly the dispatchers aren't coping very well. NSA just re-tasked a surveillance sat, but we won't have eyes-on for about fifteen minutes."

"What about the cops?" Nash said, standing up and walking closer to the screen.

He couldn't believe the story his eyes were telling. There had to be dozens of bodies on the ground. One of the train carriages was smoldering. A ticker running across the bottom of the news broadcast said: "HORROR IN COLORADO – HUNDREDS FEARED DEAD."

"Hundreds," Nash said, his voice tremulous, running a hand through thick brown hair that was beginning to gray, quicker now, ever since the start of the campaign. "My God. And the shooters?"

"We believe they're dead sir."

"All of them?"

"Yes, sir. From what we can see from this footage, along with footage from cameras on board the train that are uploaded to Amtrak servers throughout the journey, there were two shooters, one at either end. They were heavily armed. They proceeded through the train from either side, butchering everyone they came across."

"And what the hell happened out there?" Nash said, jabbing

his thumb at the screen and turning almost accusingly to the director, who was now standing again, his oversized suit making him look almost like a child wearing his father's clothes.

"A third shooter, sir. They waited until first responders made it on scene, and then picked them off one by one. Went for the cops first, which suggests they were trained. They took out anyone who could pose a threat."

"So who took *them* out?" Nash asked. "SWAT?"

"No, sir. Garfield County's SWAT team is only just gearing up. Looks like it was a local."

"A local?"

"Yes sir. A farmer, had a rifle in the back of his truck. Didn't make it on site until after the shooting started, so he hung back, managed to pick off two of them before the third detonated a suicide vest. But none of that's confirmed. The man's in shock, and we don't have anyone else on the scene."

"Okay," Nash said. "Give it to me straight, Stone. What am I looking at here?"

The director shook his head, his face drawn, looking somehow older than he had when he'd entered the room just a few minutes before.

"Honestly, sir, I've got no idea. What you saw in your security briefing this morning was everything we had. There's been no chatter from NSA. No –"

Nash's head flicked right. A woman, couldn't have been more than thirty years old, was sitting behind a small brass placeholder that indicated she was from the National Security Agency. "Is that correct, Miss –"

"Charlotte Hennessey, Mr. President." She nodded apprehensively, leafing through a thick binder on the table in front of her. "We had nothing. Since Birdseye came online two years ago, there hasn't been a single successful coordinated terrorist attack in the mainland United States."

"Until today," Nash said. Then he frowned. "Birdseye? What the hell is that?"

He felt as though he recognized the name, as though it should mean something to him. It had probably been in one of his briefings. There were so many of them, day after day, he wondered how he was supposed to retain even a fraction of the information that was fired at him on a daily basis.

Stone cleared his throat and shot Hennessey a black look. "That's compartmented information, Mr. President, and not everyone in this room has been read in. We can clear the room if you want."

"Forget about it," Nash grumbled. "It's not important. Martinez, you can fill me in on it later."

"Yes, Mr. President."

Nash glanced up at the entrance to the conference room as the door swung open for the first time since he had entered a few minutes – or a few lifetimes – before. A Secret Service agent, armed with a submachine gun, stood facing away from him and toward the doorway. The President shook his head. If someone was getting in here, he thought, then they might as well throw in the towel. The terrorists had won.

The agent tensed briefly, the barrel of his weapon flickering up slightly before he relaxed, allowing an aide into the room. Another young woman that Nash didn't recognize. She walked toward Director Stone, whispered something in his ear and handed him a small piece of white paper.

The room was deathly silent when Stone spoke again.

"Sir," he said, glancing down at the piece of paper in his hand once again, almost as though for reassurance. "There's been another attack."

11

The ride from the TD Garden Arena to 40 Sudbury Street, headquarters of Boston Police Department's District A-1 was ordinarily a short one, since the distance amounted to less than half a mile. On that day in early February, however, the streets were clogged with emergency traffic, crowds of onlookers, and abandoned vehicles – many simply left with their engines running when their owners had fled in fear.

Trapp grunted as he attempted to readjust his position from the back of the police cruiser. Since his hands were ziptied behind his back, the plastic biting into his wrists every time the cruiser bounced over so much as a dropped quarter, his attempts came to little. He thought about asking the officer to his right – a short, anxious Latino man – to cut him a little slack, but decided against it. The poor kid looked like he'd been on the job all of a week. Trapp figured if he spoke, he was likely to give the rookie a heart attack.

And it wasn't like he much wanted to speak. Trapp was no sociopath. Violence affected him as much as it would any other man – he just had a little more experience of it. But it was six months since he had last fired a weapon, and he was out of practice.

Besides, before being thrown back into the cauldron, Trapp had thought he was retired. Out of the game. He'd never expected the streets of one of America's oldest cities to be filled with blood – and certainly not to be thrust right into the center of it. Today was supposed to have been about paying a debt, about quietly remembering the best man he'd ever known, before he slipped away and disappeared for good. Instead, it had ended in fire, and placed Trapp on a path that circled right back to the life he thought he'd left behind.

The officer up front cursed as the cruiser nosed around yet another abandoned vehicle, this time a white Ford Taurus that had been left, engine still chugging, at a forty-five degree angle to the curb. Jason could see what he figured was their destination – a large red brick police station, no more than a couple of hundred yards away.

"Screw it," the officer in the passenger seat said in a thick Boston brogue.

"We'll take the rest on foot. Lopez," he said, spinning in his seat to face the man to Trapp's side. Jason figured it was nice to put a name to a face.

"You're with me. Grab this prick by the shoulder, and if you let go before I order you to, I'll have you doing traffic stops down in Roxbury for the next two years. You hear me?"

Lopez squeaked. The cruiser came to a halt, and his partner – an officer J. Doyle, according to the brass tag on the man's chest – jumped out and opened the door to Trapp's side.

"Get out," he yelled, grabbing Trapp by the scruff of the neck and yanking him so that he didn't really have much of a choice in the matter.

He didn't blame the officers for the way they were acting. All they knew was that dozens were dead, and their prisoner had been found at the scene of the crime. Their reaction was natural. And Trapp had faced worse.

They walked the rest of the way. Jogged, really, with an officer's hand gripping each of Trapp's shoulders. Behind he could hear the sound of heavy boots thundering against the asphalt, as at least another half a dozen heavily armed officers from the Boston Police followed behind.

If this were the movies, he would have been able to slip his restraints without anyone noticing. He would probably have surreptitiously grabbed the Taser from the officer to his left, Lopez, and jammed it into the side of the man to his right.

Then, in one swift movement he would have grabbed Officer Lopez by the neck, used him as cover, relieved him of his weapon and dropped the remaining six officers with the man's service weapon, leaving little more than a tightly drilled bullet hole in each of their foreheads.

Of course, this was not the movies. And while Jason had no doubt that he would be able to take on Officer Lopez, along with the kid's partner, and maybe even one or two of the chasing pack, the more likely scenario was that all three of them would end up dead, peppered by 9 mm rounds. And Trapp had no particular desire to die that day, nor send any of Boston's finest to the grave with him. Besides, he had a sneaking suspicion that if he just waited, he wouldn't be in custody much longer.

At least, not under the jurisdiction of the men of district A-1.

THEY TOOK HIS PRINTS, along with front and side pictures of his face, a swab from inside his cheek, and even a blood sample. Trapp was almost surprised they didn't ask him to squat down so they could stick a finger in his ass.

"So who the fuck are you?" a hulking detective asked, settling into a metal chair that squeaked in protest as he sat down. The interrogation room was nondescript. Two-way mirrors were a thing of the past these days, but there were cameras in all four corners of the room, and Trapp's interrogator set another one on the table in front of him.

"Just a good Samaritan," Trapp said carefully, studying the man across the table from him. "Looked like your boys needed some help."

It was hard to ignore the habits that had been drilled into him over two decades of SERE training. The acronym stood for: Survival, Evasion, Resistance and Escape, and Trapp had spent weeks of his life chained to a wall in Camp Mackall in North Carolina in the pitch black, listening to Metallica albums blasted at top volume directly into his eardrums, and shivering from repeated waterboarding sessions performed with ice-cold Gatorade, just because they could.

In short, Trapp doubted very much that an overweight Boston Police Department detective was going to extract any information from him that he didn't want to give.

"Make this easier for yourself, son," the detective said. "Help me help you."

Hell, Trapp thought. *The man's a walking cliché.*

The detective continued. "You did your country a service today, and"—he narrowed his eyes, scanning Jason's weathered face—"judging by the scars on those forearms, it's not the first time. Listen brother, I get it. I did my time. Five years with the 101st. So help me out here. Just tell me who you are, and I'll make this easy on you. Get you out of those bloody clothes. Maybe get a hot meal inside you. How does that sound?"

Jason closed his eyes briefly, let his head sink back, and exhaled.

"Listen, detective. Let me tell you how things are about to go. In a couple of minutes, your phone is going to ring. Your boss will be on the other end. He's going to ask you to come outside. A few minutes after that, a black SUV is going to pull up outside this station. Some men are going to get out. They probably won't be wearing suits, but you'll know who they are. They'll tell you to forget you ever saw me. They'll tell you that this is a national security matter, and that you need to let the professionals take it from here."

The detective looked bug-eyed at Trapp for a second, and then burst out laughing. He leaned back into his metal chair, which was bolted to the ground, just like the one Trapp was sitting on.

"Damn," he spluttered, as his last fit of laughter subsided. "Just my luck to get a crazy motherfucker like you. How the hell do you think the papers are going to spin this, huh?" The detective made a set of air quotes with his fingers. "Schizophrenic man saves hundreds. You couldn't write this shit."

Jason Trapp remained impassive. He sat back in the uncomfortable metal chair, his posture ramrod straight, his face expressionless. He ticked off the seconds inside his head. And then, just as he had said it would, the detective's cell phone buzzed.

As it happened, things didn't go quite as Trapp had thought they might. Instead of an SUV, his ride was a Sikorsky HH-60. The helicopter was better known as a Pave Hawk, and was scrambled from Hanscom Air Force Base just minutes after Trapp's prints were flagged by an undisclosed CIA "spider" program in Boston PD's servers. It was crewed by men who had done this kind of thing before. They knew better than to ask questions of their cargo, as did the CIA liaison they had picked up on the way.

The fifteen million dollar helicopter touched down gently

on the roof of the police station, maintaining some downward thrust, since the building probably wasn't rated to support its eighteen thousand pound loaded weight.

"You're Trapp?" the liaison said, raising his voice over the heavy thump thump thump of the rotors. The guy was wearing sunglasses, even though a low gray cloud had swept across the city, and held on to them with one hand, protecting them from the downdraft. He bent over almost double, ducking far lower than he needed to protect himself from the machine's rotors. Trapp knew his type. The kind of CIA officer who introduced himself as an agent, when the Agency had no such title, and who let people believe he was James Bond, when in reality his primary role was to babysit VIP helicopter transfers.

"Guilty as charged," Trapp replied.

The liaison grinned. He hadn't bothered to introduce himself, and Trapp had no particular desire to learn his name. "Guess we'll let Langley be the judge of that, huh? Seems like a lot of people have been looking for you."

Jason didn't take the bait. He climbed into the Pave Hawk, donned the protective headphones, and thankfully drowned out the sound of the man's voice. For a second, anyway. The liaison climbed in after him, strapped himself into his seat, and then tapped the microphone meaningfully as the Pave Hawk lifted off.

"What do you want?" Jason asked, thumbing a button on the side of the headset that allowed the intercom to function. His voice was curt and to the point, as it always was.

"You must be important," the liaison said, his voice crackling through the intercom, sounding tinny. "The FAA implemented a no-fly zone across the entire country about twenty minutes ago. Most commercial travel is either diverting to Canada and Mexico, or will be on the ground within an hour. Soon the only birds in the air will be painted in Air Force gray."

As the Pave Hawk lifted into the air, its nose dropping

slightly as the angle of the rotors shifted and the pilot drove it forward, course set for Langley, Virginia, a pair of fighter jets rocketed overhead, flying no higher than five thousand feet, if Trapp was any judge.

The jets were gray, and had no visible armaments mounted underneath, though Trapp knew that meant little. They were F-35s and their weapons loadout was stored internally. Each had enough firepower to turn the air force of a small European country into scrap metal.

Whatever the hell was going on today, someone upstairs was taking it seriously. Trapp thought about asking the liaison if the guy knew anything more than he'd seen on ATN, or in person in the blood-soaked floors of Boston's basketball arena. But he decided against it. If the CIA was going to this effort to retrieve him, then he figured someone would brief him soon enough.

"Huh," Trapp murmured softly, shooting the liaison the kind of look that would have quelled lesser men – or at least, those intelligent enough to understand when they were being dismissed. "Go figure."

He leaned back in his seat, the familiar feeling of the harness almost like a lover's touch around his shoulders, and closed his eyes. It didn't take very many seconds before he was asleep. A lifetime spent infiltrating the world's hottest active war zones had trained him well: sleep when you can. Because you never know when you'll get the chance next.

Unbeknownst to anyone on board, the helicopter's progress toward Langley was being tracked by a highly-classified Orion class spy satellite in Low Earth Orbit, about a hundred miles overhead. The information was downlinked to the NSA's data center in the Utah desert, and then... simply disappeared.

12

Dr. Timothy Greaves slurped from his customary Big Gulp cup, filled to the brim with sugary soda and purchased on his morning commute to the National Security Agency's Utah Data Center. The facility was known by its inhabitants as 'The Hive.'

Hive was short for Bumblehive, the codename for the NSA's newest, top-secret, and heavily-fortified installation – the NSA's very own version of a black site. Except this one didn't interrogate terrorists. It examined the entire world's data, a much more challenging – and valuable – task.

Greaves sat in front of three enormous glowing computer displays, in a dimly lit room in which red and green server lights winked on and off like Christmas tree decorations. In his wildest moments, Greaves imagined that he was sitting on the command deck of the Starship Enterprise – although the reality of his surroundings was somewhat more mundane.

The huge cup was almost empty, but Greaves reached for it again, his thick fingers almost knocking it over onto his keyboard. He caught it at the last moment, the ice rattling against the plastic walls, and his heart beat a little faster. He couldn't face going to IT again – it would've been the third keyboard he'd destroyed in the same way since the start of the year.

And it was only February.

Pushing three hundred pounds, with dyed blue hair, Greaves wasn't the prototypical government employee. He was the most senior research scientist in the entire NSA, and was currently posted at the Hive out of choice, unlike many of his fellow employees, who treated their time in the Utah desert like a tour of duty. But to Greaves, the isolated location was a blessing.

Back at Fort Meade, home to most of the NSA's vast trove of analysts and computer experts, his days were filled with endless meetings. Here, he could concentrate on his research – and by extension, making the NSA the preeminent intelligence gathering organization in the entire world.

But Greaves wasn't just an overweight eccentric with an addiction to soda. He was also a genius programmer – perhaps the best in the entire agency. And with that territory came an endless curiosity.

A curiosity that had been aroused by an anomaly he had detected several days earlier in one of the Hive's many classified subsystems – a program known as Birdseye. Almost anyone else would have ignored it – just an unexpected power draw, a minor bug in a complex system that had mostly been built by the lowest bidder, a network security company owned by the behemoth government contractor Atlas Defense Systems. They were known for producing shoddy work but had political clout at the highest levels. Their former CEO, a man called Robert Jenkins, had even recently been inaugurated as vice president. It was the kind of clout that induced most to look the other way.

But not Dr. Greaves.

The anomaly had bothered him ever since it appeared the previous week, and he'd been working on isolating the cause for hours – ever since he'd shuffled through the security turnstiles that regulated access to the Hive that morning at 6 a.m. And as soon as the debugging routine he created finished its work, he hoped he would have an answer.

He stood up, rolling his sizable neck and releasing hours of accumulated tension. He needed more caffeine, and the soda was almost empty. He decided to head for the break room to refill it. Maybe he'd go with diet this time.

When he entered the room, eyes glued to the pages of an airport thriller, he didn't immediately detect the hushed silence. A television flickered on the wall, and he had the vague sense that others were in the room, but the book was engrossing. The author mostly had it wrong – real intelligence work was significantly less exciting than the writer made it seem, at least in Greaves' experience, but it was a good read.

"Can you believe it, doc?"

"Believe what?" Greaves said, turning the page, only using his peripheral vision to make sure he didn't knock into the back of a chair en route to the soda fountain.

"You haven't seen?"

The woman's stunned tone cut through Greaves' distraction. His subconscious finally clocked that something unusual was happening. He looked up, and found the break room packed with NSA employees. Normally it was half-empty, but today it seemed like practically every member of staff was in it.

Greaves looked up at the television, and almost had a heart attack. The TV was showing ATN – aerial footage of a horrific terrorist attack. A news ticker scrolled across the bottom of the screen. 'AMERICA UNDER ATTACK.' His eyes flickered across the screen, reading the information that was scrolling past.

Dozens of attacks. Thousands feared dead. The President secure in the White House bunker. How could this be happening?

"What the hell is going on?"

No one replied. A woman sobbed silently in front of him, tears streaking down her face, and carrying her eye makeup with it. She held a cup of coffee, the absence of steam indicating that it had long since gone cold, her trembling fingers stained brown where it had spilled out.

Greaves was stunned. Most of America was in shock, too – but it was different for him. The whole point of the Birdseye system was to make a day like this impossible.

Greaves dropped his cup, all thoughts of caffeine forgotten. The plastic clattered against the ground, but no one turned around. No one appeared to notice. Every single inhabitant of the break room was glued to the television, eyes fixed on the horror that was sweeping America.

He ran back to his desk as fast as his thick legs could carry him. When he returned to his triple computer monitors, his blue hair luminescent in their glow, the debugging routine was complete. Two words inhabited the center of his screen.

INTRUSION DETECTED

Greaves blinked. This was not possible. It could not be possible. Birdseye was his baby. It took in information from every source the NSA had access to, and crunched data in ways that no human analyst could match. It had kept America safe from attack for almost two years.

Until today.

It couldn't be a coincidence. And as Greaves' eyes scanned the debugging report, as he began to process the meaning of the information on his monitor, his shock began to give way to a creeping sense of horror.

If what he was reading was true – and given the carnage on

ATN, there was no way it couldn't be – then America's largest intelligence agency hadn't just been hacked, it had been completely compromised. The terrorist attacks hadn't slipped through the net; they'd been welcomed with open arms.

His fingers felt clumsy as he reached for the secure phone on his desk. This needed to go straight to the top. And luckily for Greaves, he was a close personal friend of the NSA director, Jim Donahue. They had met when Donahue commanded the 513th Military Intelligence Brigade at Fort Gordon, down in Georgia, and the then Brigadier General Donahue had immediately recognized Greaves' prodigious talent.

When Donahue was promoted to head up INSCOM, the US Army's prestigious Intelligence and Security Command at Fort Belvoir, Virginia, he had taken Greaves with him. And then again when he was tapped to head up the NSA. Whenever Director Donahue was in town, the two men went out for a beer. And so Greaves had the man's private number. He punched it in, fingers leaden with horror.

The line rang, and rang, and rang. And then it died. Greaves dialed the number again, breathing into the microphone in short, ragged gasps. Finally, Donahue picked up. Greaves heard frantic activity in the background. When the director spoke, his voice was curt and distracted.

"Greaves, how the hell could this happen? How did we miss this?"

"Jim," the data scientist almost whispered. "I found something you need to see."

"What is it?" Donahue said. "I don't have time to play games with you. Not today. I'm on my way to brief the President. Tell me you've got a handle on this."

"Jim, I need you to fire up the jet – get down here now, and don't tell anyone what you're doing."

"What the hell are you talking about?"

"It's about Birdseye," Greaves said almost manically. "I can't say anything else over the phone. I need you to trust me on this one. You know I wouldn't ask if it wasn't important."

"This is a secure line."

"No," Greaves said quietly, running his fingers through his hair. "Not for this, it isn't."

13

The Pave Hawk helicopter cruised at an altitude of around seven thousand feet for most of the journey, and Trapp tasted burnt aviation fuel and the tang of salt most of the way. As the crow flies, the distance between Central Boston and Virginia is around four hundred miles, but the no-fly zone around New York City was impenetrable – even for the CIA – and so the Air Force pilot was forced to fly a few miles out into the Atlantic to bypass the city.

Even with the low gray cloud sitting over the East Coast that afternoon, Trapp had to admit it was a beautiful sight.

After a brief hot refuel at McGuire Air Force Base, just southeast of Trenton, NJ, during which the helicopter's rotors didn't stop turning, the aircraft was off again. In total, by the time Trapp's ride began to lose altitude a few miles out from its destination, hugging the Potomac River for the last gasps of its journey, he'd been strapped into the thing for over three hours. They hadn't even let him out to stretch his legs at McGuire. It didn't even come close to rivaling the longest time he'd spent in one of these things – that crown was taken by a twelve-hour insertion into the mountains of eastern Iran, but he had been a decade younger back then. Now the helicopter's incessant vibration was giving him a headache.

"We there yet?" Trapp snapped into his mic, on a private channel that only he and the liaison from the CIA were plugged into. He didn't want to give the guy the satisfaction of a conversation, but his ass ached like hell. Whatever was going to happen to him when he stepped off this helicopter, he just wanted to get it over with.

Thankfully, he didn't have to listen to the CIA officer's response. His headset crackled, and he heard instead the clipped, professional tones of a veteran Air Force pilot.

"Kids, this is the end of the road. We're about three miles out. My orders are to drop you guys off, and then forget I ever met you. I hope you enjoyed your flight with us today, and don't forget to fill out the survey on your way out."

The pilot circled the target coordinates a couple of times to scope out the landing site, and Trapp did the same, though for different reasons. They must've been about thirty miles from CIA headquarters at Langley, if Trapp's mental map was functioning properly.

The landing spot was in the middle of an overgrown field, the thick green grass undulating wildly from the helicopter's downwash. An old brick house stood at the north end of the field, built in the old colonial style. Trapp figured it had to be a couple hundred years old. In the field itself, he saw two men, armed with rifles, crouched low and shielding their eyes from the rotor wash.

The helicopter's rugged rubber tires kissed the earth about three quarters of a mile from the Potomac River. Trapp unclipped his harness, nodded his thanks to airmen who were doing their best to look like they weren't dying to know who the hell their passenger was, and stepped off, his boots thudding onto the ground a second later. He'd done the same thing hundreds of times before, though usually armed, and with a target in mind.

"Hold it right there, Trapp," a voice yelled out, loud even over the thundering of the helicopter rotors. Trapp did as he was told, freezing in place and surveying the speaker – a man in his early thirties, who was cradling a black Heckler & Koch HK416 submachine gun in his grip. The man's posture was relaxed, but had an intense lethality about it.

Trapp recognized the weapon instantly. It was standard issue for operators in the CIA's Special Activities Division. That made sense. It was, in fact, his weapon of choice – extremely accurate, with a manageable form factor, and most importantly of all, dependable. The thing never jammed, never malfunctioned. When an operator needed to spit a lot of lead in the bad guys' direction, an HK416 would do it forever without complaining once.

"Who the hell are you?" Trapp asked, eyeing the man with his steel-blue gaze.

The shooter was dressed in dark combat fatigues, and had the mark of a special operator about him – a cold, lethal tension that suggested he could snap into action with a millisecond's notice.

Out of the corner of his eye, Trapp saw the man's partner was dressed and armed exactly the same. Except the other shooter had his weapon raised and aimed directly at his skull. He did the math, quickly, and decided for the time being to play it cool. In all honesty, he didn't really have much of a choice. Either of the two operators could drop him before he moved a yard.

The man ignored the question.

"Get back on the helicopter," he yelled, his voice a slow Arkansas drawl.

Trapp's brow furrowed. The hell? What was the point in

dragging him halfway across the country just to send him back? And then it clicked. The operator wasn't speaking to him.

"But –"

"No questions. Get back on the helicopter, and fuck off," the shooter shouted, jerking his thumb to accentuate his point.

Trapp glanced over his shoulder, at the dismayed frown on the liaison officer's face, and a wide grin crept across his face. Maybe he didn't mind being held at gunpoint, after all.

The guy did as he was told, his hunched posture suggesting he was experiencing an intense, burning humiliation. Somehow that made Trapp feel as though everything was right with the world. Judging by the reaction of the Pave Hawk's crew, they didn't want him on board either. Either way, a few seconds later, the pitch of the rotor whine increased, and the helicopter lifted back into the air. Within a minute, it was just a distant memory.

"So, guys," Trapp said, turning back to the two armed men who had greeted him. "Either of you got a name? Because you clearly know mine, and that puts me at a bit of a disadvantage."

The operators ignored him. The one who seemed to be in charge, the man with the languid Southern accent, jerked his thumb at the brick building.

"Come on," he said.

Trapp shrugged. The operators were just muscle – they wouldn't know anything, and he didn't have the energy to mess with them.

"After you."

They fell in around him, covering him expertly, and maintaining a sufficient distance that he knew they would be able to cut him down long before he managed to grab a weapon from them. They were clearly expertly trained – and probably by the same men who had taught Trapp himself. As they reached the house, the lead operator beckoned for Trapp to come to a halt.

"Hands on your head," he said, motioning toward his partner. "Sketch, check he's clean."

The junior operator, Sketch, set his weapons down, twenty feet away from Trapp's reach. They weren't taking any chances, and he respected them for that. They clearly knew his reputation, or whoever was on the other side of the house's front door certainly did. The guy in charge kept his weapon trained on Trapp the entire time, finger resting on the trigger.

"Move your legs apart," Sketch said as he patted Trapp down.

"Usually when someone asks me to do that," Trapp groused, "they buy me a drink first."

But he did as he was told. Despite himself, he was interested to see where this went.

"He's clean," the junior guy said, stepping back and retrieving his weapons.

"Let him in."

As Trapp stepped across the house's threshold, it took his eyes a second to adjust. He could tell that there were two men inside, though whether they were armed, or he knew them, he wasn't quite sure. A second later, as a voice emanated from the darkness, everything became clear.

"Jason."

Trapp looked up sharply, clenching his knuckles from the shock of recognition. He knew the man on the left, a junior analyst named Kyle Partey. The analyst was an African-American man in his late twenties, and dressed like an Oxford professor – down to the tweed jacket, complete with leather elbow patches.

Kyle was a prodigy in the Agency, fast-tracked from the moment he signed up. He had an awkward demeanor, never made eye contact behind his rimless glasses. But Trapp had met few men who were as talented at picking apart the tangled web of strings that connected a terrorist organization as the young analyst in front of him, who was clutching a thin leather briefcase with sweaty palms. He didn't look like much, but the kid was the best the CIA had. But Kyle Partey wasn't the reason for Trapp's shock.

"Mitchell," Trapp said, his voice a grinding pit of menace as his eyes scanned the room, looking for an opening. Looking for a chance to do what he had dreamed of for so many nights. "What the hell are you doing here?"

Mike Mitchell, the deputy director of the CIA's famed Special Activities Division, eyed Trapp coolly. There was little about the man to suggest that twenty years before, he had been one of the CIA's most famed killers, before quickly climbing the ranks. He had mousy brown hair, brown eyes and was of no more than average height. Trapp dwarfed him.

"It's deputy Director Mitchell to you, Jason."

"Not anymore. Like I told you, I'm out."

Mitchell nodded, almost sadly, Trapp thought. To his side, Partey glanced at his wristwatch, and not for the first time. What had him in such a damn hurry?

"So you are, Jason," he said. "Where've you been the last six months? I thought you were dead. I thought for sure –"

Mitchell's voice trailed off, just as a wave of anger flashed across Trapp's vision. He charged forward, taking the two special operators behind him by surprise. He tackled Mitchell, who didn't resist, and flung him against the safe house's wall, pressing his forearm against the man's throat.

"You thought I had to be dead, didn't you?" Trapp said coldly. "Because if I wasn't –"

The two operators dragged Trapp backward, off their boss. One of them, he didn't see which, kicked the back of his knee, forcing Trapp to the ground. He kneeled there, glowering up at Mitchell, who was massaging his throat and wincing. Trapp knew that behind him, just out of reach, two barrels would be trained at the back of his head.

"You want us to restrain him, boss?"

Mitchell shook his head. "No. *Fuck*. Trapp, I had nothing to do with what happened to you in Yemen. I promise. I know you must think I was neck-deep in it. I figured you were coming after me this whole time. But I promise you. I didn't know. I wouldn't have sent you there, sent either of you there, if I knew it was a trap."

Jason chewed the inside of his cheek, studying his former boss's face for any sign the man was lying. Though Mitchell was as well trained an operative as Trapp was – or had been, anyway – Jason had worked for him for years. Long enough to know, he thought, whether the man was telling the truth.

"Um, sir," Kyle interjected. He glanced at his wristwatch again, before looking back up – but not quite making eye contact with Mitchell. "We don't have time for this. We need to get moving. Now."

"Kyle's right," Mitchell said. He glanced up, and to Mitchell's left. "Perkins, give me your side arm."

"Boss –?"

"That's an order."

The operator did as he was told, and handed the Glock 19 to Mitchell, grip first. The deputy director closed his eyes for a second, almost as if he was steadying himself, then his eyelids snapped open, revealing a look of determination underneath. He gave the pistol to Trapp, who looked up with surprise.

"If you're going to shoot me, Jason, do it now. If not, we need to move."

Move?

Trapp grasped the weapon, wondering if it was a trick. The pistol felt exactly as it should, but that meant little. The rounds could have been swapped out for blanks or duds, or the firing pin removed entirely. But Trapp didn't think so. Somehow, as he looked up at his former boss, he couldn't detect any dishonesty on the man's face. Maybe a little sadness behind those brown eyes, and a look of weary resignation etched into the lines on his forehead. But Trapp decided he was telling the truth.

"Fuck." Trapp swore loudly, the word ricocheting around the old colonial's four walls like a gunshot. The tweed-clad analyst to Mitchell's left visibly flinched. Trapp stood up, figuring that if they were going to kill him, they probably would've done it by now.

"Thanks." Mitchell grinned weakly. He looked at the two operators. "Perkins, Winks, open this thing up. We gotta go."

"Hell of a risk you just took," Trapp said, impressed. He still felt a tension inside him, six months of anger and thoughts of revenge coiled within him like a spring. But unless he was very much mistaken, neither Kyle Partey nor his boss had had anything to do with the death of his partner.

The two operators kicked an armchair over – the only piece of furniture in the room, and pushed it to one side, revealing a trap door underneath.

"What the hell is this?" Trapp asked, stepping over to the door, and looking from Mitchell to the entrance of a tunnel that had suddenly appeared in the house's living room.

"I'll fill you in," Mitchell said, glancing at the CIA analyst, who was now hopping from foot to foot with agitation. "Kyle – how long we got?"

"Can't say for sure, boss," the kid replied. "Maybe six minutes, if we're lucky."

"And if we're not?"

"Then we're already dead…"

14

A t the highest levels of government, the process used to identify a target, locate its coordinates and authorize its destruction is known as a 'kill chain.'

In recent years, the term has primarily been used when describing the elimination of America's most wanted terrorist enemies, and hotspots across the globe from Afghanistan to Yemen. In most of those strikes, the weapons platform of choice has been a Predator drone, or one of its later variants, such as the General Atomics MQ-9 Reaper, and the weapon of choice an AGM-114 Hellfire air-to-ground missile. Enough to vaporize a target and leave very little trace of whatever vehicle or building they previously inhabited.

A clean kill.

The decision-makers in this particular kill chain would no doubt have preferred to have commandeered an MQ-9, using code specially implanted for that precise purpose, to perform this particular mission. Fighter jets have pilots. Pilots are human. Humans ask questions. Machines don't.

On the other hand, pilots are usually among the best-trained of all America's war fighters. When the Air Force is trusting a pilot with a thirty million dollar piece of equipment, it usually pays to ensure that they are willing to follow orders.

Whatever those orders might be.

Major Oliver Peters, call sign 'Rockstar' was, at that moment, in the cockpit of his F-16 Fighting Falcon, at an altitude of about twenty-five thousand feet. A low cloud hung over the nation's capital, but his deadly airframe soared high above it. The clouds looked like a blizzard-hit mountain range as they billowed beneath him, scuttling with the wind. It was a beautiful sight – one of the many reasons that Peters loved his job. But he barely registered it today. Adrenaline pumped through his system as he rode the thundering roar of the jet turbines behind him and contemplated what he might be forced to do.

He had orders to keep the airspace around the capital empty, and he intended to follow those orders to the letter. Even if it meant shooting down a passenger airplane. He wouldn't allow another 9/11. Not on his watch.

Peters was a Quick Reaction Alert pilot, assigned to the 113th wing, DC Air National Guard. When the shooting started in Colorado, his fighter jet was idling on the asphalt at Andrews Air Force Base. As soon as reports of the wave of terrorist attacks around the nation began to break in NORAD headquarters, he had been given the go order, and he had spent the last three hours circling the empty skies above Virginia.

At this precise moment, Peters was readying himself for an aerial refueling. It was a complex maneuver, but one he had performed hundreds of times before, both in the simulator, and in the air. He thumbed his mic.

"Bulldog, this is Rockstar. I'm reading just a shade under two thousand pounds of fuel on the gauges, so you guys are looking pretty attractive right about now."

"Copy that, Rockstar," came the radio response from the boom operator of the KC-46 Pegasus air-to-air refueling tanker that had been tasked with topping him up.

As Major Peters broke away from the refueling tanker a few minutes later, waggling his wings in thanks, he received another radio transmission, this time on a dedicated secure channel.

"Rockstar, this is Colonel Craig Schofield, authenticating Victor, Tango, Oscar. How copy?"

Peters frowned. It was unusual to receive a communication from anyone other than his wingman or his own ground control team down at Andrews. But the authentication request seemed valid, so he grabbed the codebook from a pouch on his breast and thumbed through until he found the correct entry.

"This is Rockstar, authenticating Mike, Mike, Bravo. To what do I owe the honor, Colonel?"

"Son –" the radio crackled.

If it had been a handset, rather than a hundred thousand dollar unit embedded somewhere in the airframe of his F-16, Peters would have bashed it against something – the universal signal for 'Why the hell isn't this thing working right?' The sound quality was poor. It sounded tinny to Peters' ear, but hell, he could just about make out the man's voice. And after all, the Colonel had identified himself correctly, so it was the pilot's responsibility to do and die, rather than question why – a responsibility that Major Peters took very seriously.

"– I'm requesting a kinetic strike on the coordinates I just uploaded."

Peters blinked. Surely he hadn't had that right? A kinetic strike on a target in the continental United States? When he'd blasted his afterburners and taken his jet into the sky a few hours before, he had been prepared to shoot down a hijacked airliner, but this was another matter entirely.

"Say again, Colonel. Am I hearing you right?"

The tinny voice on the other end of the radio came again.

"Roger, Rockstar. I say again, you are weapons free. Proceed to your target coordinates immediately and eliminate it. Stay on station until you give me your battle damage assessment. How copy?"

"Sir, what you're asking... I'm gonna need to confirm that with my own chain of command–"

The radio went silent for a second, and then crackled again. "Son, are you questioning my orders?"

"No sir, but –"

"Rockstar, CIA has received intelligence that an ISIS cell infiltrated the Mexican border fourteen days ago, and made its way to a safe house on the eastern side of the Potomac River. A safe house at the coordinates I just forwarded you. Following so far?"

Peters chewed his lip and mentally kicked himself for questioning his orders. He decided to keep his responses short and sweet from now on, just as the chain of command usually preferred.

"Yes, sir."

"Our intelligence suggests that this particular cell has acquired a canister of a modified strain of the Ebola virus. It has a mortality rate of 53%, and they are planning to deploy it at any second. If we don't contain the situation immediately –"

The major didn't need to hear another word. He knew his duty – and he'd sat in on enough briefings on the dangers of biological weaponry to understand the stakes. The protocol was clear – it was in fact the very reason there was a two thousand pound guided bomb on the wing of his F-16. If there was a threat this close to Washington DC, it had to be stopped.

Immediately.

There was, of course, no bioweapon, and no ISIS cell at those coordinates. But Peters didn't know that. He punched down on the mic button on his control stick.

"Proceeding to coordinates, Colonel. Time to target is just over three minutes. Confirming weapons free."

15

The four men ran headlong down the long, dark tunnel, sprinting as fast as they could. The darkness was only illuminated by the flashlights mounted on the barrels of the two operators' submachine guns, which made for a surreal experience. Trapp almost felt like he was in a European techno club, the thundering of boots against the tunnel's stone floor a heavy drumbeat, the flashing lights mimicking a strobe light overhead.

Trapp didn't know why he was running. But from the look of fear that he had seen on Kyle's face, he figured there must be a good reason.

"Move, move, move," the two operators yelled from behind, almost like drill instructors at boot camp.

Trapp didn't need telling twice – though he had been out of the espionage game for the past six months, he hadn't *entirely* neglected his fitness. Nothing masked the pain of losing your partner like a grueling fifteen-mile run. Nothing except expensive scotch, that is. And he had liberally used both methods.

From time to time, one of Perkins and Winks grabbed the two CIA desk jockeys and physically manhandled them down the tunnel. A couple of times, Kyle tripped and almost fell, but before he had the opportunity to tumble to the ground and cause a pileup, he'd been yanked back to his feet and pushed forward. Through it all, the analyst kept hold of his briefcase, which was now scratched and dented from careening off the tunnel's brick walls. Trapp wondered why the kid didn't just drop it. Surely it wasn't that important.

"You stop, you die," Perkins yelled in his strangely languid drawl, and now Trapp really was back at basic training. The instructors back at Fort Benning had screamed very similar phrases at the top of their lungs, while firing off blanks from their rifles as Trapp and his fellow raw recruits belly-crawled through the mud, underneath barbed wire strung out above them to catch the unwary.

Even Trapp's well-conditioned lungs were beginning to scream out in protest by the time an opening on the left-hand side of the tunnel came into view.

"Let's go, let's go," one of the two men called out, each grabbing an arm or a leg, and physically carrying Mitchell and Partey the last few hard yards of the journey.

Trapp followed just behind the four CIA men. They dived through the doorway, entering a pitch-black room to the side of the tunnel. The second Trapp was through, Perkins slammed a heavy steel door closed, and pulled a deadbolt into place.

"Winks," he panted, ignoring the strains of his panting lungs. "Grab that crate, push it against the door."

Trapp could only see what the flashlights illuminated. The room was narrow, but went back a long way. The walls were made of red brick, but hundreds of years of seepage from the water table had rendered them nearly black. They glistened in the reflection of the flashlights. A *drip-drip-drip* sound punctuated the heavy panting now ricocheting from wall to ceiling to wall.

"Will someone," Trapp panted, "tell me what the hell is going on?"

His breath was quickly returning to normal, and he could see the same was happening with the two CIA special operators. Mitchell and Partey, by contrast, were bent double, hands on their knees, sucking oxygen through their teeth in ragged gasps.

Perkins grinned, though Trapp only guessed that from the flash of the man's teeth. He grabbed a couple of glow sticks from a pouch somewhere on his uniform, in one swift motion, and tossed them around the empty room.

"What is this place?" Trapp asked, figuring he wasn't going to get a straight answer from Mitchell until the man recovered. He looked around the room, taking in what little detail he could make out from the green glow now playing against the walls. On the floor lay rusted metal bands – almost like hoops from barrels that had long ago rotted away.

"Old Civil War smuggling route, runs right down to the Potomac," Perkins replied. He seemed to have warmed up to Trapp, ever since he hadn't shot the man's boss point blank when he'd had the opportunity.

"Most of these warehouses are bricked up now. They used to run tours down here, thirty years ago. The tunnel's still structurally sound, but most of these warehouse rooms are caving in. So they closed them off, and then eventually stopped coming down here."

Kyle gobbled in a deep breath of air and interjected. "The Agency bought the land a decade ago. The owner died, and the estate didn't care about it. Never come in useful, not until today."

"Since you seem to have recovered," Trapp said carefully, "mind telling me what's so damn important down here?"

He didn't have to wait long to find out. A muffled *crump* sound reverberated through the tunnel walls. Someone yelled

"Down," and Jason was only too happy to oblige. He knew that sound. Had heard it hundreds of times before, on battle-fields across the globe. Although usually, he was on the other side.

It was an airstrike.

When the shockwave hit, it sucked the air out of the little side room. Trapp felt the breeze on his cheeks as it rushed out. Irrationally, he wondered whether this might be how he died – asphyxiated in a dark little hole, deep under the ground. What a way to go out.

"Jesus fucking Christ," Trapp yelled, as much to steady his nerves as for any other reason. The blood sounded like a hurri-cane in his ears. His heart thundered in his chest as adrenaline surged around his body. It was a natural reaction. Anyone who's ever been on the receiving end of high explosive munitions knows that there's nothing cowardly about shitting yourself when the bombs start falling. It doesn't matter how well-trained a soldier is. There's something about an air strike that engenders complete, total helplessness. Either you survive, or you don't – and how you get through it doesn't matter in the end.

It took what felt like hours, but was probably under a minute, before the sound of the explosion faded away. Trapp looked nervously at the structure sitting on top of them. If he really was in a Civil War smuggling tunnel, then that meant it was hundreds of years old. Even new, he wouldn't have wanted to trust his life to it. In this state, they were all lucky they were still breathing, and that the bricks hadn't collapsed on top of them, staving their skulls in.

"So now you know," Mitchell said, his voice loud against the sudden quiet. His back was against the warehouse room's wall, his face a muddy gray from the dust that had fallen from the mortar all around them as the structure re-settled after the shockwave. "Trapp, someone wants you dead."

Trapp didn't reply for a second. He just blinked. Surely he hadn't heard Mitchell right.

"You're saying…"

"Kyle, run him through it. It's about time he found out what he's missed while he was away."

THE TWO CIA special operators stepped out of the dark little room, purportedly to check the tunnel hadn't caved in at the other end. Trapp had been the muscle on an operation often enough to know they were making themselves scarce so the adults could speak amongst themselves.

"You know, Mitchell, I spent the last six months deciding how to kill you," he said.

Trapp almost grinned when he saw the rabbit-in-the-head-lights look on Kyle's face as the young analyst heard what he said. He was still clutching the slim leather briefcase that he'd had up top. Trapp had to admit that he was impressed at the presence of mind the kid had to keep hold of it, when he knew – somehow – that he was running for his life.

"You know, Trapp," Mitchell replied, mirroring his tone, "I spent the last six months wondering when you were going to do it."

"Good thing I didn't get around to it, huh?"

"You're telling me."

Trapp slumped back against the brick. He was covered in gray dust and black filth. Hell, his fingers were still stained with blood from his tangle with the shooters back in Boston. He'd already been through the wringer, and this day was only just getting warmed up.

"I'm sorry," Kyle said, his voice cracking as he released the clips holding his briefcase closed. The little thoughts echoed around the dark room. "I didn't see it. I should have seen it."

"Seen what?" Trapp asked gruffly, though he thought he had an idea.

"Yemen," the analyst replied simply. "It was a setup, not a screwup. The intel was too perfect. I should –"

"The intel was dogshit," Trapp replied, his voice harsh, accusing. When he blinked, he saw the explosions from that night painted on the backs of his eyelids. He'd relived that operation a thousand times. Every time he laid his head on the pillow and closed his eyes at night he saw that warehouse go up in flames.

And Kyle Partey had sent him there. To die.

Kyle hung his head in shame. "The intel was dogshit," he agreed, for once not needing to avoid anyone's eyes – his glasses were coated thick with dust. "Perfect dogshit. I fell for it. Hook, line and sinker. You were meant to die in that warehouse, Trapp. You and your partner."

"Ryan," Trapp said, his voice raw, for once in his life tears prickling at the corners of his eyes. "Ryan Price. Best fucking operator I ever met. Best friend I ever had. And now he's dead."

Mitchell spoke. "It's my fault as much as it's Kyle's. Two years ago, the NSA started sending us mission packets –"

"I know," Trapp said, doing his best to re-establish control over his emotions after the unaccustomed lapse. "I went on enough of them. I told you something didn't feel right. The targets we were going after, the way they suddenly all had to die, instead of taking them back for interrogation. We were missing out on vital intel. None of it made sense."

"You did." Mitchell nodded. "But they were always airtight. Like something out of fucking Minority Report. Knew where the targets were going to be before they did. Knew how their money moved, what ships their weapons were on, what targets they planned to strike. We didn't know where the intel was coming from – classified above my fucking paygrade, if you can believe it," Mitchell spat.

"But frankly, we didn't care. The director was happy, the President was happy, the suits on the intelligence committee thought we walked on water. And there wasn't a single successful terrorist attack on an American target for almost two years."

"Until today," Trapp said.

Mitchell grimaced, and Trapp could see a deep sadness written on his dusty, etched forehead. "Until today. I guess they paid us back ten times over."

Kyle spoke again. Trapp had almost forgotten he was there, so lost in his own pain, memories and grief.

"They hit the Hoover building in Washington while you were in the air. Active shooters in over two dozen high schools. The thing in Boston and another five just like it. Dozens of car bombs. The attack on Amtrak Six. IEDs laid under the cover of night. More casualties than Pearl Harbor or 9/11. They're calling it the single deadliest day in American history."

"Fucking hell," Trapp breathed. He'd known it was bad. He just hadn't known how bad.

"Hell is right," Kyle said, sounding somehow more self-assured now than Trapp had ever seen him before. Like he was in his element. "You were right, Trapp. I should have seen it before. I don't know how I didn't."

"Right about what?"

"The intelligence we were getting, it was..." Kyle paused, searching for the right word. "Doctored. Manufactured. Some of it was real, but it was strung together, made to tell a story that it shouldn't have." He paused, removed his glasses and attempted to clean them with his dusty shirt. It didn't do much.

"And you believed it?" Trapp asked. It wasn't a question so much as an accusation.

"We all did, Jason," Mitchell replied. "Had no reason not to. The results spoke for themselves."

"Until now."

"Yes, until now," Mitchell agreed.

"Seems to me," Trapp said, "that someone was intentionally pulling the wool all our eyes. Feinting left so they could land a knockout blow to the right."

Mitchell nodded. "You're right. Kyle's been tracking it for a few months now."

"Ever since you died," the analyst agreed, nodding his head vigorously. "Or didn't. There was something wrong with that operation, right from the very start. But we were getting pushed from half a dozen three-letter agencies to go ahead with it."

"So you didn't do your homework?" Trapp said. "Just sent me and Ryan in there to die?"

Mitchell shrugged, interjecting. "You knew what you signed up for, Trapp. I was in your shoes once, too. You can't always wait until you have every piece of information."

"Waiting till you had just a couple of them would've been nice…"

"After the operation went sideways," Mitchell said euphemistically, "I ordered Kyle to do a full tear-down. Leave no stone unturned."

Trapp turned back to the dusty young analyst. "And?"

"I found something. Buried in the satcom records. An intrusion disguised to look like a simple buffer overflow. Easy to miss unless you squinted real hard. Someone was watching. Listening to every word you two spoke."

"Who?" Trapp asked.

He could barely believe what he was hearing. He'd spent the last six months assuming that the Agency had wanted him dead, had figured that he and his former partner were loose ends that needed tying up. It wouldn't have been unusual. Hell, that's what the safety deposit box in Chinatown was for. He'd tossed and turned at night, burning up with anger, focused on the man now in the very same room as him – and he'd gotten it all wrong.

Kyle shook his head, almost morosely. His posture changed subtly, molding into a slump against the warehouse's brick wall. "I don't know. But I went back, tore through our systems, using the off-site backups. Went back five years. And..."

Trapp motioned for the man to continue.

"It lines up with the dates this NSA system came online. Exactly. It looks like they were just probing at first. Testing our weaknesses. Listening in. But they were definitely there, on our servers. We got the first mission about three months later. A kill order, some Afghan Army colonel."

"Wasn't one of mine," Trapp said. "Why did they want him dead?"

"Who knows? The intelligence packet the NSA sent over said he was working with the local ISIS franchise. But I'm not so sure. Maybe it was just to test the kill chain, find out whether we'd carry out their dirty work. But they ramped up after that. One a month, then every couple of weeks."

Mitchell spoke up.

"The FBI was getting them too: a massive increase in the number of terrorists trying to make it through the southern border. Ten times as many as the year before. All recruited online, sent money, documents, and all telling the same story."

Trapp spread his hands. "So what? Everyone wins. We lop off the head of the snake, and send the cannon fodder to Gitmo."

"It's like you said, Trapp," Kyle said. "Someone was showing us their left hand to distract us from the gun in the right. And whoever they are, whatever they want, this goes to the very top. Unless I'm very much mistaken, this has nothing to do with Islamic terrorism. They might be the boots on the ground, but someone else is pulling the strings."

The silence hung heavy in the still, dark room. Mitchell stood up, his filthy Oxfords scraping the stone floor as he walked over to the door, and rapped against it twice. The sound echoed down the tunnel.

"Perkins," he yelled. "It's time to go."

"So," he said, turning back to Trapp. "Now you understand. I'm many things, Jason. A fool, maybe. I failed you. Failed you both. But I'm no traitor. And neither are you. So, are you with us?"

16

When FBI agent Dani Carter woke, she was blind.

A wail of sirens droned in the background, and the smell of smoke, dust and charred flesh drifted on the air accented by a harsh, medical tang that reminded Dani's dazed mind of an operating theater.

In the darkness, she panted. Her body sang with pain. She didn't know where she was. She barely remembered *who* she was. She was awake, but only barely clinging on to consciousness, her brain slowly rebooting after the shock it had experienced.

"Just stay where you are, agent."

The voice came as though from a great distance. It was a man's voice, deep and calm and clinical, though had Dani been more awake she might have picked up on a tense undertone. Its owner was stressed, but perhaps used to operating in that kind of environment. In the background, there was a low hum, like that of a diesel generator, punctuated by the violent beeping of medical devices.

"Where... where am I?" Dani breathed. She couldn't even hear herself. Moving her lips hurt; they felt dry and chapped.

She dragged her tongue across them for moisture, and tasted copper and smoke, but it didn't help.

"Here, drink," the voice said, sliding a plastic straw between Dani's desiccated lips. The touch of the cold water was blissful. She drank greedily.

"You're safe, Agent Carter."

Dani felt a flicker of irritation run through her body. The emotion signaled that she was alive. Why wasn't this person answering her questions? Who was he? And where was *she*?

She struggled to sit up, her fingers reaching out and touching the cold metal of a gurney underneath her. Her shoulder lanced with pain as she moved, and she winced.

"You need to lie down," the voice said from the darkness. "You've been out a while. You're concussed – it's dangerous to move too quickly. You need to let your brain recover."

"What happened?" Dani asked again, voice spiking with annoyance now. Why couldn't she remember anything? Had there been an accident? The last thing she remembered was driving to the Hoover Building that morning, for the ceremony. And then…

Nothing.

Just flickers of motion in the darkness. She must have hit her head. Yes, that made sense. Had she fallen?

Dani squeezed her eyes shut. At least, she thought she did. She wasn't certain whether they were open or closed. She was so dizzy. Why couldn't she think?

Her dad.

Oh God, her dad. She'd gestured for him to hit the deck, but had he understood what she meant?

Was he…

Dani reached out wildly, her heart pounding. In the distance, a machine beeped wildly. It might have been attached to her, but she didn't know. Her fingers found the man's covered arm.

"My dad," she said, her stomach constricted, her voice a wheeze of fear and pain. "Is he here?"

The silence that followed her words lasted for what felt like forever. "I'm... I'm sorry, agent. I –"

"Is he alive?"

This time, there was no answer.

Dani pushed herself up again, nausea forgotten as adrenaline flooded her system. Her heart was thundering inside her chest, the pain in her shoulder forgotten. She reached up, to her face. Her fingers scraped across the bandage, and she tore it off. The sudden brightness made her squint and squeeze her eyes shut.

As her vision came back into focus, in pieces, rather than all at once, Dani took in her surroundings. She was in a tent with a low, curved ceiling. Ribbed, like something off a military base, or perhaps a refugee camp. It was a triage tent, Dani quickly realized as her faculties returned to her. The adrenaline briefly pushed aside her panic over the fate of her father, and allowed her to think logically.

Rationally.

There had been an attack on the Hoover Building. She had seen it about to happen. Yelled at the terrorist to stop. Drawn her service weapon and shot him in the head. But she'd been too late.

She looked down at her body, for the first time checking to see if she was in one piece. It was almost an afterthought. Someone had cut away her skirt. Her jacket was gone. Her blouse, too. They'd left her underwear on, thank God. Not that Dani cared much for her modesty. You learned to compartmentalize at the Academy. The instructors there used nakedness as a weapon to mold you. You might leave Quantico, but Quantico never left you.

Her stomach was scored, a bloodied groove lanced across it. The cut was long, but not too deep, and was stained with the dark orange of iodine. She had similar cuts, similarly treated, across her upper arms, and a burn on her leg. Not too bad. She'd gotten lucky.

"Okay, agent," the man said, grappling with her in a failing attempt to get her to lie down. "I'm gonna need to inject you with this."

Dani snapped the man with a withering glaze, grabbing his arm and halting the syringe in midair.

"You stick that in me, Doc, I promise it'll be the last thing you do today."

He wilted. Dani Carter had always had that effect on men. It was to her detriment in her personal life, where she felt she was forever destined to be alone. But in situations like this it could be a highly effective weapon.

"What's wrong with me?" she said.

"I'm... I'm going to put this down, okay?" the man said, gesturing at the syringe in his hand. "It's just a muscle relaxant. You can't tense up like this. It's not safe."

Still, after she had removed her grip on his wrist, he put the syringe down. It clinked onto a metal tray. She glanced at it and saw her FBI badge was lying next to it.

"Doc," Dani said, flashing the man a glare. "Don't make me ask you again. What the hell happened to me?"

"Physically, you're fine. A couple of scrapes, some cuts and bruises. You'll feel like crap for a couple of weeks. But your head is a completely different story."

"Why?"

"Judging by your vitals, you've picked up a concussion. Grade one, probably, but maybe grade two. You'll need a couple of weeks bed rest."

"Doc, look around," Dani said, pointing at the triage tent. The sound of sirens drifted in from outside. "Someone just declared war on America. I'm leaving this tent, whether I get your permission or not."

The medic ran his fingers through his sandy blond hair. His face was marked with iodine and dried, dark blood. Whether it was her own, Dani didn't know.

"Yeah," he muttered. "I get that impression."

The adrenaline was beginning to fade, and as it did, her emotions started biting through. Inside, Dani was roiling. She had never fired her service weapon before – not in anger. She'd killed that man. Sure, he was already in the process of sending his body to hook up with the promised seventy-two virgins, but still, she'd pulled the trigger.

And she'd failed.

Dani was glad she was still seated on the gurney, because otherwise her knees might have given way. A wave of grief threatened to overcome her. Oh God. If her dad was dead, it would be her fault. She was the only reason that he'd been there, to watch his daughter receive a meaningless award she didn't even want.

If he was gone, it was her fault. *She* had asked him to come. *She* had reacted too slowly. *She* had failed to stop the bomber.

If he's gone...

The thought lingered in Dani's mind, driving all other activity away. It was like the explosion of a nuclear bomb, driving all other clouds before it, and allowing no other conscious thought.

Mitch Carter was all Dani had in the world. With her mom gone, dad was all she had left. If he was dead because of her, Dani didn't know whether she would be able to survive.

Dani turned, only one thing on her mind. She had to find out if her father was alive or dead. The medic's handsome face floated into view, concern openly written on his face.

"Doc," she said. "I need to find my dad. I need to know. If he's alive, where would they have taken him?"

⌇

GEORGE WASHINGTON UNIVERSITY HOSPITAL looked and sounded like a war zone. The walking wounded lay on gurneys, abandoned in hallways. Their faces were streaked with dirt and dried blood – and yet as Dani rushed past, she couldn't help but think they looked unbowed, and unbroken.

Afraid, and yet determined.

Dani wondered if she looked the same. She thought not. No one by the name of Mitch Carter had been admitted to George Washington, but the harried looking receptionist said that didn't mean much. They were taking patients in so fast, from attack sites all over the capital, that they were booking them in as John Does. Identification could come later. What mattered right now was saving lives.

Dani looked just like she felt – as though a bomb had hit her. She was wrapped in a space blanket that she had been given when she hitched a lift to the hospital in the back of an ambulance. Every time someone tried getting in her way, she flashed her FBI badge, and left them in her dust.

All that mattered was finding her dad.

She rushed through one hospital ward after another, hallway after hallway, only now appreciating the true scale of what had taken place today. There were hundreds of wounded in this hospital alone. Thousands of citizens had braved the streets, responding to a call for blood donations, no matter the risk to their own lives.

But as she scanned face after face, body after body, Dani's hopes faded. She had started with the lightly injured, hoping against hope that her father would be among them.

But he was not. Nor was he in any of the hospital beds that dotted the facility's overflowing wards and hallways. Mitch Carter was gone, and Dani had never felt more alone in her entire life. She sank to the ground, crouching in the middle of the hallway, the shining blanket like a cloak around her body. She dropped her head to her hands, and tears stung her eyes.

And then she saw him.

His balding head poked out from beneath the sheets of a gurney that was being wheeled out of the double doors of an operating room. A bag of blood and another of saline were hung over his limp body. His head was turned to one side, a line of stitches across his temple.

Dani sprang to her feet.

"How is he?" she asked the technician wheeling the gurney.

The man's face was harried and drawn – exhausted from a day he couldn't possibly have anticipated when he woke up that morning.

"Are you related?"

"I'm his daughter," Dani said, her voice cracking with relief – and fear. Her father looked a decade older than he had just a couple of hours before. Shrunken on the gurney, as though the old Marine had lost fifty pounds.

The technician stopped in the middle of the hallway, allowing Dani to touch her father's face with trembling, hesitant fingers. He felt so cold. How could he possibly survive this? But he couldn't leave her. She couldn't be alone.

"The surgeons did all they could," the technician said. "He took a piece of shrapnel to the stomach, and another grazed his head. They've put him into a coma."

"For how long?" Dani almost whimpered.

"I'm sorry," the technician answered. "I'm not a doctor."

"But you work here, don't you? You must have seen this before?"

The technician grimaced. "I –"

"I can take it," Dani insisted. Her knuckles were white where she gripped the metal side of the gurney. "Please..."

"It's up to him now. He'll be asleep for a few days. If he makes it through that, then..." The man shrugged. "Listen, I know you're hurting," he said, "but I need to get your dad out of this hallway. The doctors can't do anything for him here."

Dani nodded and followed the man as he wheeled her father through the hospital, not letting him out of her sight. It was an irrational reaction, almost childlike, but she would not be swayed. She followed until her father's gurney stopped, nestled between almost a dozen others that looked just the same. All surgery patients, all in medically-induced comas.

Dani clutched the blanket to her shoulders, staring at her father's limp body, her mind numb. But as she stood there, a new emotion entered her mind. The numbness broke like a wave on the shore, and in its wake foamed anger. Anger that someone had dared to steal from her the only thing that mattered in her life.

Rage that she hadn't been able to stop it.

And as the rage itself faded, it was replaced with an iron resolve. She was going to find out who was responsible for this. Not for the sake of the thousands of dead across the country – but for her father.

This was personal. Whether Mitch Carter lived or died, Dani Carter was going to bring his attackers to justice.

17

The Reservoir Hill District of West Baltimore, bracketed by Druid Park Lake to the north and West North Avenue to the south, is a beautiful area of town. Or at least, it should be. If it were somehow possible to simply lift the area, complete with its desirable Victorian rowhouses, and the green open spaces of the nearby park, and set it down just outside of New York City, the land values would skyrocket.

Of course, Reservoir Hill isn't in the Big Apple. It's in West Baltimore, in an area practically run by drug gangs. The local police had recently instituted an unofficial policy to leave the area to its own devices past nine in the evening after gang bangers started taking nighttime pot shots at police cruisers the summer before, leaving one officer paralyzed and in a medically-induced coma, and his partner on long-term medical leave.

Jason Trapp arrived in Baltimore that morning, having hitched a lift down Interstate 95 in the company of a friendly trucker. Presently he was standing in front of a safe house on Linden Avenue. It had been purchased some years before by an

Agency front company using unmonitored slush funds, and never entered into any electronic system. It was about as off-grid as it got.

On his shoulder Trapp carried a rucksack that contained little more than a change of clothes and a sleeping bag, all purchased from an outdoor supply store the day before. It didn't matter to Trapp. He was used to packing light. Had been, in one way or another, ever since he was a kid.

"Spare some change, man?"

Instinctively, Trapp's fingers felt for the cool metal of the Beretta that was currently lodged inside his waistband. His body gulped down a dose of adrenaline and he spun only to see a homeless African-American man, his wiry beard streaked with gray, shuffling toward him with his hand out. Trapp's pulse spiked, and he was forced to take a deep breath to control it.

Easy, Tiger. What's wrong with you?

To his surprise, Trapp felt shaken by the events of the past few days. He was on edge. Jumpy. Everything he had spent an entire lifetime trying to avoid. For him, control was paramount. It was why he had risen to the elite tier of US special forces – Jason Trapp could control himself where other men could not. It didn't make him better than those other men. Just different. They hadn't lived through the things he had, or grown up in a home like his.

They'd never needed to learn to hide their emotions or stifle their reactions. Control even their breathing, so when someone stumbled into the house at three in the morning, stinking of the bottle, they could avoid a fearsome beating. That was Trapp's curse, and he wouldn't wish it on anyone. But it had equipped him with a quiver of techniques that he used now to calm his breathing.

"I'm all out," he said.

He didn't want to be remembered, and figured that if anyone came asking, the homeless man was more likely to remember the one in a hundred bystanders who actually gave him some money, rather than the ninety-nine that didn't.

The man shuffled past, muttering to himself, "Asshole."

Trapp shrugged. It was a good description. He'd give the man that.

The wave of attacks on February 1 that had hit even before President Nash's administration was two weeks old were now commonly referred to as Bloody Monday. It was an apt description. The final casualty count was unknown, but stretched above five thousand dead, with several thousand more seriously wounded. Twice as costly as 9/11. The most American deaths on a single day since the Normandy landings in World War II.

But it wasn't the violence that bothered Trapp. He was used to it, unlike most ordinary Americans. It wasn't even the fact that the devastation had occurred on American soil, rather than some faraway country. It was the fact that the one certainty he had harbored for the past six months – that Mike Mitchell was the man who had wanted him dead was, in reality, untrue.

Mitchell wasn't the man responsible for putting Trapp in a Yemeni hospital. He wasn't responsible for the death of Trapp's partner, and his best friend.

And so, the single driving force that had motivated Trapp to heal, that had pushed him to stow away on a cargo plane bound for Mexico, then slip across the southern border at night, shadowing a cartel *coyote* who knew the route, had been stolen from him. He had planned to mete out his own swift brand of justice. To put a bullet in Mitchell's forehead.

And now he couldn't. The man was no traitor. In fact, unless Trapp was very much mistaken, he was a true patriot.

The thought left him cold. Empty.

Trapp was in Baltimore because Baltimore was in Maryland, and so was the NSA. And the NSA was the only connection that anyone had been able to draw between the death of Ryan Price, the airstrike, and the events of Bloody Monday. It was a tenuous link at best, but it was the only lead that took Trapp an inch closer to delivering justice.

In truth, Fort Meade was barely any closer to Baltimore than it was to DC, but Mitchell knew of a safe house in Reservoir Hill, an off the books location that he'd stored up for a rainy day. And so Trapp was standing in front of it.

He climbed a flight of concrete stairs up to the front door. He had retrieved the key from a dead drop location an hour earlier, and now slipped it from inside his jacket pocket. He carefully checked the doorway for any signs that the building had been breached, but found none. Someone had attempted a forced entry – there were deep scratches by the steel door's lock, which Trapp imagined came courtesy of a crowbar. But as far as he could tell, they were neither recent, nor the marks of a professional. Probably just some opportunistic crackhead looking for an easy score.

The safe house certainly wasn't impregnable, but neither was it an easy target. The protective bars were made from a titanium-steel alloy that would defeat almost any commercial angle grinder. Trapp glanced at its filthy windows as he turned the lock and heard a series of three deadbolts release. He knew that the glass would be impact resistant, probably bulletproof. Certainly enough to deter a couple of junkies looking to steal a television.

Trapp entered the house and secured the door behind him. He heard the insistent warning chime that signalled the presence of an alarm and located a panel by the door. He entered the code that Mitchell had given him, and it fell silent.

"Home sweet fucking home," he said, looking around.

As far as he could tell, the building hadn't been entered in at least a year. Probably not since Mitchell's people had set it up. There was a thick layer of dust on the windowsill and a stack of mail on the floor – mainly flyers for local fast food joints, and a going out of business advertisement for a nearby big and tall clothes shop.

Trapp quickly swept the house. The top two floors were empty, just bare floorboards and drawn blinds. As was the case down below, there was no sign of any recent activity, human or otherwise. Not even the outline of a rodent's paw print in the thick layer of dust.

He descended the wooden stairs, wincing as they creaked. The sound made no impact, but his life had been jeopardized too many times by the squeak of an errant floorboard for him to truly feel comfortable with it.

"What have you left me, then, Mike?"

Just like on the top two floors of the building, the blinds on the bottom floor of the safe house were closed, casting a musty gloom throughout the property. It was a sensible decision, given that there were at least two crates of firearms stacked in the living room, but it gave the place a foreboding air. Trapp flicked the light switch on the wall, but got nothing.

No electricity, huh? Bet you haven't paid the heating bill either, you cheap bastard.

The first floor of the safe house was decorated in the same minimalist fashion as the two above it. That is to say, there was no furniture at all. Just a few stacks of unmarked military crates. Trapp wondered what goodies lay inside them. An assortment of weapons and surveillance gear, no doubt. But he didn't care enough to check. Not yet, anyway – they would still be there in the morning.

Trapp tossed his rucksack to the floor and slumped down next to it. He was dog tired. He closed his eyes and thought about catching up on some sleep. But it wouldn't come. Instead, his thoughts ran wild.

What are you doing here? they asked. *You could be on a beach somewhere. Screw the Agency. You did your time, Trapp. Why go back?*

It was an inconvenient question, because there was a ring of truth to it. Trapp *had* done his time. He'd given almost twenty years of service to his country. He never expected anything in return – once you enter the Special Activities Division, you become a ghost. A deniable asset. All record that you ever existed is wiped out.

After all, if an asset gets captured, it's much easier to let them rot in some foreign jail if there's no record they were ever even born...

Trapp had known the deal the moment he signed up. Maybe not at first, with the army. Hell, he'd been barely more than a boy back then. In trouble with the law, no family left, and willing to grasp any route out that didn't involve spending time behind bars. But by the time he joined Delta, Trapp knew what path he was on.

Men like Trapp were a race apart. A dying breed, perhaps, although grumpy old men have been saying that about kids these days since tribes first picked up sticks and stones and went to war. But Jason Trapp had fought in the mountains and the desert, and two dozen more conflicts besides. He'd fought and bled and seen friends die on every continent, in every conceivable battle space.

Trapp had sent more of America's enemies to an early grave than perhaps any man alive. Or at least, any man who didn't ply the trade of war from behind the ergonomic joystick of a Predator drone, in an air-conditioned trailer five thousand miles away from the nearest bad guy.

No. It wasn't a computer game for Trapp. He was a killer. The kind that got up close and personal, and stuck the vicious blade of a KA-BAR knife into a man's brainstem so that he was dead before he knew he was in danger.

Trapp had fought and bled and barely survived so many

times his body was a patchwork of scars. His friends were either lying in shallow graves or had drunk themselves into oblivion, or worst of all, were waiting on the VA for payments that never came on time.

So Trapp asked himself the question again. Why go back? Why fight for a country that had forgotten him? A country that had left him for dead. A country that sent his best friend to die on faulty intel, and never even acknowledged it.

The answer took a long time to come.

It came with his fingers tracing a loop around the scar that marked his neck—a habit that had once died, now back with a vengeance. A memory flashed in his mind, of boot camp and Ryan Price. They were on a fifteen-mile tactical march, packs heavy on backs that were unused to hard work. It was easy for Ryan, and Trapp envied the man – for that is what he had been, when Trapp himself was merely a boy. His lanky stride ate up the ground, and Trapp pushed himself to keep pace, although it nearly killed him.

Every time he rearranged his pack, Trapp's fingers would catch on the scar around his neck. He knew it marked him out. He was already different from the other recruits, blemished by a childhood whose damage wasn't just physical, though the marks on his back would never fade, but psychological, too. The jagged line around his throat was both – the most visible reminder to all the other recruits that Trapp was *different*, and to be avoided at all costs.

Ryan had caught the action, but not said anything for the longest time. The march dragged on for hours, over hilly terrain, carrying fifty pounds on their backs, and all he did with those piercing blue eyes was watch. And when he crossed the line, ahead of all the other recruits, but with Trapp by his side, he finally spoke his mind.

"I'm gonna call you Hangman," he had said.

The name had stuck. The nickname wasn't given because

he was a killer, but in spite of it. And from that day on, Trapp hadn't minded the scar so much. It was still a visual, unmissable mark of the life he'd lived before the army offered him a new one. But instead of a reminder of the innocence that had been stolen from him, it was a promise of the man he could become.

But for a second time, that peace had been stolen from him. Ryan was dead, and someone out there was responsible for it. And Trapp knew that he would not rest until that individual met found judgement at his hand.

Finally, his eyes began to close. But before they did, Trapp remembered who he truly was.

The kind of man that stands ready in the night to do things to other men that the rest of us aren't even prepared to imagine. Though Trapp would never admit it, he was a very special kind of hero – the type that doesn't want praise, plaudits or fame. Just the quiet satisfaction of a job well done. Of mothers and children sleeping soundly because he'd saved them from the things that go bump in the night.

Jason Trapp was what he was. And, as he drifted away into the first untroubled, dreamless sleep he had enjoyed in months, his last thought was that he knew what he had to do.

18

The current Speaker of the House of Representatives, Randall Woods, mostly went by the name Randy. That's what his constituents called him. The name he plastered on his election posters. The trick he used to allay the concerns of worried junior congressman. *"Please, Jim, call me Randy. Come in and have a drink."*

Right now, Randy Woods was waiting in line at the entrance to the West Wing of the White House. And he didn't like it. Not one bit.

The speaker hated the name that politics had forced him to adopt. But he had found it useful: it gave him a man of the people persona that the name Randall just didn't.

And since the speaker was a practical man, he chose not to look a gift horse in the mouth. Randy had never claimed to be a *good* person. When he'd led the Emerging Markets Division of the famed investment bank Goldman Sachs, he had been known as a hard charger. Ambitious. Ruthless. They were just the qualities he'd needed to assume the leadership of his party in the House.

And of course, people had called him Randall back then.

The previous year, the speaker had declared an income just shy of three million dollars to the IRS. It wasn't, strictly speaking, the full sum of his earnings, but any more than that would have been difficult to explain on the campaign trail. Randall felt that his constituents needed to see him as a successful man – a businessman, the kind of guy who just gets things done. But not *too* rich.

"Just wait there, sir," a Secret Service agent said, holding up his palm to the speaker in the universal gesture to stop. He came to a halt next to a plant pot just under the white-columned portico that stretched out of the West Wing. Snow dusted the ground and a biting wind whistled through the columns, cutting through Woods' thick, two-thousand dollar Brioni overcoat as though it wasn't even there.

Woods hated it.

Ordinarily, a man in his position would have been ushered through the ring of steel that surrounded the heart of the nation's government. Waiting in line to be scanned by a metal detector was for lesser men – especially in weather like this. The speaker snorted. Next thing he knew, one of the agents would be asking to pat him down.

But everything had changed two days earlier. A horrific wave of terrorist attacks had swept the nation, leaving thousands dead, the US Armed Forces at Defcon-2, and one of the most senior elected representatives of the population of the entire United States standing in line like some peasant.

Woods glanced around, irritation building within him at the wait. The Secret Service agents around the White House no longer dressed in their usual dark suits, with their service weapon hidden in a discreet shoulder holster. No, now the place was like a military encampment, with a Marine Corps armored personnel carrier parked up outside the West Wing exhaling a thick cloud of black smoke every time it started up, and miked-up agents patrolling the grounds with submachine guns clipped to their flak vests.

"How long is this going to take?" the speaker grumbled, though he received no answer.

The start to his morning had already been far from satisfactory. Ordinarily, he would have been picked up from his official residence by the head of his security detail, Tom Warner, a detective from the Capitol Police, and driven to a local diner for breakfast. Coffee and an egg white omelette.

But Warner hadn't turned up that morning. A traffic accident, his replacement had anxiously informed Woods. The speaker didn't much care, though he pretended otherwise. It was just good sense to keep the men who might take a bullet for you happy.

Whatever the case, by the time he'd arrived at the diner, they were out of eggs. "Just cooked up the last batch," the owner had apologetically informed his most powerful customer. "Shortages, you know. Since the attacks. Ain't no drivers out on the roads right now. Won't be for a while, I'm guessing."

The speaker grimaced as a pang of hunger clenched his gut. It probably wasn't real—he'd eaten, after all—but he was a man who liked his routine. When it was broken, it screwed up his entire day.

The cell phone in the breast pocket of his suit buzzed. He eyed the line of people waiting to go through the metal detector and figured he might be there a while. He worked his fingers past the thick wool of his coat, fished out the phone and answered it brusquely. He grimaced as the cold wind chewed at his fingers. They already felt half numb.

"Woods."

"Mr. Speaker. I must say, I like your coat. Is it new?"

Randall's face creased with confusion.

"Who is this?" he demanded.

Probably a kid, he figured, who'd somehow got a hold of his cell phone number. He made a mental note to rip shreds out of his assistant when he got back to his office on Capitol Hill. Maybe fire the girl. She wasn't nearly as pretty as he'd first thought, or perhaps he'd just tired of her. It wouldn't be the first time. Maybe this was an opportunity to kill two birds with one stone.

"It doesn't matter. Randy – I can call you that, can't I? For now, all you need to know is that I am the man who's going to make you President."

"What the hell are you talking about?" the speaker murmured into his cell phone, snatching a suspicious glance around him, looking for anyone on the phone. The voice on the other end of the line had said he liked his coat, hadn't he?

Did that mean –?

"Now, now, Randy," the voice said, almost mockingly, though it was hard to make out due to its flat, empty tone. "You can't see me, but I promise, I can see you."

What the hell did that mean? The speaker wanted to hang up, to end this call, but a writhing pit of worry had snaked its way from his brain to his gut. The cold was forgotten now, replaced by the sudden heat of nervousness.

"It's Randall," Woods hissed. "And if you don't tell me what you want, then we're done."

The voice paused for a second before responding. "The Jefferson Hotel. Suite nine oh one."

The speaker froze. Of all the things he'd been expecting to hear, that certainly hadn't made the list. How the hell could he possibly know? He was careful, always had been when it came to indulging his sexual peccadilloes. He'd covered his face when entering the hotel, and paid for everything with cash. Whatever this crank thought he knew, the threat was an empty one.

"I don't know what you're talking about."

"Oh, I think you do, Randy," the voice said, lingering over the speaker's name with evident glee. "You like blondes, correct? Young. No older than twenty-one. That's what you told the agency, isn't it, Randy?"

The speaker's throat constricted. He choked out a guttural grunt. He wasn't used to being talked to like this – and especially not by someone who actually had dirt on him. The line shuffled forward a step, but he didn't move until someone banged into the back of him.

He thought fast. There was a reason he used that particular escort agency, after all. It was the same one every damn senator, congressman and cabinet member used in this town. No names. Burner phones. And young college girls from the right kind of families – the kind you could claim you were interviewing for a research job, if you ever needed to. They weren't *hookers*. No, they were far more respectable than that. And they knew the drill. If it ever came to it, they'd take the payoff and disappear.

In short, they were deniable. And that's exactly what Randall planned to do. He clutched on to the lifeline, like a dying man reaching for a rope. When he spoke, his voice was strained. He looked around nervously to make sure no one was watching.

"You've got nothing. I'm ending this call."

In his fingers, the phone buzzed, just once, signaling the receipt of a message. "I don't think so, Randy. You'll want to take a look at that message."

Hand shaking, the speaker removed his cell phone from his ear, shielded the screen so that no one could see, and tapped the message icon. He didn't know what he was expecting to see. Definitely not the video that flashed up onto the secure black iPhone's screen.

His heart stopped.

Oh, he was fucked now. And not in a good way – not in the

way he had been two nights earlier, ridden by a tight young freshman from Georgetown University. His eyes were drawn inexorably to the curve of her hips as they ground against his own, rising and falling as she most likely simulated ecstasy. Randall didn't care very much either way as his own pulse quickened, as his head fell back, and his face puckered up with carnal satisfaction.

He skipped forward a few minutes of the video, which appear to have been taken with a high definition camera from somewhere on the opposite side of the suite, from around chest height.

It showed everything.

Right now, it showed him walking over to the minibar, his cock still rigid and stiff above a thick bush of pubic hair. It showed the girl, he forgot her name, walking toward him as he popped a bottle of champagne. As he poured it into her mouth, then kissed her.

The speaker let out a low guttural moan, too stunned to speak.

He saw his political career flashing before his eyes. Hell, if he wasn't mistaken, he thought he could feel the first tremors of an earthquake shaking the tectonic plates under Washington DC. A hard-won reputation torched, just like that. He'd never be able to go to a restaurant in this town again. He noticed an African-American woman behind him shoot him a curious look and hurriedly checked to make sure the screen was covered.

Randall returned the phone to his ear, the fingers of his free hand loosening his collar, sweat beading on his face. He needed air.

"What the hell do you want?" he hissed.

"I already told you, Randy. I want to make you President."

The line shuffled forward again, and Randy realized that a gap had opened up in front of him. He glanced over his shoulder, and noticed that the graying woman behind him was looking at him with barely concealed irritation. Of course, she knew who he was, and wasn't about vocalize her irritation, but still, he was making a scene, and that was the last thing he could afford right now. The speaker saw a whole pack of curious faces staring at him from the line behind him and turned away, his head movement jerky.

What did the voice just say? Make me President? What the hell does that mean?

The Secret Service agent beckoned him forward, toward the metal detector, and a bead of sweat trickled down the groove of Randall's spine. It felt ice cold; a harbinger of his political doom.

Randall walked forward, toward the detector and the Secret Service booth that regulated access to the West Wing. He killed the screen of the phone and put it into one of the little airport-style trays to the side, before emptying his pockets and removing his belt. They clinked when he set them down, and an acrid mix of disinfectant and body odor filled his nostrils.

Normally, being treated like this would have pissed him off, but right now it was all he could do not to just turn around, and get the first plane to a tropical island where he could forget this day had ever happened. The world was closing in around him, and yet here he was, shuffling forward like a lamb to the slaughterhouse. But what choice did he have?

"Just hold there, sir," the agent said, glancing at a readout on the computer screen in front of him before gesturing him forward. The speaker stepped through the metal detector unit, and for some reason felt a sharp spike of relief when the machine didn't buzz. He was so on edge he thought the sound might have given him a heart attack.

Retrieving his cell phone, he checked the screen was still off before returning it to his ear. "You still there?" he muttered, glancing around.

He was in a hallway that led toward the lobby of the West Wing. The floor was marble, black on white, like a chessboard. The place was filled with a nervous energy – aides rushing around God knows where carrying God knows what. They moved out of his way like minnows fleeing a shark. But for the first time in a very long career, the speaker wished he was one of them. Young. Anonymous.

Randall saw a restroom to his left and stepped inside it, locking the door behind him and then running the tap to make sure he couldn't be overheard. If only he'd been this careful two nights earlier.

"Indeed," the flat, artificial voice commented.

"I was –"

"Going through security, Randy. I was watching. Remember that. I'm always watching."

How the hell did this guy know so much? Randall thought wildly. And what the hell was he talking about, making him President? It sounded like a line from a bad movie. And yet it was completely, terrifyingly real. The speaker just hoped the guy was crazy, hoped that some madman had acquired his phone number. It wouldn't have been the first time. But Randall knew deep down that that wasn't the case. There was a cold, calculating ease in the voice on the other end of the line. Madmen didn't talk like that.

"Okay, okay," he said, rubbing his forehead, his fingers slipping from the slick of perspiration now glistening on top of it. His chest was tight, and his voice came out in a desperate, pathetic whine.

"Tell me what you want. Money? I'll give it to you. However much you want. Just make that tape go away."

"I can't do that, Randy," the flat voice said. "And I've told you what I want. I'm going to make you President. And then we are going to do great things together."

"You're insane," Randall said, shaking his head with disbelief. "I should report this conversation. Go to the authorities."

"I wouldn't advise that, Randy. I'd hate to have to release that tape."

Riding a wave of inspiration, Randall gambled. It was a facet of his character that he had relied on so many times before. At your time of greatest weakness, strike. It's when the enemy is least expecting it.

"Maybe I just get ahead of it. Leak the news that I had a sex tape stolen. It'll hurt for a bit, sure. Maybe I'll lose a few donors. But the news cycle will be focused on these attacks for months. This probably won't even make page twenty in the Post."

"You can try, Randy. But you're an ambitious man; it's why I chose you. Of course, I *could* go further down the list. Write you off as a lost cause, and pick someone else. But I see greatness in you."

The voice paused, almost as though it was mulling over its next steps.

"And I'd be lying if I tried to claim to you that you weren't an easy target. A champagne party with a twenty-year-old hooker on the night of the most devastating terrorist attack this country has ever seen. Mr. Speaker, I'm no politician, but the headlines write themselves. And you know, Randy. You've been a very naughty boy. That bank account in the Caymans. Your cocaine dealer in New York. I know everything about you. *Everything.* But perhaps you need a little more motivation?"

The speaker's phone buzzed again, the vibration tickling his ear. When he spoke, his voice was raw. "Is that from you?"

"It is."

Trembling, Randall checked the message. Another video. As it filled the screen, he blinked, confused. It seemed to be the same video, from the same night in Suite 901. He slept with hookers all over town, of course, but he recognized the goldleaf wallpaper that marked out the Jefferson Hotel. It was the first time he'd taken a girl there. He'd made a note that it wouldn't be the last.

But no. The video was different. In fact, it appeared to be shifting before his very eyes. Morphing. The girl undulating up and down on his cock was shrinking. Her shoulders getting narrower, her hair changing color. She looked younger and younger.

What the hell is this? Randall thought desperately. But he knew. The girl on the screen of his cell phone now looked no older than fourteen. Maybe even younger than that. He watched again, as his stiff cock led the way to the minibar. As he popped a bottle of champagne. As a young girl's terrified face filled the screen, tears streaking eyeliner that had been liberally, if childishly applied.

And he watched as his own hand gripped her throat, holding the green-tinted bottle to her lips and forcing the alcohol through them. None of this had ever happened.

But Randall knew that face.

Riley Bennett. Christ, he still remembered receiving the Amber alert. Her face was on the side of a milk carton in his goddamn fridge, those hazel eyes always staring as the door swung closed and the light blinked out. Her distraught parents had been on TV for months, desperately appealing for some-one, anyone to come forward with information about their daughter. Real or not, if this tape hit the Internet, then it wasn't just his political career that was toast. He would be behind bars before the day was out.

"I can prove that wasn't me," the speaker said, his mind scrambling for a way out. It latched on to one. One that might end his political career, but would at least save him from prison. He'd sent most of his security detail away that night, as he always did. But not Tom. Tom was discreet, and the speaker trusted him. Not just with his life, but with the more sordid carnal pleasures that the speaker enjoyed.

"Warner. Tom Warner. The head of my detail. He was there that night. He saw the girl. Patted the bitch down. He'll testify to it. And the video is fake. I'll be able to prove it wasn't me."

"Oh, Randy," the voice said in a tone of mock sadness. "Did no one tell you? Mr. Warner died this morning."

"What?" Randall croaked.

He felt like he was being executed, a noose around his neck, and someone had just kicked away the stool supporting his feet. He just stood there, his buttoned collar seeming as though it was biting into his neck and cutting off his airway. The bathroom's walls closed in around him. For a second he felt unsteady, as though his legs were about to give way.

"Terrible, really," the voice gloated. "Traffic light malfunction. A truck crashed right into his SUV. Killed him instantly, along with his beautiful wife. So sad."

Randall's fingers scrambled behind him for the edge of the washbasin, and he leaned against it, his heart beating faster than he could remember. He was sweating heavily now. Panicking. "What do you want from me?"

"Want from you? Nothing. Not yet, anyway. You had better run along, Randy. You'll be late for your meeting with the President. And you wouldn't want to draw attention to yourself, would you?"

"I –"

"Take a good look at that desk, Randy. It will be yours soon enough..."

The line went dead. The voice owned the speaker now. And they both knew it.

19

Jason Trapp woke at about six the next morning, feeling truly refreshed for the first time in months.

In a country that was in turmoil, he might have been the only man who slept soundly that night. He had no ties, no children to care for. No wife to worry about. It didn't matter that his only pillow had been his rucksack, nor that his mattress was a hard, dusty wooden floor. Trapp had slept the relaxed sleep of a man who had his mission. A man who knew what he had to do.

Stomach growling, Trapp got to work.

He stood up and stretched, working the kinks out of his neck and shoulders and back. He had once gone almost three weeks without brushing his teeth, while crawling on his belly through the thick, black jungle mud of Cambodia's monsoon season, heavy warm rain lashing his back and thick sludge staining his combat fatigues black. He had been a younger man then. And bringing toothpaste on a kill mission wasn't exactly a priority.

But Trapp wasn't in Cambodia. Despite what Steelers fans would have you believe, Baltimore was still technically in the

United States of America. And that meant he didn't have to relieve himself in a plastic bottle, nor go even a single day without brushing his teeth.

Thank God.

He retrieved a small bag of toiletries from his rucksack and cleaned himself up before searching through the military crates that decorated the safe house's living room. After he opened his fifth, only to find it stacked yet again with military hardware the likes of which would have had any gang in the city salivating, Trapp began to wonder whether Mitchell had forgotten to provide anything with actual sustenance.

But on the sixth, Trapp struck gold.

"Mitchell, you beautiful bastard," he muttered, grabbing a selection of MRE rations – 'Meals Ready to Eat,' not 'Meals Rejected by Ethiopians,' as some less politically-correct soldiers described them. Which, when Trapp thought about it, was pretty much every soldier he had ever met.

He examined his options, looking for something that he would be able to choke down at this time in the morning. That ruled out the chili and macaroni, beef and black beans, and *definitely* the vegetarian ratatouille that some sadist had included, in what Trapp could only imagine was a dark practical joke.

Trapp shook his head as he chose the least worst option, the chicken pesto pasta, and ripped open the tan packaging. He ate it cold, mostly without tasting, which was probably for the best. Just about the only good thing about MREs was their high calorie content. Well, that and the peanut M&Ms. He shoved those in his rucksack for later.

Finally clean, fed, and sated, Trapp took stock of his position. He had a plan. Or at least, if not an entire plan, then at least the sketch of one. He knew that he was in a unique position. He might be the only man alive who could achieve what he had to do. Not because of any particular set of skills, although Trapp knew himself to be supremely capable when it came to almost any type of weapon or style of martial art – at least the effective ones—but because the world thought he was dead.

And, after the events on the bank of the Potomac River Trapp imagined that the target he had in mind thought him dead twice over. Since he had no idea who that individual was, it wasn't much of an advantage – but it was all he had.

Trapp grabbed the components of his burner phone from the rucksack, clicked the battery and sim card into place, and powered the unit up. It took a few seconds before it was ready for use, and Trapp used the time to chase his breakfast pasta down with a swig of energy drink from the MRE pack. The ingredients combined to create a seething pit of indigestion in his stomach.

When the phone was ready to use, Trapp tapped an icon on the home screen. It called up a simple app, which immediately requested a password. He entered an eleven digit number from memory, and the app allowed him access.

Mitchell's analyst, Kyle Partey, had shown Trapp how to install and securely delete the app. Trapp could – and probably would – toss the burner at any time, but as long as he could get his hands on another device, he would always have a line of communication open.

Trapp had worried about whether the app was secure. After all, they suspected that the NSA was compromised. It was the reason they weren't using the secure government phones, several of which Trapp had come across while searching through the supply crates. But Partey had assured him that the encryption protocol was so strong that it would take the Fort Meade's fastest supercomputer longer than the known age of the universe to crack even a single intercepted message. That was good enough for him.

Trapp glanced down at the screen. There was no list of

contacts, just a chat window. He tapped a message in with slow, clumsy fingers – a million miles away from the kids he saw these days, who seemed to have been born with devices surgically attached to their hands.

Anybody home?

The text appeared on the screen. Trapp settled back, prepared to wait for an answer. It was still early, and as far as he knew, Mitchell only had himself, Kyle and the two Special Activities Division operatives with him.

But a reply came quickly.

Authenticate.

Trapp keyed in an authentication sequence from memory and waited for the corresponding reply. Formalities out of the way, he got down to business. He typed in another message and pressed send.

Give me a sitrep.

This time, the reply took a little longer to materialize.

Kyle has a backdoor into the Agency's computer systems. As far as we can tell, nobody has any idea who is behind the attacks. ISIS claimed responsibility, but it looks opportunistic. The White House has no idea what to do.

Trapp chewed his bottom lip. There was a whole lot he wasn't seeing here, he was sure of that. Someone wanted him dead – badly enough to first send him on a suicide mission in Yemen six months earlier, and then to commandeer a US Air Force jet and carry out an airstrike on American soil. Was it all because he had started asking the wrong questions about the intelligence they were receiving? Was that why Price had died?

Something about this didn't add up. Trapp didn't for one second believe that a bunch of Islamic goat herders had managed to pull off the most sophisticated terror attack in history. The only way it could have been done was if the NSA itself had been penetrated – but Trapp didn't buy that either. But what did that leave?

Trapp cracked his knuckles, the sound echoing around the empty safe house. His shoulders were tense, his ears still slightly ringing from the airstrike just a day earlier.

Trapp typed another short message.

What about the NSA?

The reply came quickly.

Director Donahue took an unscheduled flight to the NSA's Utah Data Center shortly after the attacks commenced. He then went radio silent. Washington was unable to establish contact for over 24 hours.

Trapp glanced at his watch and grimaced. It was at least a two-day drive to Utah, and that was if he went without sleep.

I don't suppose you can hook me up with the USAF again?

The reply was swift.

No need. Donahue came back online about an hour ago, and requested a meeting with the President. His plane lifts off in about twenty minutes. Flight plan is filed for Andrews.

Trapp rubbed his forehead and groaned audibly, the deep sound echoing around the silent and empty safe house. He had no idea what was going on. But as he thought it over, pieces of the puzzle began to fall into place. The visit to Utah was unplanned. Something must have shaken loose after Bloody Monday. And if Donahue was somehow involved in whatever the hell was going on, then the last place he would go would be the White House. Which only left one option.

He knows something.

Trapp wondered what the hell Donahue could have discovered. Going radio silent on the President in the midst of an unprecedented national crisis was unheard of. It would be a career ender for any man, no matter how high up the greasy pole of Washington's bureaucracy he climbed. The fact that Donahue had made it to the lofty heights of the head of the National Security Agency only made it worse.

That's what we figure. Get to Andrews. Get eyes on Donahue. We need to know what he's up to.

Trapp grimaced. He had to move fast. If he calculated right, the flight from Utah to Andrews would take about three hours. Maybe a little longer. It meant he didn't have much time.

20

Gunfire crackled in the distance, punctuated only by the sound of grunting men. Andrew Rawlin surveyed the scene in front of him with satisfaction. The occasional ray of sun broke through the clouds overhead, glinting off a fast flowing river that passed through the encampment, the calming hiss of which was completely at odds with the chaos sweeping the country. Pilgrim, South Dakota might be a long way from anywhere, but the satellite phone in his pocket had an Internet connection, and with it, the world was small.

He had watched the devastation, and heard in it the tidings of a new world.

Rawlin wasn't worried about anyone hearing the sound of gunfire. The encampment sat on a parcel of land that measured almost a hundred square miles. He had purchased it almost two years earlier and had spent months, and several million dollars, making sure the land was securely fenced. At best, the sound of a gunshot can be heard from three miles distant. It was close to seven miles to the nearest fence, and another ten to the nearest town.

"Just you wait, Drew," a man next to him snarled. "I'm going to take this revolver, grab one of 'em ragheads and blow his fucking brains out."

Andrew, as Drew was now attempting to style himself, closed his eyes briefly before turning to face his conversation partner. His hair was short and a mousy brown, his left cheek swallowed up by a large purple birthmark.

The man standing on the wooden porch next to him was stocky, of medium height and a forgettable build. His teeth were stained yellow and black from the effects of a flirtation with methamphetamines. It was a condition known as 'meth mouth,' and it wasn't pretty.

"You're not going anywhere, Gibson," Drew chided, pushing the hand holding the man's weapon downward. The wintry air of South Dakota in February bit at his fingers, almost stinging. He briefly considered relieving his old friend of the six shooter, but decided it wasn't worth the trouble.

"We've been through this."

"And why the fuck not, Drew? This country's at war. You seen it, I know you have. What's the point in us building all of this," Gibson said forcefully, waving his tattooed arm out and gesturing at the growing, snow-dusted encampment, "if it's not to get ready to fight? Them dune coons, you know what they did to me, Drew. Know what they *took* from me."

Rawlin bit his bottom lip, savoring a burst of pain that drew a tear from his eye. They were approaching the end game of his plan, and he couldn't afford to make mistakes. Even when that meant disappointing his oldest friend.

As boys, they had lived in the same shitty trailer park just east of Albuquerque, New Mexico. They had each watched their parents succumb to drink and drugs, sold to them by Blacks and spics, and both had vowed it would never happen to them.

They joined the army on the same day, forging their

parents' signatures on consent forms that the recruiter barely glanced at. They were just sixteen. By their late twenties, both men had done multiple tours in the sandbox, from Afghanistan to Iraq. They had served in the same unit all that time. Served honorably, as each lost friends – the kind of men you would give your life for without thinking.

And then, two weeks before their unit was due to ship home, Gibson's Abrams armored vehicle hit an IED buried beneath the road. He lost his leg to the ragheads, and then five years of his life to the drug that made the pain go away.

"I know what you lost, brother. I was there, wasn't I?" Andrew said, glancing down at the pale, slightly scarred skin of his forearms.

Not so long ago, they had been covered with tattoos, just like Gibson's still were. Eagles clutching swastikas; flaming crosses of hate. But now the visible evidence of his dalliance with some of America's least subtle white nationalist groups was hidden, lasered off, the last remnants covered by thick, dark body hair.

It had been done onsite, several months ago, at the instruction of the mysterious voice on the phone. He had purchased a laser removal device, complete with a sympathetic operator, and had it shipped all the way to the ranch near Pilgrim. Andrew grimaced just thinking about it. The procedure felt like thousands of rubber bands being snapped against his skin all at once. The operator had been busy ever since.

"You were," Gibson conceded. "So you know what they took." He pointed at the carbon fiber prosthetic strapped to his knee. "I'll never get it back, Drew. I want to see the fear in their eyes before I kill them. Make them feel how *I* did."

"You'll get your chance," Andrew assured his friend. "Soon. But not today."

"And why the hell not?" Gibson muttered. He didn't usually speak this way to his friend. There was an unspoken understanding between the two men – that Rawlin was the leader, and Gibson wasn't. No matter their past together, on this ranch, Andrew Rawlin's word was law.

"You know I'm good, Drew. One leg or no, I'm the best shot you got. Put a rifle in my hand and I'll send those fucking Arabs to their Paradise. The streets will run red, I ain't stoppin' till they're all dead, or someone puts a bullet in my forehead."

It was true, Andrew knew. Darren Gibson was a deadly shot. The best sharpshooter in their whole damn battalion, in his prime. It was why he'd recruited him, when the sensible decision would have been to let the man rot from the inside out, courtesy of his favorite poison.

It had been a good decision. The first couple of weeks were tricky, of course. Rawlin had chained his friend to a metal bed frame and sweated the meth out of him. It had almost killed the man. But he survived, was stronger for it.

And Rawlin's organization was stronger for it, too.

Gibson had swapped one addiction for another – crystal meth for hard work. Gratitude for his life, and hatred of the animals who had taken it from him, drove him harder than any army marksmanship instructor. He'd made Rawlin's men train until their trigger fingers cramped up. Until they were almost as good as he was.

And so, yes, Rawlin knew, saving his friend had been sentimental. But it was also worth it. But even so, they were too close to the completion of his benefactor's plan to take any risks. Gibson could be unstable, increasingly so now they were nearing the culmination of all their hard work.

Rawlin wouldn't let it all go to waste. If it came to it, he'd put a bullet in the back of his friend's head himself. The fate of the nation was at stake. It mattered more than one man. Any man.

"You'll do what I tell you," Rawlin said, his lip curled. "I'm too close to let you fuck it up, Darren. You understand that? I saved you from yourself once, but I won't do it again."

Gibson shot his friend a look that Rawlin had never seen before. His face was twisted in a combination of frustration and compassion. Rawlin paused, and let him speak.

"I always trusted you. You know that, right?"

Rawlin nodded.

"And you never steered me wrong, not once. Even after all the dumb shit I done, even at my lowest, you always been there for me, Drew."

Andrew, Rawlin thought, a grimace crawling across his face, distorting the birthmark until he presented a fearsome sight. But Gibson carried on, eyes darting all over, but mainly focused on the ground.

"Maybe it's time I was there for you."

Rawlin's voice was tight. "What does that mean?"

Gibson looked up, fixing his friend with a look of deep concern. Rawlin sensed that the man's earlier bravado had been his way of working up to this very moment.

"Like I said, we grew up together, right?"

"Right."

"So I *know you*, Drew," Gibson said, waving his arm vaguely around the frozen training camp. "I know you didn't put all this together yourself –"

Rawlin's lip curled. For a moment, the civilized mask he tried to portray slipped.

"You better be real goddamn careful about what you say next."

Gibson stopped dead, fear and indecision carved onto his sallow, gaunt face. He gulped, as if building up the courage to speak his mind. When he spoke, his voice was soft, boyish, as if unconsciously appealing to their shared childhood.

"All I'm sayin' is who's paying for all this, Drew? What do they want? Because I been in militias before, back when I was still smoking up, and believe me, they ain't anything like this. Just a bunch of guys like me, hopped up on crystal and running through the woods. But what you built here, it's some real shit. And I been there before, man. When it looks like a good deal, it always comes with strings attached."

Rawlin gritted his teeth. Gibson was a fool, he thought. He should never have brought him in on this. What they were building here was too important for the junkie's broken mind to grasp.

And yet...

Was there something to his friend's concerns? What did he truly know about the man who had helped make all this possible? They'd never met; he was just a voice on the phone. He paid the bills, sent supplies, and whispered of a brave new world.

A world in which a man like Rawlin could be king.

Rawlin didn't know how his benefactor had arranged for Bloody Monday to occur, though he didn't doubt the truth of it. When he'd first been told of what had to happen, his reaction was one of revulsion. But his eyes had been opened to see that the old world had to die so that a new, better one could be born. The Muslim hordes wanted nothing more than to destroy America and everything she stood for, even as his beautiful country was choking itself from within. He now understood that there was no shame in his benefactor working with the Arabs, because he was not. He was using them. America needed an enemy in order to summon the will for the cleansing that was needed. And right on cue, one had stepped out of the shadows.

Gibson looked at his old friend, cringing as he awaited a response. The sight of the man's weakness stiffened Rawlin's resolve. How could he doubt his benefactor now, when they were so close to achieving the ultimate prize?

Rawlin closed the distance between the two men, his movement catlike and graceful. He prodded his friend's chest, his finger jabbing outward in a vicious, biting stab.

"You don't know what the fuck you're talking about," he said coldly. "There's shit going on that you don't understand, because you're not capable of understanding. Your brain is fried, and that's on you, not me. But if you get in my way, in the way of what I'm doing here, believe me – the fact we grew up together don't mean shit."

Gibson looked back, his dark eyes broken. Rawlin's anger burned off him, and every time it sparked, his friend flinched.

"I –"

"Now, Gibson. Are you going to disappoint me?"

Gibson shook his head furiously, face flushed with embarrassment. "No," he choked. "I promise you, Drew. I'm with you, one hundred percent. I shouldn't have said anything. It's not my place."

Rawlin stared long and hard into his old friend's eyes. He warned every new recruit that no matter who they were, or what they had done in their past lives, it didn't matter. Their old selves were dead. The recruits were reborn by promising their lives to the new Aryan nation. He warned them that in the new world, the world they were to build, every white man, woman or child would be equal. And he warned them of the consequences of disobeying his orders.

There would be no second chances.

Rawlin stepped back, grinning, the spell of anger broken like a summer squall. He patted Gibson on the cheek. "Good man. I knew you wouldn't fail me. Come on, let's do the rounds."

Although the bulk of the ranch that Rawlin had purchased was flat, empty pastureland, he'd built the main encampment around the bend of a narrow, fast-flowing river that had cut a deep ravine into the landscape. His benefactor had assured him that strings had been pulled at the very highest levels of American law enforcement to conceal the camp, but Rawlin was a paranoid man and figured that since the terrain was already there he might as well use it to help disguise what they were doing.

"You checked the camo netting?" he asked Gibson as he strode forward, off the wooden porch, his boots crunching on an inch of fresh snow.

Gibson smiled, pleased that his friend's anger had broken.

"Did it myself," he said. "Gave a good shake, too, got some of the snow off it. It was hanging a little low."

The netting was strung clear across the ravine. It shielded most of the training facilities, weapons ranges and living quarters from overhead surveillance. Not that Rawlin had any reason to believe he was being watched. But he didn't trust the government. And what they were doing was too important to take any chances.

"Good," Rawlin said.

They walked in silence for a couple of minutes, until the sound of gunshots grew louder. They neared the outdoor tactical firing range, a maze-like structure built from low walls, and laid out like a village. Rawlin quickly bent over to grab two bright orange hunting bibs from a box. He tossed one in Gibson's direction.

"Put this on."

The two men stood and watched as an instructor put a group of four recruits through their paces. The recruits – all men – were dressed in the green fatigues of the FBI's Hostage Rescue Team, complete with the Bureau's three-letter acronym stenciled both front and back. To complete the picture, each of the men had a forty-five caliber 1911 pistol strapped to their hip and a 9 mm MP5 submachine gun clipped to their vest.

As the recruits made ready, strapping on their helmets, Andrew's eyes studied them. He noticed the hair on their heads most of all. When they arrived, months before, each man wore his hair short, cropped to the skull, and had tattoos decorating faces, chests and forearms. Now they resembled America's finest – the kind of men you wanted your daughter to marry.

"On my mark," the instructor yelled, hands in his pockets to protect them from the biting cold, "you will assault the building. There are an unknown number of tangos inside. Your orders are to neutralize them. Hostages are to be considered expendable."

Rawlin nodded his approval.

The instructor had once been a member of a SWAT team in Brooklyn. The Department received one too many complaints of excessive force, and after being assigned to the case, Internal Affairs noted that the incidents all involved members of Brooklyn's large African-American community. In Rawlin's view, what happened next was political correctness gone mad. What were the police for, after all, if not to keep the Blacks in check? But the NYPD thought differently, and the man found himself out on his ass.

But the New York Police Department's loss was Rawlin's gain. Between Gibson's prowess with long weapons and this man's evident experience with close quarters battle, Rawlin's military vanguard of the coming Aryan nation was quickly proving to be meticulously well-drilled. He might not have the numbers – yet—but Andrew Rawlin would wager on any of his men in a one-on-one encounter with the tyrannical forces of the US government.

And besides, Rawlin knew, the numbers would come. After Bloody Monday, it was inevitable. As if on cue, the satellite phone in Rawlin's pocket rang. The instructor glanced over in his direction, but Rawlin waved at the man to continue.

He answered the phone gruffly. "Hello?"

As always, the voice on the other end of the line sounded flat and tinny. Rawlin didn't know what kind of scrambler the man was using, but it seemed to suck any hint of life from his voice.

"You know who this is," it said simply.

A few yards away, the instructor stepped up onto a raised platform in order to get a better view of proceedings and yelled, "Mark!" Rawlin retreated a little, so that the conversation wouldn't be lost in the sound of gunfire, but still kept the range in eyesight.

"Is it time?" Rawlin replied. An unaccustomed wave of nerves threatened to overcome him, starting in his stomach and quickly radiating around his body. He felt tense, like a predator waiting to strike. In a way, he supposed, he was.

In front of him, the four men of the ersatz FBI Hostage Rescue Team lined up against a low wall. He watched as the first man unclipped a dummy fragmentation grenade from his belt. The man behind him reached out his left arm and gripped the leader by the shoulder, leaving his weapon free. The two men behind him did the same. Rawlin watched as the team leader counted down on his fingers before tossing the grenade through the structure's open door.

He turned away, and the sound of gunfire peppered the air.

"Almost," the voice said. "Your men are ready?"

"They are," Rawlin replied, bouncing from foot to foot with nervous energy. "What shall I do with the recruits? The ones who aren't ready."

The reply came quickly. "I don't care. Kill them, if you need to. If you think they can be useful, let them live."

The answer might have shocked Andrew Rawlin. It was a callous way to describe men and women who had flocked so eagerly to their righteous cause. But if he were the kind of man who was easily shocked, then the voice would not have chosen him.

"Very well," Rawlin said, lowering his voice more as a precautionary measure than from any real fear of being overheard. His breath danced in the air, and snow crunched beneath his feet. Anyone not directly involved in a training assignment was sensible enough to be inside, where it was warm.

"And the rest?"

"Send them to their staging areas. Immediately. You received the secure comms equipment I sent?"

"I did."

"Make sure every team has a backup. I will coordinate mission assignments directly." The voice paused, and Rawlin wondered whether it was finally time.

"You've done well, Andrew." It continued. "Are you prepared for your own task? You are vital to what comes next."

"I'm ready," Rawlin said. As the words left his lips, he knew it was the truth. What was coming would be the culmination of his life's work. And if he didn't live to see the new world, then it was a sacrifice he was willing to make.

"Good. Your country thanks you. And Andrew?"

"Yes?"

"Before you go, make sure you tie up any loose ends."

Slowly, sadly, Rawlin turned, and his eyes fell on his oldest friend. He would do what he had to.

21

Trapp worked fast.

He found two large duffel bags in one of the crates and filled them with weapons and other gear, throwing in an MP5 submachine gun, several pistols, ammunition, a bulletproof vest, and a first aid kit in a small green plastic box. The last item looked out of place as it sat on top of the arsenal of death, and Trapp figured if he needed it, then he was probably already screwed. Still, it felt better to have it than not.

Almost as an afterthought, he grabbed a small black rectangular plastic device from one of the supply crates and slipped it into his back pocket.

He placed the two bags by the safe house's front door and checked his watch. It was 6:53 a.m. He'd learned about Donahue's flight only fifteen minutes before, which meant he had about three hours before the director's plane landed at Andrews.

He left the safe house and locked the door behind him. He glanced around, checking whether anyone had seen him, but neither noticed nor sensed anything amiss. Trapp's instincts were usually finely honed, and he trusted them with his life. They had repaid that trust many times over.

This morning, which had dawned fine and bright, though extremely cold, they were telling him nothing. In truth, the Reservoir Hill neighborhood was quiet that early in the day. The only people awake were the slouched, shuffling homeless, protected from the cold by thick, rancid blankets draped across their shoulders. The sunlight only served to accentuate the neighborhood's ruin – glinting off shattered glass and providing a glimpse into the gloomy depths of long-shuttered storefronts.

Trapp walked fast, heading for a parking lot that he had noticed on his way to the safe house the day earlier.

"Morning," he mouthed at a woman passing by, the Subway baseball cap on her head indicating that she was probably on her way to work. She glanced up with a look that was somewhere between shock and disdain.

Trapp couldn't blame her. Though a woman had once told him he was handsome, the last few months had challenged her description in practice. His split, wraithlike eyes were as compelling as they had ever been, but his face wore new scars, marked by the burning warehouse in Yemen. They would fade in time, just like the one that marked his neck like a hangman's noose, but never completely disappear. Right now, he wouldn't be winning any beauty contests.

He shook off the thought and covered the distance to the parking lot in just a few minutes without encountering anyone else on his way.

The lot was almost empty, and Trapp chewed his lip for a second, wondering if it would have what he needed – a car new enough to be vulnerable. He slipped the black device from his back pocket and touched a light gray button on its side. An LED light on the device blinked green. He long-pressed the button once more, and waited.

The device was an Agency special. Unknown to the public, the CIA had long ago compromised almost every major car manufacturer across the globe. Unlike the radio frequency 'man in the middle' attacks ordinary car thieves used, which relied on scanning the airwaves for the unique code emitted by a car's key fob in order to copy it, the black device was preprogrammed with hundreds of master keys. It meant Trapp didn't need to wait around. Just a few more seconds, and...

"Jackpot."

The device's LED flashed green at about the same time as the brake lights on an SUV on the other side of the lot blinked. A tone chirruped, echoing off the boarded-up, decrepit houses that surrounded the parking lot.

Trapp had never stolen a car in the US before. Well, at least not since he was a teenager, growing up on the wrong side of the tracks. Now, it felt wrong. This car would be someone's mother's only route to work, or a nurse's only way to get to the hospital.

But as Trapp approached the 2017 Toyota RAV4, he forgot those concerns. The vehicle was painted matte black, with tinted windows and alloy rims. In this neighborhood only one profession was likely to be able to afford a car like this. And given that Baltimore had one of the highest rates of opioid abuse in the entire United States, Trapp suddenly didn't feel nearly so guilty.

He opened the vehicle's door on the driver's side and got in. He tossed the black device onto the Toyota's console, where it mimicked the vehicle's key fob, closed the door and gunned the engine.

His watch read 7:02 a.m.

‿

THE SUN HAD BARELY RISEN over the White House and President Charles Nash was already exhausted. He sat behind the Resolute desk in the Oval Office, mind numbed by the horrifying parade of statistics he had been exposed to over the past several days. America was at war.

But with what enemy, he did not know. No one, not the NSA, not the FBI, not the CIA, had yet discovered who was behind the horrific wave of attacks on Bloody Monday. No one except ISIS had claimed credit, and they popped up every time a car exhaust so much as backfired. The cable networks were whipping up a panic, and yet Nash had no way to cool it. He needed answers, or at least the face of an enemy he could show to the American public.

Even his VP was thousands of miles away, secured in Texas by the Secret Service to ensure continuity of government. Jenkins had been his rock through the campaign even after Nash defeated him in the primaries, which might have been enough to sour a lesser individual. He'd tapped the older man to add experience and intellectual heft to his administration. Robert Jenkins had chaired the Senate Intelligence Committee for over a decade before joining the private sector. What he had forgotten about the various foreign and domestic enemies that threatened the United States wasn't worth knowing. Right now, the president could use his friend's advice.

Instead, he was adrift. The power of his office was as unparalleled as it was insufficient. In truth, Nash felt no less impotent than he had when George was in the throes of his battle with painkillers.

His fingers curled into a fist, nails biting into his palms. The pain helped, some, but couldn't mask the tidal wave of grief that assailed him. And through the grief, a single, nagging question. If he couldn't save his own son – what made him think he could serve his country any better?

Nash looked up as someone entered the room. A Secret

Service agent now stood watch inside the Oval Office itself, twenty-four hours a day. The man's eyes didn't waver as Martinez, his chief of staff, approached the desk.

"Mr. President," she said. "How are you this morning?"

"I feel a lot like I look," Nash groaned, his throat thick and heavy. Fawning press reports through the campaign had painted a description of a candidate who was blessed with movie star good looks, a man who had risen from nothing and triumphed through adversity. But Nash knew those days were gone. He had been president for less than two weeks, and his eyes were already weighed down with dark bags, his face pale and drained. Whatever the outcome of the present crisis, the man Nash had once been was long gone.

"I'm afraid I've got bad news for you, sir," Martinez said. The President looked up, studying her face sharply. She looked drawn – was probably operating on even less sleep than he was.

"What is it now?"

"Sir, the Attorney General just received a dossier from the NSA."

"What dossier?"

"It claims that the FBI has been compromised. That's how the terrorists managed to catch us with our pants down. They had help from the inside."

"Not possible," Nash said, shaking his head. "Rutger's a goddamn American hero."

"Director Rutger is clean, sir. But the AG has incontrovertible evidence that almost a hundred of his agents aren't. We need to get ahead of the news cycle. We have maybe four hours until the press gets a whiff of this. It's going to be a shit storm either way, but maybe we can at least mold the narrative. I'm coordinating with the US Marshals as we speak."

Nash slammed his fist down on the polished surface of his desk. The impact hurt, but the pain only fueled his rage.

"What the fuck is happening, Emma?" he spat. "Thousands

of Americans are dead and no one has seen my NSA director in two days. Are you saying he's finally come up for air?"

Martinez nodded. "That was the other thing I came to tell you about. Director Donahue just reappeared. He's on his way to the White House as we speak."

Nash fixed her with a glowering stare. Martinez didn't deserve to be the target of his rage, but she was here, and Donahue sure as hell wasn't.

"What the fuck does he want?"

"I don't know, Mr. President. But it's urgent – and he wouldn't speak to anyone except you."

22

By 2011, the Congressional Research Service estimated the cost of keeping a single American soldier in Afghanistan had reached $3.9 million.

Per year.

For Colonel Benjamin Peretz, that number had sounded very sweet indeed. He had bumped into an old friend of his from their days as young men, commandos in the elite Sayeret Matkal Israeli special forces unit, while at a drinks party in Jerusalem.

The man, a certain Solomon Abrams, had retired from the Israeli Defense Forces with the rank of Major, so Col. Peretz knew that while his pension would be comfortable, he certainly shouldn't have been able to pay for a Tom Ford suit. Nor the thirty thousand dollar Rolex that occasionally glinted out from beneath his perfectly pressed white shirt cuffs.

When Peretz asked his old friend what had changed, Abrams simply smiled, and uttered only two words.

"The Americans."

After doing a little digging, Peretz discovered that the American military was paying a staggering four hundred dollars per gallon to get gasoline hauled from the Pakistani border all the way to the Afghan capital, Kabul. The very next day he walked into the General Staff building on the Camp Rabin military base in central Tel Aviv and resigned his commission.

By the end of the month, he was living in a corrugated iron shack in Karachi, Pakistan, running security for a small fuel trucking company. At the time, the company was losing a fuel truck every three weeks in Afghanistan's heavily contested tribal lands. In the four years in which Peretz handled security, he didn't lose a single truck.

Those had been very good years indeed for Colonel Peretz. By the time the war in Afghanistan began to wind down, he was handling security for almost a third of all fuel deliveries to American forces in the country. Drivers flocked to work for him, because he was the only man who could guarantee that they would not die. Even the Taliban knew not to screw with the man with the jagged red scar across his left cheek.

It wasn't worth it. What their commanders quickly came to understand was that Israelis didn't play by the same rules as the weak, feeble Americans. Perhaps it came from living in a hard, desert land, surrounded on all sides by enemies who didn't just want to defeat them, but wanted to literally wipe them from the face of the planet.

Whatever the case, after a convoy under Benjamin Peretz' protection came under attack in late 2012, he personally led a mission into Kandahar Province that left two dozen Taliban fighters either dead or permanently crippled, and their leader nailed to a wooden door by his crotch.

The warning was received in the manner it had been intended, and for the rest of the war, the Taliban would attack convoys both in front of and behind Peretz' own, while leaving his unscathed.

And so, when Peretz returned to Israel, he was a very rich

man. He could have idled away his days living in the lap of luxury. Superyachts off the coast of Monaco. Summering in the Hamptons. But within months, Peretz got the itch. He was a killer, not a housecat, and he needed to get back into the game.

Shortly after that, an entire unit of Sayeret Matkal commandos decided to leave the Israeli military. They did so with the blessing of the General Staff, and an understanding that if Israel ever called, in her hour of need, Peretz' men would answer. They were mercenaries, but also patriots. And they were the best of the best.

At that precise moment, Benjamin Peretz and that very team of Israeli commandos were sitting in three black Mercedes SUVs, all complete with tinted windows, and were dressed in dark combat fatigues and bulletproof vests. Four men in each vehicle, twelve in total. The heating in Peretz' vehicle was blasting out on its highest setting, but it was still too cold. He yearned for the dry warmth of the desert.

Each of his men was equipped with an Israeli-made IWI TAR-21 assault rifle, chambered for 5.56 mm ammunition. The weapons were chunky, with a heavy stock, and were each mounted with their operator's preferred sight.

As if on cue, the colonel's phone buzzed. He answered it without hurrying. Inside, he was deadly calm. The scar on his cheek danced as he spoke.

"This is Golan," he said in perfect, if slightly accented English. "Go."

"Benjamin," the voice on the other end of the line said calmly. The compression on the scrambled phone made it sound flat, almost dull. Devoid of emotion. "You received my introduction, I take it?"

Peretz cleared his throat in the affirmative. He had indeed received the man's 'introduction' – a twenty million dollar payment into a numbered offshore bank account. Half for his men, and the rest for him alone. The transfer had come with no strings attached. Only the promise of a very lucrative client. And in Benjamin Peretz's world, money spoke loudest. He had only one rule: he would not harm the interests of the state of Israel.

Everything else was fair game.

"Good," the flat voice said. "I see you are at the location I specified."

"Indeed."

"Mr. Peretz," the voice said. "I need you to kill a man for me."

"Naturally."

A flat, distorted sigh came down the line, and into Peretz' ear, as if its owner had come to a painful decision.

"Benjamin, I need you to eliminate the Director of the National Security Agency. And I need it done this morning."

For once in his life, Benjamin Peretz was rendered speechless. He had killed on every continent except Antarctica, both for his country and for himself. Some of his targets had been very powerful men: CEOs, generals, warlords.

"That," Peretz said, buying himself some time to think, "sounds like an extremely expensive proposition."

"Name your price."

Peretz looked around the inside of the Mercedes SUV. His men were sitting, looking relaxed, but in truth pretending not to be listening in. They knew that their newest client was what was known in the business as a 'whale.' The kind of customer who could significantly speed up the date of their retirement.

They were hard men. Some of the best fighters that Peretz had ever met.

But at the same time, he understood that his time with them was naturally drawing to a close. Peretz knew himself to be a rare breed. Most men fight for one of three reasons: money, patriotism, and pride. The second of the three is the only one that can be sustained at the very highest levels for any true length of time.

Pride dulls, and men who fight for money get sloppy given sufficient time. When they reach whatever number they decide is enough, they don't subject themselves to sufficient risk. And the willingness to undertake personal risk is what separates elite special operators from ordinary men. It's at the border between life and death where a man truly finds himself.

"Twenty-five," he said. "Each."

Around him, his men's eyes snapped open with barely restrained shock. The number was in American dollars, as it always was. It was enough to retire on. Enough for them to live as rich men until the end of their days. But with a number that large came risk, and that meant danger. Peretz studied his men's' eyes. Were they still hungry? Would they still fight for him?

The flat voice didn't hesitate, and Peretz kicked himself, breaking his train of thought. He thought he had been pushing it. But whoever this client was, he clearly wasn't concerned with money. Peretz wondered how high he could have gone.

"Done. And another fifty for you, Benjamin. Half now, half after the job's done. Paid into the usual account."

"How do I contact you?" Peretz replied, quickly regaining his normal equanimity. "When it's done?"

"I'll be watching."

"Where will he be?" Peretz asked.

"He lands at Andrews Air Force Base in an hour. His motorcade will be waiting for him. Six bodyguards from the NSA's Scorpion team, traveling in armored vehicles. He's heading for the White House. It is imperative that he is not allowed to complete his journey. Do you understand?"

Peretz chewed his lip. This was going to be one hell of a

dangerous operation. After it was done, he and his men would need to disappear. Assume new identities. Travel one by one to South American plastic surgery clinics and acquire new faces. It would be expensive. Then again, they were about to be extremely rich men.

"I do. We'll need an exfil route. Top cover. The second we start shooting, every police officer, soldier and mall cop in a fifty-mile radius will converge on our location. We need support, or we're dead men."

The voice paused.

"Understood. Benjamin, your men are carrying encrypted radios and cell phones, correct?"

Peretz frowned. It was uncanny what his newest client seemed to know. Almost as though he had a spy in Peretz' own team, although the canny Israeli mercenary knew that was impossible.

"You are correct."

"Ask them to check whether they have any signal."

Peretz did as his client instructed. One by one, he watched as his three men checked the signal on their cell phones, then tried their encrypted radios. Nothing worked.

"Are you still there?" he asked into his scrambled cell phone, expecting that like those in the hands of his men, his phone would no longer be functional.

"Yes, Benjamin. Before the operation starts, I will bring down every cell tower in a three-state radius, jam every radio frequency, and throw up hundreds of false positives on every radar screen from here to California. The authorities will be so busy chasing their tails, they won't have any idea the attack is taking place until it's already over. Is that sufficient?"

"Can you leave our channels open?" Peretz asked.

He didn't truly believe that what his client was promising was possible. Not without having a couple of US Air Force EF-

III electronic warfare planes hovering overhead, and no matter how wealthy their client was, no matter his reasons for wanting Director Donahue dead, and no matter how much he was willing to pay, Peretz didn't believe he could order US Air Force assets into the air.

But the wily colonel had no intention of ordering his men into action unless his contacts confirmed that their client had delivered on his promise. If he didn't get that confirmation, then he and his men would be on a private jet headed out of the country within hours.

"It's already done," the voice replied. "You'll want to confirm before you give the go order, of course."

"Of course."

"Happy hunting, Colonel Peretz."

The line went dead.

ALTHOUGH TRAPP DIDN'T KNOW it, Peretz' plan was simple. He sent three men to Andrews Air Force Base: a sniper, a spotter, and a driver. Peretz knew that the second Director Donahue made it into his armored SUV, his job would become significantly harder. It would be far easier to eliminate the man with a single well-aimed head shot.

If his sniper got his man, then at $350 million it would probably be the most valuable single fifty cal round ever fired.

Peretz was, however, nothing if not careful. And since a fifth of that sum was personal upside, he was *extremely* motivated to get this operation right.

He also knew that in order to get from Andrews to the White House, Donahue's motorcade would have to cross one of three natural chokepoints: either the Frederick Douglass Memorial Bridge to the east, the John Philip Sousa Bridge, or the 11th St. Bridge to the west.

The leader of Donahue's security team would not make the decision until the very last second. And so in order to intercept his target, Peretz would need an ace up his sleeve. An ace of the aerial kind.

And an ace he intended to acquire.

23

Trapp gunned the engine of the black Toyota RAV4, driving as fast as he could, while remaining within the speed limit. The last thing he needed would be for a cop, jumpy and trigger-happy after the terrible events that had so recently rocked America, to pull him over and accidentally put a bullet in his head.

He headed directly for Andrews Air Force Base, absently rubbing the faded scar that circled his neck. Recent events had dredged up memories he'd long ago bottled away. Memories of fear, and pain, and the ammonia stink of a young boy's terror. Memories of the first man he ever killed; too late to save his own mother. Then later, too slow to save his partner.

Trapp exhaled and pushed the darkness away. He didn't have time to indulge his own demons right now. There would be time later to wallow in the past—if he survived.

Andrews was only a forty-minute drive from the safe house. Either he was too early for rush hour, or Baltimoreans were still too spooked from Bloody Monday to feel comfortable venturing far from home.

Either way, the roads were clear and he made good time,

the RAV4 eating up the gray concrete roads with ease. The snow-dusted country zipped past on either side, reminding Trapp of the view from the Millennium Falcon as it entered hyperdrive, the growl of the engine noise and vibration of the tires only adding to the sensation. He grinned to himself. Now that was a memory that dated him.

Trapp stopped briefly to set up his communications link. He had a feeling that whatever happened today, events had a possibility of going sideways very quickly, and a direct line to Mitchell might come in useful. Beneath a plain navy blue baseball cap, pulled backward over his head, he was wearing a throat mic and ear piece linked to the secure app on his phone.

"Control, this is Hangman. Give me a sitrep."

Kyle Partey's calm, assured voice replied immediately. Trapp had always found it strange that a man who seemed so anxious in person was always so comfortable when directing complex operations. He supposed it was simply the man's comfort zone. His element.

Just as Trapp himself knew that, if their roles were reversed, he would probably not last a week in the young analyst's shoes. He wasn't a cubicle-drone kind of guy. The thought of trudging to work every morning, stopping to buy coffee at Starbucks, and then slogging through nine hours behind a keyboard filled him with dread.

"Reading you loud and clear, Hangman. What's your position?"

"I'm about three miles out from Andrews," Trapp said, stepping on the gas to overtake a jalopy that looked like its engine was about to fall out. "Where is the target?"

"Director Donahue is set to touch down in about forty minutes, Hangman. His motorcade will meet him on the runway and proceed straight to the White House. I don't have any information for you on his route."

"No," Trapp said. "They'll play it by ear."

It was what he would do, Trapp knew. Routine was the greatest enemy of effective personal protection. Routine allowed assailants to figure out where their target would be, at what time, using which method of transport. It allowed a crazy man to get close enough to take a shot at the President.

Or, as Trapp himself had done many times, it gave a team of highly trained special operators an opportunity to eliminate or capture a high-value target.

"Tell me about Donahue's detail," he said.

"He always has six with him. From the NSA's Scorpion team. The motorcade is composed of three vehicles: heavily armored Chevrolet Suburbans. Windshields should stop anything smaller than fifty caliber, and they've got their own air supply. As long as he's traveling in the continental United States, NSA satellites will be on overwatch the entire time."

"Shit," Trapp muttered. His voice was low, but barely needed to be audible for the throat mic to pick it up. "Any way you can fix that? They'll make me immediately."

"I'll see what I can do," Kyle replied.

Trapp got off Route 495 from Baltimore at Forestville, a small community just a couple of miles from Andrews. All around, Trapp saw signs of the area's high population of military personnel. American flags fluttered from windows, flagpoles and front porches, and young men with close-cropped haircuts drove cars they couldn't afford. He'd been one of them once. Suckered into buying a muscle car in one of the many dealerships that clustered together just off-base, catering to young men with too much money and not enough sense.

It felt somehow comforting, like returning home after a long vacation. Trapp had lived most of his life in places like this. At least, when he wasn't deployed. As he drove, farmland flashing past out of his right window, the chain-link fence that surrounded Joint Base Andrews now fast approaching on his left, he mulled over the situation in his mind.

Donahue's six-man protective detail was a small one, no matter how you cut it. Even a longshot presidential candidate might have as many as fifty Secret Service agents assigned to them for protection, with many of those working overtime when their charge was on the move. Add to that local cops and other federal agencies, there could be a ring of steel around the candidate that was hundreds of officers deep.

No matter how good Donahue's Scorpion guys were, and no matter how infallible the NSA satellites providing overwatch might be, in Trapp's view six men wasn't even enough to protect a kindergarten, let alone the director of the National Security Agency.

Trapp figured it was because of the bean counters up at Congress. No doubt the bureaucrats had raised hell at Donahue's protection budget. The thought sickened Trapp. After the President himself, there weren't many people America's enemies would rather get their hands on than director Rick Donahue.

The problem, as far as Trapp saw it, was that given a couple of days and a Barrett fifty caliber M107 sniper rifle, he was certain he would be able to get a clear shot at pretty much anyone – and that included Donahue. In fact, Trapp had often wondered why terrorists spent so much time and energy trying to take down highly protected airliners and federal buildings, when shooting a man from a distance of a thousand yards would have been just as effective, and far safer.

Hell, the Washington sniper had shut DC down for weeks. Trapp shivered as he thought about the prospect of what fifty such sharpshooters could do. Or a hundred. Or more.

They could tear the country apart.

24

Dani Carter returned to work three days after Bloody Monday, about ten ahead of schedule. The doctors didn't like it, but while there was no doubt that the agent had been knocked senseless, her vital signs had recovered remarkably quickly.

As for the rest of her injuries: the cuts and scrapes and bruises that marked her body like a toddler had gone hog wild with a fingerpainting kit, those were just flesh wounds. Not pretty, but not life-threatening either.

"Identification," a uniformed FBI agent snapped as she stepped up to the offices of the Bureau's field office, on DC's 4th Street. The roads immediately around the squat, pale ten story office block were cordoned off, to guard against vehicle-borne attacks, and she didn't have to look hard to see signs of FBI sniper teams on the rooftops.

More accurately, Carter thought as a foul, rotting meat stench wrinkled her nostrils, the streets weren't cordoned off, but blockaded by DC's hulking garbage collection trucks. It was a common enough tactic, one usually employed by the police when protecting events like parades. Carter had no doubt that within a couple of days, the trucks would be replaced by large concrete slabs. She wondered how long it would be before the roads reopened to traffic – or if they ever would.

She handed her badge to the uniformed agent. He stood just shy of six foot tall, with dark black hair and remarkably hairy fingers. He glanced down at it, still cradling his primary weapon, a black Colt M4. His partner, on the other side of the large entrance to the office, was equally alert. His weapon wasn't raised, but Carter knew it would take only a second. Both men wore black bulletproof vests, stenciled with the letters *FBI*, which only served to make their impressive frames even thicker.

Jesus, she thought, studying the ring of steel around the field office. *Is this what we've become?*

She felt more like she was entering Baghdad's Green Zone than an office building in Washington DC.

"Agent Carter," the man said, handing her badge back with more than a hint of recognition in his eyes. "I didn't realize it was you."

Dani kinked her eyebrow. "Have we met?"

The agent grinned, and his posture noticeably relaxed, though his eyes never stopped roving the street behind her. He let his M4 hang limply on its sling, and crossed his arms over it.

"No, ma'am. They flew me in from Cincinnati just this morning. Guess the people upstairs figured Ohio is pretty low on the threat matrix. But I know who you are." He jerked his thumb back at the field office behind him.

"Doubt there's an agent in there who doesn't. We're damn proud of you, believe me. Ain't much to feel good about right now, so you're about all we got."

Dani frowned, and then immediately regretted it, as a scrape on her face that had only recently scabbed over delivered a vicious lance of pain.

"Thanks, I guess. I didn't do anything you wouldn't have."

The agent shook his head. He nodded his head down, dark hair bobbing at the weapon underneath his arms.

"I doubt that, ma'am. I'll let you in on a little secret. I've never fired this thing. In anger, I mean."

Dani returned her badge to her waist. "Until Monday," she replied softly, "neither had I."

Her cubicle was on the fourth floor, and after negotiating a second ring of security just before the elevators, along with a couple more excruciating displays of gratitude which Dani was entirely unprepared for, she made it up there.

Only to be greeted with a standing ovation.

The fourth floor offices were a hive of activity. Whiteboards had been wheeled in from the basement and were covered with barely legible hieroglyphics that Dani presumed were supposed to be words. It looked like every agent in DC had been pulled back to headquarters. All leave canceled. There were two agents for every desk and several more waiting in the wings. Suit jackets hung off the back of wheeled office chairs, and a cacophony of ringing phones, printer sounds and nervous excitement filled the air.

Dani walked toward her cubicle, cheeks flushing red at the unaccustomed attention. "Please," she said once or twice, "stop. I didn't mean to interrupt..."

But it was no use. Perhaps the agent guarding the front entrance was right. There was little enough to be cheerful about right now in America. Maybe Dani Carter was all they had. Especially the agents in this very room, who had no doubt lost friends and colleagues during the attack on the Hoover Building. As she made it to the gray walls of her cubicle and threw her rucksack down, a familiar face stepped toward her, shaking his white-topped head.

"Carter," Olsen said, enveloping her in a bear hug – easy enough, since he was almost a foot taller than her. "What in the hell are you doing here?"

"Doc gave me the green light," Dani replied, slightly stretching the truth.

The doctor hadn't exactly cleared her, so much as given up hope of preventing Dani from returning to work. No more than two hours a day, and no physical activity for at least a week, he had said, probably knowing it was futile even as the words escaped his lips.

Dani was a woman on a mission. Someone had reached out and attempted to harm not just her, but the only person in her life who mattered. She wouldn't stand for that. Whoever was behind Bloody Monday, they were going to pay. They might not know that yet. Probably didn't even know her name. But they would pay, nonetheless.

"Believe me," Olsen said, "you're a sight for sore eyes."

"It's just good to be back."

"How's your old man?" Olsen asked, tired eyes narrowed with concern.

Dani grimaced at the reminder of where she'd spent most of the past three days – at her father's bedside as he fought for life. That was why she was back at work. She needed a distraction, and this was it.

"In and out of consciousness. The doctors think he'll make it, and I guess that's all that matters."

"It'll take more than a bit of shrapnel to kill that old bastard," Olsen grinned. "Trust me."

Dani matched his smile. "I hope you're right."

She glanced around the office floor. Every couple of seconds, an agent would come and clap her on the shoulder and say something like, "Always knew you were a fighter" or "Good to have you back."

She felt uncomfortable from the attention, but judging by the hunched-over posture and tension most of her fellow agents were carrying, she decided to roll with the punches. If it made them feel good, then so be it.

"So," Carter said, "fill me in. Where are we on the attacks? Put me to work, boss. I can't face another day on the bench."

Dani noticed Olsen almost wince as she asked the question. He looked tired, and older than he had just a couple of days earlier, his gray hair looking drab and lifeless, the lines on his face more pronounced.

"Up shit creek without a paddle," he admitted.

"That good, huh?"

"You better believe it," the experienced SAC replied. "So far we've tracked almost a hundred separate attacks across thirty-two states, involving upward of three hundred terrorists. We've got over five thousand dead and twice that many in the hospital."

Dani knew all of this. Or at least, most of this. Although the precise number of perpetrators hadn't been released by the authorities, the cable networks and news websites were running with the rest of the information Olsen had given her. For the last seventy-two hours, the grim statistics of Bloody Monday's tragedy had been replayed on a loop, the blue light thrown off by ATN flickering like a candle in the darkness of her father's hospital room.

"So why the long face?" Dani quipped, her analytical mind revving up into high gear.

She abstracted herself from the horrifying truth that lay at the bottom of the statistics Olsen had rattled off – the funerals that were already taking place across the nation. The children who would never walk again. The wave of suicides that would follow for years as grieving parents, mothers, fathers, brothers and sisters all finally gave up and stopped fighting.

She had failed them already, by letting the attackers not so much slip as saunter through the net. Carter vowed that she would not allow herself to fail that way again, digging her fingernails into her palms and savoring the pain that resulted.

The only positive Dani could take out of the scenario was,

paradoxically, the sheer number of attackers. Few had been taken alive, and if history was any guide it wouldn't be easy to make them talk. Torture works better in the movies than real life. But as both her time in the Academy and then the last eight years in the field had taught her, nothing beat physical evidence.

On September 11, 2001, nineteen Al Qaeda hijackers seized control of four civilian airliners, killing over two thousand people. Until Bloody Monday, it was the worst terrorist attack in American history. But practically before the bodies had stopped falling from the Twin Towers, the FBI had already identified eleven of the men from passenger manifests. Within a week, they knew everything there was to know about the rest, from their sexual predilections to the size of their shoes.

With three hundred such leads to chase down, Dani felt an almost primal hunger overtake her. She would be the one to crack this case, she promised herself that. She owed it not just to the Bureau, but to her own father.

"We got nothing, Carter," Olsen admitted with a grimace.

It took Dani more than a few seconds to process what her boss was saying. To put it bluntly, it didn't make sense.

"What are you talking about?"

Suddenly the atmosphere in the FBI field office started to click into place. There was an uncomfortable tension in the air. Every agent had a strange, haunted look, not from tiredness, as Dani had initially assumed. Not exhaustion from working triple shifts for days hunting down terrorists. No, she saw what was missing – that hungry, determined look every good agent got when she was running down a lead.

"Read my lips, Carter. We haven't done full work-ups on all of the perps yet. But we're halfway through, and each time we're coming up empty. These guys were ghosts. We don't know how long they've been in the country, how they crossed the border, or what they've been doing since they got here. I mean

Christ, we're running DNA analysis just to find out what fucking continent they came from."

"And chatter?" Dani asked, her mind cycling through the list of possibilities.

What Olsen was saying simply didn't compute. An attack on the scale of Bloody Monday would have required millions, maybe hundreds of millions of dollars to finance. It would involve not just the three hundred attackers, but thousands more in support. Like a cruise ship disappearing into the Bermuda triangle, there was simply no way something this vast could have been missed.

Dani lowered her voice. Strictly speaking, she wasn't supposed to know about the NSA's latest and greatest intelligence gathering system – but it was a poorly kept secret in the law enforcement community. The intelligence packets that landed on desks across DC every morning were sanitized, but that only went so far.

"What about Birdseye?"

Olsen shook his head. Dani felt a pang of sadness overcome her as she studied the once proud, now almost broken man standing before her. She knew how much he loved his job. Knew that just like her, in the early hours of the morning instead of sleeping, he obsessed every night over how he could protect America better. Dani knew that his failure would have cut him deeply.

"Zip," he said. "They didn't see this coming either."

That didn't make sense. Unless whoever pulled this off had coordinated the attacks via carrier pigeon, the NSA's keyhole satellites must have picked up something. Dani frowned, her face creasing as her tenacious mind tackled the problem.

"What about their weapons?" Dani asked. "They had everything, right? Military grade. We must've found fragments of serial numbers, bomb casings, their rifles..."

"Dani, believe me," Olsen said, gesturing around the office, "if there's a rock to look under, we've been right down there, with the beetles and the lice. Serial numbers registered to weapons consignments that either never existed, or were destroyed. No link. No idea when or if they were sold or traded. It's like someone's gone in to every database we have and fragged them."

As Dani closed her eyes, processing everything she had been told, it felt almost as though the ground beneath her feet was swaying. She didn't know whether it was from the head injury, or the realization that the Bureau wasn't infallible. That right now, the Washington DC Field Office, hell, maybe the whole damn Bureau, didn't know anything more than the talking heads on cable television.

"Okay," Dani said slowly, the words forming on her tongue before they really crystallized in her mind. "So we know what we don't know, right?"

"Right," Olsen agreed, in a tone that suggested he didn't really want to talk about it. Dani guessed he hadn't slept in days. His face was sallow and gaunt, hands trembling from exhaustion, teeth yellowed and stained from his coffee intake.

"So let's go with what we do."

Olsen threw his hands apart with frustration. "Weren't you listening, Nadine? What part of we've got nothing, zip, nada, did you not understand?"

Dani shot Olsen a cold, dissatisfied look at the use of her given name. He'd known her long enough to know better than that. He grimaced an apology.

She leaned against the wall of her cubicle, her slight weight not posing much of a problem for its structural integrity, and let her mind race.

"Think it through, boss," she said. "This was too big for Al Qaeda to pull off, right? As far as we know, all they've got left is fifteen illiterate tribesmen and a goat in some shit-stinking Afghan cave."

"As far as we know..." Olsen replied, his tone suggesting exactly what he thought about the reliability of American intelligence right now.

Dani sprang forward, the excitement of her hypothesis causing her to bounce from foot to foot. "Same goes for ISIS. Even at their peak, they weren't capable of coordinating something this big outside of the Middle East. Remember that truck plot we stopped in Newark?"

Olsen nodded. "What about it?"

"Everything!" Dani replied, frustrated that he wasn't on her wavelength. "It doesn't fit. None of this does. The Air Force was bombing them back to the Stone Age in Syria, and when the bombs were dropping, SEAL Team Six was going in night after night and snatching their top people. We had them on the run. Best they could do was recruit some kid off the Internet, fill his head with religious mumbo-jumbo, and get him to mow people down in a truck. Just like they did in France."

She continued. "You're expecting me to believe that they went from hiding out in caves to nailing an operation like this? I don't buy it. It would've cost tens of millions of dollars just to plan. Hundreds, maybe. To get into our systems, they'd have needed the best hackers in the world – and all without us noticing."

"So what are you saying?"

"This wasn't Al Qaeda, or ISIS. It has to be bigger than that – state sponsored. Maybe Saudi intelligence, or the Pakistanis. We know the Saudis funded the 9/11 hijackers, and Pakistani intelligence sheltered Bin Laden for years. Maybe they decided to step things up."

"But why?" Olsen said, a fire burning in his eyes for the first time since Dani had stepped into the field office that morning. "To what end?"

Dani Carter never got an opportunity to answer that question. As she opened her mouth to reply, mind racing over the possibilities, a cry split the humming, tense office, silencing it in an instant.

"Federal agents!"

Dani's head snapped to the source of the sound. Instinctively, her hand went for her gun, only for Olsen to grab her wrist and give her a subtle shake of the head.

What the hell is going on?

Men and women in dark navy windbreakers began to flood into the cubicle farm from both emergency stairwells and the bank of elevators Dani had stepped out of only moments before. The only thought that went through Carter's mind was that the terrorists had come back to finish the job. But that didn't make any sense. On each of the men and women now circling the field office, printed front and back in white, were the words *United States Marshall.*

A gruff, bald marshal, his service weapon drawn but not raised and fury in his eyes began to yell in a gruff, hoarse voice that echoed around the brightly lit office.

"Get your hands behind your heads. Any of you sons of bitches so much as touches your weapon, it'll be the last thing you do."

Special Agent in Charge of the Washington DC Field Office of the FBI, Rick Olsen, stepped forward from his post beside Dani, his hands raised in a conciliatory gesture.

"Marshall, you better have a God damn good reason for this. Tell your men to lower their weapons and get the fuck out of my office in the next twenty seconds, or I'll have your head –"

"Richard Olsen," the federal marshal replied, cutting the SAC off in a tone of barely concealed disdain. "On the orders of the attorney general, you are under arrest on suspicion of aiding and abetting enemies of the United States of America. Anything you say can and will be used against you in a court of law. You have the right to talk to a lawyer..."

As the marshal continued reading Olsen his Miranda

rights, something both Dani and he had done hundreds if not thousands of times, Carter looked around the field office with shock. The process was being repeated in cubicle after cubicle, where dozens of agents proclaimed their innocence as their rights were read out, or just stood gawping with dumb astonishment as their colleagues and friends were taken away. The metallic clink and rasp of handcuffs filled the air, punctuated by the thud of confiscated handguns hitting desks.

"Carter," Olsen said urgently, locking eyes with her as the bald marshal began to lead him away in cuffs. "Get to the bottom of this."

"I will," Dani said, almost choking over the words. By the time she was composed enough to say anything else, Olsen was gone, and the field office was left in a state of stunned silence.

What the hell had just happened?

25

"Control for Hangman, over."

Trapp spoke into his throat mic, eyes still scanning left and right for any sign of Donahue's Air Force-operated C-40 Clipper private jet. He was on at least his third circuit around Joint Base Andrews, and he had nothing. Overhead, the sky was split every few minutes by a peal of thunder as a jet took off from the airbase. Trapp couldn't imagine how anyone could live here. The sound was like a physical assault on his eardrums, forcing him back against the leather seat of the Toyota.

"I read you, Control. Got something for me?"

"You bet," Partey's assured tone replied. "I just picked up three black SUVs heading east on Allentown Road."

"That's them," Trapp said with quiet relief. He spun his eyes to the left, picking out his route.

"We concur," came the reply, though from Mitchell this time rather than his analyst. "What's your plan, Hangman?"

Trapp thought for a second before replying.

"How are we for overwatch?"

"Limited," Mitchell replied. "Kyle's hacked into the traffic

camera network, but we don't have any access to the base's
security systems."

"I'm working on it," Kyle added, though he didn't sound
particularly confident of success. "But right now the best I can
promise you is the odd glimpse. I can't maintain a visual."

"Then I need to get eyes on," Trapp determined quickly. "I
need a structure, tall enough to overlook both runways. Ideally
something with a bit of cover."

It was a plan, but Trapp knew it wasn't much of one. If the
security around Joint Base Andrews was any good, which it
would be, given the frequency with which high-value administration officials flew from it, then spotters would be scanning
every rooftop. Especially right now, with the military at
Defcon-2.

There was a short pause, and Trapp heard the sound of
fingers dancing across the keyboard in his earpiece. It sounded
like heavy rain plinking on a thin tin roof.

"I just got another hit on the motorcade. Looks like they just
turned off Allentown into the base using a service entrance on
the northwest corner. Just give me a second."

Trapp remained quiet but dived off Allentown, turned the
RAV4 around in the parking lot of a McDonald's, and gunned
the engine in the opposite direction. The fast, tight maneuver
swept up litter in the SUV's wake, and left Trapp feeling slightly
lightheaded.

"Okay," Kyle said. "I've got a Quality Inn Motel, three stories
high, with an HVAC unit on the roof. It should make for decent
cover."

Trapp had seen the motel on his first spin around the base.
It was a squat building, painted a dirty yellow, and if he recalled
correctly it was advertising rooms for thirty-nine dollars a
night. Given its proximity to Andrews' round-the-clock jet take-
offs and landings, and its no doubt paper-thin walls, Trapp
imagined the only customers management would be able to

sucker into renting a room would be military personnel who didn't have much of a choice.

"Got it."

Two minutes later, Trapp was at the motel. That was when he caught his first lucky break. His eyes flashed across a black Mercedes SUV that was pulling into the motel's parking lot just as he began braking to do the same. Its dark, tinted windows were almost impenetrable through the swirling clouds overhead.

"Control," he said into his mic. "Are you seeing this?"

"Negative, Hangman. What have you got?"

Trapp took his foot off the brake and stepped on the gas. There was a diner a couple of hundred yards up Allentown, and instead of pulling into the Quality Inn, he ditched the RAV4 there instead. The vehicle was as inconspicuous as a drug dealer's car could hope to be, but he wanted to play it safe. If the driver of the Mercedes was here to assassinate Donahue, they probably weren't expecting to meet any resistance. But that was exactly what Trapp was programmed to provide.

"I'm not sure yet," he said, popping the Toyota's trunk. He glanced around to make sure no one was paying attention, but there was nothing but the rhythmic hum of the kitchen's extractor fan, and the taste of maple syrup and bacon fat on the air. It felt like a sleepy place, and with the military base so close by, no one was looking for trouble.

Trapp unzipped one of the black duffel bags. He already had a pistol in a shoulder holster underneath his jacket, but something about the Mercedes SUV had prompted his instincts to go into overdrive – screaming out a warning that he needed more hardware.

It was at least a ninety thousand dollar car. Trapp wasn't really into German engineering, but he knew enough to get by. No one with that kind of money would stay at a rat-infested motel like the Quality Inn unless they had a gun to their head.

It couldn't be a coincidence that the Mercedes had parked up next to the only building with a clear line of sight to where Donahue's jet was about to be. The only remaining possibility was that the vehicle was operated by the NSA Scorpion team, but that didn't fit either.

"You said Donahue's motorcade was three vehicles, right?"

"That's right."

"Suburbans?"

Trapp didn't quite have an eidetic memory, he wasn't a savant who never forgot anything, but he was pretty damn close. He remembered exactly what Partey had said about Donahue's motorcade. When he was on a mission, his brain filed away every piece of information it came across, just in case it was needed later.

"Yeah that's right. What are you seeing, Hangman?"

"I think maybe another player just entered the game," Trapp said. A jolt of adrenaline hit his system, as it always did before he went into battle. He didn't know for certain that was what was about to happen, but he had a pretty good idea.

"Who?"

"If I knew that, I wouldn't be asking all these questions, would I?"

Trapp was already carrying two fifteen-round magazines in addition to the one in his Beretta, but he threw in a couple more, just to be certain.

He thought about picking up the MP5 submachine gun, but decided the prospect of someone noticing was too high. If base security was alerted to his presence, then he'd have a squad of military police on his ass before he could blink.

Finally, he took a suppressor for his pistol out of the bag, slipped off his jacket, donned the bulletproof vest he'd packed, and put the jacket back on. He placed the gun accessory in its pocket.

"I'm proceeding to the motel on foot," he said. "How long till Donahue's flight lands?"

"It's about five minutes out. Have you got an active threat down there? We can get in touch with Andrews, get the plane to go around?"

Trapp considered the suggestion, but dismissed it. They needed a lead on whatever the hell was going on more than they needed Donahue alive. He would prefer to achieve both objectives, but if figuring out who was behind Bloody Monday meant the director had to incur a little bit of risk, then it was one Trapp was willing to take.

He could apologize to Donahue later. Or put a bullet in his forehead, if things turned out that way.

"No," Trapp replied. "I'll handle it. See if you can get any eyes on the motel."

"Copy."

Trapp walked toward the motel, the sound of traffic loud in his eardrums as cars streaked past just yards away. Every minute or so, a military jet either took off or landed on one of Andrews' two runways. Twice, he heard the telltale shriek of fighter jets slamming on their afterburners and taking to the skies – evidence of the heightened state of alert that the military was operating under.

Right now, though, the noise might play in his favor. He fingered the suppressor for his Beretta in his jacket pocket. Contrary to popular imagination, a suppressor is not a silencer. You can't just make a pistol, submachine gun, or rifle's report sound like a high-pitched squeak, as watching James Bond would have you believe.

The accessory helps dissipate the gas leaving a weapon's barrel, quieting the bang. Not enough to allow Trapp to sneak into a target's bedroom at night and eliminate them without waking their wife, but in an area like this, with the clamour of fast-moving traffic and even faster-flying jets, it would probably mask enough sound that Andrews' base security wouldn't notice gunfire.

If it came to it, of course. Hell, Trapp thought, maybe he was just being paranoid. Although since someone really was out to get him, it was probably a healthy reaction.

"Coming up empty, Hangman," Kyle said. "You're on your own on this one. No cameras in the vicinity of the motel. At least nothing hooked up to an Internet connection."

"Copy that," Trapp replied. It didn't surprise him. The Quality Inn looked roach infested and decrepit, its outer walls decorated with dark streaks of rust, and in desperate need of a fresh coat of paint.

"Stay off the line. I'll call you if I need something."

He was on his own now. And in truth, that's the way he liked it best. Although he had formed a deadly two-man team with his deceased partner, Ryan Price, Trapp was even better flying solo. He had a predator's instinct for prey, and prey's instincts for trouble.

Trapp approached the motel, hands deep inside his pockets, posture slouched. He knew he didn't have much time. If someone had sent an assault team to this location, then it was for only one reason: the fact that the Quality Inn Motel had the only unobstructed view of the runways at Andrews anywhere on the northwest corner.

He hugged the walls as he reached the motel, staying tight so that someone looking down from overhead would be less likely to notice him. He saw the Mercedes SUV parked in a space near the rear entrance of the motel, and the sight provoked a sharp intake of breath as he struggled to control that familiar bout of nerves. He would have to walk directly past it to reach the emergency stairwell that led to the building's roof.

As he rounded the vehicle, his slouched posture ensuring he looked a couple of decades older than he really was, he noticed a man sitting in the driver's seat of the SUV. Trapp kept his eyes down, but looked sideways, his eyes probing.

Gotcha.

The driver was dressed in a civilian jacket, presumably so that a passing cop didn't think that anything was out of the ordinary. But nothing could hide his close-cropped haircut, or the military bearing with which he held himself.

Trapp considered his options. He didn't have time to take out the driver. His only option would be to put a bullet through the man's skull, and he figured the vehicle was probably armored. Even if it wasn't, the sound of the gunshot might attract unwanted attention – and given that the Andrews runways were almost a thousand yards away, if someone was here to kill Donahue, then they would be a crack shot. The last thing he needed was someone with those skills turning their attention on him.

When he was clear of the motel, he spoke into his throat mic, careful to keep his voice low. "I'm approaching the motel," he said. "We've definitely got company. I'm going for the roof."

Kyle's reply was short and sweet. Trapp remembered why he liked the young analyst. The man was a cool customer. And most importantly, unlike so many desk jockeys with a height-ened sense of their own self-importance, he didn't bother oper-ators like Trapp when they were in the field.

"Copy."

Trapp walked around the building, out of view of the SUV, and found the access stairwell that ran straight to the roof. He bent down to tie an imaginary shoelace, scanning his vicinity as he did so, and sensing no immediate danger. The stairwell was old, painted black, but not recently. Much of the paint had chipped off and lay in small piles underneath the metal frame. Trapp gritted his teeth with frustration. He sensed the thing would creak and rattle with every step he took – like climbing a rickety wind chime.

As he stood back up, he glanced upward, looking to see if someone was covering the stairwell. The climb would be the most dangerous part, unless of course he encountered a full team of shooters on the roof. They would have the high ground, and even an incompetent gunman would be able to put half a dozen rounds through his chest before he could so much as send one up in reply.

Trapp reached into his jacket, felt the comforting cool metal of his Beretta, and drew it from its holster. With his other hand, he calmly screwed the suppressor into place. And then he began to climb.

He didn't know what he would find up there. But he was about to find out.

26

cold February wind bit against Trapp's face and numbed his fingers, sending clouds scuttling across the face of a steel grey sky. He crept up the rickety metal stairwell that led to the motel's roof, acutely aware of the cries of protest emanating from the rusted steps underneath him. It was stained with bird shit and felt like it might collapse at any second.

The incessant roar of military jets taking off from the runways that were just a few hundred yards away finally came in useful. As yet another jet soared into the sky, momentarily sending a deafening, thunderous roar rolling across the Maryland countryside, almost every other sound was rendered impossible to hear. Trapp took advantage of the opportunity to climb an entire flight of stairs, putting him only a few steps from the top.

After his sudden movement, the sound of the jet engine faded away, leaving a stillness in its wake. It was as if the few birds hardy enough to survive an East Coast winter, rather than migrate down South, had been stunned into silence. And the traffic, too. Trapp froze, straining every sense as he wondered whether he had been detected. The quiet felt heavy, pushing down on his shoulders, his mind painting every whisper of wind as a threat.

Trapp held his 9 mm Beretta out in front of him, the weapon freezing cold to the touch. The suppressor added almost an extra half a foot to the length of the barrel. It changed the way the weapon felt in his hand, moved its center of gravity a little, but Trapp had fired tens of thousands of rounds using devices just like it, and he was confident of his ability to adjust his aim.

He crept another step up the stairwell, and as he did he caught a snatch of conversation on the breeze. It sounded like Arabic. Trapp froze. He started to wonder what the hell was going on here. Could it be the same terrorist organization that had been responsible for the attacks on Bloody Monday?

But then he caught another scrap of dialogue, before the heavy thump of a landing helicopter broke the stillness once more.

Not Arabic. Hebrew.

Trapp didn't speak the language, but recognized it nonetheless from a training mission in the Negev desert some years before. It was a curious tongue that sounded almost like a mix between Arabic and French. Throaty, and yet somehow beautiful.

He didn't stop to work out what the presence of a Hebrew speaker on the motel's roof meant. The conversation hadn't sounded like a warning – there was no harshness to it. It was softer. An update, perhaps. Trapp figured that meant he probably hadn't been made.

Stealthily, Trapp climbed the last few steps, freezing at the faintest squeal of metal against metal and lowering his body so that his head did not crest the lip of the motel's roof. By the time he crested the summit, he was in a three-legged crawl – the only limb not in contact with the stairs was the arm holding the suppressed Beretta.

He froze as a sound cut the quiet, as loud to him as if someone was standing right next to him speaking into his ear.

"Hangman, Donahue's plane just landed. It's taxiing, but the motorcade's coming out to meet it. You're on the clock."

He almost breathed a sigh of relief, but caught himself. It was only Kyle on the radio, thankfully providing the one piece of information he had desperately wanted to know. He needed to move fast.

As far as he could tell, the most likely answer for what he would find on top of the motel's roof was a two-man sniper team – shooter and spotter. If that was true, it meant he had only moments before Donahue would step out of his C-40 passenger jet and meet an untimely demise, courtesy of a fifty caliber round to the skull. By the time he hit the ground, there would be little of his brain left, the gray matter decorating the white paint job of the airplane like a spray of vomit.

Trapp needed to confirm what he was up against. He risked a peek over the lip of the roof.

Shit.

He'd been right. Two men were lying prone on the opposite side of the roof. He could see the soles of their boots, toes facing the ground, like tiny smokestacks sprouting from the rooftop. Their bodies were hidden beneath gray urban camouflage blankets.

But that wasn't the bad part. The motel's roof was covered with a few inches of loose gravel. The first step he took would scream a warning, stone scratching stone like a mountain rock fall.

Trapp swore silently, his heart racing, and adrenaline pounding in his system as he tried to figure out what the hell to do next. The two Israelis had to be thirty feet away, at the edge of his accurate range with the suppressor. There was no way he could rush them, not without at least one of the Israelis spinning around and putting a bullet in his chest.

Although he couldn't know for sure, Trapp was pretty confident that the spotter would be equipped with an assault rifle. At this distance, if he allowed the Israeli to get off a shot, the 5.56 mm ammunition would slice through his bulletproof vest like wire through cheese. He would be dead before he hit the deck.

Trapp cycled through his list of options in his head, his heart sounding like a drum kit on a washing machine spin cycle. He could make the shot with the pistol, he knew. Had done so on the range thousands of times. Though the cold wind was turning his fingers to icy blocks, he'd made far more difficult shots in far worse conditions.

But dead men couldn't answer questions. And right now, Trapp needed answers; needed to know why someone had tried to kill him – twice. Needed to understand what could possibly be so important that it justified the death of the best man he'd ever known. And how everything tied in with the events of Bloody Monday.

"Hangman, it's Mitchell," his earpiece buzzed. "Kyle's managed to get access to some of ATC's runway cams. You got about thirty seconds."

Shit.

Trapp realized he didn't have time to think. He had to act. He paused, studying his breathing, letting his pulse fall below forty beats a minute. For an untrained individual, this might take as long as fifteen minutes. But for Trapp, who had a resting heart rate of thirty-five beats a minute, which would be considered excellent for an Olympian rower, and who had practiced meditation for years, it was child's play.

The time counted down, the metronomic beat resonating in Trapp's skull.

Three.

Two.

One...

He took one last, deep breath, then exploded up, and fired two well-aimed shots into center mass.

27

The second the bullets left the Beretta's muzzle, Trapp charged. The gravel on the roof crunched beneath his heavy bootsteps, but he didn't hear it. In that moment, his world was limited to the cold metal in his grip, the rushing blood in his ears like surf thundering against a rocky coast, and a burning desire to get the job done.

As he moved, the spotter yelled out something guttural and harsh in Israeli that Trapp figured had to be a cuss word. To the man's left, the Israeli with the sniper rifle collapsed to the deck, fingers reaching around and clutching his wounded back. He let out a loud, catlike keening whine.

Trapp's honed instincts quickly catalogued the shooter as the lesser threat. The man had a pistol strapped to a holster on his hip, but made no move to go for it. His Barrett fifty caliber sniper rifle had toppled over amidst the commotion and lay like an oil stain on the gravel. Trapp breathed a sigh of relief. Donahue was safe.

For now, at least.

The spotter to his left twisted, grabbing an assault rifle from its position next to him, and began rising into a shooting position. Trapp had managed to cover half the distance between the stairwell and the two men. It wasn't enough.

Shit.

Trapp skidded to a halt, stones flying in every direction, and crouched, bringing the Beretta up into a two-handed grip. It seemed like he was doing that a lot these last few days. He wasn't used to playing so fast and loose, especially not with hot lead flying in the air.

He didn't yell, "Freeze!" After all, this wasn't a Hollywood movie. Instead, he depressed the Beretta's trigger twice. The Israeli spotter slumped back against the roof, two small dots of red appearing on his forehead.

The second Israeli was more sensible. Either that, or the man was already dead. Whichever it was, he stayed perfectly still.

"Don't fucking move," Trapp said, raising his voice to be heard over the sound of a passing jet.

"Don't shoot," the man said in throaty, accented, but perfectly understandable English. It was clipped with pain.

Trapp rose to his feet. From this angle, he could see that the wound in the man's back was oozing blood onto his black combat fatigues. They glistened, like the inky black eyes of a jungle predator.

"Don't give me a reason to," Trapp replied. "Did I hit anything important?"

The man didn't reply for a second, as though confused by the direction this conversation had taken. Hell, Trapp could understand that. After all, a second ago the guy probably thought he was on the easiest mission of his life. Ten seconds later, his partner was dead and he was about fifteen minutes from bleeding out.

"I don't know," the erstwhile sniper said, his voice catching as he spoke. "Maybe."

Trapp closed the distance between him and them. He kept

his Beretta trained on the injured man the entire way. He had eleven rounds left. It would only take one to end this man's life for good.

"Do you want to live?" Trapp asked.

"You'll kill me either way."

"Now why the hell would I go and do a thing like that?" Trapp asked, crouching down and picking up the fifty caliber rifle that was lying on its side to the sniper's right. He ejected the chambered round and then the magazine, tossing both out of the man's reach, then dropped the rifle.

The Israeli whimpered with pain. Trapp looked down at him with little sympathy. He was lying on his front, as he had been when lining up a shot at Donahue's head. He had the curled wire of an earpiece running down the side of his neck, and toward what Trapp assumed was a radio attached to his vest.

"Are you transmitting?" Trapp asked gruffly, his pistol trained on the man's skull. "Just give me a reason."

"No! I promise." The injured soldier moaned.

"Keep pressuring the wound," Trapp instructed the Israeli without a trace of emotion in his voice. "Can you see it?"

The man tried to twist his head round but began to whimper from the pain. He shook his head.

"Looks to me like you'll bleed out in the next twenty minutes," Trapp lied.

As far as he could tell, the Israeli had gotten off lightly. Sure, his back would probably give him hell until the day he died, but he'd walk again, and unless Trapp was mistaken he wouldn't die today. Then again, bullets could do funny things after entering a man's body.

"Help me," the Israeli cried out plaintively. "I'll tell you whatever you want to know."

"I told you what I want," Trapp said plainly. His aim was unwavering on the back of the man's head. "Keep pressing down on that wound. I'm going to take that weapon off you and then frisk you, okay? One wrong move and I'll paint these stones with your gray matter and leave you up here for the HVAC guy to find this summer."

The Israeli moaned his assent. Trapp crouched down, unfastened the man's holster, grabbed the pistol, and tossed it aside. He did the same with the man's earpiece, yanking the wire out of the radio it was attached to before throwing it over the edge of the roof.

He glanced up as he did so, looking down at the runway in the distance. He thought he might be able to see Donahue's C-40, surrounded by its black motorcade like ants around a fallen French fry, but from this distance it was hard to make anything out with any detail.

"Who sent you here?" Trapp asked, grabbing his prisoner by the man's bulletproof vest and rolling his body over so he could relieve him of his radio. He took it, then stepped back and away from his injured prisoner. "And why were you planning on killing Donahue?"

"Money," the man said, spitting out a bloody globule on to the motel roof before continuing. His chest heaved from the effort. "Twenty-five million dollars."

Trapp let out a low whistle. "Jesus. You want to split it?"

The Israeli looked up at him with hunted brown eyes. Sweat beaded his face, and a dark smear of blood marked his forehead where he had attempted to wipe it off. Trapp had seen that expression before, dozens of times. It was a human being in survival mode; a man who would do and say anything in order to preserve his life.

"What?"

"I'm kidding. I need Donahue alive. Tell you what, let's make a deal. You tell me who sent you, and I'll call you an ambulance. Lie to me and I'll tie you up and let you bleed out, right here."

"I don't know," the man cried out. His face was white, his fingers stained a dark red by the blood seeping out of his back. "I just go where I'm sent. Watch who I am told to watch."

"And kill who you're told to kill," Trapp said flatly.

He was about to say something else, ask the man who was running the show, when the radio in his hand crackled. A voice emanated from the small black encrypted unit. Again, it was in Hebrew.

"What did he say?" Trapp demanded.

"He's checking in. Wants to know if the job's done." As he finished speaking, the man started panting heavily from the pain.

Trapp considered his options. He could put the barrel of his pistol against the back of the sniper's head and threaten to kill him if he tipped off the man on the other end of the radio. But that plan was fraught with risk.

"Who's *he?* Your boss, or your getaway driver?"

The prisoner froze.

"Yeah, I know about him," Trapp said.

Still, the thought played on his mind that at any moment, the third man might interrupt this pleasant little tête-à-tête. He didn't have time to screw around.

"My boss," the sniper moaned. "Benjamin Peretz."

Trapp squinted. Maybe the name rang a bell, but he couldn't be sure. Israel pumped out mercenaries like no other country on earth. It was a hazard of pressing every man and woman into active military service.

"What happens now?" Trapp asked. He knew the Israelis had to have a backup plan, in case the sniper was unable to get a clear shot.

"I don't know," came the reply.

Trapp cleared his throat menacingly. "Don't play games with me," he said. "I don't want to have to kill you."

Judging by the low, depressed moan that escaped the

Israeli's lips, he didn't desire that outcome either. Trapp knelt, putting his knee on the opposite side of the mercenary's back from the bullet wound to hold him in place. He leveled the Beretta and pressed it hard against the man's temple.

"I promise, I swear it, I don't know –"

The radio crackled again. More Hebrew. Trapp couldn't understand a word, but he knew the sound of a worried officer when he heard one.

"What did he say?"

"He's worried we've been compromised," the Israeli said, his accent getting thicker as his breathing grew more labored. "Ordered us to change frequencies."

Trapp tossed the radio aside. It was useless to him now. Besides, he had more important things to worry about, like the driver of the Mercedes down below. Except, as he found out just a second later, he didn't. He heard the squeal of tires, and the revving of a high-performance engine, and as he peered over the motel's roof, he saw the SUV speeding out of the parking lot, a black streak against the gray concrete road.

Trapp grinned. "Guess you guys never got the memo about never leaving a man behind."

He quickly searched the rest of the supplies the two Israelis had brought with them and found a roll of duct tape in the rucksack by the Israeli's side.

"This is going to hurt," he said.

He pulled up the man's shirt and used some of the excess fabric to mop up his blood. He tore off a strip of the tape and pressed it down over the man's wound. Next, he bound the man's hands and legs.

Trapp tapped the button for his throat mic. "Control, you still there?"

"What's going on, Hangman?"

"We've got a problem. These guys were only an advance element. There's a backup plan. Either my new friend doesn't know what it is, or he does and he's not talking. I don't have time to find out."

"What's your plan?" Mitchell replied in a clipped tone.

"I'll leave this guy for you. He's an Israeli merc, said something about a Benjamin Peretz. If you can send one of your guys for him, great, he might be useful. If not, send the feds. I don't want him freezing to death out here. He's injured, so whichever you choose, do it quickly."

"On it," Mitchell said. "I'll send Perkins."

"Great. I'm going after Donahue. These guys are going to hit the motorcade, I'm betting before it gets to the White House. Tell Kyle to get me a heading. We don't have much time."

28

The RAV4 ate up the outer loop of the Beltway as Trapp stomped his foot on the gas. Cars flashed by left and right as the black Toyota sped past, flashes of color in Trapp's peripheral vision. An old pickup truck ahead spewed out clouds of black smoke from its exhaust, filling his nostrils with the smell of burnt oil, and then it was but a distant memory in the rearview. The smell lingered in the cabin of the SUV.

He was in hot pursuit of the motorcade, heading east, which either meant that Donahue's protection detail was intending to cross Woodrow Wilson Memorial Bridge and head through Alexandria, or else they were planning to fake right at the very last minute, and turn onto Route 295 instead of crossing the Potomac.

Trapp figured they would choose the latter option, but he couldn't be certain. After two decades operating at the tip of the spear, working alongside the very best surveillance assets the US military and intelligence services had to offer, he wasn't used to operating like this – almost blind. It felt like he was fighting with one hand tied behind his back and a fifth of cheap whiskey running through his veins.

"Keep me in the loop, guys," he said, his voice tense with anticipation. The White House, Director Donahue's destination, was just fifteen miles away from Joint Base Andrews, about a half hour drive with the usual traffic. He was already ten minutes into the pursuit, which meant that if someone was planning on hitting the motorcade, it could happen at any moment. He needed to be there when it did.

"Where are they?"

"Kyle has them on the traffic cams," Mitchell replied through his earpiece, his voice just audible over the growl of the overstretched engine. "They're about a mile ahead of you."

"What are my options here?"

He had run the scenario a dozen times in his head. He was pretty sure that the Israeli mercenaries would attempt an ambush at some point in the next ten miles. He didn't know why, but for some reason it was imperative that Donahue not make it to his meeting with the President.

"You need to keep him alive, Hangman," Mitchell ordered. "Whatever it takes."

"Thanks for the armchair quarterbacking, Mike," Trapp retorted sarcastically. "I was hoping for something a little more concrete."

"Then you shouldn't have joined the Agency," Mitchell replied, deadpan.

"I told you, I'm out. What's Kyle got?"

The voice of the analyst sounded in Trapp's earpiece. "I concur with your assessment, Hangman. They're going to strike at one of the bridges. They're natural chokepoints. But beyond that, I've got nothing. I'm not picking up anything out of the ordinary on my end, but all I have access to right now is the traffic cams. They could be anywhere."

"Crap," Trapp muttered.

He glanced down, into the footwell on the passenger side, where he had dumped the duffel bag containing the Heckler and Koch MP5 submachine gun. It was just out of sight, but close enough that he could reach over and grab the weapon in a matter of seconds.

The speed on the red needle of the glowing digital odometer in front of him read a hundred and ten miles per hour. The wind tore at the SUV's windows, generating a dull roar that mostly blocked out the blaring of horns as he swerved through traffic.

"You're closing in on the motorcade fast, Trapp," Kyle warned. "You're about five hundred yards back. Slow down so they don't make you."

Trapp did as he was advised, stepping off the gas and allowing the Toyota to slow. He settled in behind a red Ford Bronco that had to be a decade old, with rust spots dotting the trunk. It had Virginia plates.

Trapp saw a shock of long blond hair behind the steering wheel, and wondered where the woman was heading. Maybe to work, or to pick up her kid from school. He hoped he wasn't about to ruin her day – along with a few hundred other commuters. He let his eyes rove across the other cars, searching for another of the black Mercedes SUVs, just like the one that had held the sniper team at Andrews.

He found nothing, although that didn't mean much. The Israelis were masters of disguise. They could be anywhere, hidden in any of a hundred cars, just waiting for the right moment to attack. Hell, for all he knew the blond woman was one of them. Just waiting to pull out an RPG and open fire.

Trapp wracked his brain for a plan. Right now, all he was doing was speeding toward disaster. In a matter of minutes, the lead Chevrolet in Donahue's motorcade would be engulfed in flames. He could already see it: an IED, maybe, or a heavy machine gun loaded with depleted uranium rounds. A contrail of smoke in the air, and then the weighty *crump* of an explosion. Enough firepower to rip right through the vehicle's thick armor plate and turn everything and everyone inside into ground chuck.

The Israelis would close in after that, getting near enough to open up on Donahue's vehicle. They'd need to confirm his kill in order to get paid, as well as to ensure the director didn't have anything in his possession that might compromise their employer. Trapp had been on the other side enough times to guess how the next few minutes would play out.

The operation would be over in minutes, no matter the outcome – had to be, this close to DC. A protracted gun battle is rarely in anyone's best interests, especially when it comes to collecting and spending a twenty-five million dollar bounty. No amount of money is any use to a merc if they end up dead. Trapp figured that this operation had to be the biggest score the Israeli team had ever encountered. One last payday before they blew town for good. It explained why they'd been distracted enough on the motel roof to allow him to close to within shooting distance.

"Can you patch me into Donahue's detail?" Trapp asked. "We need to throw a wrench into their plan. Get him heading in another direction. Doesn't matter where, just anywhere that isn't one of those fucking bridges."

"I'll see what I can do," Mitchell replied.

Minutes of relentless tension followed, as the clock counted down ever closer to catastrophe. The sound of the wind beating on the RAV4's frame competed with the whine of the engine. To either side of the Beltway, spaced out houses and green fields gave way to more densely-built condominium complexes and retail outlets. The Toyota sped past a collection of fast food joints just off the freeway, all signs that Donahue's date with disaster was approaching fast.

"The Wilson Bridge is only a couple of minutes away, Kyle,"

Trapp said, the tension evident in his clipped voice. "Tell me you've got something."

"Got it," Kyle crooned with satisfaction. "It took me a while. Don't have access to my usual systems."

Trapp didn't care why it'd taken so long. He knew he only had a few seconds before everything went to shit. "Patch me in."

"Done."

Trapp yanked the steering wheel, overtook a battered pickup truck that had seen better days, and began weaving through traffic again, making up lost time. In the distance ahead of him, he could see the flashing blue lights concealed behind the grilles and rear windows of the NSA vehicles.

"NSA protection detail, do you read?"

No answer.

"I say again, NSA protection detail, this is CIA officer Jason Trapp, do you read me?"

The CIA officer bit was technically a lie, but it didn't matter. Again, there came no reply. Trapp beat the Toyota's dashboard with frustration and pushed the stolen car to its limits. Ahead of him, just as he had predicted, the motorcade peeled away from the Potomac crossing at the very last second and took Route 295 instead, traveling parallel with the river. It glinted in the patchwork February sunshine, darker spots occasionally shadowing the surface of the muddy torrent.

"Kyle, what the hell's going on? I thought you said you patched me in?"

The line was dead. He was on his own.

Trapp swore, taking the same offramp onto Route 295 and following close behind Donahue's motorcade, now just a hundred yards ahead. They began weaving in and out of traffic, just like he was. Good – it meant they'd noticed the Toyota driving like a madman behind them. It would at least put them on alert. But it wouldn't help them, not if the Israelis turned up with as much firepower as Trapp was sure they would.

What the hell is happening?

Trapp pulled his phone from his pocket, leaving one hand on the steering wheel. He glanced down at the screen and saw it had no bars of signal. The needle on the odometer in front of him nudged past a hundred and twenty miles an hour and kept climbing. Ahead, the motorcade was engaged in its own evasive maneuvers – but instead of evading the Israelis, they thought *he* was the threat.

"Fuck."

At this speed, Trapp's RAV4 was eating up a mile every thirty seconds. The more powerful NSA Suburbans ahead of him were moving faster still, and by now the first of the three bridges across the Anacostia River was barely a heartbeat away. Everything was going to hell, and quickly. The Toyota vibrated beneath him as he zigzagged through traffic.

Trapp didn't know what the hell to do. He was driving deaf, dumb and blind. He had no way of getting in contact with Mitchell, the rest of the CIA thought he was dead, and his phone had chosen this precise moment to bite the bullet.

Or had it?

Trapp was an intelligent man, and his years in the field had taught him that there was exactly no such thing as a coincidence. Trapp had never believed in chance. He quickly grasped that someone was jamming his comms. And not just his – Donahue's, too.

His own were just caught in the crossfire. Trapp reached forward for the RAV4's dashboard and fiddled with the digital car radio to confirm. He got nothing, on any of the hundreds of channels that were normally available. Whoever was doing this had access to some serious tech.

Overhead, Trapp heard the familiar *thump-thump-thump* of a helicopter's rotors. Joint Base Anacostia was close, and though as far as Trapp knew it was mostly home to ceremonial military units, he wondered if somehow Mitchell had come through with backup. If he had, Trapp promised to swallow every curse he'd ever flung at the man.

Ahead of him Donahue's motorcade screamed off Route 295 and through a section of roadworks that stood between the freeway and the Frederick Douglass Memorial Bridge. The motorcade slowed fractionally, but only for a distance of a couple of hundred feet, and within seconds they raced clear through and onto the bridge.

Trapp followed, blood pounding in his ears as he watched the inevitable occur. Ahead of him, the bridge exploded in fire.

29

The helicopter rose high over the Frederick Douglass Memorial Bridge, flying directly in front of the sun as rubble rained down from the impact of the anti-tank missile. It had missed the target, but turned a nearby Corolla into scrap. Trapp covered his eyes as he looked up at the aircraft. It was painted a dark blue, and its distinctive shape marked it as having rolled off an Augusta Westinghouse production line, though he didn't recognize the precise model. It was commercial, not military, he knew that much.

"Damnit."

Trapp couldn't believe that this was happening in the United States of America. Hell, if an attack as brazen as this had taken place in war-torn Somalia, he would have found it hard to believe. The bridge over the Anacostia was just five miles from the White House, a similar distance from the Capitol Building, and all those other august monuments to American democracy. And yet right now it was lit up with fire, reminding Trapp of the opening scene of *Apocalypse Now*.

Trapp watched almost as if in slow motion as the helicopter's forward motion ceased and it began a stationary hover, the blades cutting through the air with a heavy, rhythmic beat. He noticed that on either side its doors had been removed. It was hard to make out from this distance, and with the sun beating down on his eyeballs, but he thought he saw heavily armed commandos harnessed into the helicopter, just black specks in the distance.

A second rocket trail streaked out of the side of the open aircraft and made it rock. At that distance, it was like shooting fish in a barrel. The lead Chevrolet suburban went up like a firework, rendered into a shower of burning metal in an instant and incinerating everyone unlucky enough to be inside.

Trapp tried raising Mitchell again, though he knew it was futile.

"Control, this is Trapp. Do you read me? I say again, Control, this is Trapp. I need backup. Get the cavalry here, now."

He hit the brakes hard. The RAV4 slowed instantly, momentum throwing him forward, and leaving black streaks on the gray concrete road surface. All around, cars were screeching to a halt, some smashing into others as they attempted to avoid the carnage ahead, but only adding to the glass, metal and carbon fiber debris that now littered the surface of the bridge.

The sound of grinding metal filled the air, punctuated only by the *rat-tat-tat* of bullets striking their target. Overhead, two commandos had opened up with their rifles and were sending down an unrelenting wave of bullets at the bridge. They fired indiscriminately, not seeming to actively search out civilian targets, but not caring much if they hit them either.

Trapp grabbed the duffel bag from the passenger floorwell, then dived out of his door, keeping low and away from the worst gunfire. He knelt on the concrete surface of the bridge, the heavy weaponry louder now that he was out of the false security of the Toyota.

He looped the sling of the MP5 around his neck and shoulder, wishing he had thought to take the fifty caliber rifle from the motel roof. At this range, the MP5 would be useless against the aircraft hovering overhead, whereas the Barrett fifty cal would have punctured the unarmored chopper with the ease of a holepunch.

But there was no point thinking about what he could have done, what he should have done. He needed to get moving. The cold air was already thick with smoke, painting the back of Trapp's throat and making him choke.

Trapp grabbed as much of the submachine gun's ammunition as he could carry, stuffing magazines into every spare pocket of his jeans and jacket. If he'd planned this better, he would have double-taped them end to end. But he hadn't truly believed that something like this could happen. Not on the streets of America. That old motto drilled into him at the Farm swam through his mind in a mocking chorus.

Fail to prepare, prepare to fail.

Trapp vowed that if he ever made it out of this, he'd never fail like that again. He dropped to the ground to peer beneath the RAV4's chassis, and saw Donahue's motorcade screech to a halt. In the distance, the helicopter briefly touched down, offloading several commandos before returning to the sky. The Israelis found cover and unleashed a barrage of fire at the motorcade.

And that meant at Trapp himself. Bullets pinged off metal and shattered glass windshields, the sound adding to the harmony of horror that was being unleashed all around him. The screams of terrified civilians split the air as he looked over at what remained of Donahue's motorcade.

"Move," he muttered.

The two remaining Chevrolets did as he urged, reversing slowly at first from the onrushing Israelis and their relentless rate of fire before they began to accelerate. Their bullet resistant windshields and run flat tires were taking a beating, but proving their worth. Trapp looked up again at the helicopter still buzzing overhead and saw one of the Israeli commandos preparing another shoulder-launched missile tube.

Screw it.

He needed to move. If he stayed here, he'd end up a dead man either way – but more importantly, so would Donahue. And Trapp couldn't allow that to happen.

He would not.

Trapp brought the MP5 to his shoulder and charged forward, firing short, controlled bursts in the helicopter's general direction – more out of hope than expectation. He used the cover of crashed and abandoned vehicles, their former occupants now running in every direction, desperately attempting to hide from the relentless gunfire. Lead chewed up the concrete in a straight line that ended just yards from his feet, shards of it ripping at his jacket and cheek. A spray of bullets whipped the air around him.

Eyes closed, he threw his body against the bullet-ridden chassis of a nearby sedan and waited for the killing blow to strike.

But it never came.

One final bullet pinged off the sedan's ruined wheel well before the helicopter gained a few feet of altitude, and spun away in a long circle, briefly removing itself from the equation.

Trapp turned his attention to the two remaining Suburbans in Donahue's motorcade as he fought to regain his breath. They were attempting to accelerate away from danger, but the bridge was so littered with abandoned vehicles it was almost impossible to maneuver. And with the Israelis up ahead, they couldn't go forward either. The teeth of the trap were slamming shut, trapping them inside.

The rearmost Suburban hit a shattered pickup truck with a deafening screech of metal on metal and crunching glass, and briefly rocked onto two wheels before coming to a halt. For a few seconds, nothing happened. And then Donahue's protective detail rolled into action, finally reaching the realization that the only way out was by foot.

The two front doors of the rear Suburban opened, and two heavily-armed black-clad commandos jumped out of the vehicle, the sound of their boots thudding onto the bridge's scarred surface somehow distinct amidst the chaos. One exited the other surviving SUV. Trapp figured one would have stayed with Donahue as a last line of defence. That mean the other two were already dead.

"Covering fire!"

The yelled order split the air. Two of the men began firing up at the helicopter. Trapp recognized the distinctive silhouettes of Heckler and Koch G36 automatic rifles in their hands. He punched the air with satisfaction, knowing immediately that the heavier caliber weapons had a significantly better chance of inflicting damage than his own pea shooter. He stayed low and kept moving forward into the danger zone, his heart thudding yet his mind somehow startlingly clear.

"Get the Stinger!"

The NSA bodyguard's voice carried over the sound of battle, over the licking of flames on the destroyed lead Suburban, and over the sound of gunfire rattling in the background.

Now that's what I'm talking about, Trapp thought.

Until now, Trapp's estimation of their tactical position was, put simply, that everything was fucked. With the helicopter, the Israelis had the high ground. But the sudden appearance of the FIM-92 Stinger surface-to-air missile was a game changer.

"Friendly incoming," Trapp yelled over the sound of battle as he closed on their position. One of the NSA commandos spun around, sensing a new threat. Trapp ducked behind an abandoned gray minivan and cried out again. "I'm CIA, don't shoot!"

Since the NSA operative didn't immediately rip him apart with a hail of gunfire, Trapp figured he might as well take a chance. If they didn't work together, they'd all end up dead anyway. He unclipped his MP5 and held it above his head to signal he wasn't a threat.

"Come here. Point that thing in my direction and I'll put a bullet in your head," the operative barked. His face was bearded, eyes hidden by a pair of reflective Oakley sunglasses. The bodyguard was a real cowboy, but from the way he carried himself Trapp guessed he could handle himself in a scrap.

"Coming out," Trapp replied clearly and urgently. He hoped that the man would keep his word. He didn't want to end up dead. Especially not today. He had shit to do.

Trapp closed the distance between him and the cowboy. As he moved, the NSA commandos began laying down suppressive fire at both the helicopter and the Israeli mercenaries now pinned down further up the bridge. Trapp knew that this lull in the fighting couldn't last. The enemy would need to move fast – even with communications jammed, they couldn't linger here long without the cavalry showing up. The eye of the storm was about to close on them and sharpen into the vicious stiletto point of a twister.

Trapp reached the NSA shooter who had beckoned him over. As he arrived, ducking in behind the now wounded, bullet-ridden vehicle, he found the man's rifle aimed directly at him.

"Now exactly who the fuck are you?" the man yelled.

"Easy, buddy," Trapp replied evenly. He jerked his head in the direction of the Israeli mercenaries. A bullet chewed up the ground a few yards from his toes. "I'm not with them."

"You're the guy who was chasing us," the man said suspiciously. His eyes darted left and right every couple of seconds as he scanned for fresh threats to his principal.

"I'm the guy who tried to warn you the shit was about to hit the fan," Trapp said, not flinching as a bullet ricocheted off a car abandoned nearby and snapped only inches past his ear.

The NSA operative gestured at the carnage all around. "Nice work."

He took his eyes off Trapp, which the former CIA special operator took as a sign that he didn't consider him an immediate threat. Trapp pressed his momentary advantage as the whine of the helicopter increased and the aircraft began to close in again.

"I took out two shooters at Andrews," he said. "They had a Barrett fifty cal aimed at Donahue's head."

Instantly, the man's eyes snapped back to him. "Where?"

"Quality Inn Motel, just opposite the base."

The bodyguard's eyes flicked upward, as if remembering, and then back to Trapp. His posture softened – still tense and alert, but noticeably less suspicious. Trapp had always possessed an uncanny ability to read people. It was an invaluable asset to have in his line of work. He suspected that the man opposite him shared it.

"Yeah, I remember passing that. I guess we owe you one. You can call me Will."

"Won't do either of us any good unless we get Donahue out of here," Trapp fired back immediately, raising his voice over a renewed hail of gunfire.

"That's fair," Will replied. He stood up, sheltering behind the suburban, and fired several short bursts at the Israelis. "Jake – where are we with the Stinger?"

Another of the NSA bodyguards spoke up. Trapp saw that he was crouched over a hardshell case, assembling a missile launch tube. "Give me twenty seconds. Then I'm gonna need some cover."

"You got it." Will raised his voice. "Okay team, we've got a friendly visitor from the CIA, so be advised we do not, I repeat we do not want to stick a bullet in his head unless we absolutely have to. Got it?"

One by one, the other two NSA commandos snapped a look at Trapp, and then resumed firing.

"I'll take that as a yes," Will grinned. "Next order of business, Jake's up for a little pest control. Get ready to open up."

Trapp switched out the magazine in his MP5, wishing he had a weapon that packed a little more punch. The second Will gave the signal, he stood up and unleashed a volley of fire at the Israelis advancing toward them on the bridge. One of them collapsed, painting the gray concrete a dark red.

He watched as the NSA shooter with the Stinger launch tube stood up, brought the sight to his eye, and took aim. Trapp hadn't fired one for years, but knew the system did most of the work. They were designed to be fired by grunts, and in these hands there was little chance of the missile failing to hit its target.

There was a click as the Stinger was ejected from his launch tube, then a rush and a roar as the solid fuel rocket motor ignited, and the missile streaked upward. Trapp's body was filled with a rush of adrenaline as he realized he might just get out of this after all. A second later, his veins turned to ice.

"Incoming!"

30

The two missiles crossed paths in midair, their contrails painting train tracks in the sky. The Stinger screamed upward, impacting the stolen Augusta Westinghouse helicopter just two seconds after it was fired. The fragmentation warhead inside, which consisted of almost seven pounds of high explosives, penetrated the helicopter's chassis before exploding. Colonel Peretz died on impact. His brain didn't even have the time to process the image of the missile speeding toward him before it winked out for good.

The aircraft seemed to hang in midair, its blades wobbling as a man was ejected by the force of the explosion. A metallic screech filled the air as the rotor itself spun loose, plunging into the Potomac several seconds later.

There was little left of the aircraft by the time it hit the ground.

Trapp threw himself to the deck, clamping his hands to his ears the second he heard the word *incoming*. It was a reaction ingrained in him through years of training. It probably saved his life.

The Israeli Spike fire-and-forget anti-tank guided missile hit the bridge at almost the very same instant its operator was cremated in the skies above. It missed Donahue's Suburban, striking instead the abandoned SUV that had prevented it from moving any further. As the vehicle exploded in flames, a wave of shrapnel pinged out in every direction that eviscerated two of the NSA commandos and severely wounded one more.

The SUV flipped up, incredibly rising almost fifteen feet into the air, where it seemed to hang for a second as it reached the very top of its arc. Trapp watched in open-mouthed horror as it began to fall – and then as it toppled directly onto the Chevrolet Suburban containing the man he'd come here to save.

Time halted after the two massive explosions. Trapp lay on his back, still clutching his ears as a wave of flames rolled over his body and bit greedily at his skin. His chest rose and fell rapidly as an instinctive panic swept across him, his body sucking in greedy breaths of super-heated air that stung his throat. He smelled burning jet fuel and singed hair and tasted burnt aviation fuel. And then the noise returned as time sped back up. Low at first, hoarse cries of pain and his own strained breath. The screech of rending metal. The *ping-ping-ping* of bullets ricocheting off vehicles all around him.

The Israelis.

Although they had stopped firing after their ride disappeared in a ball of flame, the mercenaries had opened up once again. And with the NSA commandos mostly out of commission, no one was firing back.

Get up. You move, or you die.

It was instinct that propelled Trapp. Not conscious thought. In the days and weeks that followed, he would not even remember the actions he took in that moment. He rolled over onto his front, hauling himself up onto hands and knees. The

NSA shooter who had introduced himself as Jake was lying next to him, blood speckling his face, whether dead or unconscious Trapp didn't know.

He didn't have time to care.

Trapp took the man's assault rifle and several magazines from his combat webbing. He ejected the half-empty magazine from inside the rifle, slapped a new one home, and brought the weapon to his shoulder. His ears were ringing and the ground felt unsteady beneath his feet. Bullets tore the air apart all around him.

And yet he was not hit. In Trapp's mind, the world was still.

Somehow, all he knew was that he had to buy time. With the helicopter destroyed, the Israelis could no longer make a quick getaway. They would have to move fast to make one last push to eliminate their target before the cops arrived and they were forced to leave empty-handed. Whether Donahue was alive or dead, Trapp did not know. The SUV that had landed on top of the Suburban had crushed the front of the vehicle, but the rear half was less damaged. It was possible that he had survived—or if not, that he was carrying vital intelligence.

Either way, Trapp knew what he had to do: push the Israeli mercenaries back for long enough for them to realize that no bounty was worth spending the rest of their lives in Supermax.

He brought the assault rifle to his shoulder, moved forward through the hail of gunfire, and crouched behind the half-destroyed Suburban that contained Director Donahue. His first burst after popping back up cut down an onrushing Israeli commando. The man was only a dozen yards away when the first bullet to strike him sliced open his carotid artery. The second hit his shoulder and spun him around, the combination of impacts cutting loose a spray of blood that painted the bridge a dark red.

Trapp felt no elation, just grim determination. He had a job to do, and no one was going to stop him completing it. He kept firing until there were no more targets to hit, until two more Israelis lay dead on the bridge and the rest of their brethren were in full retreat.

It took his battered, exhausted brain a few seconds to realize that the sound of gunfire had died off. The world was still, except for a soft hissing as gas leaked out of the burning vehicles that dotted the bridge and began to ignite. There were no civilians around to cry out with terror. Anyone who could run was long gone, and anyone who couldn't was dead.

The mercenaries had stopped coming. Trapp had cut half of them down; the rest had cut and run. Trapp himself slumped to his knees, holding on to his rifle for support. The world spun around him and almost slipped away.

Don't stop.

That voice again. Insistent. Trapp knew that it spoke the truth. If he stopped moving, he would slip into unconsciousness. If that happened he would be found and questions would be asked. He didn't know if any of Donahue's bodyguards had survived the assault, or whether the man himself was alive. There would be no one left to vouch for him.

If he allowed himself to drift away, if he was found here, then the whole thing might be pinned on him. And the real perpetrator would steal away.

Move.

The voice was louder this time, but it was as though Trapp had found an inner reserve of strength. He gripped the rifle, its barrel still warm, and clambered to his feet. He gritted his teeth as a wave of pain rolled through him, his fragile body protesting the orders it was given.

He ignored it.

Trapp checked the NSA commandos for signs of life, but one after another he found the men lying in pools of their own blood.

Until the last.

It was Will, the one he'd spoken to. The man was unconscious, seemingly having sustained a blow to the head and a gash that had opened it up from temple to jaw. His breathing was shallow, and his pupils were dilated and unresponsive when Trapp gently pulled apart his eyelids, but he was alive.

He left him slumped against the damaged SUV. He had to check on Donahue, had to know if the man was still breathing, and whether all of this had been for nothing. Trapp limped forward to the half-crushed Suburban. The adrenaline was fading now, and his limbs felt like lead weights, his boots catching on the scarred concrete surface of the bridge.

Trapp circled around the front of the Suburban, and as he drew closer he grew more and more certain that no one inside could possibly be alive. The entire front cabin had been crushed by the falling SUV that now lay balanced precariously on top of it. The smashed windscreen was decorated with thick rivulets of engine oil, and the stink of spilled gasoline was thick on the air.

Despite the exhaustion, he urged himself on. He had to know.

He yanked at the passenger door, but it held fast. The fallen SUV had crushed the metal around the handle, preventing the mechanism from opening.

"Crap," Trapp hissed. Why wouldn't anything come easy today? He knew he didn't have a lot of time. In the distance, a chorus of sirens was already beginning to fill the air. The attack itself could only have lasted a few minutes, five at the most. Still, he was surprised that there hadn't already been a police response to an attack this close to the seat of government.

Trapp hefted his rifle and inserted the barrel into a gap between the door and its frame. He hefted with all his might, but the thing was stuck tight. He tried again, every muscle, sinew, and ligament straining in unison. Finally, slowly, it began to move, metal squealing in protest. With one last heave, Trapp popped the door open. He almost vomited when he saw what was inside.

The front two seats of the Suburban were empty. Trapp remembered he'd seen two commandos exiting the vehicle to help repel the attack. They must have been sitting up front.

But two men lay lifeless in the back seats. One bodyguard, his head staved in by what looked like an SUV's rear axle, was still clutching his rifle and covering his charge even in death. He had at least died quick. His brain matter splattered the black leather seats of the Chevrolet, and rivulets of blood were already beginning to thicken on his fatigues.

Donahue was equally dead. He wore a suit, black, his collar open, and a tie hanging loose out of the seat pocket in front of him. The force of the Spike missile's explosion had propelled the axle into the cabin of the former NSA director's armored vehicle, and through the man himself.

Trapp swore, too exhausted by the events of the past few days to be truly sickened by the gruesome sight in front of him. He was more angry than disgusted.

He'd come all this way for nothing.

Trapp knew he had to get out of here, that it might already be too late. He began to turn away, before something drew him back. He scanned the cabin of the Chevrolet, looking for a briefcase, a rucksack, anything. But it was empty. As the wail of sirens grew closer and closer, accompanied by the thump of yet more rotor blades, Trapp thrust his body into the vehicle, kneeling in blood, his breath loud in his ears. He searched every plausible hiding place, but came up empty.

Acting on one last impulse, Trapp searched Donahue's body. The man's suit pants were wet with blood and his hands came away sticky. There was nothing in the pockets. He wiped his fingers on the white shirt before running his hands across the front of the jacket.

It crinkled.

There was something there. Trapp's heart raced as he reached inside, where he found a letter. When he drew the envelope from Donahue's jacket pocket, he almost choked.

It was addressed to the President.

31

D ani Carter was sitting in an empty conference room in the FBI's DC field office, scratching barely legible letters into an after-action report on the events at the Hoover Building when her phone buzzed, causing it to dance on the dark mahogany table.

It was ridiculous that the Bureau had her filling out paperwork when the entire country was in lockdown. But that was Washington for you. The bureaucrats here would still be completing forms in triplicate when the nuclear warheads started flying and mushroom clouds sprouted next to the damn Washington Monument itself.

The empty desks that spotted the DC field office, all folders and computers removed by federal marshals, were a heavy reminder of the arrest of dozens of FBI agents across the nation on charges of aiding and abetting terrorism. The remaining agents shuffled around the office like zombies, each plainly wondering if they would be next.

Dani gritted her teeth just thinking about the arrest of her boss—and mentor—Rick Olsen, along with all the other agents who had been frog-marched out of the DC field office, hands cuffed behind their backs like common criminals.

They were good people, good, honest men and women—and valuable agents. The country needed them running down leads at a time like this, not rotting in federal jails. But the evidence, supposedly, was incontrovertible. Phone, bank and travel records linked each of the arrested agents to sleeper cells that had committed heinous acts of terror. The NSA had even discovered voice recordings that each arrested agent swore blind were fake, though all expert analysis said the contrary.

Put bluntly, Dani thought it was all a load of crap. If the NSA had so much intelligence, why had they only shared it after the attacks, and not before? There was something off about the whole situation. And Dani intended to get to the bottom of it.

But that hadn't stopped the twenty-four hour cable networks from calling the FBI arrests "the most thorough penetration of any law enforcement agency since Aldrich Ames betrayed the CIA." Those words had been spoken by one of the most level-headed pundits on television, Jim Anderson, who headed up ATN's breakfast coverage. Talk radio was sending out a much harsher message. And there was no way Dani was even glancing at the toxic cesspool that was Twitter.

Carter's tired emerald eyes didn't immediately recognize the number on her phone screen, and she considered not answering. She relented, releasing a heavy sigh of frustration as she realized it could be the hospital, and pressed the green call button.

"Carter."

"Agent Carter, please hold for the director."

The director?

Dani froze, a jolt of adrenaline sweeping through her system like a tornado. Surely the curt, businesslike voice on the other end of the line hadn't meant *the* director, as in the director of the FBI?

For that matter, how had they even learned the number for her private cell? Her FBI issued unit was missing, probably bagged and tagged and sitting in some Bureau evidence lockup with the rest of the Hoover Building debris, and with all the bureaucratic drama over the past few days, they hadn't got around to issuing her a new one.

Dani thought fast. Perhaps she was a person of interest? After all, if someone had set up Olsen, she might be their natural next target. Everyone knew how close she was to the former special agent in charge. A thin sheen of sweat formed on her forehead as her body's natural fight or flight response kicked in.

"Is that Agent Nadine Carter?" a gruff voice asked before she had a chance to decide to flee.

"Dani," she corrected automatically. "I mean—yes, sir."

"You can cut all of that," Rutger said, sounding low, throaty and tired.

Dani recognized his voice from dozens of press conferences. Seizures of drugs and weapons from Mexican cartels, thick, white blocks of interdicted cocaine set on tables before the national press and paraded on national television. The arrest of senior Italian mafiosi in New York. But none of it fit – why the hell was he calling her?

"Yes sir—I mean... Okay." She cut herself off and flushed with embarrassment, rapping the knuckles of her free hand against her head.

Foot, meet mouth.

Rutger chuckled tiredly. Dani wasn't surprised. He must have been pulling eighteen-hour days since the attacks started. The whole country was at breaking point, and every false alarm strained nerves even further. A lull had chased the initial wave of attacks. But somehow that made everything worse. Everyone was just waiting for the next domino to fall.

"Listen, Carter. I don't have long. I wanted to thank you for what you did. You might have saved a lot of lives at the Hoover Building."

Dani slumped her shoulders, thankful the director could not see her. She still felt guilty about her actions that morning. She could have done more. *Should* have done more. One question haunted her: if she had acted sooner, could she have saved more lives?

Would her own father be safe right now, instead of occupying a Georgetown hospital bed, fighting for his life? An image of Mitch Carter swam across Dani's exhausted mind. Her father, his barrel chest shrunken in his dotted hospital gown, a red sutured scar tearing his skull from temple to jaw. She blinked away a tear.

"Yes, Director. Thank you, sir."

"I told you –" the director started. "Forget it. Carter, I wanted to ask you what you thought about Olsen."

Dani's political antennae went on to high alert despite the emotions running high inside her. She knew Rutger's reputation, that he was a straight shooter. He didn't play political games, except to help the Bureau get its mission accomplished. He was honest with his agents, and never threw them under the bus. But even with all of that, this was a dangerous topic of conversation.

"Sir –?"

"Answer the question, dammit," the director said, his tiredness becoming more apparent.

Dani shrugged. She didn't have anything to lose. After all, as much as she hated the publicity, hated being the center of attention, she knew her reputation within the Bureau was at an all-time high. Hell, she had even received a letter of commendation from the White House, and was just about the only agent in the entire FBI who wasn't being treated like a traitor on the networks.

You asked for it.

"Honestly sir, I think it's a crock of shit. The SAC is the best agent I've ever worked under. If he's a traitor, then God help the rest of us."

The line went silent. Dani held her breath. Had she just torn her foot from her mouth only to aim it right for the shit? As the seconds dragged on, she thought maybe she had. And she didn't give a crap. Sometimes you needed to do what you thought was right—even if it meant sacrificing your own career.

"Carter," Director Rutger said forcefully, "I'm making you SAC. *Acting.*"

Dani's mind froze. Surely she hadn't just heard him correctly? Had Rutger just promoted her to head up the DC field office? He couldn't have – she was almost a decade too young, even in her wildest dreams. Too green.

"Sir, are you sure—?"

"I'm not doing you a favor, Carter. Right now, the politicians on the hill"—he spat the words out with disgust—"are baying for our blood. They won't stop at budget cuts, or congressional hearings. Not this time. I'd be surprised if by the end of the week some grandstanding senator isn't calling for the whole damn Bureau to be shut down."

"But why me?"

"Bluntly, Carter, I need someone whose reputation is unimpeachable, and right now those scars on your face mean you're all I got."

"Thanks for the pep talk," Dani said.

"Don't blow smoke up my ass, Carter. I know you're young, but I also know your reputation. If Olsen was right about you, you'll ruffle a lot of feathers by the time you're done. I'm counting on you, Carter. Find out who the hell is framing my Bureau."

The line went dead.

She had barely a second to respond before a commotion broke out in the main office. Agents rushed to their feet, grabbed their weapons and began hurriedly throwing on blue windbreakers and bulletproof vests. Dani stood, still unsteady from the whiplash of events. The last few days had tossed her around like she was stuck on the end of a bungee cord, plunging down and down into the gaping maw of the Grand Canyon, red stone walls streaking past on either side.

And now she was the special agent in charge of the FBI's DC field office. Either she was about to hit the ground hard, or ping straight back. God, she hoped it was the latter.

No, not the SAC. You're just filling his shoes, Dani corrected herself.

But SAC or not, Dani was no longer lost. She'd regained a sense of purpose. She knew what she had to do.

Find out who framed Rick. And put the asshole behind bars.

But right now, something else was going on. Dani stepped out of the conference room, leaving the paperwork on the long meeting table, and knowing that particular problem was only going to get worse.

Great.

"What's happening?" she asked an agent rushing past.

"Someone hit us again. Hard..."

32

Dani arrived on scene at the Frederick Douglass Memorial Bridge less than an hour after the shooting had started. The air still stank of fumes, smoke and death, jarring against the cool river breeze. Most sirens had been silenced by now, but one still sang a lonely tune, accompanying the hundreds of sets of emergency lights that fought off the oncoming gloom.

"My God," Dani whispered.

The bridge over the Anacostia River looked more like something out of a World War II action film than a piece of American transport infrastructure. It was covered with brass ammunition casings which glinted in the floodlights that the FBI and Metropolitan PD were beginning to set up. The light penetrated the dusk and revealed a bridge that was scarred with black scorch marks and strewn with chunks of rubble from large craters that pockmarked the concrete.

Firefighters were on site as well, hosing down burning vehicles, as well as the charred husk of a helicopter. Dani winced as she realized they were spraying suppressant foam. The chemical was a real piece of work when it came to preserving evidence. Then again, aviation fuel was equally destructive, so she figured that on balance it was a trade worth making.

Thankfully, once the cyber-attack that had crippled communication networks and slowed emergency response times up and down the East Coast ceased, it became clear that there was only one attack site, not the dozens that had initially been feared. Dani offered up a silent prayer – if there had been more like this, there wouldn't be much of an America left.

"What have we got?" Dani asked, flashing her badge at a uniformed cop.

The man eyed her suspiciously once he saw what agency she was from. Dani quickly realized how challenging her position might be. It wasn't unusual for agents to get involved in a jurisdictional cockfight on a crime scene. Normally, the person with the FBI badge came out on top, especially in the District. But right now, that outcome wasn't nearly so certain. Dani's face creased with irritation. She'd dreamt for years about making SAC – but never like this. Never with the reputation of the Bureau in tatters around her.

The officer shrugged. "I'm not sure I should say."

Dani closed her eyes, cracked her neck left and right, and let her eyelids flash open, fixing the man with a piercing green glare. "Listen, officer, what's your name?"

"Riley."

"Listen, Officer Riley. You see these marks on my cheek?"

The cop nodded uncertainly as a helicopter roared overhead, its blades ripping the air apart as it turned, the downwash foaming the surface of the Potomac and sending a cloud of dust swirling across the bridge.

It was a news helicopter, Dani saw from the logo on the side. Just great. She made a note to find out who at the network had given the okay on that one. The pilot was breaking the no-fly zone. He'd be lucky if the FAA ever let him take to the air again.

"Three days ago," Dani continued, snapping her attention back to Riley and pouring all of her anger into her gaze, "I put a bullet into a terrorist's brain. I've spent the past two recovering from a fucking explosion. So if you think that messing with me right now is a good play, be my guest. But maybe you wanna think a little bit harder about the next word that comes out of your mouth."

Officer Riley gulped and looked like he would rather be anywhere else in the world right now than in front of this crazy, scarred bitch who was ripping him a new one.

"I apologize, ma'am."

"Accepted. Now tell me what you got."

Riley shrugged, a look of puzzlement crossing his face.

"Honestly, it's got me beat. I did two tours in Afghanistan, and never saw anything like this. There's over a dozen dead shooters, half of them armed with German hardware, half of them with Israeli. Looks like they beat the crap out of each other. But we've got no idea why."

Dani looked at Riley sharply. "Wait, you're telling me there was a firefight?"

The information she'd picked up en route had been fragmentary, and that was putting it kindly. Dani had pictured an attack just like the ones several days before: aimed at a soft, defenseless target, and designed to spread terror. But this sounded different.

Riley nodded, the floodlights glinting off the handcuffs at his belt.

"Sure looks like it. Hell, there's a freaking Stinger launch tube over there." He gestured toward a destroyed Chevrolet Suburban, crushed by another dark SUV that was lying – inverted – on its roof. "We got pulled way back to wait for EOD to give us the green light."

"Did any of the shooters survive?" Dani asked, her forehead

creased with confusion. This didn't fit the pattern established on Bloody Monday.

What the hell is going on?

"One. Found him near that Suburban, but he's in bad shape. They took him to George Washington. But you won't get squat from the poor bastard anytime soon."

Dani thanked the officer, and whistled for one of her agents, Adrian Ward. He was a dark-haired, lanky agent, like her wearing a navy-blue windbreaker. And he too was getting the third degree.

"Looks like we're public enemy number one, huh, Dani?" Adrian said, throwing her a mock salute to recognize her newfound authority.

"Cut that out. Tell me what you see here. Because from where I'm standing, none of this makes a lick of sense."

"Sounds about right," the agent replied. He pulled a latex glove from inside his windbreaker and used it to pick up an ammunition casing from the concrete bridge. "We've got nine and five fifty-six mil ammo all over the place. An MP5, a whole bunch of Heckler & Koch automatic weapons, and some Israeli hardware I've never even heard of. We're running prints now."

Dani shook her head. "This was no terrorist attack," she said, her mind racing as it attempted to construct a jigsaw puzzle in the dark, with what seemed like every other piece cut in half.

"It was a shootout. Two sides, somewhat evenly matched." She pointed at the destroyed Suburban. "Looks like there were two, no, three of those Chevrolets. So it was a motorcade. Which makes those guys"—she gestured into the distance—"a protective detail. The question is, who was the HVT?"

HVT stood for High Value Target. Dani needed to know who the attackers had been after. What could possibly have been so important that they would risk launching an attack in broad daylight in the middle of Washington DC? If it hadn't been for the cyber-attack, it would have been a suicide mission.

Which meant that Dani was now certain the timing of the cyber-attack was no coincidence. It was a feint. A distraction. But from what?

"Come with me," she said, ducking underneath the police tape.

"Hey, Dani," Adrian's voice rang out, sounding an octave higher. "Don't you think we should wait for the bomb squad?"

"What? And miss all the fun?"

ONCE DANI SAW the face of the passenger of the crushed Suburban, she knew what had happened here. This was an assassination.

The director of the National Security Agency had been murdered in broad daylight, along with a protective detail comprised of half a dozen well-armed commandos. Whoever had carried out this attack had known exactly what they were doing. They attacked from the air, according to the witness statements that were beginning to filter through. Fired some kind of missile.

That's when things got disjointed. The human memory is unreliable at the best of times, and the center of a major American city being turned into a warzone is definitely not one of those.

Some of the witnesses swore that an unknown hero had joined the firefight and changed the course of the battle. But Dani wasn't sure she believed them. The whole 'good guy with a gun' thing was a myth, ninety-nine times out of a hundred. Normal people don't just appear out of the blue and take on a squad of well-trained commandos.

And besides, none of the civilian corpses were armed. So

either this mysterious good guy had disappeared, not wanting to claim the credit for his heroism, or he had never existed.

Dani's experience had taught her that the simplest explanation is usually the best one. And the simplest explanation, in this case, was that the witnesses had seen what they wanted to see. They were desperate for the cavalry to arrive, and so their minds had conjured the memory of someone doing exactly that.

And since they hadn't been separated, the story had spread like wildfire. Dani was sure that by the end of the day the networks would be running pieces on the 'Hero of Anacostia', turning this shitshow into even more of a media circus than it already was.

Dani glanced over her shoulder, startled by the loud rumble of truck engines, and saw that EOD had finally arrived. She grimaced, chewing the inside of her cheek. "Adrian, go find out if the guys running prints have got anything. I've got a feeling we're about to be kicked off this crime scene."

The agent did as he was told. Dani looked for what she was missing. She searched her brain for anything that was out of place. A piece of evidence that didn't fit. And then she found it.

The MP5.

Dani spun on her heel and headed directly for the FBI's forensic science tent. She entered a second later and saw that a field lab had been set up inside. She didn't know what half of the machines did, but the small space was humming with activity, with white-coated technicians taking shots of numbered pieces of evidence from every angle, the camera flashes periodically turning the confines of the small white tent a brilliant shade of white.

"Adrian, the MP5."

"What about it?"

"It was the odd one out, right? The only one you found."

Adrian nodded.

"Let me see it."

Adrian beckoned over one of the technicians, a short blond woman with thick glasses, and she led them to where the MP5 was laid out, along with an assortment of empty ammunition magazines.

"Have you run prints on this one already?"

The technician shook her head.

"Do it, now."

In modern forensic science, running prints is child's play. High resolution scanners, huge databases and high-speed Internet connections mean that what only a couple of decades before might have taken hours, now took less than two minutes. Dani watched impatiently as the technician pulled an adhesive strip off the weapon, scanned it, and began the search. Her stomach was tied in knots as she waited.

Dani was onto something. She knew it. What it was, she didn't know – but she had a feeling it might hold a clue to all of this.

"Okay," the technician said. "I think we've got something."

"A name?" Dani asked quickly.

The technician shook her head, her blond ponytail dancing from side to side. "No. A police report filed a few days ago in Boston."

33

"We're fucked," Mitchell said.

Trapp found it difficult to disagree with the man's assessment. It had taken him hours to reach the safe house that the CIA team was holed up in. Shortly after the attack, a ring of steel had descended on Washington DC.

Trapp had ditched every scrap of military gear he was carrying, switched his jacket for a denim alternative taken from an abandoned vehicle on the bridge, and made a break for it. He made it into the city just in time, before the area was swamped with cops, federal agents, and military personnel.

Still, he doubted he would have been able to arrive at the safe house without help. The hideout was situated in the Great Falls country suburb, about twenty miles out from the District. Mitchell had sent one of his two CIA special operators to come grab Trapp. Luckily, Perkins had come equipped with a counterfeit Metropolitan Police Department badge and spirited Trapp out of the clutches of the quickly growing search net.

"Up shit creek without a paddle," Trapp agreed.

The safehouse was an old farmhouse that was currently

being redeveloped. The developer had run into financial diffi-
culties, and the building was currently in the middle of a legal
tug-of-war between two different banks, which meant that
work was stalled indefinitely. Add to that a little bit of Kyle's
wizardry, and no one would ever think to look for them there.

It also meant that there was little furniture for Trapp to
slump down on, just a few folding chairs, and trestle tables
loaded with weapons, laptops and communications gear. The
place stank of epoxy and fresh paint, sawdust, and the faint but
lingering body odor scent of working men.

Right now, Trapp would trade his life savings for a comfortable couch. He was exhausted. It was that very particular type
of fatigue that all men who put themselves into danger know so
well – the aftermath that follows when the tide of adrenaline
retreats. When the mind and body is left to pick up the pieces,
to somehow recover after the hell they had been through.

"Want a beer?" Mitchell said, opening a fridge and tossing
Trapp a bottle of Budweiser before he had a chance to answer.
Trapp plucked it out of the air, popped the cap, and lifted it to
his lips as Mitchell took several more bottles from the well-
stocked cooler and handed them out around the muted room.

"What the fuck happened out there?" Trapp finally asked,
the bottle drained in seconds. He set it on the stripped-back
concrete floor and fell gratefully into a folding chair. Its legs
scraped against the concrete as Trapp settled.

Mitchell shrugged. "World War III."

Trapp glanced around the room. He wondered what the
men he saw looking back had been doing for the past few days.
What battles they had fought – for they looked as tired as he
felt. He grimaced. Part of him wanted to just give up. Pretend
none of this had ever happened. Sleep for a week, drink the
fridge dry, and wake up in a new America where someone else
got paid to fix the problems.

Shit, he wasn't even on payroll anymore. Except for the men

in this very room, the rest of the Central Intelligence Agency –
those with clearance high enough to know he ever existed in
the first place – thought he was dead.

"Specifically," Trapp said, his voice clipped.

A twinge of adrenaline flushed through his veins, his
exhausted, almost empty adrenal glands responding more to
the former CIA man's relentless desire to keep fighting than
anything else.

He knew this feeling. The seething anger and crippling
depression that burned through his body like a wildfire whenever he tasted defeat.

Trapp was like an Olympic athlete, the kind of insanely
driven individual who trained day after day, year after year,
decade after decade with an unrelenting, unbending desire to
be the best. To beat the best.

All he wanted was to serve his country, no matter which
dusty shithole that took him to, no matter who he had to kill,
no matter what river of shit he had to crawl through to get the
job done.

Jason Trapp was born to complete his mission. And when
he couldn't, the failure cut him deep. It stole the thought of
sleep from his mind and left him unable to contemplate taking
any other action except heading back into hell and trying all
over again. Retracing his footsteps, finding out where it all went
wrong, and then making sure that all memory of that failure
was wiped from the face of the earth.

Mitchell sighed. His face was lined, his eyes small and dark,
with thick bags underneath. The mood in the room was equally
somber. Only the best of the best made it into the Agency's
Special Operations Group. None of the men Trapp saw were
used to being on the losing side. And yet that was precisely
where they found themselves.

"You want specifics? All we have is specifics. Details.

Nothing actionable. No bigger picture. No threads tying this whole shit show together."

"Humor me."

Mitchell shrugged and gestured at Kyle. Somehow the young analyst was still dressed in a tweed suit, although he had at least forsaken his tie.

"By the time Perkins got to the roof, the merc was dead. Internal bleeding—there was nothing you could have done. He brought back everything the guy had on him, but nothing useful. We know from what you told us that he was Israeli, probably led by a man called Benjamin Peretz, a former colonel in their special forces."

Trapp nodded. He hadn't expected the Israeli to die on that roof, but felt no particular guilt at the man's passing. He had chosen his path. Trapp had never liked men who killed for money. Sometimes it was necessary to work with them, but he never trusted them.

Once a man can be bought, his loyalty is temporary, and only owed to the highest bidder. And that is not always – or even often – the United States of America. If anything, he felt irritation that they hadn't managed to get any more intel from the mercenary. He ground his fist into his thigh with irritation.

Kyle continued. "As you know, shortly before the attack on the motorcade commenced, there was a massive jamming attack up and down the Eastern Seaboard."

Trapp hadn't known this. "Wait, you're telling me it wasn't localized?"

Kyle shook his head. "Not by a long shot. Every cell tower in a hundred-mile radius went down three minutes before the attack. That's right about when we lost communication with you. Shortly after that, hundreds of phantom signatures appeared on military air defense radars, heading for high-value targets including the White House and dozens of military bases, including both NORAD and the alternate site at Cheyenne Mountain."

"Jesus," Trapp breathed.

He blinked a couple of times, trying to process what this new information meant. It was almost impossible to understand. He had spent his entire career hunting down terrorists, weapons dealers, assassins—some of the most evil men who had ever stood in opposition to his country. He had prevented the release of a biological agent in downtown Charlottesville, and killed a man seconds before he opened fire on a presidential debate.

But Trapp had never come up against an enemy like this. It was like fighting a superpower. They were outmatched, outgunned, and outnumbered. How the hell could five men in a room possibly go up against an enemy they couldn't even identify, much less hope to match pound for pound?

"You got it," Kyle agreed, his voice hoarse. Trapp wondered if the kid had slept in days. He guessed not. Judging by the half-crushed cans of Red Bull that littered the laptop-strewn trestle table, he had pulled more than one all-nighter.

"That's why law enforcement's response time was so slow. Most units were routed toward the White House and the Capitol Building, both of which went into lockdown. False information came on the net that the attack on Donahue's motorcade was a diversion from the real target."

"Who has the technical capability to pull something like this off?"

"Except for us?" Kyle replied. He counted off a list on his fingers. "The Chinese, the Russians, the British, the French, and that's about it."

"We can pretty much rule out the Brits and the Frogs," Mitchell said. "We thought it might be the Russians—it fits their MO of sowing discord and fear, tying us up at home so we can't mess with them abroad—but as far as we can tell, there's not a single link between this set of attacks and Moscow. Beijing, either. And with Donahue dead, we don't have a single lead."

"Maybe we do," Trapp said cryptically. His fingers slid into the right-hand pocket of his denim jacket, knuckles brushing the rough material, and fingered the letter he'd taken from the NSA director's still warm corpse.

Everyone's gaze was suddenly on him. Each man shared the same pinched look. It was an expression that spoke of the need to assuage their guilt at failure. It was doubtless etched into his own face, too.

"What are you saying?"

"Donahue was dead by the time I got to him."

The posture of the men around him slumped slightly with disappointment. Perkins spoke up in his slow Arkansas drawl.

"What about his detail? Those boys have anything to say?"

Trapp shook his head, pulling the envelope from his pocket and brandishing it. It drew eyes like moths to a flame.

"No, but Donahue had this on him."

Mitchell's voice was low and hungry. "Have you read it?"

"Not yet."

"Then stop dicking around."

Trapp did as he was told. He slid his little finger into the opening at the end of the sealed envelope, and pulled it back, tearing the paper open. Inside was a single sheet of unlined paper, decorated with a thick, purposeful handwritten scrawl. It looked to have been written in fountain pen ink – almost as though the author was intentionally signaling his avoidance of technology.

He started reading.

Mr. President.

I hereby tender my resignation as Director of the National Security Agency. As we discussed earlier today, I have failed both you and my country. There is a cancer within the Agency that has been providing succor to our enemies. Hiding them in plain sight. Casting doubt on loyal Americans: killing some and blackmailing others to do God knows what. For years I fought to expand the NSA's powers, championed the Birdseye program and believed that if there was nothing that we could not see, then there would be no place for our enemies to hide.

I was wrong. Instead of protecting America, I have created a weapon more deadly than any we have ever faced.

I have instituted efforts to root out the conspiracy that I have allowed to grow under my nose. But I must warn you, Mr. President, that the tendrils of this sickness run both broad and deep.

It has been the greatest honor of my life to serve both you and my country. I can only apologize for my failure in this matter. I stand ready to assist in any way that you ask, and will bear every punishment that I rightfully deserve.

Gen. Rick Donahue.

In contrast to the rest of the letter, the signature was messy, as if the author had had enough resolve to make it most of the way through writing, only to falter at the last.

"Donahue spoke to the President already?" Trapp asked, frowning. His brain was struggling to process the enormity of the words he had just read.

Kyle shook his head vigorously. "No. He must have had it prepared to hand over after his meeting."

Trapp ran his fingers through hair that was thick with sweat, grease and soot. Christ, he wanted a shower. And a soft bed, and to lie down and not get up and not deal with any of this shit for a month. But that wasn't an option right now. The men in this room were the only people alive who had even an inkling about what was really going on. They had been right all along – the NSA's Birdseye program was compromised, though by whom, and for what purpose was still unclear.

Chillingly, with Donahue dead, they might be the only

people left who knew. They might be America's last – and only – line of defense.

"So now we know why they wanted him dead so bad," Trapp said. "He uncovered this conspiracy. This was never about a bunch of Arab terrorists making a bid for Paradise. Someone out there is making a play for power. Donahue found out, tried to warn the President, and they killed him for it."

"Now we know," Mitchell agreed. "But what the hell are we going to do about it?"

The room went silent, punctuated only by the background hum and beeping of Kyle's servers and computer towers. Trapp knew that he neither would nor could stop fighting. The memory of that little kid's eyes in Boston haunted him every time he closed his own.

Someone out there had put that boy's life at risk, killed his father, unleashed a wave of terrorist attacks across America, and all for what?

The silence lingered for a very long time. Trapp was tense, his muscles exhausted and yet at the same time primed to explode. Trapp's body was his best, most reliable weapon. He was desperate to use it in the service of his country, and his body responded to his brain's desire. But they were all out of leads. He had no one to fight. And the silence dragged on.

It was only broken by the chime of a laptop on the other side of the room.

At first, no one responded. Each man looked the way Trapp felt: shellshocked and stunned by what they had learned – and yet at a loss as to what direction they should take next. But the laptop chimed again, and this time Kyle stirred to life. It was as though he could not resist the siren call of his technology. He stood up and walked over to the chirruping device.

"What is it?" Mitchell asked.

Kyle's expression wrinkled with surprise before he looked up. "Looks like a new player just entered the game."

Trapp's own voice was gruff with tiredness. "What are you talking about?"

"Someone just ran your prints."

"Who?"

Kyle tapped his keyboard. "The FBI."

34

The man's name was Sean Bolton. Presently, he was in Bluffdale, Utah, not far from the NSA facility known as the Utah Data Center, and he was waiting for instructions.

Sean had been a nice boy, once, from an ordinary middle-class family in a safe suburb of New York City. They were never rich, yet growing up he never wanted for anything. He was a sweet child. Made his mom pancakes on Mother's Day, never acted up in school. But over the years, he changed. Became a man his mom didn't recognize, then one she was ashamed to admit she was related to at all.

Sarah Bolton hadn't spoken to her son in almost a decade. Not since the night where he got into a bar fight and left an Asian man paralyzed.

He did time for that. Nine years on Rikers Island. The experience changed him. In his eyes, it was for the better. He found a kinship inside that was unlike anything in the outside world, where races mixed with each other like rutting dogs.

And then he was released and found himself circling the drain. He didn't have a place on the outside. After all that time, he didn't know how it functioned. When he first went behind bars, the smartphone didn't even exist. By the time he got out, the world was addicted to them.

It was only a matter of time before Sean would find himself either behind bars again, or perhaps dead. He was lost, and he started lashing out. Couldn't get a job, not an honest one, anyway, and fell in with a crowd that pushed drugs and practiced violence. In a crew of dangerous men, Sean Bolton quickly gained a reputation as the kind of man you didn't want to cross. If you looked at him the wrong way, you might find a razor-sharp four-inch blade slipped between your ribs.

Maybe enough to kill. Certainly enough to hurt.

Six months earlier, word of Sean's particular predilection for violence and his utter disregard for the cost of human life had passed up a particular chain and found its way into the ear of a man named Andrew Rawlin. The meeting that followed shortly after changed Sean's life.

If Sarah Bolton could see her son now, she might think that the experience of prison had changed him for the better. Given him the opportunity to atone for his crimes. Showed him a spiritual path out of his darkness.

For Sean was wearing the dark brown, wide-toed shoes, black pants and white shirt of a Mormon Elder, complete with an identifying name tag clipped to his left breast pocket. He looked every inch a man of God. He sat behind the wheel of an old, rented sedan car, painted white, and could have been one of a million such men, returning from a day spent proselytizing in the service of his Lord.

The disguise was a good one. In Utah, sixty-two percent of the population is Mormon. They don't—ordinarily—drink, and they prefer to deal with their issues in-house. And of course, the enormous power wielded by the Church of the Latter-Day Saints meant that police in the state tended to give its congregants a wide berth. It was just easier that way.

Less paperwork.

If the police had pulled him over and searched the vehicle, which they did not, they might have found either the loaded Sig Sauer pistol taped underneath his seat or the can of gasoline in the trunk, or both. But none came his way, and Sean gave them no reason to suspect anything, anyway. His tattoos were long gone, his close-cropped hair now grown out. He even spoke differently. Enunciated his letters. Sounded like he'd gone to private school.

As the sun began to sink in the sky of a cold, gray February evening, Sean received a message, sent to a secure communications app on his phone.

It was brief. Just an image of a man with blue hair, an address, and a time. 8 p.m.

Sean knew what he had to do.

DR. TIMOTHY GREAVES sat in a stunned, numbed silence. He was in the garage of his Bluffdale home, surrounded by what looked more like a server farm than the contents of an ordinary home. Interspersed with the blinking lights and vast amounts of heat given off by rack after rack of servers and hard drives were stacks of DVDs and pieces of *Star Wars* merchandise, most of them still in their shrinkwrap packaging.

Greaves' blue hair was stuck limply to his forehead, thick with two days of unwashed sweat and grease. He had not returned to his office at the Hive since the death of his friend, Jim Donahue, nor taken a shower, or so much as brushed his teeth. His fingers and wrists were on fire from two days of almost uninterrupted typing.

The desk in front of him was littered with crushed soda cans and empty coffee cups, dark rings staining the ceramic material. The scene was more reminiscent of a high school gaming convention than a grown man's working environment.

But Greaves didn't see any of it.

He had done the impossible. He had hacked the NSA. Or, to be more precise, had created a tool that would access the agency's servers with ease. Even the ones he wasn't supposed to know about. The ones that *nobody* was supposed to know about.

His finger hovered over the return key. Every test he had run indicated that his hunch had paid off. But right now, at this very moment, he had a choice. He could still walk away and pretend that none of this had ever happened. Pressing that button might end his career. The National Security Agency doesn't look too kindly on people who penetrate its systems— not even when the masked intruder is one of its own employees.

If Greaves had been running this test by the book, he would have done it from a clean room inside the security of the Hive itself, or perhaps from Fort Meade in Maryland. Not from his own garage, and certainly not surrounded by the detritus of an uninterrupted two-day coding marathon.

But Greaves knew he had no other choice. He had known Jim Donahue for over a decade, and the two men had become friends. And Greaves had caused the man's death, as surely as if he had pulled the trigger himself. There was no way he could take that back. But maybe he could make it right.

The grief hit him now. He had been able to hide from it when he was staring at the glowing computer screen in front of him, his fingers dancing across the keyboard at lightning speed. He'd thrown himself into the impossible and come out the other side. But ignoring the problem could only work for so long. Now Greaves had to face the consequences of what he'd done.

His throat closed up, and great, wracking sobs overcame

him, though his hand never moved from his position over the keyboard. It took long seconds for him to compose himself, as raw cheeks stung with hot tears and the collar of his T-shirt was quickly stained with salt.

And then Greaves pressed the button.

The screen took several seconds to load. When it did, he was presented with a sight he had seen thousands of times before: the threat matrix created by the NSA's Birdseye system.

It was a list of America's enemies, thousands long. Birdseye sifted every single classified and unclassified source of information there was, drawing together clues that could not be linked by an instrument as blunt and limited as the human mind. It was able to detect threats to the homeland with unparalleled accuracy, even recommending the most effective course of action– down to the very assets estimated to be most likely to eliminate that threat.

Although Greaves didn't yet know it, Birdseye had flagged a warehouse in Yemen six months before and recommended the CIA task a team that was led by one of their best operators. It was on that mission that Ryan Price had died, setting into motion a chain of events that was still unfolding.

Except this time, something was different. The threat matrix Greaves saw in front of him was not the one he had worked on for the last two years. Gone were the Islamic terrorists, the far-right militias, the North Korean hardliners and the Russian oligarchs who ordinarily populated the ranks of the matrix.

Greaves' gaze was drawn unerringly to the face that topped the list. The man's eyes were compelling, both inky black and a chilling gray. His face was clean-shaven and a scar marked the width of his neck, faded, but still very visible from the flash of the camera.

But it wasn't the man's Caucasian features that caught Greaves' attention. It was his profession: he was an employee of the Central Intelligence Agency. His name was Jason Trapp.

Greaves scrolled through the threat matrix, noting with mounting horror the names of the targets. They were not terrorists. They were not enemies of the state. They were not enemies of America at all.

They were FBI agents. CIA officers. Members of Congress, police officers, soldiers, sailors and Marines.

They were patriots.

He blinked, trying to process what this meant. On a second screen, he logged in with his usual access credentials rather than the ones he'd created as part of his hack, and the normal threat matrix returned. The realization hit him with a flash. The system was showing him what he was *supposed* to see. It was Potemkin list of targets, displayed to make Birdseye's stewards think it was operating as designed.

"Who are these people?" He hissed as he turned back to the hidden list. He scrolled madly up and down, trying to pick a pattern out of the chaos.

And then, with an almost physical shock, Greaves saw another face.

His own.

He moved the mouse, his hand feeling like it was encased with concrete. Greaves clicked on the file and his eyes scanned the contents, reflecting the glow of his computer monitor as they did so. They widened. A gasp of air escaped his lips, and a chilling cold entered his veins.

He read the words with horror. Read the name of the asset who had been tasked with his own murder. A man named Sean Bolton, who would be dressed like a Mormon missionary. Greaves looked at his watch, knowing without needing to check that the time was now. His life was forfeit. He choked out a sob as grief curdled within him to terror.

And then he heard the knock at his door.

35

Vice President Robert Jenkins looked out on his West Texas cattle country ranch and wrinkled his nose. He hated cows. Hated the way they stank, the way they shit, even the way they looked at him with their huge unblinking brown eyes. Like they knew he didn't belong here and weren't taken in by his good ol' boy charm.

Which was the truth.

Jenkins hated the country. He was a city guy, more at home among the swirling cigar smoke of a wood-paneled Manhattan lunch spot than this backwards corner of America. But owning a ranch played well in the press. So Jenkins had sucked it up. Besides, the second he had decided to make a run in national politics, he realized the drawbacks of being born in Delaware. The state had only three electoral college votes.

Texas brought with it thirty-eight. So now, Vice President Robert Jenkins clothed himself in the Lone Star flag of Texas.

Jenkins had been stuck on the ranch for almost a week. The Secret Service had decided that right now it was the safest place for him, at least until law enforcement discovered whoever was behind the current wave of attacks. They had 24/7 support overhead from a pair of US Air Force F-35 Lightning fighter jets, and heavily-armed agents patrolled the grounds. Snipers on the roof provided overwatch. In short, Oakdale Ranch was a fortress.

But it also stank of shit.

"Mr. Vice President?"

Jenkins turned around and saw an aide whose name he barely recalled. She was fresh-faced, blond, probably a Georgetown graduate and barely twenty-two years old, if he was any judge. And when it came to establishing a woman's vintage, the vice president was very practiced indeed.

"What is it?"

"Your two o'clock is here. The journalist."

Jenkins grunted his assent and walked back through the porch doors into his study. The Secret Service hated the fact that he hadn't allowed them to hermetically seal the doors, but Jenkins had quickly pulled rank. What was the point in owning a thirty-million-dollar ranch if he couldn't at least enjoy the view? And it was one hell of a view.

"Send her in."

On a clear day, he could just about make out Guadalupe Peak, the highest natural point in Texas. Today was just such a day, and as he waited for the reporter, Jenkins turned to face it, hooking his fingers inside the waistband of his denim jeans. It was decorated by a single white cloud, shaped like a soldier's beret.

The woman's name was Rita Mason. She wrote for the *Wall Street Journal*, and before that had interned at the *Washington Post*. Jenkins had done his research carefully when he selected her. She was no friend to the administration, neither the nascent one he currently served in, nor the last. Though she was young, still in her twenties, she was already getting a reputation on the Beltway circuit for her hard-hitting, immaculately researched investigative journalism.

Sadly for Rita, the *Journal* had recently announced layoffs – and her head was on the chopping block. She needed a way out of her predicament, and the vice president intended to provide one—on his terms.

"I'm sorry I'm late," Rita said as she entered the vice president's airy study. She was flustered, that much was immediately apparent, but was attempting not to rush.

"Don't be," Jenkins replied, examining the reporter appreciatively. His chief of staff hadn't mentioned that the woman was a perfect 10. The headshot that accompanied her byline made her look older and more severe. Jenkins wondered how many hours she put in at the gym to achieve that toned figure. Endless miles on the treadmill, no doubt, a habit that he did not share.

What was the point in all those years spent in the pursuit of endless fortune and power, after all, if he was forced to starve himself? To deny himself the pleasures of the world? Robert Jenkins was not a man who enjoyed denying himself anything at all.

The vice president motioned for her to sit on the leather couch next to him. He crossed his legs and leaned back, settling into an open, relaxed pose. By contrast, Rita sat straight upright, as far away from him as she could manage while still remaining on the couch, with her back at a ninety degree angle to her thighs. She looked off-balance. Her red hair was pulled back into a simple ponytail, and Jenkins wondered what it would look like dancing across her shoulders as she kneeled before him.

"Thanks for coming on such short notice," he said, plastering a wide, fake smile on his face. Might as well put the woman at ease before revealing his cards.

"It was no problem at all," Rita replied. "And again, I'm so sorry for being late. It's hard to travel with all the restrictions."

"I hope my staff assisted?"

Rita nodded. "They did. But even so, there aren't many planes in the air. After the FAA grounded air traffic, a lot of the planes got diverted to Europe or Asia. They're still bringing them back."

"Ah. Of course."

It had been so long since Jenkins had flown commercial that he often forgot that most people didn't have at least a Gulfstream or Learjet at their beck and call. During his long tenure as CEO of Atlas Defense Systems, he'd been flown in palatial luxury in a converted Boeing 737.

If anything, the Air Force jets he now flew in were a step down. The VP didn't ever travel on Air Force One. It was a fact that grated on Robert Jenkins. An insult. He brushed it aside. He needed to concentrate.

"Do you know why I asked you here?"

A look of puzzlement briefly crossed the young journalist's pleasant, red-cheeked face as Jenkins studied her intently. Her eyes were a sparkling shade of blue, her lips lightly dusted with a rouge gloss – just enough to catch the eye. The more Jenkins looked at the young reporter, the more he liked what he saw.

Perhaps, he wondered, he might be able to kill two birds with one stone. His accession to the vice presidency and the concurrent increase in scrutiny meant that Jenkins was now forced to forsake many of his former passions. The pursuit of desirable young women was, unfortunately, chief among those.

Rita shook her head.

"I thought not," Jenkins said. "I trust you're happy for this conversation to proceed off the record?"

With a hint of reticence she said, "I suppose so."

Jenkins leaned back and let the luxurious cushioning of the couch embrace his frame. A predatory smile stretched across his face.

"Good," he said, elongating the word in his adopted Texas

drawl. "Ms. Mason, I wondered if I might be of some assistance to you?"

Rita flushed, betraying her inexperience.

"You..." she stammered. "To me?"

"Indeed," Jenkins said, splaying his legs apart and letting the silence stretch out before he continued. "Tell me, Rita, how long have you been at the *Journal*?"

"Two years," she replied with a quizzical frown. "Two years next week."

"Not long."

"Depends on your perspective," Rita replied with a shy smile, showing off a set of perfect pearly whites. "Feels like a lifetime to me."

Jenkins grimaced. Intentionally or not, Rita Mason had just reminded him of the disparity in their respective ages. He was not a man who wore his encroaching years well.

"It would," he said, thin lipped. "And have they told you if you are on the list?"

"The list?"

"Of layoffs," Jenkins said, taking satisfaction at the look of shock that rippled across Rita's young face.

"No," she choked, clutching onto her notepad as she attempted to regain some composure. "I didn't know any were planned."

"That's how it goes," Jenkins agreed. "Bad news travels fast, so they'll keep it locked down until they march you out carrying a cardboard box. Have you put any thought into your own position?"

"My position..." Rita whispered.

Her straight-backed posture was beginning to collapse. Though no one had briefed her exactly why Jenkins had requested her, she'd assumed it had something to do with Bloody Monday, or the administration's plans for the first hundred days. This, though, was something else entirely.

Jenkins smiled broadly, reveling in the girl's discomfort.

"First in, last out," he said. "And unfortunately, my dear Ms. Mason, I think that includes you."

Rita blinked rapidly several times and swallowed hard. Her eyes glistened – and though Jenkins didn't know exactly what she was thinking, he took a wild guess. She had the fresh-faced look of an idealist. Top of her class at Emerson College's School of Journalism, she'd no doubt dreamt of breaking the next Watergate since she was not long out of diapers.

And now, Jenkins thought, he was threatening to rip that prize from her grasp. As he studied the reporter, who was barely holding it together, her fingers clenched in white-knuckled claws, her freckled cheeks now drained of color, he knew it was time to offer Rita Mason a lifeline.

"But maybe I can help." Jenkins smiled. He shifted up the couch a few inches, then a couple more. He could feel the heat of Rita's thighs now, was close enough to reach out and stroke her cheeks.

"How?"

"Do you know what political editors can't get enough of?" he asked.

"What?"

"Highly placed sources in the administration. Particularly those willing to give scathing quotes."

Rita's eyes flashed, her journalistic instincts battling with her and momentarily coming out on top. "On the record?"

Jenkins shook his head with a wry smile. "That's not how this works."

"I don't even know what *this* is!" she protested.

Jenkins reached out and toyed with a stray strand of her red hair, tucking it gently behind her freckled ear. He was close enough to smell her perfume now. Just the ghost of an aroma, but one that had him unaccountably excited.

"Mr. Vice President," Rita whispered, an expression of discomfort creasing her young face. "What are you doing?"

Jenkins took a deep breath before answering, drinking in the smell of Rita's perfume, her sweat and her fear. He dragged his tongue across his thin lips and smiled. It was a hungry expression that died without ever reaching his small, flinty eyes.

"Getting to know you, my dear. We'll be spending rather a lot of time together, after all. Now, let me tell you a story about President Nash."

36

Jason Trapp was driven with an intensity the like of which he had rarely experienced. Particularly in the past few years, during which he had begun to suspect that the targets he was being given were flawed. That the men and women he was being sent to eliminate were not America's enemies, after all, but unwitting obstacles standing in the way of a far greater plan.

It was the day after Donahue's assassination, and Trapp found himself riding the back of a surveillance van not far from Dani Carter's H Street apartment. The van was a rental, not designed for its current task, but had been quickly converted for an altogether different purpose. Trapp sat behind a bank of screens that fed him half a dozen camera angles, each a wintry scene, as snow now dusted the streets. He watched as nervous commuters hurried home, desperate to get out of the open before night fell.

The more Trapp learned about the wave of terror sweeping across America, the more he thrust himself into the center of the maelstrom, the more he began to understand that it was all connected. The missions toward the end of his time at the CIA.

Amtrak Six. Bloody Monday. The attacks in Boston, and the assassination of the director of the NSA.

Each was linked by a thread whose entire length Trapp could not yet see. But it was a thread on which he was beginning to pull.

And when he found the end, when he found the person or persons responsible for unleashing hell upon America, he would return the favor tenfold.

"This is Hangman, radio check," he said.

The microphone was mounted around his neck, and picked up the slightest of vibrations, meaning there was no need for a headset, or the Secret Service tactic of running the microphone through an agent's sleeve to the wrist.

"Redneck, coming in loud and clear." That was Perkins' chosen callsign. Trapp hadn't inquired, but figured it was because the deadly operator sounded like a Grade A hillbilly.

"Sketch, ditto."

"Good job, gentlemen. Let's stay frosty out here. Agent Carter doesn't know she picked up a new set of guardian angels. Let's keep it that way."

The plan was simple. It was a Hail Mary play, in some respects. It relied on waiting and watching, sitting in place until something happened, rather than the infinitely more appealing option of going out, rattling the cages and *making* something happen.

But right now, they were out of leads. Donahue was dead, law enforcement was chasing its own tail, and his team, formerly of the CIA and now operating as unpaid interns, was right out on its ass. In the end, they didn't have a choice.

It was Trapp's idea.

He realized that this conspiracy, whoever they were, had a pattern. They had tried to eliminate him twice – first in Yemen, and then a second time on the banks of the Potomac, and then followed the same playbook with Donahue. They were ruthless when it came to operational security. If there was even a chance that someone suspected what was going on, as Trapp himself had first begun to, all those months ago, then that person had to be eliminated.

And since the director was dead, and Trapp himself was in the wind, that only left agent Nadine Carter.

And although she didn't know it, by searching his prints—by merely displaying an interest in him—she had made herself bait.

SURVEILLANCE OPERATIONS MIGHT LOOK exciting in the movies, but Trapp knew from bitter experience that in reality they were anything but.

You spent long hours on your ass in the back of a van that was either freezing cold, or hotter than Death Valley due to the heat ejected by the surveillance equipment. You only ate fast food, or you didn't eat at all. You had to stay sharp for hours as your body cramped up and your mind started to wander, just in case you missed that one second in which the shit hit the fan.

But there was one constant.

You always pissed in a plastic bottle.

The sun had set, and the early February evening threatened to be a cold one. Fat snowflakes fell from the sky, not in great numbers, but that would follow soon enough. The sky was a dark, ugly gray before the sun finally disappeared past the horizon. A storm was setting in. Of course, Trapp thought. It had to be snow.

The white stuff would make everything more difficult. When it got thick enough, it could play havoc with the directional microphones. Unlike rain, it could prevent a man from seeing across the street. Cameras were rendered almost useless.

Trapp had a feeling that before too long, they would be stuck with just the human eyeball, Mark 1.0.

"Status update," he said into his throat mic, mainly to make sure the surveillance team was paying attention.

Trapp's back was in agony from hunching over the monitors the back of the van. On the other hand, things could always be worse. Perkins was currently on top of the building the opposite side of the street from Carter's apartment, manning a suppressed M2010 Enhanced Sniper Rifle. The weapon was accurate for an ordinary marksman at around thirteen hundred yards. Perkins could hit a man at almost two thousand yards nine times in ten.

It was overkill, of course. But better safe than sorry.

"I'm freezing my ass off here," Perkins replied. "Any sign of our target?"

"I'm trailing her now," Winks said, his voice low and professional in Trapp's earpiece. "She went to the grocery store. Got a sixpack of Bud Light and a filet mignon. My kind of girl."

"Keep your distance, Sketch," Trapp said. "I don't need to know what she's eating for dinner, just that she's there. Any sign of trouble?"

"None yet."

TROUBLE DIDN'T COME until almost three in the morning. It arrived in the form of a man dressed in a long black wool overcoat, a dark brown briefcase at his side. Trapp's immediate impression, from his position behind the monitors in the surveillance van, was that he was a civil servant. Maybe a lowly bureaucrat at the State Department – and not the kind that meant they really worked for the CIA.

In this neighborhood, which was overwhelmingly populated by a middling rank of administrators and civil servants, he didn't look out of place. Except, of course, that it was well past midnight, a time when any right-thinking government employee was long since tucked up in bed.

"Target approaching," Trapp murmured into his throat mic.

"I've got a shot," Perkins said as the newcomer stepped into the bright halo thrown off by a streetlight. Snowflakes danced in its glow, hovering and spinning and soaring on gusts and flurries of wind. The crunch of the man's footsteps carried on the directional microphones, and was deafening in Trapp's ear.

He contemplated turning down the volume, but stopped himself. He dared not miss a thing, not with a woman's life in his hands. Ever since he had failed to save his mom all those years before, Trapp had had a weakness for women. Not in the way most men did, but in a willingness to subject himself to desperate harm to save a member of the fairer sex.

"How's our girl?" Trapp asked, his eyes glued to the bright screens in the back of the van. He watched the man slow fractionally as he passed the stairs that led up to Carter's apartment. It was hard to tell from this angle, but had his eyes flicked up toward her door, just momentarily?

"Her blinds are down, so I can't see much, but there's still a light on inside. Either she's passed out on the couch, or this chick is all kinds of dedicated."

Trapp grew concerned that Carter had slipped the net. That somehow she had made the surveillance that was tailing her and executed countermeasures of her own. He shook it off. They had set up cameras and motion sensors on every possible exit, and barring a couple of false alarms caused first by the snow, then some kids darting out of the fire escape, no one had left.

Trapp's fingers caressed the cool metal of his holstered Beretta as he tried to figure out what the hell to do. He wished he hadn't sent Winks back to the farmhouse to get some rest.

He wished there were a dozen more men under his command. He wished America wasn't under attack at all.

But wishing wouldn't make it so.

Trapp followed the man in his screen as he crunched a solitary path through the snow. Maybe it was nothing. Perhaps he was just seeing things.

And then a new sound filled the van's cabin. Trapp's heart stopped. Slowly, he moved his head to survey the new threat. It was emanating from one of the silent alarms he had set up. He checked the handwritten tag under the warning LED, and saw that it was attached to the apartment complex's rear entrance. This couldn't be a coincidence.

"Crap," he whispered. "Redneck – there's a second tango."

37

C arter couldn't sleep. She hadn't had a moment to think all day, and now her mind was running wild. Less than half a week in charge of the DC field office had cured her of any lingering hunger for promotion to one of the Bureau's top jobs.

Paperwork. So much damn paperwork. Carter was a field agent. She belonged out in the weeds, with her badge around her neck and her gun on her hip. She was considerably more at ease kicking in a suspect's door with her weapon drawn than she was filling out endless bureaucratic forms.

And so though it was long past the witching hour, Dani found herself behind the screen of her secure laptop—finally doing the kind of work that mattered.

Though she didn't know it, it was Jason Trapp's face that glowed out from her laptop screen. A mug shot taken by Boston PD, thick stubble on his chin and a smear of dried blood on his forehead, the scar around his neck just visible at the bottom of the frame. Dani had spent hours staring at that handsome, haunted face. Running searches on prints that simply didn't exist on any database known to man. Hell, even the report that Boston PD filed was supposed to have been deleted.

They'd gotten lucky.

"Who the hell are you?" she muttered, moving her mouse and running a new search, with expanded parameters.

The guy had to be former military. Maybe a spook. He had that look about him. The Boston cops she had spoken to had mentioned burn marks on his forearms, and eyes that flashed both black and gray.

As Dani studied his mug shot for the thousandth time, she saw an easy confidence, a self assurance that he could take on every man in the holding cell, probably single-handed. It was kind of attractive. Her mystery man had a rugged charm.

And what have his looks got to do with anything, Dani? she chided herself. She was supposed to be hunting for clues, not a new boyfriend. Although it *was* late. Maybe she'd simply been working too long. Tomorrow was already gonna be hell.

Her laptop chimed to acknowledge the receipt of an email. She wondered who the hell could possibly be messaging her at this time of the morning, and almost didn't look at it, assuming it would be spam. She was glad that she did.

"Jackpot."

Apparently Carter wasn't the only one working late. She thanked the anonymous FBI technician matching her midnight oil in the Boston field office. She had what she was looking for. The footage from the CCTV cameras inside Boston's TD Garden – the site of the terrorist attack at which this mystery man had first shown up.

Dani downloaded the footage from the FBI's secure email program onto her desktop, and then clicked play. She watched in rapt astonishment as the mystery man entered the events arena, weapon drawn. She noted the way he moved with a lithe, predator's grace. Every step he took was considered. He didn't rush, but moved quickly nonetheless. Didn't expose himself to unnecessary danger yet didn't linger.

The camera angle changed, and now he was creeping up a set of concrete stairs, the camera looking down at his face. He was determined, set. There was no expression of fear. This was a man who had been in similar situations too many times to count. Another angle change, and Dani recoiled in horror as she saw the flash of a rifle. The killer's victim died off screen. Or perhaps lived; without sound it was hard to tell.

"Come on," Dani muttered, although she knew that all this had already happened.

She'd read the Boston PD reports, knew that when SWAT had arrived on scene, the terrorists were already dead. Knew that even with the special weapons team's excellent reaction time, had it not been for this mystery shooter, many more would have died.

Who the hell are you? And why didn't you take credit?

As Dani watched a basketball arc up through the air, then the terrorist on the court turn and slump to the ground, staining the polished wood with his blood, Dani realized she knew why.

This man, whoever he was, was just like her father, and all his veteran buddies. Not in age, nor build. But in his single-minded focus on helping those in peril.

But there was more to it. The basketball trick spoke to an intelligence that hadn't come across in the dry, bureaucratic language of the police reports. It was out-of-the-box. Something a cop probably wouldn't try – something Dani knew that she herself would never have thought of.

Outside, the flashing lights of a police cruiser drove slowly past, coloring the walls of her darkened apartment even through her closed blinds. Dani subconsciously wondered whether it was anything to be concerned about, but the increased police presence wasn't exactly out of the ordinary in

Washington DC right now. Hell, they had the National Guard on the streets, patrolling in pairs with loaded rifles, and armored vehicles protecting every major monument and federal building in the city.

Which was a lot.

Though she didn't pay the sight much attention, it primed her subconscious to stay alert. She watched her laptop screen as the mystery man looked over his shoulder, placed his weapon on the ground, and laced his fingers behind his head. He didn't seem surprised to be shoved against the wall, cuffed, and frog marched out of the arena.

Carter didn't blame the officers as the footage ended and the laptop screen cut to black. They saw a man with a weapon and neutralized him. Hell, the mystery hero was lucky he didn't meet his end in a hail of lead. Although perhaps it wasn't luck, merely his innate understanding of what would happen next.

He'd analyzed the situation, known exactly how it would play out, and made a decision to minimize his risk of being caught in the crossfire. It was a mark of intelligence.

Dani sat back on her couch, fished a now warm, half empty bottle of beer from the coffee table in front of her, and gulped from it, wincing at the brackish taste of the warm liquid. How long had she been sitting here?

She knew her instincts were right. The mystery man definitely had military training. American, presumably, given the police reports regarding his accent. He had seen combat, judging by the scars on his forearms. And given that Dani couldn't find any trace of him on any law enforcement database known to man, she would bet her life that he was either special forces, in some deep black SOCOM program she never even heard of, or a spook.

But where the hell did that leave her? And how had he shown up in the middle of the terrorist attack in Boston? Was it by coincidence, or had he known it was going to happen? And then, days later, how had he also been first to arrive on her crime scene in DC?

What the hell is going on?

Dani wished she could call up her boss, Rick Olsen. If that's what he still was. She hated to picture him as he would be now, his white hair in stark contrast with the orange prison scrubs. He'd been her mentor for years, pretty much ever since she left the Academy. She'd barely made a career decision in all that time he hadn't had at least some input on. She asked herself the question: WWRD.

What would Rick do?

But she came up empty. Right now, Dani was flying blind. The Bureau itself was under attack, and she wasn't sure she had either the experience or the skills to get to the bottom of who was behind it.

Outside, a sound caught her attention. It was barely audible over the sound of sirens in the distance, the faraway noise of traffic traversing H Street, and the noise of her laptop fan, but it was there. The sound of a fire alarm sounding for just a second before being silenced. But why had it drawn her attention? Why that sound, not any of the others thrown out by the normal hum of a large American metropolitan city?

You're just being paranoid, she thought, even as her hearing sharpened enough to pick up the sound of boots crunching through the snow.

There was something about them. Not the fact that someone was walking at this time of night, but their cadence. Their urgency. Their owner was hurrying. But what could there be to rush for at this hour?

Dani stood up slowly, her mind racing. After realizing that someone had assassinated Donahue, she had considered a scenario just like this. She knew something wasn't right about this whole sequence of events, everything since the first attack on the morning of Bloody Monday to now. None of it added up.

The terrorists were ghosts, smuggled into America on routes that no law enforcement agency had yet identified. And though the NSA's Birdseye system hadn't marked a single one as a high priority for surveillance in the previous two years, paper records suggested that before that, they were on watch lists maintained by every law enforcement agency from the CIA to the damn Coast Guard.

The pieces clicked into place in Dani's mind. This was no ordinary terrorist plot. Maybe it wasn't a terrorist plot at all, at least not in the ordinary use of the term. Someone had set the whole thing up. Planned a bloody series of attacks. Provided the weapons, and somehow hidden the perpetrators from law enforcement.

And they had killed to preserve their secret. Not just anyone, but the leader of a major US intelligence agency.

So what might those same killers do to her?

Dani's heart was racing at what felt like a thousand beats per minute. Her palms were sweaty, and she wiped them on her thighs. She was wearing little more than a white T-shirt and a pair of tight Lycra workout shorts that she wore to bed, so the contact when it came was skin on skin. Her palms felt cold and clammy.

She quickly went to the window, pressing herself against the wall as she nudged one of the slats of the blind upward. She peered out, hoping against hope that she was imagining things. But even before she saw the outline of a man disappearing around the side of her apartment building, bracketed by the streetlight and the swirling snow, she knew she wasn't.

Dani sprinted, wishing she hadn't locked her service weapon in the gun safe. It might be good practice, but right now it felt like a foolish mistake. She rushed into her bedroom, went to the safe that was next to her bedside table, and began punching in the six digit code to unlock it. Her fingers slipped, and she keyed the last digit in wrong.

"Fuck."

The gun safe buzzed a harsh warning. Dani knew she only had three chances to get this right, and she'd already lost one. She knew the code, punched it in twice every day, before heading to the office and after returning home at night. Yet in her panic, she'd already screwed up once.

Come on.

Her fingers trembled, but seeing the scrapes on the back of her hand gave her renewed confidence. She'd survived these terrorists once. She would do it again. Her fingers danced over the keypad, and this time the safe buzzed a tone of success. The lock clicked, and she dived for her weapon. It wasn't loaded. She always made it safe before locking it up.

Another mistake.

There was another sound. Boots thudding in the hallway. Dani knew she wasn't imagining things now. Someone was coming. For her. And they were coming now.

Her weapon finally loaded, Dani spun, exploded out of her crouch and went looking for cover. She needed something solid, something that would absorb a beating. The couch, maybe, though faced with any serious caliber of ammunition it would provide little resistance.

The sound that filled her living room a second later was so unexpected that it nearly gave her a heart attack.

It was her doorbell.

38

"Redneck, what have you got?" Trapp muttered in a muted voice into his throat mic as he ran down a hallway in Carter's condo building, motion activated lights springing to life as he moved. Christ, that was one way to blow his cover. The fucking things were lighting up like the Christmas decorations in Times Square.

"Nothing good," the special operative replied. "I've lost him. He walked straight past, and round the corner. Sorry, Hangman."

"Don't apologize," Trapp grunted. "Keep your eyes peeled, and the second the fucker so much as blinks at you wrong, put a bullet in his head."

"Roger that," Perkins agreed, a hint of glee in his voice. Trapp understood it better than perhaps anyone else on the planet. The man was an elite CIA Special Operations Group killer. He was used to taking action. To fighting America's enemies wherever he found them.

And for the last few days, he'd been sitting on his hands as the whole country descended into chaos. It wasn't what he had trained for all those years. The man would have been burning up with ambition to play his part.

And now he could.

"Wait... Hangman, he's back; climbing the emergency stairs. Got 'im heading for the roof on my side of the street, taking up an overwatch position," Perkins updated.

"Copy," Trapp said into his mic as he spun round a corner. "Take the shot the second he presents a threat. Understood?"

"My pleasure, Hangman," came the terse, determined response. Trapp knew that he didn't have to worry about Perkins's shooting. Whoever this second attacker was, he'd sign his death warrant the second he touched his weapon.

Trapp mentally shunted that part of the operation to one side. He didn't need it taking up valuable real estate in his brain. Right now, he had only one focus – get to the other assailant before the man got to Carter.

And ideally, take him alive.

Trapp slowed, remembering from the blueprint of the condo building that Carter's apartment was around the next corner. He moved as quickly as he could while still retaining a modicum of stealth. As he reached the corner, he stopped and pressed himself against the wall.

He listened. Charging in half-cocked could cost him his life, and that meant Agent Dani Carter might wake up to a bullet in her forehead. The hallway was quiet, and Trapp began to wonder whether he had made a terrible mistake. Perhaps the shooter had taken a different route.

And then he heard it. The chime of a doorbell. Then again, more insistently.

It had to be hers. The shooter was at Carter's front door. Trapp saw the events of the next few seconds playing out in his head like a movie. Carter would be asleep. The doorbell would rouse her. She would worry – after all, who calls on someone's apartment in the middle of the night? She would imagine that something had happened to a family member, that the police were at her front door to deliver her some terrible news.

The agent's mind would be dulled by sleep. She wouldn't be expecting the visitor at her door to pull a weapon. Or to fire.

She would stumble back, crimson blood staining her pajama top. The killer would take a step forward, over her nearly lifeless corpse, and fire one more bullet into her skull. Just to make sure.

Trapp blinked, and from around the corner he heard a distant, muffled voice, squashed by the woman's front door. She sounded sleepy, just as he had imagined. "Just a second..."

Trapp knew he had to move fast. He checked his weapon and rounded the corner, creeping low. It was a horrible operational position – the hallway was lit brightly by motion sensitive lights that worked on a timer, and the attacker was almost twenty feet away from him. He had maybe thirty seconds before they would flick back into darkness. On any other mission, that's what he would have waited for. The moment the lights went dark, he would have crept forward and taken the attacker by surprise.

But he didn't have the time. Before that, Carter would come to the front door. She'd open it, and then it would be over.

Trapp might still get his man, but at the cost of a good agent. And that had to be avoided at all costs. Too many brave men and women had died already, fighting an enemy they did not know and could not hope to understand. Trapp had to put an end to it. But he wasn't willing to bear any cost. Not *this* cost. So he began to edge forward, taking silent half steps, his weapon leveled and ready to fire.

He watched his target tense. The man had a pistol in his right hand, held low, almost at waist height, so that it could not be seen in the door's peephole. The man was focused so intently on Carter's front door that he had not yet noticed Trapp creeping toward him.

Trapp began a count in his head. He figured he had maybe ten seconds before Carter opened her front door, but he could not be certain that the attacker would wait until she opened it. Maybe the second he heard her approach he would fire through the door.

Hell, that might be the way Trapp would've done it himself.

Screw it, Trapp thought. He didn't have time for this. He needed to save her, now. And so he charged. The intention in his mind was to tackle the man at the waist and slam him against the door. With the element of surprise, he might just startle the attacker, giving him the second he needed to take advantage.

And then things started to move very fast.

Before Trapp had covered half the distance the man glanced his way. Shock flared on the attacker's face at the sight of the armed man charging toward him. He flinched, began to turn, his weapon rising through the air. And then Carter's front door opened. The attacker's gaze snapped back, his brain processing the new input.

But too late.

A bottle of beer smashed against the man's weapon, exploding and sending a spray of foam and broken glass battering the walls of the hallway. Then a leg swept out, knocking the man to the ground, and Dani Carter was crouching over him, her weapon pointed at the man's temple just as Trapp arrived himself, weapon drawn.

"Don't fucking move," she growled. Then, with alarm, she realized that her attacker wasn't the only presence in the corridor. Her gaze flicked up, and the hand holding her pistol flinched, but did not draw back.

Dani Carter looked up at Trapp. For a second, no recognition lay in her brilliant green eyes. And then it was there. They widened just fractionally, but Trapp was nonetheless impressed by how well she handled the shock of the situation. And then she spoke, her voice mostly calm, barring a small tremor from the adrenaline that must've been surging through her veins.

"We have a lot to talk about."

39

P erkins' voice crackled in Trapp's earpiece. "Hangman, he's lining up a shot."

Trapp spoke into his throat mic, still matching Carter's gaze. "Take him."

"Roger that."

A second later, Perkins drawled with the consummate insouciance of a practised CIA professional. "Tango down."

"Copy. Get the body into the van, and get ready to move. I'll be with you soon. Things didn't..." He paused.

"Things didn't exactly go as we planned."

The man lying underneath Carter's knee groaned, a few rivulets of blood beginning to blossom on a hand that was still pressed into shards of smashed glass on the hallway carpet.

"Maybe we can take this somewhere a little more private?"

Carter tilted her head. "Maybe you can tell me who the fuck you are?"

Trapp grinned. Looking down at the FBI agent, he noticed for the first time how attractive she was. Not conventionally pretty, not the kind of girl you might see on a Milan catwalk, but nevertheless Trapp's kind of woman. Her green eyes were piercing, and he got the very real sense that she was profiling him in just the same way he was her. He shrugged.

"Jason Trapp. Nice to meet you. I would shake your hand, but—" He glanced first toward the Beretta in his own grip, then the prisoner underneath Carter's knee.

"Okay, Jason Trapp, why don't you give me one good reason I shouldn't arrest you right now?"

Trapp studied Carter intently. She seemed remarkably unfazed by the scene that had just taken place. He realized that she couldn't have been sleeping when she heard the chime at her door, but even so he was impressed by her reaction time. Most people, hell, even most law enforcement agents would not have reacted in the same way.

She'd been not just instinctive, but decisive. Identified a problem, then solved it. Hell, when it came to it, she hadn't even needed his assistance.

Trapp grinned. "Well, I was gonna say I just saved your life, but it doesn't look like you needed much help."

A ghost of a smile flickered on Dani's lips before she extinguished it, consciously turning her gaze hard. "What just happened here, Jason?"

Trapp held up his weapon, palm facing outward in a gesture of peace, and then slipped it into the space between his belt and the small of his back. He pulled a set of flex cuffs from his pocket and glanced at Dani's prisoner.

"May I?"

She gestured her consent.

Trapp quickly crouched, secured the prisoner, and whispered a threat into his ear.

"Your friend is dead, buddy. If you cry out, I'll do the same to you."

He caught the look on Dani's face as he stood back up. She wasn't from his world. She was an FBI agent. They played by a different set of rules. He saw a battle playing out on her face.

One part of her was hungry. It desperately wanted to know not just who Trapp was, but *what* he was, and most importantly what he was doing there.

The other part was the law enforcement side of her personality. Trapp had read Carter's file. She'd aced every test she'd ever taken. She was the kind of agent the Bureau didn't get their hands on very often – because mostly, people with those kind of smarts joined a bank on Wall Street, or a tech firm in the Bay Area. That part of her was by the book.

He wondered which would win out. He didn't have to wait long.

"Why don't we take this inside?" Carter said. She jutted her chin at her one-time attacker's weapon. "Grab that and hide the glass."

Then, turning to the restrained prisoner, she smiled a mirthless smile. "Don't expect me to stop him."

A minute later they were inside her apartment and the prisoner was secured to a dining chair with another set of plastic restraints. He grabbed a dirty washing up cloth from inside the sink and stuffed it into the man's mouth.

He took a step back, checking his handiwork, and noticed the would-be attacker was wearing a counterfeit FBI badge around his neck. It looked indistinguishable from the real thing, at least to his eye. A fake like that would have been neither cheap nor easy to come by. It meant that whoever he was, the man had connections.

"Now," he said. "Let's talk."

Dani nodded. Trapp noticed that she was trembling slightly now that the adrenaline was fading from her system. Her upper arms, the backs of her hands and her face were marked with cuts, scrapes and bruises that stood out against her golden skin —though none were fresh. Trapp glanced at the couch.

"You should sit," he said. "It'll help."

"Thanks for the advice," Carter replied in a tone of voice

that suggested she didn't intend to take it. She held her weapon loosely by her side, but Trapp picked up on a tension in her posture. He knew she was prepared to use it at a moment's notice. Judging by how she had responded to the threat at her front door, he wasn't entirely sure that he would have that situation handled.

FBI agent Dani Carter was a firecracker. Trapp liked what he saw.

"You never gave me a reason not to put you in cuffs," she said, keeping her tone sufficiently restrained to avoid it carrying to their prisoner.

Trapp raised his eyebrow. "You think you could?"

Carter didn't respond to his barb. "You're a person of interest in an ongoing investigation, Mr. Trapp," she said. "You played the hero in Boston before disappearing in an US Air Force helicopter, and then you showed up on my crime scene in downtown DC."

Trapp nodded. "I did."

"That's all you're going to say?"

"Habit, I guess."

"You're a spook," she said. It was a statement not a question. "CIA?"

Trapp figured there wasn't much point in playing games. He wasn't with the Agency, not anymore, at least not officially.

"I used to be," he admitted.

"And what are you now, Jason? A contractor?"

He shook his head. "Retired."

"You don't seem very retired to me."

Trapp grinned. "I guess not."

"Since you're feeling chatty, why don't you tell me who's on the other end of that radio in your ear? More friends from your retirement village?"

Trapp glanced at the prisoner, who was testing his restraints and staring at Carter with barely restrained fury. "I don't think he likes you," he said.

"The feeling is mutual," Carter replied. "And that wasn't an answer."

Trapp sighed. "I told you the truth. I'm retired. Was retired, maybe. No one's paying my bills."

"So what the hell were you doing outside my front door at three in the morning?"

"I guess I was in the wrong place at the wrong time."

"That seems to happen to you quite a lot, Jason."

"I guess you could say that. Boston was an accident. The rest kind of spiraled from that."

Carter's eyes widened as she realized he'd finally thrown her a bone. "A happy accident."

"Not for the terrorists."

"I guess not."

Carter scanned him seriously. She looked as though she was coming to a decision. Her emerald eyes flickered left and right, and then stopped dead center on Trapp's face.

"Maybe you can tell me what the hell is going on out there. Because I know one thing. This wasn't Al Qaeda. This wasn't ISIS. It's something new. Something different. I feel like I'm looking up from the bottom of a well and seeing the sky and thinking that it's all there is to the world."

"I know the feeling. And you're right."

Trapp paused for a second to consider his options. The plan had never been for Carter to become aware that an operation was going on around her. It was supposed to be a simple surveillance job, with a snatch and grab at the end of it. In an ideal world, they would have been in and out without ever being noticed, but with an asset to interrogate.

But nothing about the past week had been ideal. And right now, looking at the scars on Carter's body, Trapp knew that if he couldn't trust her, after everything she had been through in the service of her country, then he couldn't trust anyone in the world.

"Okay, I'll show you my cards," he said. "You were right, I was with the Agency. For more than a decade. But I left six months ago."

"What happened six months ago?" Carter asked, unable to disguise the gleam of intrigue in her eye. She was a born FBI agent, Trapp noted, and perhaps it would make her a valuable ally.

"My world ended," Trapp said, pulling his throat mic loose and letting the wire hang limply from his collar. "I had concerns with the intelligence I was receiving. The people they were sending me to kill. I sent it up the chain, and the usual bullshit came back down. Everything carried on as normal. Until Yemen."

Trapp gritted his teeth as the images of that night came back to him once again. He wondered if they would ever fade, if the shock of yellow in the nighttime sky would ever fade to black, and whether the explosion that had cut through the docks in the port city of Aden would ever stop burning his skin. Whether the nightmares would end, or the memories fade. Not of the pain, but of what he had lost.

Who he had lost.

His voice was dull and hoarse when it came. "It was supposed to be the last job for a while. Just a quick in and out on a warehouse. Looking for some Russian military hardware that was being cross shipped to the North Koreans to get past the sanctions. The whole thing was a setup. There wasn't anything there, just a hornet's nest of rebels left to lure us in, and half a ton of explosives to make sure we never made it back out."

This was the first time that Trapp had said these words out loud. The revelation felt somehow calming, as though a weight was no longer pushing down on his shoulders.

Carter didn't respond for a long beat. Then she spoke as tactfully as she could. "So what does any of that have to do with what's going on now?"

Trapp let out a curt, angry laugh that bounced off the small apartment's walls. "Everything. Nothing. What the hell do I know? All I know is someone tried to kill me. Murdered my best friend. Then when I showed my face on Bloody Monday, they tried again."

Carter's eyes narrowed. "What?"

"After the Air Force dropped me off. Mitchell –" He paused, not quite ready to reveal the whole story.

"The people I'm working with, they figured something might happen, and it did. An airstrike, right down by the Potomac."

Carter froze. She'd heard something about this, seen some news footage of smoke rising from the banks of the Potomac, but in the carnage of the last few days, and the chaos of her own recovery, it hadn't come up again.

"What did you just say?"

Trapp nodded. "Yep. Guided munitions, probably a two thousand pounder. Only made it out in the nick of time."

"Jesus," Carter breathed. "Who the hell is behind all this?"

Trapp glanced at the trussed-up prisoner on the opposite side of the room. "I'm guessing you don't believe the FBI was really infested by a bunch of traitors, right?"

Carter's response was fierce and immediate. "Hell no."

"Good," Trapp said, jerking his thumb at the prisoner. "Because I think it's time we got some answers. Don't you think?"

"Yes, But not here."

40

They traveled back to the Forest Hills safehouse without any trouble from the police. Trapp wondered what he would do if a cop stopped them and found a dead man in a body bag lying next to a man whose mouth was covered by duct tape and had a black hood over his head.

Luckily, there were no problems. Trapp opted against making Agent Carter wear a hood. The location of the safe house would be burned if, for any reason, she decided to turn them in. But he didn't think that was going to happen. And besides, if the proverbial shit really hit the fan with the cops then having an FBI agent with them might get them out of a sticky spot.

"We're here," Trapp said as the van drove down the potholed private road that led to the isolated safehouse, bumping and jarring the whole way. The trees lining the road cast long shadows in the van's headlights, shadows that were born and grew and died in seconds as the vehicle bumped past, its suspension squealing with protest. Winks met the three of them as they disembarked the vehicle, and Trapp told the two

operators to get the prisoner inside and get set up for an interrogation.

"What are we going to do with the body?" Perkins asked.
"Want me to bury it?"

Trapp glanced at Dani. He wasn't 100% sure how she would
react to a suggestion like that. In his world, and Perkins', bodies
were an unfortunate by-product of doing business. If they
became an operational hazard, they were buried, burned, or
crushed into nothing in a scrap yard. But the FBI had a
different attitude. To them, life was a little more sacrosanct
than to their cousins down at Langley.

"Don't look at me." She shrugged, a nervous tremor in her
voice giving away her true feelings. "We've gone way past 'lose
your badge' territory. I'm looking at a ten-year stint at ADX
Florence for dereliction of duty. So I guess I'm all in."

Trapp was used to operating on the outskirts of the law, at
the very edges of what most ordinary people thought was
acceptable human behavior. Agent Dani Carter was not. This
was virgin territory to her, and though so far she was taking it
like a pro, Trapp wondered how long that would last.

"Leave it in the outhouse for now. It's thirty degrees out
tonight. Won't be much warmer if and when the sun shows its
face. We've got time."

As Perkins and Winks manhandled the prisoner inside,
Trapp gently grabbed Dani's arm. She was dressed in black
jeans, a warm jumper and an FBI windbreaker. The last item
had been just in case they got pulled over. Still, it added a layer
of absurdity to what was about to happen.

"You're okay with all this?" he asked.

"What's going to happen in there, Jason?" Dani replied. He
liked that she was about the only person he knew who didn't
refer to him by his last name. It felt familiar, almost as though
they had known each other for longer than they really had.

Focus, he reminded himself. This was no time to be falling for a pretty girl, though there was no doubt that Dani Carter was definitely that. Right now, they had significantly more important matters to be focusing on.

"What?" Trapp grinned. "You're happy with aiding and abetting murder and a side of kidnapping, but a little Q&A session is where you draw the line?"

Dani shot him a fierce, angry, perhaps even slightly guilty glare. He winced and made a note not to do that again.

"I won't do anything that you're not comfortable with," he assured her. "And it's not because I'm worried about having an FBI agent watching what I'm doing. Torture doesn't work. When you inflict pain on a man, he won't just tell you everything he knows. He'll tell you what he thinks you want to hear. And right now we don't have time to be led on some wild goose chase. We need answers."

"So what *are* you planning to do?"

Trapp let a smile crease his face, though it didn't reach his eyes. "A little fear never hurt anyone, did it?"

WHEN TRAPP and Dani walked into the basement where the two CIA operators had set up a makeshift interrogation room, Mitchell glanced at the FBI agent, then shot Trapp a hard look. One that said: *Don't you think you should have run this by me first?*

Trapp just shrugged. He wasn't in the Agency any longer. This was his game. It was time to play by his rules.

The interrogation room, by the looks of things, was once intended to be a home cinema. It was finished better than the rest of the house. Against the wall the prisoner was facing was a large screen, and a video projector was mounted on the ceiling. The rest of the room's occupants were leaning against the opposite wall, out of the prisoner's line of sight.

Trapp walked over to Kyle and muttered something into his

ear, glancing up at the projector. The young analyst nodded and got to work. He set up a small camera in front of the gagged prisoner, whose eyes were glancing left and right and back again, rapid and panicked with fear as they scanned the room for any clue as to what was going to happen next. He then hooked it up to the projector, so that the prisoner was left staring at a blown-up live feed of his own face.

"Now that's better," Trapp said, walking into the man's field of view. "Don't you think?"

Beads of sweat dripped down his face, no doubt acrid with fear. They looked gargantuan on the video projector. Light glinted from two flood lights positioned in front of him at a forty-five degree angle to his face.

Trapp leaned down next to the man, grabbing him by the shoulder with one huge hand and squeezing tight. Tight enough to remind the prisoner of his enormous strength, but not hard enough for it to be mistaken for an attempt to inflict pain. He ripped the duct tape off the man's lips and the prisoner squealed. He tried to bring his hands to his face, but only succeeding in rattling his metal cuffs.

Trapp's expression darkened at the sound. A memory struggled to the surface, of himself as a boy. Of spending ten long days in a dark, cold outhouse chained by the foot to the wall. It jangled every time he moved, sending his father's dogs into paroxysms of rage. Their frantic barks and yelps as they clawed at the door were the soundtrack to his nightmares for months afterward, and all for smashing a worthless piece of crockery. An icy chill brushed the back of Trapp's neck. He hated becoming one of those dogs.

"Who the hell are you people?" the prisoner panted, snapping Trapp to the present. He realized his palms were damp and wiped them across his jeans. The muscle at the hinge of his jaw pulsed. He had to do what he had to do. He could process it later.

The man's tone was flat, perhaps Midwestern, but difficult to place. Like his dead friend, his hair was flat and shapeless, as though not too long ago it had been trimmed back close to the skull, and though now grown had not yet acquired a style of its own.

"I could ask you the same question," Trapp replied. "But I don't have much time. So why don't I start by telling you what I do know? Maybe we can play a game of hotter/colder. How does that sound?"

The prisoner glowered at Trapp, then glanced at his image on the projector screen. He seemed entranced by the sight, squinting to make it out behind the harsh lights trained on his eyes. Good. That's what Trapp wanted. Every time the prisoner saw himself, saw the state he was in, it would redouble his fear.

"Or maybe I should start with me," Trapp said. "Tell you a little about myself."

That got the man's attention.

"You see, I think the person you work for killed a friend of mine. A very good friend. Someone I swore I would avenge."

"That's got nothing to do with me."

"Yes," Trapp agreed. "And no. You see –" He paused, frowning and looking intently at the prisoner, forcing him to stare directly into his cold, hard eyes. "I'm sorry, I never asked your name. How rude."

The change of direction startled the man. He answered automatically, like all humans abhorring an awkward silence, before clamming up. "James, James –"

"Well, it's nice to meet you, James. You see, yes, my friend's death has nothing *directly* to do with you. But right now, you're the only lead I have. So you see, it really *is* your problem, because I can't let you out of this room until I know who you are working for."

"You'll just kill me," James said, eyes wild, spittle flicking out of his lips and arcing in the bright floodlight. "If I tell you anything. Or he will."

By the tone of the man's voice, Trapp knew that 'he' wasn't anyone in this room. It was whomever the prisoner worked for. Whoever was next up the chain.

"Hey, Carter," Trapp called out, purposely looking over James's head and toward the back of the room. "What was the name of that prison you were telling me about?"

Dani blinked with surprise before answering. But when she did, her voice was equally cold. She was playing the game masterfully. "ADX Florence."

"And tell me, what's so interesting about Florence?"

Dani picked out the reasons on long, slender fingers that James could not see. Still, the physical action slowed her response, giving it an emotionless tone.

"You mean, aside from being the most secure prison in the federal system? They've never had anyone escape. No one's ever even bothered to try. Inmates spend twenty-three hours in your cell every day, with one hour yard time. Oh, and even that's in a cage, all on their own."

Trapp turned so that he was out of the prisoner's eyeline. He winked at Dani before speaking, then crouched down in front of him.

"You know, James, I went to Florence once." It was a lie, but the man could not possibly know that. "Looks like hell on earth. Most of the prisoners go mad within a year. I saw a man bashing his head against the concrete wall of his cell, just to feel alive."

"It's better than being dead," James replied, though his voice had less conviction now.

"You know, most of the prisoners think that. Until they get there. By the end of the first year, the ones who are still sane, all they do all day is work out how to kill themselves. Can you imagine that?"

James trembled, the cuffs clinking against his metal chair.

"But the guards take your shoelaces. Your cell has no fittings. No bars, just a plexiglass window. No sheets to make a noose. Nothing to hang it on, even if you succeeded. No wires with which to electrocute yourself, and a sink too shallow to drown a kitten in. You'll eat with your hands like an animal – no cutlery. That's what sends you over the edge in the end. Twenty-three hours a day in your cell, working out how to die, and never succeeding."

Trapp let the prospect hang in the air, let the man chew on the prospect of losing his entire life. He knew the kind of man who was sitting in front of him. Knew the man was a coward. Could tell from the scars around his neck. They were from a tattoo removal procedure. He knew what this man was.

"You're a neo-Nazi, aren't you, James?"

Slowly, the man's attention returned to Trapp's face. He looked unsure now. Second-guessing himself.

"What is it you call yourselves these days?" Trapp said, pretending to think. He snapped his fingers with feigned satisfaction. "That's it – white nationalists."

James didn't bother trying to deny it. "How did you know?"

Trapp shrugged. "The scars, the hair. You can try and hide it, but not from me."

"I don't want to go there," the man whimpered.

A wolfish grin stretched across Trapp's face. He had his man. Hadn't even threatened to waterboard him yet. Christ, at least the Arabs put up a good fight before they inevitably cracked. He spread his hands wide and crouched down so that he was on James's level.

"Then it's your lucky day. Tell me what I want to know and I'll let you go."

He was telling the truth. He didn't give a crap about James or what he had done in his life. He was a little fish. A pawn. Of no real importance.

"What do you want?"

"Names. Dates. Locations. Targets. Everything you know, James. I want it all."

41

Dani couldn't remember the last time she had felt this exhausted. She'd arrived at the field office straight from the safe house, but her mind was so amped up on adrenaline from what she had learned she wouldn't have been able to sleep even if she'd had the opportunity. The groan of the florescent tube lighting was giving her a headache and she massaged her throbbing temples even as her mind kept spinning.

She was in Olsen's office—that's how she still referred to it —sitting behind his glass desk, using his computer. The bronze-backed, black-etched nameplate on the front of the desk might have changed, and now read *Acting SAC, Nadine Carter*, not *SAC Rick Olsen*, but Dani knew it wasn't hers. Not really.

The implications of her attacker's story were staggering. He'd claimed that his white nationalist group was being funded and supplied by some outside party on an industrial scale, just like the terrorists who'd struck across the country the previous week. Her theory that the attacks of Bloody Monday had been staged was looking more and more plausible by the second. It was beyond belief that two such financiers could exist, each backing a different horse.

But that meant that both the Islamic terrorists from the initial wave, the Israeli mercenaries who'd killed Donahue, and now these white nationalists all inhabited the same stable— even if they didn't know it.

But who was behind it? And why?

That was the stumbling block upon which Dani's theory fell apart. And in truth, she didn't have a lick of hard evidence to back it up. The testimony of the punk that Trapp and his CIA accomplices currently had shackled to a chair in the basement of a safe house wouldn't exactly stand up in court.

Hell, although Dani was horrified when Trapp suggested to the prisoner that he might cut him loose, she was beginning to come around to the idea. After all, she couldn't exactly arrest him. It was that or put a bullet in his head – and Dani knew she wasn't the kind of person who could execute someone in cold blood, no matter what crimes they had committed.

Besides, the man had sung like a canary, spilling everything he knew. Trapp was chasing down one lead and Dani another. They had split the targets according to what each brought to the table. In Dani's case, as acting SAC, that was a hell of a lot. The first thing Dani had done after getting to work was to set the wheels in motion.

Now it was a waiting game, and Dani Carter wasn't any good at it. Her stomach was a pit of acid and her fingers drummed against the desk, combining with the hum of the lights to produce a not unpleasant tune.

She scanned her email inbox without paying much atten-tion and scrolled past the email at first. Her eyes were blurry with sleep, and her mind was distracted by the previous night's events. It took a few seconds for the subject line to process, and then a couple more before she scrolled up to locate the email again.

It was a memo from the Salt Lake City field office.

All agents be advised, it read. *An NSA employee was reported missing in the early hours of February 5. A man was found shot dead in his vehicle, which was subsequently set alight. We do not yet have a positive identification of the body but suspect it may be Dr. Timothy Greaves. At this stage we do not have a suspect. Our working hypothesis is that the murder is connected with the events of Bloody Monday.*

Everything stopped in Dani's mind when she read the cold, businesslike text of the memo. To whichever agent in Salt Lake City who had written it, the man's death would have meant nothing. The murder might be connected with Bloody Monday and the assassination of the director of the NSA, or it might just have been perpetrated by a junkie looking for a score.

But Dani knew better. She got that same feeling she had experienced in the lobby of the Hoover Building, when she first felt that something was wrong. A single neuron firing in her brain.

A warning light.

Somehow this was all connected. Donahue had flown to the NSA's black site, the Utah Data Center, shortly before he died. It stood to reason that he'd gone there to meet someone, from whom he'd learned something so vital to national security he'd requested an immediate, in-person meeting with President Nash. And now that it was very possible that his source was dead.

Quickly, making sure she wasn't being watched through the glass doors of Olsen's office, Dani snapped a picture of the memo on her screen. She loaded the app that Kyle had installed on her phone the night before and forwarded the image to Trapp. Maybe it would mean more to him.

The phone on Olsen's desk rang. She picked it up and held the receiver to her ear.

"Carter."

"Ma'am, the operation you requested is about to get underway. We've got everything set up in command ops."

THE COMMAND OPS room in the DC field office building was a rare example of its kind – it looked like something out of a Hollywood movie. Mostly, in Dani's experience, operations were run out of stuffy motel rooms, the beds removed and replaced with desks, computers, and enough empty cans of soda to make the agents on duty run to the bathroom every thirty seconds.

The room in front of her, however, looked like the nerve center it was. Large flatscreen monitor panels covered the walls on the opposite side, and almost a dozen agents and technicians manned computers that were set up on desks in a horseshoe pattern around the room, tapping away at keyboards and speaking in hushed tones into headsets.

"Where did you get the tip, Dani?" Adrian asked, sidling up to her, his eyes on the screen.

Dani paused a beat before responding, her attention on the room itself. There was a strange tension in the air, an excitement. When she had first contacted the field office in Minneapolis that morning, it hadn't taken a whole lot of arm-twisting whatsoever to get the local SAC to greenlight an operation.

It wasn't just her field office that was a wounded animal. Federal Marshals had invaded almost every FBI outpost across the country, frog marching good agents out the door. Dani's blood boiled at the thought. She knew that the marshals were just doing their job – and that getting angry at them would achieve nothing. It was the person responsible for all this who she was desperate to catch.

So when Dani informed the Minneapolis field office, which

had operational responsibility not just for Minnesota, but also both South Dakota and its more northerly neighbor, that she had information on a potential terrorist camp operating within the borders of the United States, the agents in Minneapolis jumped on the opportunity. Satellite photos were examined, probable cause identified, and a warrant quickly issued.

They were ready to get some. To prove their worth. To prove to the whole of America that the Federal Bureau of Investigation might be down, but it sure as hell was not out.

But for Dani, it was personal. Her father was in a hospital bed and her mentor in a jail cell. She owed both of them, and vowed to do whatever it took to make things right.

"That, Adrian," Dani said with a tight smile, "is between me and the man upstairs."

"You've really put your neck out on this one."

"Gee, thanks for the vote of confidence."

Dani didn't pay much attention to the unintended slight. The operation was starting. A technician working on a dual-screen monitor in front of her began giving a play-by-play. The imagery was up on the enormous battery of screens in front of them.

"The UAV will be on site in three, two, one – and we're live."

Dani's eyes were focused on the screen. The drone was flying at a height of just a couple of hundred feet. The footage was crystal clear. It showed what looked like a fast-running river cutting through an expanse of snow-covered fields. Dani felt a chill just looking at it. White caps crested on the top of the water as the drone footage panned around, revealing a series of low, single-story huts in the distance.

"What's the status of the SWAT team?" she asked.

All of this was new to her. She had sat at the edge of rooms just like this one many times before. But Dani had never been the one issuing orders. She tried to give off an air of confidence, but her stomach was fizzing.

"The aerial element is two minutes out. They've got ground support if it's needed, but the incident commander was concerned that the area might be mined with IEDs."

"Understood."

The SWAT team was flying in on two Bell 412 EP utility helicopters, painted black, with FBI lettering in yellow on the sides. They were flown by highly trained pilots from the FBI's Tactical Helicopter Unit, which recruited many of its pilots from the US Army's famed 160th Special Operations Aviation Regiment, a group known as the Night Stalkers. The pilots were the best of the best. Dani hoped they wouldn't need to be.

She watched the footage, marveling at how times had changed since she'd joined the Bureau. Even a few years before, none of this had been possible. Back then, agents at headquarters had to sit on their hands and wait for a phone call from the agents on the ground.

Now she could watch footage shot from the chase helicopter and monitor chestcam feeds from cameras mounted on every single SWAT team member in either helicopter. It was like playing a video game.

"I'm not seeing any signs of life here," said the technician studying the drone footage. "We've got recent signs of activity, track marks in the snow, but no heat signatures. Looks like they might have already cleared out."

Dani wanted to remind the agent in charge of the SWAT team to not get cocky. Just in case this was an ambush. She bounced from foot to foot, the adrenaline which had faded for the last couple of hours now resurgent. She cracked her knuckles and ignored her selfish desire to get involved. The men on that helicopter were as well-trained as anyone could be. They didn't need her help. They had this.

"Helicopter insertion in five."

Dani watched as a dozen highly-trained FBI SWAT team members fast-roped from the two Bell helicopters, six from each. Two snipers remained on each aircraft, providing over-watch, constantly scanning for targets.

There was a segment of a TV screen on the wall assigned to each of the agents' chestcams and numbered accordingly. Dani held her breath, hoping that in the next few seconds none of them would go black.

"Cover right, cover right," she heard, and then, "clear, clear."

Dani watched as door after door was kicked in, each time the sound echoing like a gunshot through the operations room's tinny speakers as one cabin after another was searched, cleared, and found unoccupied. She breathed out a sigh of relief. It looked like the encampment really was empty. She didn't know if that was a good or a bad thing.

Maybe it really was just a corporate team building facility after all. Closed for the winter, because what kind of nut job visits South Dakota in February if they don't have to? Maybe the man who had shown up at her door last night was just some wacko.

And then she saw it.

"Holy shit."

Dani realized that the speaker was one of the SWAT team agents. It was hard to disagree with the man's assessment. The image transmitted from his chest camera was shocking. The building looked just like all of the others on the Pilgrim encampment. But where those had mostly contained sleeping quarters, bathrooms and cooking facilities, this...

This was an armory.

The agent moved around the room checking for booby-traps. Dani's eyes were glued to the image. There must have been hundreds of identical AR-15 rifles. Dozens of military-style green ammunition crates. Tables stacked with submachine guns, grenades, Semtex, C4. The room was in a state of chaos, as though the occupants of the camp had left in a rush.

Dani pictured the scene. Skinheads tooling up. Getting

ready for war. And going – where? Where were they now? What targets were they preparing to strike?

Adrian breathed out. "If this is what they left behind..."

Dani's head fell forward. She hadn't known what she was expecting, but it certainly wasn't this. There was enough ammunition in that one hut alone to mount a medium-sized war. Adrian was right. If the white nationalists had been able to leave this much hardware behind when they cleared out, what the hell had they taken with them?

"Command, we've got something else."

"What is it?" Dani said. "Put it up on the main screen."

The technician did as ordered and footage from a new chest camera replaced that of the armory. It showed a dead man in the snow, his face pale and his lips blue with cold. He lay face down on the ground, his body partly buried by blown snow. He was wearing denim jeans that looked frozen stiff as boards, and a shapeless plaid winter jacket. The white ground was painted a splattered red, but the man had died instantly from a gunshot to the brain, so there was little additional bleeding. Dani figured the corpse would have frozen solid within an hour.

"Search him," an agent commanded. The speaker's rifle danced in and out of the frame, both covering the body and searching for fresh targets. Dani watched as another SWAT team member frisked the body, his movements efficient and professional.

"Nothing. He's clean," the agent reported. "No weapon, no papers, nothing. But he looks like a veteran. He's got a unit tattoo, along with some other real hinky shit, and what looks like a VA leg."

What the hell does this mean?

Dani bit her lip, trying to figure out what to do. The body was a red herring, but it didn't change anything. If the camp was empty, that meant God knows how many terrorists were on the loose – and they were equipped with enough lethal hardware to make Bloody Monday look like a rehearsal.

"We need to run this up the chain. The director needs to know. Get him on the line. Now."

The technician who had been monitoring the drone footage looked up at Dani, her face ashen.

"I think it's already too late."

42

The mega-church was situated in the Timbergrove neighborhood of Houston, Texas, and had a weekly attendance approaching thirty-five thousand souls. Time Magazine had recently profiled its minister, the Reverend Rafael Tucker, describing him as "the nearest thing to a superstar in the entire African Methodist Episcopal Church."

The congregation was primarily black, although it had begun to reach out into the broader community. Building bridges, the good Reverend Tucker preached, was the same as loving God.

Like everything that had happened up to this point, the church was part of a far greater strategy. It was chosen because it was over one thousand two hundred miles away from Washington DC, in America's heartland. It was a distraction. The eyes of the world would turn to Texas. Americans would be crying out for their President to reassure them, and he would not be able to resist the call.

The initial wave of Arab terrorist attacks had shocked America out of her complacency. No longer did Americans think themselves safe, whether they lived in the countryside or the city. They could be killed anywhere. On the street, on a train, at a basketball game. Even at home.

Rawlin scratched his birthmark unconsciously as he checked his men one last time.

There were six, including himself, all dressed in the green fatigues and black combat gear of the FBI's Hostage Rescue Team. Each man was Caucasian, and no longer bore the traces of the arm and face tattoos that had marked them for so long. They sat patiently, facing each other in the back of a stolen utility company truck that was parked just off the North Loop freeway. Each of the men had a large rucksack held securely between their legs. The bags contained death.

"You good, Steve?" Rawlin asked, patting the man next to him on the shoulder. He was pale, sweating slightly, and kept soundlessly mumbling to himself.

Rawlin grimaced. He had chosen these men carefully, but Steve was making him wonder if he'd messed up. Each had killed before, and not in a drunken bar fight, not in a prison brawl, but in broad daylight, just because they didn't like the color of another man's skin. Or another woman's skin, for that matter. Rawlin wasn't squeamish with details like that, not with so much to play for.

They were the best of the best. Rawlin's elite, fighters he had hand-picked from the hundreds of similar men who had graduated his Pilgrim training camp.

Steve nodded, almost as though to convince himself. His hands gripped his rifle, white knuckling it. "I'm good, boss," he said. "You don't need to worry about me."

"Who said I was worried?" Rawlin grinned.

It was the truth. He wasn't worried in the slightest. Even if Steve lost his nerve, he had four other men with him who wouldn't. Hard men. Men who had done time, spent years of their lives in prison gangs, fighting for scraps of food, for respect, and simply for the right to see another day. Men that

his nameless benefactor had sprung from jail and sent his way
for a reason.

They would not fail him.

"Everyone remember the plan?" Rawlin asked.

Five heads nodded in unison. They had been through it so
many times that some of the men had begun to recite the steps
in their sleep.

"You don't need a speech from me. Just know that I'm proud
to fight alongside you. If we die today, then so be it. We fell
firing the first shots of a revolution. And if the tree of liberty has
to be refreshed with the blood of patriots, then I can't think of
anyone better to die alongside."

One of the men made a fist and punched his chest. "Fuck
yeah!"

It wasn't quite as eloquent a riposte as the moment
demanded, but it did the job.

"Damn straight. Everybody check your camera feeds, and
let's do this."

THE CHURCH WAS MORE like a sports arena than the house of
God that Rawlin had grown up attending. The sound was
different than he remembered. Not a calm, reverent choir
singing hymns of praise to the Lord, but loud gospel music,
punctuated by shouts of "hallelujah" from the good reverend
himself. The doors to the main hall were closed, so the music
was still somewhat subdued. The bass, however, was not. It
reverberated through the building, Rawlin's boots and his
entire body.

"Can I help you?" a man asked. He was dressed in a light
gray suit, oversized for his frame. His eyes were narrowed with
a mix of curiosity and fear.

Rawlin growled a curt response. "FBI."

As he barged past the greeters, his men filing behind him into lines, their weapons pointed at the ground, faces set with grim determination, his face puckered into a scowl. The place sickened him.

It wasn't the blacks. Hell, you could say a lot about them, but at least they knew their place. Stuck together, instead of mixing with good, honest, white folk. No, for once it was his own people who made him want to hurl. Why the hell did they voluntarily come to a place like this? Out of the corner of his eye, he saw a blond girl, pale as milk, linked arm in arm with her boyfriend. What the fuck did she see in him? How could she betray her own race this way?

The bitch deserved to die. Rawlin made a note to end her himself if he got the chance.

"This place fucking stinks," one of the men behind him groused. Rawlin spun and shot the man a glare. He couldn't allow anything to compromise the chances of this mission's success. Whether he agreed with the man's statement or not, he couldn't let one man screw up the mission.

Two enormous double doors led into the mega-church's huge atrium. The men split into two teams, one heading for each of the sets of doors. Around them, confused faces were turned in their direction, but Rawlin believed in the power of authority. Those three little letters stenciled on his men's combat vests would get them in anywhere.

God bless the FBI.

Rawlin gave the order. "Go."

His men shouldered the doors. On each side one hung back to guard the exit. Two more men ran straight to the other side of the room, cutting off the emergency exits. Rawlin strode confidently down the aisle toward the enormous raised pulpit, his weapon slung calmly across his chest.

The preacher fell silent, taking the music with him. He was squinting up at Rawlin and his men, his hand over his eyes in order to see past the floodlights shining down on him. A gospel choir stood behind him, arranged in raised rows. They looked at each other nervously. Behind him were two massive screens, upon which the man of God appeared, blown up to hundreds of times his normal size.

Good, Rawlin thought.

No one in this room would ever forget what happened today. No one who survived, anyway. And if he did his job right, there would be few enough of those.

"What is the meaning of this?" the Rev. Tucker roared into his microphone. "Sir, this is a house of God. I implore you to take your weapons outside."

Rawlin was filled with a vicious, animalistic glee. This was what he had been working his entire life toward. The pain of his childhood. The army. Those years spent lost in the wilderness before he found his true calling.

Fuck your God, Rawlin thought.

But he didn't say it. Not yet. He needed these people compliant and pliable. If the congregation turned from mild alarm to panic, which could happen in a matter of seconds when dealing with such large numbers of people, then things would become infinitely more difficult.

Rawlin raised his hands, palms facing forward in a gesture that signaled he came in peace. He was, of course, a wolf wearing sheep's clothing, but they didn't know that.

Not yet.

He jumped up onto the stage that looked out on the enormous mega-church. His eyes were a little blinded, just as the Reverend's were, but it did not matter. He did not need to see the crowd of worshipers to know they were there. A nervous energy filled the room now. Voices called out, asking who they were, and what they were doing. But Rawlin simply remained silent.

"Door one secure," came a voice in his earpiece.

"Two."

"Three checking in."

"Four is locked and rigged. We're good to go, boss."

Rawlin clenched his fist with quiet satisfaction. Everything was falling into place, just as he had planned. His name would go down in the history books.

"Reverend Tucker, I apologize for charging into your place of worship like this," Rawlin lied. "The Bureau received reports of an active shooter in this area, and given that your congregation is such a high-value target I was sent directly here to protect you."

The minister blinked, his eyes glistening from the reflection of the flood light overhead. He tapped a button on his lapel mic before speaking – clearly not wanting the whole congregation to listen in to his conversation with the heavily armed man who had just invaded his service.

"The Bureau?"

Rawlin nodded and lifted a faked Bureau badge and ID from around his neck, briefly flashing it at the reverend.

"Yes, Reverend, the Federal Bureau of Investigation."

"Shouldn't we evacuate?"

"No, Reverend –" Rawlin held his finger up and then touched it against his earpiece, pretending to receive a transmission. "That was the Houston field office. They just confirmed two dead. It's best we stay right where we are."

"My God," the reverend exhaled. His black forehead glistened with beads of sweat underneath the relentless heat of the lights. *Disgusting*, Rawlin thought. But the man was convinced now. He would be putty in his hands.

Rawlin nodded seriously. "Perhaps you could ask your congregation to sit down. We've got agents outside, and my men are covering each of the entrances. Everyone will be perfectly safe – as long as they stay inside. The worst thing we can do right now is panic."

"Of course, of course." The Reverend nodded. Then he squinted at Rawlin, looking at something on his vest. Rawlin's blood chilled. Had he missed something?

"Something wrong?"

"Not at all. It's just good to see the FBI wearing body cameras at long last. I'm a member of the National Convention Against Police Violence, and the Bureau was quite resistant."

Rawlin exhaled gently. An easy speedbump. One he could navigate. "It's a trial. My men were selected to participate given the frontline nature of our role. Now, perhaps you could make the announcement?"

The Reverend nodded and spoke into his microphone. Below him, Rawlin's fifth man, Steve, the one who wasn't currently guarding one of the exits, jumped up on the stage and grabbed something out of his pack. He fiddled with it, keeping the device obscured from both the stage and Reverend Tucker.

The minister's voice boomed out on the church's sound system. "There is no reason to be alarmed. We have a slight situation outside, and these fine men"—he gestured at Rawlin himself—"have been sent to keep us safe. If everyone could remain seated, I'm sure we'll all be out of here in no time at all."

Steve looked at Rawlin and nodded.

A surge of adrenaline pumped into his veins. It was time. Two years of planning, every night dreaming of this. It had all fallen into place. No one could stop him, not now. The doors were rigged with explosives, fifty pounds of Czechoslovakian Semtex packed with ball bearings for maximum effect. The second someone attempted to open the doors, whether to save these hostages or to escape, the charges would detonate and send a wave of steel hurtling toward the audience. Cutting them apart.

Potentially toppling the structure itself.

The only way out was through the service access behind the stage. And Rawlin himself had it covered. If things went well, it would be their exit route. He unclipped his side arm. Steve's signal meant that the satellite uplink was working. Everything they said and did was being transmitted out of Houston, and broadcast around the world.

"I'm sorry, Reverend," he said, striding forward, pulling the Glock into his hand. "I'm going to have to cut you off."

The man's eyes widened in alarm. "Is something wrong?"

"I'm afraid so."

"What?"

Rawlin snarled. "You."

In one swift movement, Rawlin raised his Glock, set it against the minister's temple, making sure that he was in full view of Steve's body camera, and pulled the trigger.

There was a brief moment of calm.

Then shrieks of terror.

And then the chattering of gunfire as Rawlin's men joined in the fun.

43

Randall Woods was not a proud man. That is not to say that the current speaker of the House did not have an ego—he did, and a big one. But he also knew that the game of power was a greased pole, and he was in danger of losing his grip.

He sat in his luxuriously appointed office on Capitol Hill, shining Oxfords resting on a polished mahogany desk, and pretended that he was still running the show. A grandfather clock against the wall counted out the seconds, loud in the silence of the old stone building.

"You understand what you have to do?" the voice asked.

As always, it was flat, all life drained out of it by whatever compression software its owner used. The speaker hated that he didn't know who was on the other end of the phone. Detested not knowing who was pulling his strings, making him dance to their tune.

It had been a very long time since Randall Woods had not been in control of the sheet music.

And yet the prize on offer was too big to ignore. All the trappings of the office of the leader of the free world: the jet, the White House residence, Camp David...

Besides, it wasn't like ignoring his predicament would make it go away. The dirt the voice had on him, both manufactured and real, would be enough not just to end his political career but his life as a free man.

The speaker had briefly considered fleeing the country. He was wealthy beyond most men's wildest dreams. Two decades at the summit of Goldman Sachs is enough to provide for a very comfortable retirement indeed. He could have summoned a private jet and been sipping cocktails on the beach of a South American country without an extradition treaty in a matter of hours. Lived a life of luxury, switched expensive Italian wool for tailored linen suits and a straw fedora, the whole nine yards.

But Randall dismissed that option out of hand. He hadn't needed reminding that whoever the voice was, he was the kind of man willing to risk everything on a throw of the die. Whoever it was would not let him live, knowing what he did. He could go to the press, but say what? That it was okay, he had screwed a whore, not an underage girl who'd been kidnapped from her parents?

Yeah, good luck getting out of that one.

"I understand," Randall replied.

It wasn't much of an ask, really. After all, the President hadn't just agreed to the address to both Houses of Congress already; he had requested it himself. Spent the transition twisting arms on Capitol Hill to make it happen. Of course, the circumstances had changed, but wasn't Nash a man of his word?

"This is how it begins, Randy," the voice said, and even through the compression algorithm, the speaker thought he detected a hint of pleasure in the man's voice. "This is how you become the leader of the free world."

Randall paused. There was a worm in his stomach; it had

been gnawing at him for days. "And what then? What will you ask from me?"

The voice took a long time to reply. The speaker wanted to know what the quid pro quo was. Why was the voice offering to make him President? Gifts of that magnitude didn't get handed out like candy. There was always a quid pro quo. You scratch my back, I'll scratch yours. The speaker wanted to know what he would have to give up.

The answer was simple. "Everything."

RANDALL WOODS STRODE out into the cramped House of Representatives press briefing room, feeling not so much a spring in his step as lead weights glued to his soles. If he said what he had been instructed to say, acted as he was instructed to act, then there would be no going back. He would cross his own personal Rubicon and have to live with the consequences.

But did he have a choice?

And anyway, wasn't this the game? The reason everyone came to Washington DC. Not for riches or celebrity – but *power*. The power to shape lives, and for one man, sitting behind the desk of the oval office in the White House itself, the power to end them.

If he so wanted, to end every life on earth.

It wasn't just fear that propelled Randall forward. It was avarice. The dream of total, unconditional power.

The briefing room was pleasant, if cramped. It was carpeted with a thick blue material, and behind the podium were shots of the dome of the Capitol Building and flags bearing the insignia of the House of Representatives.

"Thank you for coming here today," he said, leaning forward and into the microphone. In front of him was a smattering of journalists, maybe a dozen of them, seated on folding chairs set out for twice that number.

It stung Randall's ego, but it didn't matter. Soon enough, he would exchange the House press briefing room for the one in the White House. And then, the seats would be full. He would remember those who had shown him respect today, as well as those who hadn't.

"Today has been another horrible day in American history," he said, puffing his chest out and assuming a Churchillian gravitas. "After Bloody Monday, we all hoped we would never see such tragedy again."

Randall looked down, beyond the podium and at the assembled reporters, few of whom were paying much attention at all. Many tapped away on laptops. He imagined that most of them had sat through half a dozen similar briefings today after the news of the atrocity in Houston had begun to filter out. Hell, maybe some of those briefings had taken place in this very room. The reporters before him were probably filing copy to their news desks at this very moment.

"But see it we have," Randall continued. "An act of terror more horrifying than any of those that preceded it. Americans have a right to be safe in their homes, their communities, and their places of worship. I pledge the power of this great House, and that I will give everything to protect the American people and preserve their way of life."

More boredom. A polite cough. The rainfall plinking of keyboards. Randall wasn't having quite the impact he had anticipated when he practiced the speech in the mirror that morning.

"In times of terror such as these, I believe it is important – no, *vital*—that we show that we are not afraid of these terrorists. We do not fear the evil they hope to spread. We can and we *must*"—he pounded his fist against the flat of his open palm—

"show these animals that we will not allow them to disrupt our daily lives, or prevent us from doing the things we love."

He paused for effect, knowing that even if the reporters in front of him were not paying attention, that by the evening this footage would be on every news network.

"And so, Mr. President, I invite you to address both Houses of Congress in a Joint Session. We must show the American people that we are not afraid. And that neither is their President. Thank you."

PRESIDENT CHARLES NASH was in the Oval Office, re-reading the *Wall Street Journal* hitpiece for the thousandth time when he saw Speaker Woods' red-faced grandstanding on a muted television in his office. The words of his speech flashed up on the screen.

At first, the President barely glanced up. When his subconscious finally finished processing what the speaker was saying, the ember of rage already smoldering in Nash's mind went supernova. Bloody Monday, the death of Director Donahue, the attack in Houston, and that morning's article in the *Journal* – each event was a body blow more desperate than the last.

And now *this.*

He punched the intercom button on the phone that sat on top of the Resolute desk. "Karen, get Martinez in here now."

Before he lifted his finger his chief of staff burst through the door of his private study, which adjoined the Oval Office. Her dark skin was flushed, lips tight with frustration.

"Mr. President, you need to see –"

Nash cut her off. "Emma, I thought Homeland Security told us the address to a joint session of Congress was too great a security risk?"

Martinez nodded. "They did, sir. The Secret Service agreed

that it was a no-go. You'd be too big of a target, and one they couldn't guarantee to protect without stripping the cupboard bare and leaving the rest of the city at risk. We were calling it off. Quietly, so it didn't make the press."

"Well, it's too late for that. What the hell is Randall doing?" Nash snapped. "He's supposed to be our guy!"

"I don't know, Mr. President," Martinez said through gritted teeth. She was clearly embarrassed, and although Nash would ordinarily cut her some slack, it was her job to stop things like this happening.

"And you didn't know he was planning this? This... *stunt*."

The redness on Martinez's cheeks doubled. Nash took no joy in humiliating his chief of staff, but sometimes a display of authority was necessary. Events were not supposed to surprise the leader of the free world. Martinez should have been on top of it.

And yet, here they were.

She ground her teeth together. "I'm sorry, Mr. President."

"Don't be sorry, just don't screw up again," Nash said. He sat back down behind the Resolute desk and let out an angry sigh. "Belay that. I shouldn't have let anger get the better of me."

Martinez accepted her boss's apology with a tight-lipped smile. She didn't look like she wanted it. Then again, Nash reflected, that was why he had said it – knowing that with her type A personality, anything less than complete success was a miserable failure.

"Well what the hell are we going to do about it?" He said. "And what's in it for him? Airtime?"

"We have to do it," she said. "You'll have to give the speech, or the whole country will think you're a coward and you'll be a lame duck from the opening bell. There's no way around it. But I'll find out what game he's playing, Mr. President. You have my word."

"See that you do," Nash said, returning to his desk. "And Martinez?"

"Yes, sir?"

Nash picked up the well-thumbed copy of the *Journal*. Every sinew strained as he attempted to control waves of not only anger, but long restrained grief. You never recovered from the death of a child, merely learned to process the pain. Some days were better than others. Anything could bring back a memory: a scent, the memory of a meal. But it wasn't often the culprit was a front-page article in the *Journal*. The black print had hit Nash like a garbage truck.

"Find out who the hell Rita Mason is. And why she's writing about my dead son."

Martinez nodded and spoke quietly as she left. "Yes, Mr. President."

Nash stood alone in the center of the Oval, biting his tongue to distract himself from the pain. Even three years later, the image of his son's once handsome, then gaunt face filled his mind. All prior memories of his beautiful boy growing up were forever pushed aside by that one horrible crime scene photo of George with a needle in his arm, lips blue, collapsed on the floor.

In truth, Nash knew, George's death was what had driven him through the campaign. Though he claimed to his wife that he wanted to stop other families going through the devastation they had, the truth was that for Nash, the presidential campaign was an all-encompassing distraction. A distraction from his grief, and from his mounting troubles at home.

Through the campaign, most reputable news outlets had skirted the topic of George's death. But that honeymoon was clearly over. The *Journal* article claimed that he was in a state of numbed panic inside the White House, refusing the counsel of advisors and letting the country burn around him. A modern day King Lear—not broken by grief, but cowed by it into a state of dangerous indecision.

And yet, Nash knew, though the article was a hit piece, a collection of lies and distortions, it also contained a kernel of truth. He *was* sleepwalking to disaster, and allowing events to dictate the course of his Presidency, rather than the other way round.

The American people expected better from their President, and Nash desperately wanted to be the man they deserved. The man they thought they had voted for. He needed to stop playing defense.

To go on the attack.

But the question was – *how?*

44

"**Y**ou cannot be serious," Trapp groaned.

He hated politicians. Even if he had spent his entire adult life defending their right to exist. To hold press conferences. To bloviate, pontificate, procrastinate and generally stand in the way of American progress.

Unfortunately, there was nothing more American than free speech. Trapp would spend his life to defend it. Even if that meant men like Randall Woods had to be allowed to share in the privilege. Still, Trapp could have avoided his present heartburn if only he hadn't turned on the radio in the surveillance van. If only he hadn't listened to the speaker's press conference.

What kind of idiot, Trapp wondered, would consider holding a Joint Session of Congress at a time like this? At a time when there were more bodies littering American streets than any time since the Civil War. It was a giant flashing 'come and get me' sign, a neon target on the back of a country that was on the brink of total disaster.

Trapp knew the answer. A politician.

As far as he was concerned, there was only one good lawmaker in the whole country and that was the president,

Charles Nash. He seemed like a good man, not interested in political gameplaying, horse trading, pork barreling, and the usual exploits of the Capitol's power players.

No, Nash seemed trustworthy. He was a veteran, and while that wasn't an automatic seal of approval in Trapp's book, it was certainly a step in the right direction. And he seemed driven by the death of his son rather than personal gain, though Trapp couldn't honestly say he'd followed much of the campaign.

But then again, maybe it was just because Nash was new. Perhaps he would end up no different from the rest of them. Weak. Greedy. Trapp guessed only time would tell.

But either way, it wasn't Trapp's business. He was chasing down a lead – running down a list of locations the prisoner had given them the previous night. The first two had been a bust.

He just hoped he'd have more luck with the last.

"IT'S A SHELL GAME, TRAPP," Kyle said through his earpiece.

"The warehouse is owned by a corporation registered in the Cayman Islands. But I pierced the shield on that one, and it led to another shell company in Singapore, then one in Germany. I'll keep looking, but I guarantee it's a dead end."

Trapp was in the back of a van parked on Vine Street, in a mixed residential and business district just north of Washington, DC. The area was rundown, and Trapp got the sense that it had never even seen better days. Tufts of green pushed past the paving stones and the road markings had long faded away. Potholes scarred the road, reminding him of the surface of the moon.

"I'm guessing that's not normal," he replied, peeling his eyes away from a set of binoculars. The day was settling into an evening gloom, and it was getting difficult to make out the warehouse at this distance.

"Seems unlikely," Kyle agreed. "Have you seen any activity?"

"Not a whole lot," Trapp admitted. "But there are a couple of vehicles parked outside. A black SUV, and a gray sedan. Could be someone holed up inside."

Then again, it could be nothing.

They had prised the warehouse's location out of the would-be assassin. Their prisoner claimed that it was a staging area, although he didn't know for what. He was still at the safe house, chained to a chair. Trapp had no intention of letting him go unless this lead panned out.

"What else have we got?" Trapp asked, setting the binoculars on the man's floor and picking up a night vision scope, which he raised to his eye. "If this doesn't work out."

Kyle paused before replying. "Not a whole lot. Agent Carter sent over an FBI memo a few hours ago that I've been looking into, but it's not much of a lead."

"Dumb it down for me."

"Local police found an NSA employee murdered two days ago near the data center in Utah. The same day as Donahue was killed. The guy was called Greaves. I've heard of him before. He was a legend."

"He must've been who Donahue went to meet," Trapp mused.

"That's what we're thinking. The locals found drug paraphernalia near Greaves' vehicle and chalked it up to a deal gone wrong. For some reason nobody noticed he was gone for a couple of days, until this morning. The Bureau sent someone down from Salt Lake to check it out, but Dani hasn't sent anything else over yet."

"Did the Israelis get to him?" Trapp asked.

"Your guess is as good as mine. If you don't find anything at the warehouse, then I guess we'll have to find some way of getting you down to Utah. But I don't see how we can get you in the air, not without someone noticing."

"And driving will take a day and a half," Trapp growled. "We don't have time for that."

"Precisely," Kyle agreed. "So let's hope you turn something up tonight. And there's something else."

"Go on."

"Dani's going directly to FBI Director Rutger on this. It's our only shot at stopping this address to Congress. But we don't have anything solid. Right now we need a smoking gun, and you're the only one who can get it."

45

Washington DC was in lockdown. If security had been tight before the assassination of the director of the NSA, it was ironclad now. The combat air patrol in the night skies over the capitol had been doubled, then tripled, and it seemed like almost every thirty seconds the terrifying roar of a fighter jet passing over the city could be heard, the glow of their engines just visible against the darkening sky.

The National Guard had been federalized, and armored vehicles were all over the DC area. Grunts with automatic weapons were sitting on every airfield bigger than a postage stamp from DC to Boston. Nothing was getting in the air, let alone close to the District of Columbia, without being shredded by a hail of lead.

Agent Dani Carter wondered whether it would be enough. Ever since her father had landed in the hospital, she had begun to question the old certainties. The old leatherneck was the toughest guy she'd ever known, her rock throughout her lonely childhood. For all intents and purposes, he was invincible. And yet their faceless enemy had reached out and gotten to him in the heart of the FBI. Maybe nowhere was safe.

She watched, throat thick with worry, as the lead elements of FBI Director Vince Rutger's motorcade came into view. A dark painted FBI armored vehicle was at the front, with an agent manning a fifty caliber M2 Browning machine gun hanging out the top. Behind that were almost a dozen identical black SUVs, one of which presumably contained the director himself.

Dani gulped. She traced her path backward. How the hell had she ended up in this situation? Just a couple of weeks ago she was working mid-level terrorism cases. Now she was the acting special agent in charge of the Washington DC Field Office – a position ordinarily held by an agent with well over a decade of seniority on her.

The armored vehicle screamed past her, its engine coughing up almost enough black smoke to choke her. It didn't stop, nor did the next three SUVs. Dani wondered if they had forgotten they were supposed to pick her up. A pebble skittered past her black shoes.

Finally, the fourth SUV slowed to a stop by the curb and an agent jumped out, clad in black military-style fatigues, combat webbing, and armed with a rifle. On the other side of the vehicle, she heard another set of boots, and presumed the man's action was being mirrored by another agent.

"Get in," an agent growled at her, stepping out of one of the SUVs and bringing a black rifle to his shoulder. He jerked his finger at the SUV that had pulled up just behind his, then panned the weapon in search of targets.

"That one. Move!"

She did as she was told, half-running to the SUV. An agent climbed out, opened the back door, and practically bundled her in. Before the door closed behind her, the convoy started moving again. The whole thing went like clockwork, and as

Dani craned her neck to look back, she realized that neither the vehicles at the front or rear of the convoy had ever stopped.

Because that's what it was, Dani thought. A convoy, not a motorcade. She never imagined she would see something like this on the streets of America. It seemed more suited to wartime Iraq.

But then, that's what this was. Wartime. And the enemy could be anywhere. Heck, that's exactly what she was here to talk about.

"Thanks for joining me," Director Rutger boomed, his thick, gruff voice almost filling the inside of the SUV. He grinned. "Sorry about the charade. They're taking my security very seriously after what happened on the bridge."

"That's understandable," Dani agreed. She felt off-balance in the director's presence.

He was a bull of a man, she noted. Even though he was in his early 60s, with white hair to boot, underneath his gray suit jacket his chest was that of a college crew rower. She thought she remembered reading a profile of him from just a couple of years before in the New York Times, in which he'd proudly boasted of a two-thousand-meter sprint time of just over six minutes.

Not bad, Dani thought, wryly remembering her last experience on a rowing machine, which had ended up with her on her ass, red as a lobster and almost passed out from dehydration.

"Terrible what happened to the man, of course," Rutger growled, "but all this is a little unseemly, don't you think?"

Dani nodded, noticing the man's well-spoken, almost old-world tone. It sounded strange, paired with his deep, gruff voice. "It doesn't feel very American."

"Ha!" The director's loud explosion of laughter startled Dani. "Nail on the head, Agent carter. The sooner we can wrap these terror networks up and get back to our normal lives, the better. Which brings me," he said with a gleam in his eye, "to the reason you are here, Carter. Exactly why did you need to speak to me so urgently?"

Dani wiped her suddenly clammy hands against her pants. If she went through with this, if she told the director what she knew, or even what she suspected, the inevitable question would be how she had come across the information. And the answer to that particular question could easily have her spend the rest of her life in a maximum security federal prison.

Dani asked herself seriously – was that a risk she was really willing to take?

The answer came immediately.

Yes.

"Sir, I need to apologize to you. I've placed you in a lot of danger by asking for this meeting."

Rutger frowned.

"Carter, I am the director of the Federal Bureau of Investigation. My detail heads off at least a dozen threats to my life each month. So I'm used to being a target, believe me. And you know what they say in Baltimore?"

Dani shook her head quizzically.

Rutger grinned. "You come at the king, you best not miss."

"I didn't realize you were a fan of the *Wire*," Dani said with surprise.

"Be very careful about what you say next, Agent Carter." Rutger smiled. "I'm not that old. Yet."

"No, sir," Dani grinned. She was beginning to like the director. He seemed like a take no shit kind of guy, which was rare enough in Washington DC, in her experience. And they needed a man like him right now. Because at the moment they were fighting with one hand tied behind their back.

"My wife got me into it. I usually hate those crime dramas. So unrealistic. But every man has his vice. Now, why don't you start by telling me what was so urgent?"

"Yes, sir," Dani agreed. She swallowed nervously, and then began. "Director. I need your help."

"Go on."

"We need to stop the President from speaking to Congress."

"You're telling me..."

Dani paused. That wasn't the reaction she had expected. She had anticipated a battle, not immediate agreement. "Wait, you're on board?"

Rutger snorted. "Are you kidding? I don't know whose damn fool idea it was, but that's politics for you."

He leaned toward Dani and continued. "Every three letter agency I can think of advised against this event. CIA, NSA, CTC, DHS, DIA, even the fucking Coast Guard, for all I know."

"So why's it still going ahead?" Dani asked with a frown.

"Politicians," Rutger spat. "The second Randall Woods offered that invitation up to the President, he couldn't refuse it. He would have looked weak, and believe me, if there's one thing the American people hate, it's a weak President."

Dani shrugged. "Better weak than dead."

"You would think so," Rutger said. "But that's not how things work in this town. And I'm not so sure I agree." He furrowed his brow and settled back against the leather seat of the SUV, eyeing her with renewed interest. "But that is beside the question. Why are *you* so dead set against it?"

This was it, Dani knew. The moment of truth. The last second she could back out without revealing everything.

But the decision was already made. All this was just window dressing. Dani knew that she wasn't the kind of person who could sit on something this big just to save her own hide. She imagined what her father would say if he knew she'd considered something like that. The look on his face. The shame.

"Sir, I've been running..." Dani paused, stretching for the

correct terminology. "I suppose you could call it an unconventional sort of operation."

"Go on."

"Director, about six months ago, a CIA agent named Jason Trapp was reported dead after a building his team assaulted blew up."

"And?"

"Earlier this week, Jason Trapp shot two terrorists dead in Boston, saving hundreds of lives. A few hours later, an F-16 discharged a two thousand pound air-to-ground guided munition after a military communication system was penetrated. The target was Trapp. A few days after that, we picked up Trapp's prints on a weapon that was found at the scene of Director Donahue's assassination."

"Why the hell haven't I heard anything about this?" Rutger growled.

Dani gulped. Keeping information from a man with as fearsome a reputation as Director Rutger was not something many agents tried to do – and if they did, they sure as hell didn't admit it directly to his face.

"Sir, this is where things get"—Dani paused, reaching for the word she had used a couple of seconds ago—"unconventional. Two nights ago, I apprehended a man who attempted to kill me while I slept."

"My God!" Rutger said, looking truly shocked. Dani knew that the man bled Bureau blue. The idea that any of his agents were in danger was anathema to him. "You're lucky to be alive."

"It wasn't luck, sir, it was Trapp," Dani replied. "I managed to get the drop on a shooter at my front door. But there was a backup. A sniper. And Trapp's team took him out seconds before he was able to get a shot at me."

The director didn't speak for a few seconds. When he did, his voice was low and thoughtful. "I see what you meant by unconventional, Agent Carter. Where is this man now? Because as far as I'm aware, he's not in the Bureau's custody."

"No, Director. That's why I needed to talk to you. I don't have the hard evidence. Not yet. But I think whoever is responsible for all of these attacks has a bigger plan. I think they are planning to kill the President."

A silence stretched out inside the director's armored vehicle.

"Well as it so happens, Agent Carter," Rutger said, finally breaking it, "I'm on my way to see him right now. Perhaps you'd care to join me."

46

Sunset at Washington DC's latitude fell that night just before six in the evening. Trapp would have preferred to wait until the early hours of the morning before conducting his assault. He knew that no matter how well-trained a fighter is, their reactions are dulled in the middle of the night. It is an inescapable fact of human biology.

But he didn't have a choice. Trapp needed evidence, and he needed it fast, or the address to Congress was going to go ahead. And although he had no proof, Trapp knew in his gut that something was going to happen on Capitol Hill. He didn't know what, but he knew when: two nights from this one. And since the whole world seemed to have gone mad, he might be the only person who could stop it.

If this lead came to anything, of course.

"Hangman, your window of opportunity is coming up in about thirty seconds," Kyle said. "Happy hunting."

Trapp acknowledged the analyst, and then contacted his backup. "Redneck, sitrep," he said into his mic.

"I'm on the roof of the scrapyard opposite the warehouse.

I've got eyes on the vehicles and the front entrance, but nothing around the back. Sorry, Hangman, it's the best I can do."

"Copy," Trapp replied tersely. His wraithlike eyes studied the gloom, looking for any sign of life. But as yet, there was nothing.

Winks was back at the safe house with Mitchell and Partey, babysitting their prisoner. Trapp knew that the team was stretched thin. He didn't mind working alone, but usually preferred to have the cavalry not too far away, just in case something went wrong. Because something always went wrong.

Trapp donned his GPNVG night vision goggles. The acronym stood for Ground Panoramic Night Vision Goggle, and the device was the favored option of America's most elite war fighters – tier one special operators like SEAL Team Six and Delta. When Team Six kicked down the door of Bin Laden's hideout in Pakistan back in 2011, this is what they were wearing.

At sixty-five thousand dollars per unit, the goggles were not available to most soldiers. Not even most special operators. But Mitchell had planned well. The goggles blended ordinary night vision with an infrared heat display. When combined, the output made targets stand out as if they were painted in neon.

"I'm on the move," Trapp said. "Redneck, if anyone comes out the front, drop them."

He lowered the goggles into place, knowing that if anyone saw him he would look like an alien. But the advantage was worth it – and besides, the area was empty. Most of the warehouses were abandoned, and this close to the train tracks wasn't exactly prime residential land.

Trapp left the van, closing the door behind him quietly, and made one last check of his weapons. He was carrying an MP5, a KA-BAR knife strapped to his left thigh and a pistol holstered on his right. A pack slung over his shoulders contained a shaped demolition charge and a couple of flash bang grenades.

Trapp went over his operational plan one last time. It was simple. Blow the back door and go in all guns blazing. He didn't like it, but he didn't have a choice.

He took the fifty-yard distance between the van and the side entrance to the warehouse at a slow run, following the train tracks. Right on cue, a freight train passed, traveling at no more than twenty miles an hour, but creating enough noise that Trapp knew there was no chance of his footsteps being overheard.

The night was clear and he didn't truly need the goggles yet, with most of a full moon shining overhead. But there was no light emanating from within the warehouse, so he knew they would be vital inside.

He reached the side of the dilapidated building just a few seconds later, his heartrate barely elevated. It wasn't that his fitness was returning—even at the worst of his recovery Trapp had maintained a reasonable base—but his comfort with situations of extreme danger. A one-man assault on a warehouse containing an unknown number of tangos certainly counted.

"I'm in position," he murmured into his throat mic, so low that he could barely hear himself.

"Copy," Perkins replied. "Still nothing out front."

Trapp took a deep breath, then lowered the pack from his shoulders. He extracted the breaching charge – a small amount of C-4 plastic explosive. He was no demolitions expert, so the amount of plastic might be an overkill. But Trapp figured that it was better to use too much than not enough.

Through the scope of his goggles, the world was lit up in a green glow. Unlike cheaper models, the GPNVG did not noticeably narrow Trapp's field of view. His situational awareness would not be perfect, but it would be a damn sight better than anyone on the other side of the warehouse's corrugated iron walls.

Trapp took a few seconds to master his breathing. That

sense of unease began to rise in the pit of his stomach. The sense that this time he would finally screw up. That someone would put a bullet in his skull, instead of the other way round. He didn't fight it.

He *savored* it.

There was a reason he was so good at his job. Trapp feared death, and he would do anything to escape its clutches. The fear made him feel alive, made him pay attention to sounds and smells and movements most other men would miss.

His pregame ritual complete, he pressed the plastic explosive into place around the door's lock. The door itself was metal, and he wondered if it would be barred on the other side. Perhaps he should have added more plastique.

Demolitions was a science unto itself, and its foremost practitioners were highly skilled. Trapp was merely a layman. To him, more equaled better. Even so, he knew the basics. The shaped strip charge would cut through the lock, and hopefully anything else holding the door in place. It was ignited by a radio-controlled detonator, the control unit for which he held in his right hand.

"Good to go," he whispered. "Breaching in three."

Trapp got to cover. This was the downside of explosive breaching. Unlike ballistic methods, a complex term for an action that can be better described as battering a door down, using explosive charges involves some risk for the operator. Risk like losing a limb. But more importantly, because Trapp couldn't get so close to the door, it added a few seconds in between the moment of the breach and the entry – neutering the element of surprise. That was what the flash bangs were for.

After a silent countdown, Trapp depressed the switch in his hand. A millisecond later, the charge ignited, blowing the door open. The sound was deafening, and he felt the impact of the shockwave as a physical blow. He sprang into action, pulling the pin from the flash bang grenade with one movement, and charging toward the door with another. He threw it inside, then stuck his fingers in his ears and sheltered behind the wall.

Smoke filled the air, both from the flash bang that detonated with a heavy *crump*, and the earlier C-4. Trapp hefted his MP5, finger on the trigger, and stepped into the warehouse.

He moved fast, the stock of the weapon at his shoulder, his feet moving almost like a dancer's – elegant and graceful. He cleared left, then right, moving in a choreographed routine.

The inside of the warehouse was lit up in a ghostly green. Trapp felt like he was playing a videogame. His hearing still rang slightly from the impact of the double set of explosions. Adrenaline surged through his system, giving him the edge he didn't so much need as crave.

But there was nothing. As Trapp entered the room, nobody fired back. He saw no one. As far as he could tell, the warehouse was empty. It was pitch black, though his goggles minimized the impact of the darkness. Crates were stacked near the walls at the far end of the warehouse, and a piece of equipment seemed to cut the large space in two. It looked like a conveyor belt, Trapp thought.

Trapp spoke quietly into his throat mic. "Control, I think this might be a bust."

As if the sound of his voice had broken a truce, the warehouse lit up with gunfire. Bright streaks flashed in Trapp's night vision, and he dived behind a concrete stanchion for cover. Bullets pinged against the warehouse's far steel wall, and several more chewed up the concrete floor where he had only just been standing. Dust and smoke coated his mouth. The gunfire was coming from two directions, at opposite ends of the warehouse.

"Scratch that, I've got contact. Two shooters."

Trapp cursed himself. He'd lowered his guard, and it nearly got him killed. He vowed not to screw up again. But he didn't have time to think. Only to react. The warehouse was lit up in flashes, as though by a photographer's camera. He crouched low behind the stanchion and let his mind tackle the problem.

Two shooters. They had been lying in wait. No lights, so they knew someone was coming. It was an ambush, and they had nearly got their man.

But not quite.

Trapp listened out for the source of the gunfire. The shooters were well-positioned, set up behind cover at the opposite side of the warehouse, each manning a different corner. Their fields of fire were clear – and he was right in the middle. In front of him the stanchion was getting chewed up by a hail of lead, chips flaking out and covering the floor like snow. Trapp knew it was only a matter of time before the shooters would hit him.

Crap.

Jason Trapp wasn't good at a lot of things. Holding down a steady job that didn't involve killing men for a living, for example. But he was damn good at thinking on his feet. A savant when it came to surviving situations that few other men could. He grabbed the one remaining flash bang grenade from his left thigh pocket and readied it in his hand. He waited for a break in the firing, and then screamed at the top of his voice.

"Charlie team, flank right!"

The sound of his hoarse voice cut through the momentary silence in the warehouse. Trapp almost saw the confusion on his opponents' faces. But he didn't stop. He pulled the pin from the flash bang and tossed it toward the gunman farthest from him. He counted to three, averted his eyes and plugged his ears.

The second the flash bang detonated, Trapp rushed the nearest shooter, sidestepping the abandoned conveyor belt with his MP5 submachine gun pressed to his shoulder. He fired a three-round burst and the man fell to the ground, dead before he even realized that Trapp had moved.

Trapp knew that the advantage of surprise would only last so long. He rushed down the center of the warehouse, using the conveyor belt for cover. The darkness was daylight to him, and the second shooter hadn't yet resumed firing. He heard the man's voice.

"Jake? That you?"

Trapp mumbled noncommittally. The man shouted out again, peeking up over a row of crates that he had been using for cover. His voice was tight with fear. Trapp didn't have time to get a bead on him before his head ducked back down.

"You see him? I can't see him, man. You get him?"

Trapp didn't answer. The second he reached the end of the conveyor belt, he withdrew a magazine from his thigh pocket, threw it to his right and sprinted to his left, rounding the crates. In the green glow of the night vision, he saw the man staring toward the source of the sound in the darkness. And then he put a bullet in his brain.

Trapp didn't stop. He cleared the rest of the warehouse, checking behind every crate, every piece of disused machinery. But the place was empty. For real, this time.

"Control, Hangman. Both shooters are dead. I think that's it."

He returned to the body of the man he had so recently killed, crouched and patted him down. The man was carrying nothing, bar extra ammunition and a wallet filled with cash, but no credit cards or identification. Trapp flicked up the scope of his goggles, pulled out a flashlight, and checked the body. The man was Caucasian and had the telltale scars of removed tattoos—just like the men they'd encountered the previous night.

Mitchell replied, not Kyle. "Copy that. You got anything else?"

Trapp scanned the warehouse with a flashlight. There was evidence of recent activity here that was at odds with the derelict front of the building he'd spent most of the afternoon scoping out. Scrapes on the floor. Recently disturbed dust. Trapp got the sense that there had been more people here than just the two shooters, perhaps many more. But whoever had been here, they were thorough. They had left behind no clue for him to follow, no leads to chase down.

Another dead end.

"Fuck!"

The fury rose in Trapp, and he kicked out at a wooden crate, releasing it as the thin material shattered against his strength. Every step he took, he stumbled. The body count kept racking up but for what? Nothing they did got them closer to an answer. Nothing helped bring Price's killers to justice. It was like building a jigsaw puzzle in the dark.

"Hangman?"

He let out a deep sigh, the anger fading and leaving him empty. "Nothing."

"Okay. Get photos of the bodies, and then get the hell out of there before the cops show up."

Trapp's earpiece buzzed again. But this time, it was Perkins.

"Hangman," he muttered. "We've got company out front."

47

The smoke inside the warehouse was beginning to thicken, making it difficult to breathe. Trapp was relieved to escape it, even if that meant jumping straight from the frying pan into the fire.

"Redneck, tell me what you've got," he said, biting back a cough. He exited the warehouse the same way he had come in, to shield his movements from this new threat. A stack of wooden pallets had started to smolder and he could already see flames bursting into existence. Another few minutes and the whole warehouse would go up.

"One vehicle. Driving fast. I only see a single occupant," came the reply.

"Armed?"

"Unclear."

A second voice joined the conversation – Mitchell's. He was apologetic, but firm.

"Guys, I'm sorry to interrupt, but if you're going to get me something, I need it now. Carter just checked in; she's about five minutes out from the situation room, and we'll only get one shot at convincing the President of this."

Trapp moved around the side of the warehouse, thinking fast. Was the new arrival a cop, attracted by the sound of gunfire? Possibly, but Kyle hadn't reported anything on the police scanner. He considered the option that it was another of the white nationalists coming to assist the ambush, but that didn't compute either. Why not station more men in and around the warehouse instead of sending two lambs to the slaughter?

"Copy, Control. No promises. Redneck, I'm coming out front. Don't light me up."

"Understood."

Trapp made it to the front of the warehouse and saw the vehicle Perkins had warned him about. It was driving fast up the potholed road that led to the warehouse, with its lights on. Trapp fought the impulse to relax – the fact that the car was lit up like Times Square probably indicated that it didn't pose a threat.

But then again, it might be bait for an ambush, and one of those had already come close to getting him killed tonight. He didn't intend to make that mistake again.

"He'll be on you in about twenty seconds," Perkins warned.

Trapp clicked the button of his radio twice, ejected the half-spent curved magazine in his Heckler and Koch submachine gun and replaced it before chambering a round. Whatever this new threat was, he was ready.

He lowered his night vision goggles over his eyes, and once again the world was bathed in green. The car's headlights cut two streaks in the night sky. The car came to a stop in his field of view, lamps reflecting against the warehouse's metal loading doors.

"Redneck, any other tangos?" he asked quietly, bringing the MP5 to his shoulder and training it on the windshield of the car. It was a drab sedan, Japanese, and looked like a cheap rental – beaten up, and painted in a dark color.

"Negative. Just one guy behind the steering wheel. I have a shot."

"Do not engage. I repeat, do not engage. We need him alive. I'm moving in."

Trapp stood slowly to avoid attracting attention. As he rose up, the driver of the sedan came into view. He had one hand still on the steering wheel and was twisting in his seat, fumbling for something on the passenger side.

"What's he doing?" Trapp asked. "Have you got a visual?"

"Negative."

Trapp used the two vehicles parked out front of the warehouse as cover, pressing his body against the chassis of the nearby SUV and ensuring his head wasn't visible through the windows. He would have to show himself over the last five yards, he knew that. It was inevitable.

"Moving in."

He steadied his weapon against his shoulder and prepared to rush the vehicle and drag the driver from behind the wheel when he froze.

"Wait!"

Trapp's mind took a long second to process what the hell had just happened. He didn't recognize the voice in his ear. Which was impossible. He crouched, reassessing the situation, but edged to the end of the SUV in front of him and trained his weapon on the driver. What was going on? Had someone hacked their communication system?

"Who the hell is this?" Trapp spat into his throat mic, careful not to take his finger off the trigger. He glanced left and right, sampling the air like a dog in case this was a trap. But he sensed nothing. Still, that didn't mean anything. This could be a suicide run, with the vehicle rigged to blow. Trapp had seen enough of those in Iraq to know better than to let his guard down.

"Don't shoot," the voice cried out in his earpiece. "I'm here to help."

Trapp squinted through the goggles. The light thrown off by the headlights made it difficult to make out any detail, but he was pretty sure the driver's lips were moving, indicating he was somehow communicating with them. How was this possible? Only five people should have had access to the secure frequency they were using, and whoever this guy was, he wasn't one of them.

But Trapp knew one thing – they were on the clock, and it was counting down faster than he would like. He had to make a decision, and he made it fast.

"Redneck – still got your shot?"

"Affirmative," came the reply.

"I'm coming out. If this guy so much as blinks, take it."

"Copy that."

Trapp knew that their uninvited guest would have heard that whole exchange. He hoped that it would make him pause before pulling out a weapon – if that was indeed his plan. It didn't make any sense, but then, a lot about the last week didn't seem to make sense.

"I'm not armed," the voice insisted. "I promise. Please, just don't shoot. I'm no use to you dead."

Trapp rose and spoke into his radio with a deadly intensity. "Kill the engine and place your hands on the wheel. If you move, it will be the last thing you do, you understand?"

Instantly, the driver's hands returned to the steering wheel. Which meant that no reply was forthcoming, because in the green glow of his night vision Trapp could see a radio handset clutched against the wheel. The man nodded, fast and anxious to communicate his message.

Trapp paced toward the now silent vehicle. He could hear flames licking against the contents of the disused warehouse. Within just a few minutes the place would go up like a firework.

By morning, all that would be left would be a skeleton of concrete and metal, with anything that could burn long gone.

He also knew that the second the warehouse went up in earnest, it would trigger a second countdown, one with more practical consequences. Emergency services would arrive on scene within minutes. The sound of combat had seemingly not been heard by the locals. Or at least, not reported. But fire is different. Not only can it be seen from a great distance, especially at night, but it triggers an innate human desire to call for help.

"Keep your hands where I can see them," Trapp said, his voice low and controlled, though his heart was racing. At this distance he was able to make out a few more details about the driver. He was large – both tall and significantly overweight. The sedan sat low on its suspension. Trapp didn't take him for a killer. He was practically trembling.

He touched a button on a device attached to his MP5 and a green laser beam lit up. The targeting system was ideal for use with night vision goggles, which rendered depth perception difficult, but that wasn't why he had turned it on. In fact, he flicked the goggles away from his eyes as he closed on the car. The glare from the headlights was too bright at this distance, making it difficult to see.

No, he'd turned the laser on because if his instincts were correct, the man in this vehicle was a civilian. He sounded terrified that at any moment someone might open up and send him to an early grave. The laser dot was an easy, visual reminder of the danger that Trapp posed to his life—a warning not to step out of line.

He pulled the door handle open and got his first good look at the man. Sweat shone on his brow, visible even in the darkness. He was almost three hundred pounds, and there was a big gulp convenience store cup stuffed in an undersized holder between the two front seats.

"Are you armed?" he asked, keeping the weapon trained on the new arrival.

The man shook his head, flinching as one of his hands briefly left the steering wheel. He clamped it back immediately. "No. I have a handgun in the glove compartment, but nothing on me."

"Why don't you start by telling me who the hell you are," Trapp said evenly, staring the man in the eye. "And then maybe I'll decide whether or not I'm going to kill you."

THE MAN, it turned out, was named Dr. Timothy Greaves. Three days ago he had been gainfully employed by the National Security Agency at its Bumblehive data center in Colorado. Now he was a dead man.

Except he wasn't.

He was currently sitting in the back of Trapp's van, clutching a heavy black duffel bag as they sped away from the burning warehouse. As sirens streaked past in the opposite direction, Trapp ensured he was glued to the speed limit. The last thing he needed right now was to be pulled over. As Mitchell kept reminding him, the meeting at the White House had just begun, and if Greaves was going to prove useful, it had to happen fast. He pulled to the side of the road the second the coast was clear.

"So," he said, clambering into the back of the van, where Perkins stood watch over Greaves. "Why don't you start by telling me how the hell you just hacked into our comms?"

Greaves locked his gaze on Trapp. And then, slowly at first – as though he was building up the courage, and then faster, he shook his head. "We don't have time for this."

"Who's we?"

Greaves looked at him like he was an idiot. "Oh, I don't

know," he said, clutching the duffel bag to his oversized frame. "Maybe the people trying to stop a coup in the United States of America? But I'm serious ~ we don't have time for this."

"What I don't have time for," Trapp insisted, his voice low and dangerous, "is making a mistake that gets someone killed. So humor me, Doctor. Why don't you start at the beginning?"

Greaves grimaced, frustration turning his cheeks red to add to his already sweaty brow. "Fine. Have you heard of Atlas Defense Systems?"

"Should I have?"

Greaves shrugged, not seeming surprised at Trapp's lack of comprehension. "Atlas is the biggest defense contractor no one's ever heard of. Like Berkshire Hathaway, except for guns and bombs. Thirty billion dollars in annual revenue. Everyone from the Marines to the CIA has contracts with companies they own."

Trapp thought he might understand where Greaves was going. "Including the NSA?"

Greaves nodded. "*Especially* the NSA. Intelligence is where they started. Their bread and butter."

"So what the hell has Atlas got to do with these attacks?"

Greaves looked at Trapp, as if imploring him to believe what he was about to say. "*Everything*. I think someone at Atlas intends to attempt a coup. They're planning to attack the President when he addresses Congress. And we need to stop them."

"Have you got any proof of this?"

"Not exactly. But I think I can get it..."

48

Vice President Jenkins stood in a secure communications facility built into the bedrock underneath his Texas ranch, waiting for an Air Force technician to set up the link to the White House. He was dressed in a pinstripe suit, which was slightly tight around his waist.

The vice president was ordinarily a sushi man – only the best bluefin tuna, flown in directly from Japan. Easy on the lips, and the same on the hips. In comparison, the food on the campaign trail was barely edible. All those pitiful diner photo ops with ordinary Americans where he was forced to tuck into a slice of apple pie or a hockey puck of a burger and pretend to enjoy it. He hadn't, and yet he was stuck with the evidence of the forced indulgence. At his age it would take months to lose the extra pounds. The thought rankled.

"How long is this going to take?" he grunted.

The technician, a kid in his early twenties who clearly wanted to be anywhere in the world right now except the presence of the surly VP, didn't turn around from his computer as he replied.

"Just a few more seconds, sir."

"Hurry up."

A short while later, with the frightened Air Force computer technician long gone, Jenkins took a seat in a comfortable, handmade leather-backed executive office chair and waited for the communications link to initialize. He glanced down at his suit once again. It was ridiculous, he thought. There was no sign of civilization for miles in any direction, unless you counted farms, which Jenkins certainly did not. He might be the only man wearing a suit for a hundred miles.

It was ridiculous, Jenkins thought, and yet it was important to make the right impression. He would have preferred to have been in the Situation Room, along with the President and the Joint Chiefs of Staff, and all those other decision-makers. Jenkins had always thought that you didn't know what a man was thinking unless you looked him in the eye.

But there was a reason that VP Jenkins had acquiesced to the Secret Service request that he stay on his ranch until the security situation stabilized. And that reason was worth the sacrifice of being forced to endure the smell of cow manure, the paucity of edible food or intelligent conversation. It was worth everything, and he knew he didn't have much longer to wait.

The conference initialized, and several video feeds appeared on the big bank of screens on the opposite wall. The largest was an image of the White House Situation Room, stretched across four linked displays.

Several additional monitors displayed images from US military combatant commands across the globe, as well as the CIA's Counterterrorism Center. Jenkins noted with irritation that the feed of him currently be displayed in the Situation Room would be the same size.

"Thanks for joining us, everyone," President Nash said, striding into the room and causing everyone to stand. He motioned them down with an almost embarrassed gesture.

Jenkins thought it was unbecoming. He would never act like that. The presidency was as much an act as a position. You didn't just become the leader of the free world because someone handed you a briefcase containing the nuclear codes. It was in the way you composed yourself. How you treated other men.

Nash sat and gripped the edges of the mahogany conference table for a second, collecting his thoughts. He looked up, and an unseen camera at the other end of the table must have been pointed directly at him.

"Jenkins, generals, good of you to join us," he said. "Bob – I understand you're to be the designated survivor on Friday night."

Nash's casual use of Jenkins's first name rankled the VP, but he didn't let the irritation show.

"Wish I could be by your side, Mr. President," Jenkins said, pasting a determined smile onto his face. "But the Secret Service insisted."

Nash flicked away his comments with another tiny gesture of his fingers. Jenkins leaned back in his own chair, glowering.

"Ryan," Nash said to Ryan Stone, the director of the National Counterterrorism Center, "why don't you brief everyone on the latest developments?"

Stone nodded. His features were set with an expression that Jenkins took to be embarrassment.

The vice president wasn't surprised. Every three-letter agency the US government had was chasing their tails. Some of them had bigger budgets than entire nations, and yet they were each as lost as the next. He allowed himself a tight smile of satisfaction. Events were unfolding in precisely the way he had planned. Of course, there had been setbacks—the former CIA officer Jason Trapp was quickly becoming a thorn in Jenkins's side—but nothing he couldn't handle. He was just two days away from achieving his ultimate goal – and after that, nothing would be able to stand in his way.

"Yes, Mr. President. As you know, two days ago, the director of the National Security Agency was assassinated just a few miles away from here. As yet, CIA, NSA and DHS are not clear who was behind the attack."

"And where is Director Rutger?" the president asked.

"A few minutes out, Mr. President," an aide replied from somewhere off-screen. "His motorcade got held up."

Nash grunted.

A man Jenkins recognized as General Jack Myers, the chairman of the Joint Chiefs of Staff, spoke next. Like the VP, he was being beamed in, in his case from Raven Rock, the military bunker near Blue Ridge Summit in Pennsylvania that was informally known as the underground Pentagon.

"Ryan, what about the shooters?"

"Israeli. Mercenaries. The Secretary of State has spoken with President Shimon, and he has assured us that the state of Israel did not participate in this attack."

"And you believe him?"

"I do, Jack. The Israelis had nothing to gain from killing Donahue. This was a contract job. We might not know their identity, but whoever is funding and coordinating these attacks has deep pockets, and they are not playing by the normal rules."

Myers snorted. "No shit."

Nash cut in. "Enough. Let's be productive. Do we have any idea what they might be planning next?"

The silence in the Situation Room spoke volumes. Jenkins could hear it all the way from Texas. He hid the expression of satisfaction that threatened to stretch across his face. Nash was spinning in the wind.

"This is simply not good enough, people," Nash snapped, slamming his hand down on the Situation Room conference table. "This country spends sixty billion dollars a year on the intelligence community – and you're telling me that with all those resources you've got *nothing*?"

Jenkins was somewhat surprised by Nash's vehemence. He didn't think much of the younger man, but he was displaying some unexpected spine, the vice president had to admit that much.

He frowned, wondering if this might present a problem. He had always thought of Nash as a neophyte—entirely unsuited to run a kindergarten, let alone the entire United States. But he assured himself that it was merely a speedbump. He'd covered his tracks well. It was just a matter of time.

"Mr. President, we're –"

"Ryan, two days from now I will be standing underneath the Capitol dome broadcasting live to the entire country. What am I supposed to tell them?"

Another silence reigned. It was broken only by the opening and closing of the wooden doorway leading into the Situation Room. Jenkins' forehead creased as he tried to work out who had just joined.

And then his blood ran cold.

"Director Rutger," Nash said coldly. "Good of you to join us."

It wasn't Vince Rutger who had the vice president spooked. It was the woman who had entered the Situation Room alongside him, and who was now seated against the walls of the room along with aides from the other agencies represented around the conference table.

Her name was Nadine Carter. And if his men hadn't screwed everything up, she would already be dead.

"My apologies, Mr. President," Rutger said. Jenkins squinted, attempting not to look too interested in the new arrivals. The FBI director looked tired, but Jenkins couldn't make out any further details of the man's expression. He consciously forced himself to relax into his executive chair. He couldn't do anything from here. He would have to let this play out.

"Perhaps you have something to add. The Bureau is leading the Douglass Bridge investigation, is it not?"

Rutger nodded. "It is, sir."

"And have you found anything?"

Rutger glanced over his shoulder, back at Nadine Carter. Jenkins held his breath, heart barely beating as he waited for the ax to fall.

Vince Rutger turned back, his massive frame hunched over with disappointment. "No, sir. It's a dead end."

49

"Trapp," Mitchell growled the second he walked through the front door of the safe house with Perkins and Greaves in tow.

"You better have a damn good reason for making me call off the dogs."

Trapp was asking himself the same question. He had been forced to make a split second decision: Allow the Joint Address to Congress to go ahead, putting the President in danger, or let Dani and Director Rutger try and stop it. He had chosen the first option, and Mitchell had backed his play, contacting Agent Carter and calling her off at the very last second.

It was a risky move, and they all knew it. If it went wrong, then Nash might end up dead, and his attackers achieve every single one of their goals. But it was the only way. There was far more at stake here than the life of a single elected official—even the President himself.

Trapp shrugged. "I guess we'll have to find out."

He was exhausted. His back was beat-up from hours crammed in the back of the van. His feet felt like they were encased in concrete. He hadn't slept the whole night through in days – and it wasn't like the six months before that were anything to write home about.

The only benefit of getting back in the field, as far as Trapp could tell, was at least the nightmares he had been having ever since Yemen were on a temporary hiatus. If only because he wasn't getting a chance to close his eyes.

Then again, those very same dreams were beginning to invade Trapp's waking hours. For the first time in his life, though he might be fighting for his country, he was not wearing its flag. For two long decades, a moral certainty had guided his every action. Serving his country had also served to pull Trapp out of the darkness of his own tortured childhood. It even helped him atone for his own original sin.

Ever since he met Ryan Price, Jason Trapp had become an avenging angel—funneling his own dark thoughts into action, his guilt into goodness. But now he was lost. His friend was dead, his nation had disowned him.

Mitchell turned his glowering gaze on Greaves. Compared with the usual occupants of this safe house, he was an outlier. Where Trapp and the other two CIA operators were lean and muscular, he was anything but. His large frame was topped by tousled blue hair that needed a cut, and his nervously flickering eyes suggested that he was currently wondering if he had made the right decision in allying himself with Trapp.

"Who the hell is he?"

Trapp shot Greaves the kind of look that said *Shut the hell up and let me deal with this.*

He knew that Mitchell would ease up. He was just throwing his weight around. They just needed to wait out his frustration. The former deputy director of the CIA Special Activities Division didn't like being out of the loop, a feeling that Trapp sympathized with.

But Trapp also knew that sometimes in the field it was necessary to make a decision on the fly. You didn't always have the luxury of time. Sometimes you had to go with your gut. And that is what he had done.

Trapp grinned. "You don't recognize him? He's a dead man, just like us."

"What the hell is that supposed to mean?"

"It's my pleasure to introduce you to Dr. Timothy Greaves. Formally chief scientist of the National Security Agency."

Mitchell ran his fingers through his hair and closed his eyes. A couple of seconds later they reopened, and Trapp sensed that the man had come to a conclusion. It didn't surprise him. Before joining the executive ranks on the CIA's seventh floor, Mitchell had been an operator just like him.

One of the key character traits required in a job like that is complete conviction in a chosen course of action. But when the facts change, so must you. Operators who hang on to misplaced anger tend to end up dead.

"I guess we better hear you out, Dr. Greaves."

Greaves glanced at Trapp anxiously. It was fair enough, Trapp thought. He didn't know Mitchell from Adam. Hell, it wasn't like Trapp had a long relationship with the man himself – less than an hour ago, he had a submachine gun aimed directly at the scientist's head. But high-pressure situations have a way of short-circuiting ordinary social conventions. Trapp and the doctor had gone into a crucible as strangers and exited it as allies.

"Go ahead," Trapp said. "Tell him what you told me."

Greaves allowed his duffel bag to fall to the floor, catching it at the last second to avoid damaging whatever equipment was inside.

"Any chance we could sit?" he asked, shrugging down at his body. "Only, I've had a long couple of days, and..."

Mitchell gestured irritably at a trestle table surrounded with chairs. They all took a seat and waited for the doctor to begin.

"Okay," Greaves began, shifting his frame as he searched for a comfortable position in the folding chair. "Have you heard of an NSA program called Birdseye?"

Mitchell nodded. "Of course."

"It first came online about five years ago and has been steadily upgraded since. Every single piece of data the NSA has access to is fed into the system. Intercepted domestic telephone calls, text messages, all the stuff we are not supposed to have access to. Live feeds from every single Internet-connected surveillance camera on the planet. Every bite of data that crosses the Internet. If you can dream it up, we have access to it."

Trapp watched Mitchell closely. So far, so nothing. Greaves wasn't telling them anything they didn't already know, or at least suspect. Everyone knew that the NSA operated far outside of its congressional mandate. That was no surprise. After all, the CIA did the same. Someone had to make the hard decisions that kept America safe, even if that meant doing things the politicians were too weak to sign off on.

"Sure," Mitchell agreed. "You guys at Fort Meade have been feeding us intelligence for years. Birdseye just kicked it up another level."

Greaves nodded. "It did. The algorithm was able to process data in a way we didn't have the capability to do before. It saw connections between discrete pieces of intelligence that would ordinarily require a human analyst to draw."

"So if humans can do it, why the machine?"

"Scale," Greaves replied. "Cases that would have taken a dozen analysts hundreds of man hours took Birdseye just a few seconds. It was designed to be an exponential leap in our capabilities. And it worked. Better than any government program I've ever been involved in. But then something changed."

"What?"

"A few weeks ago, I started tracking some unusual power

fluctuations. What you have to understand is that the Utah Data Center is essentially just a giant computer. It guzzles electricity like you wouldn't believe. We have a gas turbine power plant on site, powerful enough to supply sixty-five thousand homes with electricity."

Trapp leaned in. "What was so unusual?"

"I almost didn't catch it. The servers that Birdseye is hosted on were spinning up in quiet periods and doing... something."

"What?"

Greaves shrugged. "Well, that's the million-dollar question. At first it wasn't much of a priority. Most of the technology at the Bumblehive is still highly experimental. When you combine that with government contractors bidding bottom dollar, you end up with a hot mess. But the weird thing was that none of the power draws were showing up in the logs. They weren't just being deleted, but actively falsified."

"By who?"

"That's what I started digging into a few days ago. I kept it quiet until I reached out to Director Donahue." Greaves's posture sagged at his mention of the man's name. "Maybe that's what saved my life. I have no doubt that whoever is behind all this would have tried to eliminate me much earlier if they knew what I was up to."

Mitchell ground his teeth together. "What the hell *were* you doing? I'm done playing twenty questions, Doctor. Give me a straight answer."

Greaves looked at Mitchell like he was a Neanderthal. Trapp had met many men like the doctor over the course of his career. Scientists were a different breed to trigger pullers. For Greaves, context was just as important as the core of the information itself. Mitchell and Trapp just wanted to know the bare minimum—what they needed to do.

Who they needed to kill.

"Okay, I'll dumb it down for you," Greaves said acidly.

Trapp disguised a smile. He was beginning to like the man.

"I thought the Russians were behind this at first. Maybe the Chinese. As far as I know, they're the only two countries with a cyber program advanced enough to hack the NSA. It made sense for them to be firing up the servers at night and deleting the evidence before the day shift arrived."

Kyle chimed in. Trapp almost jumped at the sound of the man's voice. He'd almost forgotten he was there.

"That's what we thought. It fits the Russian MO – sow chaos without leaving fingerprints that we can directly trace back to them. But you're saying it wasn't them?"

Greaves shook his head. "No. I did some digging, and it goes too deep. What I'm saying is, no one hacked us. This code was already there, built directly into Birdseye. Like a Trojan horse, just waiting to be used."

The room went silent. Trapp had already heard some of Greaves's suspicions, but the detail was startling. If he was telling the truth, and he had no reason to doubt the man's honesty, then the events of the last few days were just the climax of a long-planned conspiracy to destabilize the United States.

"So you're saying the NSA is behind this?" Mitchell said, standing up and pacing around the room. He was a ball of nervous energy. "To what end?"

"No, not the NSA," Greaves replied. "I considered that, but it doesn't make sense."

"Maybe you did," Mitchell said, casting Greaves a pointed look. "Or maybe this is your crisis of confidence. You saw what you had unleashed and had second thoughts. Are you looking for absolution, Doctor? Because I'm not the right man to give it to you."

Red anger filled Greaves's cheeks. He stood up, knocking his chair from behind him. It fell to the ground with a clatter that echoed around the sparsely furnished safe house.

"Go fuck yourself," he spat. "The second I found out I did something about it. A good friend of mine ended up dead because of it. Then they came for me. I'm here to help. But if you don't want it, then please, tell me now."

"Mike, cool it," Trapp said, shooting his former boss a black look. The man zipped his lips but glowered back. "The doc has a theory. Hear him out."

Greaves nodded his thanks. "Like I said, Birdseye wasn't *compromised*. The code was there all along."

A light flashed in Mitchell's eyes. "So who built Birdseye?"

"Atlas Defense Systems," Trapp said, raising his eyebrows. "Heard of them?"

Mitchell nodded. "Who was in charge of the contract?"

"A man called Neil Patel," Greaves replied, shaking his head sadly. "I was at MIT with him. Even attended his funeral a couple of months ago."

"He's dead?" Mitchell yelled, slamming his fist on the nearest table. Kyle's computer equipment jumped, and the analyst's eyes widened in alarm. He dived forward, snatching up a hard drive inches before it hit the floor.

"They're all dead," Greaves said softly. "Heart attacks, aneurysms, anaphylactic shock. Over the past six months, every key member of the project team has died."

"They're tying up loose ends," Mitchell said. His jaw was set, his eyes heavy with defeat. "Is anyone left?"

Greaves shook his head.

"Then we're fucked," Mitchell grunted. He sank back into a folding chair, kicking an empty beer bottle as he did so. It skipped across the concrete floor and smashed against the far wall. The explosion silenced the room.

"Maybe not," Trapp said cryptically. "Tell him, Doc."

"I managed to code a backdoor into Birdseye. That's how I found you guys in the first place. Right now you're the system's public enemy number one."

Mitchell fixed him a glare. "Way to bury the lede. You're telling me you know who's behind this?"

"It's not that simple," Greaves replied, shaking his head. "My access to the system is limited, especially now I can't hard link directly into the servers. You've got to understand how much data Birdseye processes every second. When I'm not hard linked to the servers, it's like trying to drain the Mississippi River with a paper straw."

Mitchell ground his teeth. "So what *do* you know?"

"Several days ago, whoever is behind this conspiracy contacted Randall Woods. As far as I can tell, it was for the first time."

"Wait," Trapp muttered slowly as his brain tried to process the magnitude of what Greaves had just said. "The Speaker of the House is tied up in this?"

Greaves nodded.

Trapp stayed silent for a short time, absently scratching his thickening stubble. Greaves's revelation explained why Woods had called his press conference. Why he'd put the President in a position where he had to attend Capitol Hill and paint a target on his back. He didn't know why the speaker had done such a thing, and he didn't know Randall Woods, but he'd met many men like him. Trapp knew how they worked.

And it gave him an idea.

50

Speaker Randall Woods lived in the affluent Foxhall suburb of Washington DC. His house was large, almost six thousand square feet, and certainly could not have been purchased on a government salary, not even the speaker's comfortable $223,000 annual stipend. It was a red brick colonial, its walls locked in an embrace by vines that were brown and lifeless as a result of the winter cold, their few remaining leaves coated with a hard frost.

Although the Speaker of the House is entitled to a palatial suite on the grounds of the Capitol, all expenses paid, courtesy of the hard-done-by American taxpayer, even that lap of luxury wasn't good enough for the former Goldman Sachs banker.

No. Randall figured that if he wouldn't shit where he ate, he sure as hell wouldn't work where he slept.

Not for him either was the practice some parsimonious—and ostentatious—Tea Party speakers had adopted in years gone by, sleeping in cots in their offices in order to demonstrate to their constituents that they *weren't* wasting taxpayers' money. Randall Woods had no intention of behaving that way. It was no way for a representative of the people to act.

As Jason Trapp crept into the sculpted grounds of the speaker's mansion, a Beretta 9 mm strapped into a holster around his thigh, dressed entirely in black, he didn't pay attention to any of that.

"Movement at your six, Hangman," a voice said, crackling into his earpiece. "Hold tight."

He thumbed the microphone button twice to signal that he understood.

Woods ordinarily had a six-man protective detail, but after the events of Bloody Monday and the untimely death of the head of his detail, along with the man's pregnant wife and child, the detail was doubled. That presented Trapp with a challenge, but one that he was confident of overcoming.

"Okay," Kyle said over the radio. "You're clear."

Three SUVs with the markings of the Capitol Police sat on the curb outside, along with a cruiser from the Metropolitan PD. It was three in the morning, and having worked back-to-backs all week, the cops inside appeared half-asleep. If Trapp screwed up, he had no doubt they would be first on the scene. But if he was careful, they would never know he was here. He'd waited until a foot patrol had finished before entering the grounds, and didn't expect another for at least twenty minutes.

He crept through the grass garden that led up to the French doors at the back of the house, careful to check for any hidden sensors, pressure plates or tripwires that might have been installed since the most recent set of plans the speaker's close protection detail had submitted to their superiors. He found nothing he hadn't expected. The lights inside the house were off, except a single bulb burning somewhere on the second floor.

No glow spilled out into the sheltered garden.

This was mostly at the speaker's bidding. He liked to bring women back to the mansion. The garden was covered by tall pine trees, and the only possible vantage points were nearby houses whose owners were as wealthy as they were discreet, which meant there no way for the press to see what he was up to.

But after his protective detail responded to a false alarm one too many times, embarrassing the speaker with his night-time visitors, he'd ordered that the security system be scaled back. It was music to Trapp's ears.

The most difficult obstacle to overcome was the thin layer of snow that lay on the ground. It had fallen several days ago and then frozen hard, meaning that each of Trapp's footsteps was met with an answering crunch, loud in the quiet of the night. He compensated by exerting sufficient control over the movement of his boots that he set them down millimeter by millimeter. He probably didn't need to. The speaker's detail was wrapped up warm inside their vehicles. But Trapp was a careful man.

He keyed his microphone and spoke in barely more than a whisper. "Is the alarm system active?"

The addition of Dr. Timothy Greaves to the team was a welcome one. The man was a certifiable genius when it came to anything technological. After all, as the National Security Agency's most senior research scientist for almost a decade, he had a hand in almost every security measure designed to protect America's leadership.

"We're ready to bring it down on your mark, Hangman."

Trapp closed the last few yards to the French doors, his feet beating a different tune as they kissed the surface of the marble patio. He paused there for over five minutes without moving, bringing his heartrate down below forty beats a minute so that the sounds of the night were crystal-clear, without so much as the rush of blood in his ears to distract him.

It was a ritual he had performed more times than he could count, on every continent, in active war zones and countries with which the United States has no diplomatic relations, and probably never will.

Nothing would rush Jason Trapp in that moment. A dead operator is no use to anyone, least of all himself. There were hours until the sun came up. If necessary, Trapp was prepared to use them all.

Trapp listened for any sign that his infiltration had been detected. The crunch of boots on snow. The sound of a man panting, or the click as a rifle was readied for use. He heard nothing, save the whistling of wind through frozen branches, and the mournful caw of a bird that hadn't fled for warmer climes.

"Do it," he whispered.

He grabbed a pick gun from a pocket in his black combat vest. The lock that held the French doors fast was Austrian, the best of the best. But the pick gun had been developed in an Agency lab and would be more than up to the task.

He moved fast.

He had to. The alarm system would be down for no longer than sixty seconds – any longer than that would trigger a subroutine that would alert the Capitol Police Department, and their procedure was to sweep the house. A workaround to defeat that particular safety feature would have taken several hours longer than they'd had.

Trapp held the gun to the door and waited for the telltale click to sound. The lock was based on a cylindrical design, rather than the more common pin tumbler models common to most households. Harder to pick by hand, but no match for the gun Trapp was cradling.

His earpiece buzzed. "Forty seconds."

A freezing cold wind bit at Trapp's face as he waited. He didn't need the reminder. The time was counting down in his own brain, every bit as accurate as the mariners watch on his wrist.

"Thirty seconds."

Still, Trapp waited for the gun to do its work.

"Nine, eight, seven..."

And then he had it. The click seemed to reverberate around the mansion's frozen garden, though Trapp knew that the snick of the lock opening was no louder than a muted cough. He pulled the door open, stepped inside, and pulled it fast just in time.

"The system is coming back online. Hold."

Trapp waited with bated breath. He knew if the alarm sounded, then he had no choice but to make a break for it. His mission tonight relied on stealth, not brute force. And he had no intention of using the Beretta that was currently strapped to his thigh. That was for show. No matter what happened tonight, no matter the cost, Trapp would rather die than kill a cop who was just doing his duty.

"Okay, you're clear, Hangman. Time to wake up Sleeping Beauty."

Trapp clicked the radio twice. Now was no time for Hollywood wisecracks.

He cleared the room, and the entire ground floor, without once drawing his pistol. He didn't unclip the strap that held it in its holster until he was mounting the stairs. Trapp knew there wouldn't be a member of the speaker's security detail at the top of the stairs. The Speaker of the House of Representatives is not the President, nor does he merit such extensive security precautions.

Although perhaps he would after tonight.

The master bedroom was the second door to the left of the top of the stairs. The door to the suite was slightly ajar. He held at the top of the stairs, waiting just as he had done before entering the house for any sign of movement, of life. When he was completely assured there was none, except the rhythmic sound of the speaker's snores, Trapp stepped forward, bringing his boot down lightly on the hallway, waiting for a giveaway creak, which would not be unusual in a house of this age.

The shriek did not come until his third step. Trapp froze. Waited. Listened out for any sign that the metronomic snoring had altered in any way. It hadn't. For once, he was in luck. Randall was a heavy sleeper.

He entered the bedroom without causing any further floorboards to protest. He paused briefly, pressing himself against the wall just to the left of the doorway, and waited. The speaker kept snoring.

Finally certain he was undetected—and aware that Dr. Greaves had disabled the speaker's panic alarm—Trapp walked casually to the speaker's bedside with his Beretta steady in his hand. And aimed it at the man's head. The heavier steps provoked a groaning chorus and the speaker stirred, his sheets rustling, but did not wake up.

Trapp sat down on the bed. The mattress was high-quality and barely sank, despite Trapp's muscular bulk. He noted that the curtains were closed and decided to flick the bedside lamp on. Randall Woods' features came into sharp contrast. His eyelids flickered, as his waking brain puzzled over this new input. Trapp didn't bother waiting. He placed his Beretta between the man's teeth and hissed a greeting.

"Rise and shine, asshole."

The speaker's eyes burst open. Trapp couldn't make out their color in the light thrown off by the lamp, but the panic in them was unmistakable. He mumbled something that Trapp could not make out, due to the cold metal of the pistol that was currently occupying the space where the man's tongue should be.

"Listen close and listen well," Trapp said. "Mr. Speaker, I'm going to call you Randall. And Randall, unfortunately for you, you fucked up. When I remove my weapon from between your teeth you are going to have two options. The first is that you cooperate. If you do, I won't be forced to put a bullet in your brain."

Trapp left the second option unspoken. The widening of the man's eyes told him that he grasped the concept. He pulled the gun from Randall's mouth and dried it on his sheets.

Randall's voice, when it came, was weak. "Who the hell are you?"

"That"—Trapp smiled thinly, his wraithlike eyes flashing in the dark—"is the wrong question."

"Well what the hell's the right one?"

"What's that old saying?" Trapp asked. "Ask not who the hell I am, but what you can do for me. Right now, Randall, what you can do for me is squeal like the little pig you are."

Randall didn't say a word. His eyes were wide, fingers clutched so tightly that his knuckles turned as white as his thousand thread-count Egyptian cotton bedsheets.

Trapp raised his eyebrow. "Cat got your tongue?"

To be honest, right now Randall Woods was about the only politician Trapp had ever come across who had had the good grace to shut the hell up. He kind of liked it. But then, he also had questions, and those questions needed answers, and those answers might well save the United States of America herself, so you could say he was on the clock.

Trapp cracked his neck.

"No," Randall squealed, slithering back a few inches in fear. "I just don't know what you want."

"Randall, I want answers. And right now you are the only person who can give them to me. I think you know exactly why I'm here."

"I promise you I –"

Trapp bared his teeth in a considered attempt to be menacing. In all honesty, with the hangman's scar around his neck, the weapon in his hand, and the fact that he had woken the

Speaker of the House of Representatives up in the false safety of his own home, it wasn't needed.

But it worked. Randall flinched, drew back, pulled the covers tight against his neck as though they could somehow protect him from the force of Trapp's wrath.

"I don't have time for empty promises, Randall. What I want to know is who you are working for. If you lie to me, or tell me you don't know what I'm talking about, I will knock both your front teeth out before you're done lying. You have ten seconds."

Trapp was telling the truth, and from the look in Randall's eyes, he knew it too. The terrified speaker did not know that Trapp hated acting like this. A childhood spent acting as a punching bag can send the victim in one of two directions: pacifism or psychopathy. Trapp was a strange chimera of both. He was no stranger to inflicting pain, of course, but he used it as a tool, not an end in itself.

He began the count, staring Randall down and daring the man to test him.

"Ten."

"Stop," Randall whispered. "I believe you. I'll tell you everything. But he will end me if I do."

"I'm okay with that," Trapp replied indifferently. "Start talking."

The speaker swallowed nervously, still gripping the bedspread with trembling fingers. He closed his eyes, as if preparing himself for what would certainly mean the end of his career.

"Okay. I first heard his voice five days ago –"

"Give me a name."

"I don't have one, or any way of contacting him. He contacts me. That's the way it works."

"What does he sound like?" Trapp asked, thinking on his feet. "Young? Old? Does he repeat any turns of phrase?"

Randall shook his head. "It just sounded tinny, as though he was using something to obscure his voice. I don't remember him saying anything memorable."

"What did he want from you?"

Randall exhaled deeply before replying, his ashen face and shivering limbs evidence that he knew he was a man who is going away for a long time.

"It's not what he wanted from me. It's what he wanted *for* me."

Trapp raised the pistol, making sure Randall could see he was done messing around.

"Which was?"

"He said he was going to make me President."

51

Cal Cooper was a Detroit native, even if his new partner at the Capitol Police force told him he sounded like a surfer bro from Orange County. Until nine months before, he had never even left his home state of Michigan.

Cal had worked for a company called Productiv, which was an auto parts supplier for Toyota. He had no great dislike for the blacks, or the Jews, as so many of his comrades at the Pilgrim training camp did; his hatred was reserved for the Asians.

Specifically, the Japanese.

Cal's grandfather had fought with the US Marines at Iwo Jima. He lost a leg and gained a lifelong hatred of anyone with what he called "slitty eyes." Cal's father had shared the same instinct, but for most of his childhood, Cal himself grew up not particularly caring one way or another for his family's grievances.

Until two years before.

That was when Toyota shipped most of its production south, into Mexico, and although they claimed it was for supply-chain reasons, Cal knew the real reason: cost. The Hispanics were cheaper than Americans. Worked longer hours, because they knew they had to, or they would be out of a job.

Cal didn't even really hate the Mexicans. Hell, what choice did they have? If it was a straight tossup between joining a cartel and working for Toyota, he knew which he would pick. But even so, words like "spic" began to creep into his vernacular.

But Cal's greatest anger was reserved for the Japanese. They were the ones who had undercut the American automakers in Detroit, forcing them out. They were the ones who had killed off the unions, when Ford and General Motors couldn't compete with their underhanded business tactics. They were the ones who had offered him a job, offered him a chance at a life with a wife and kids, and then cruelly snatched it away.

He had been so close. He'd had a girlfriend, Rosa, and they were talking about starting a family. And then he lost his job. And in Detroit in 2017, getting a new one wasn't nearly as easy as the politicians on TV always made it sound. There was no work. And then there was no girlfriend. She hadn't liked him much, afterwards. Hadn't liked the man Cal Cooper had become.

"You gonna hog that shower all morning, Coops?"

The voice belonged to his partner, Andy Douglas. He was African-American and had been with the Capitol Police for about ten years. Cooper had to admit that he was a damn fine officer. He had a nose for every little thing that just wasn't quite right on his beat.

"Be right out," Cal replied, raising his voice over the sound of falling water. He rinsed off the last of the soap suds, grabbed a towel, and stepped out of the shower cubicle, drying himself as he moved.

The locker room was in the basement of the large Capitol Police station on the street. It stank of mildew, and his locker didn't close properly. There was only one station for over two thousand cops, and that meant you never got enough time in the shower. Even when you just needed a few moments to think. Even when life was speeding up around you, and you needed to make a decision, but you just didn't know what to do.

"Hey," his partner said, as he passed and stepped into the shower. "The lieutenant was looking for you."

Cal froze. A vision entered his head, the same one he had been worried senseless over for months. That someone had run a background check and discovered that he wasn't who he said he was. Or rather, that he hadn't done the things he said he had.

He kept his voice even. "Did he say why?"

Andy shrugged. "Hell if I know. You do something to piss him off?"

"Guess I'll find out…"

THE LIEUTENANT to whom Cal Cooper reported had an office somewhere on the fifth floor of the vast sandstone police station. He waited outside the door, drumming his fingers nervously against his thick leather belt.

"Enter."

Cal opened the door and sat down where he was told. The lieutenant was in his early forties, and already beginning to gray at the temples. His eyes were piercing blue, and Cooper knew that because right now, they were locked on his own.

"You have friends in high places, Cooper?"

"Uh, I don't think so, boss?"

The lieutenant flicked a printout of an email across the desk between them. "Then explain this."

Cooper reached forward and nervously retrieved the email.

His eyes scanned from left to right, and then he understood. "I don't know anything about this, sir," he lied.

"Sure you don't," the lieutenant snorted. "Listen, Cooper. I don't care who you had to blow, don't throw me under the bus like this again. I don't want to be getting emails from the chief of police about some rookie cop, understood?"

Cal knew sometimes it was better to stay silent, and decided this was one of those times. He held his breath as he waited to hear the lieutenant's judgment, half-hoping his decision would be made for him, one way or another.

The lieutenant exhaled forcefully, then ran a hand through his graying blond hair. "Screw it. I'm not gonna mess with the chief on this one. You'll be posted right outside the House chamber. Don't do anything, don't say anything, just keep your mouth shut and your eyes front. Understood?"

"Yes, sir."

"You better, Cooper. Because if you step out of line, I will have you doing traffic stops for the rest of your career."

52

Trapp entered the Capitol Building with an uneasy spring in his step. His brown Oxfords echoed where they landed on the polished marble, and his tan chinos and tweed jacket helped him blend in as much as possible—given the marked difference in both height and bulk—with the hundred other scurrying aides and reporters moving with equal haste through the vast stone edifice. He was carrying a drivers license issued by the Tennessee DMV that said his name was Donald Hayes, and he had press credentials around his neck from the *Chattanooga Post*.

All the details checked out when he went through the checkpoint run by the Capitol Police. Greaves had seen to that. Donald Hayes wasn't so much a cover as a real person, as far as any database in the entire United States knew. Articles under his byline had even appeared on the *Post's* website – a fact that would convince even the most thorough vetting process.

Donald even had a meeting with the Speaker of the House of Representatives – notionally his hometown Congressman.

The plan was simple. It was one that Trapp's long career with the Central Intelligence Agency had prepared him for very well. He had an asset—Randall Woods—and he was going to squeeze him until the pips squeaked.

Greaves's backdoor into the NSA's Birdseye system went in two directions. He could suck information out, as he had done several times before.

But the other direction was just as interesting.

He could seize control of Birdseye for a short time – perhaps thirty minutes. During that window, the members of Trapp's off-books team of misfit intelligence and law enforcement personnel would be able to hear everything the terrorists said and did. Discover their precise locations.

Even transmit false instructions.

Greaves had cautioned Mitchell that if he used this option, it would be strictly a one-time thing. Either the person controlling the system would become aware of the intrusion or the system itself would fight back – or both. So for their plan to work, they had to remain in the shadows doing the hard yards for as long as possible. That's what today was about. They needed to identify as many of the terrorist operatives as they could. Unveil the fine details of the plan for the attack on Congress they knew was coming.

In short, it was like a game of chess. They needed to move their pieces into place before the final strike – and hope like hell that their intentions weren't noticed. And stage one in their plan was to draw the mysterious 'voice' into the open. To bait him into making a mistake. That was Trapp's job.

"Okay, do you read me?" Greaves said, his voice breathy in Trapp's ear. The communications unit was a tiny one, hidden in Trapp's ear canal, and the battery would only last ninety minutes, but that should be enough.

Trapp pressed a cell phone to his ear, thanking the fact that the world was obsessed with the small devices these days. It made undercover operations significantly easier. He still just about remembered the days before cell phones, when talking to yourself in an empty hallway made people stare at you like you were crazy. Now everyone was doing it.

"Loud and clear, Doc," he replied. "I know you're not used to this kind of thing, but if you could move a little further away from the microphone?"

"Sorry," came the embarrassed reply. "I'm new at this cloak and dagger stuff."

Trapp went through several more layers of security before reaching the speaker's office. There was no way that he could have gotten this close with a weapon on him. He lost count of the number of times his identification was checked, and he was patted down.

In the end, the speaker didn't leave him waiting long. Randall Woods's secretary looked surprised when the speaker poked his head around the heavy hardwood door of his official office just moments after she announced the arrival of Donald Hayes from the *Chattanooga Post*. It wasn't exactly a heavyweight news organization, and by the look on her face, she wasn't used to her boss dealing with anyone of lesser stature than the chief features editor at *Vanity Fair*.

"Don," the speaker said as he greeted Trapp with a nervous smile. "Good of you to come. You made it up here all right?"

The second the hardwood door closed behind Trapp, cutting off the sound, he gestured at the speaker to drop the act.

"How you holding up, Randall?" He grinned. "You remembered your lines. Atta boy. Ever thought about a career in acting?"

He watched the speaker's eyes flicker up and down his body, perhaps looking for a weapon. He wouldn't find anything more dangerous than a ballpoint pen, but then again, it wasn't like Trapp needed a gun to accomplish his task. And both men knew it.

"How the hell do you think?" Randall said, his eyes lidded

and dark. "You've got my balls in a vise. Don't act like you give a damn about how I'm feeling."

Trapp shrugged. "I was just making small talk, Randall. But you're right. Let's get down to business."

"Why couldn't you have done this over the phone?" the speaker asked, studying Trapp carefully. "If he finds out I've spoken to you, that's it. I'm a dead man."

Trapp nodded, attempting to convey an air of sympathy. He had to let the man's anger burn out. Once it did, Randall Woods would realize that he really didn't have any other choice.

"He'll kill me. Or release the tapes, and then I'm as good as dead. You know what they do to child molesters in prison?"

"I have an idea."

"I won't last a week. I'll be begging them to finish me off by the end. I didn't even fucking do it!"

Spittle flew from the speaker's mouth, his finger jammed into the air as he carried himself on a wave of emotional energy. And then, just as Trapp had known it would, the tide broke. Woods's shoulders slumped. He sat back behind his desk and lowered his head into his hands.

"Doesn't that feel better?" Trapp said, keeping his tone light. He had to admit, he was kind of enjoying this role reversal. It was usually politicians who put him in harm's way, not the other way around.

"Fuck off."

"I will, soon," Trapp agreed. "But you need to do something for me first."

Randall didn't bother raising his eyes to Trapp as he spoke. "What?"

"I need you to call Agent Dani Carter at the FBI and tell her you're being blackmailed. Tell her all about the voice. What it told you."

Trapp leaned forward across the desk and flicked a scrap of paper with a phone number on it toward the speaker, a brilliant white against the scuffed maroon leather finish of the man's desk. "Use that number."

Woods shot upright, his face bloodless, panic in his eyes. "I can't," he choked. "If I do what you ask, I'm signing my own death warrant."

Trapp shrugged. "The thing is, Randall, if you don't do what *I* ask, I'll kill you right here and now, in your own damn office. So you have a choice. Trust that I know what I am doing, and do what I say, or take your chances that I'm not a man of my word."

Randall locked eyes with him, probing Trapp for any hints that he was lying. Trapp gave him none. The truth was, it would give him great satisfaction to finish Randall off. He probably wouldn't actually go ahead with it. But even he didn't know for sure.

"You're a psychopath, you know that?" the speaker whimpered. "What the hell happened to you as a kid?"

Trapp remembered a length of barbed wire twisted into a noose biting into a little boy's neck. But he blinked away the memory. He couldn't let it keep exercising its power over him. Price was dead, but his legacy wasn't. Trapp had beat his darkness once, and he could do it again.

"That is none of your concern, Randall," Trapp replied evenly. "Now, are you ready to make the call?"

The speaker leaned back in his chair, his breath uneven, his chest rising and falling in ragged waves. Trapp almost shook his head. How the hell had someone like this risen so high in the US political system? Why would people vote for a man like Woods?

That was a question for the ages. But right now, it wasn't one Trapp had time for. He spoke out loud, knowing that Greaves was listening to everything he had said. "Are you ready, Doctor?"

"Who the hell are you talking to?" Randall groaned.

Greaves's reply was to Trapp alone. "I'm ready, Trapp. The backdoor into Birdseye is active. As far as the cameras in the Capitol are concerned, you don't even exist. If everything goes well, we'll know exactly who he's talking to."

"Dial the number," Trapp said, his voice hard, his eyes communicating one simple message. *If you do not do what I tell you to do, you will suffer.*

For one long second, Randall looked like he might have grown a backbone. And then he crumpled. He picked up a landline on his desk, his fingers trembling in the air before he punched in the numbers, but not for long. Just before he punched in the last digit, Trapp delivered a warning.

"Remember, Mr. Speaker. The only chance you have of getting out of this alive is if you work with me. You understand?"

Randall locked eyes with him once again. But this time, they were the eyes of a broken man. He was Trapp's now. They always were in the end.

Trapp mouthed the word "speaker," and the speaker looked puzzled for a second before his expression cleared. He punched the button on the phone unit and replaced the handset in its cradle. Trapp listened to the phone ring, and ring, and wondered if there was any chance of this plan actually working, since everything else they had tried so far had failed spectacularly.

"Dani Carter."

The FBI agent's familiar tones filled the speaker's palatial office. Randall looked up at Trapp for confirmation before he spoke.

"Agent Carter. This is Randall Woods, the Speaker of the House."

"Yes, sir," Dani replied, missing half a beat as though through surprise. "How can I help?"

And then the line died. A *beep-beep-beep* resonated out of

the speaker unit. Behind the congressman's desk, Trapp clenched his fist with satisfaction. He didn't let it show. They were not yet done.

"I've got something here, Trapp," Greaves said.

"Replace the handset, Mr. Speaker," Trapp ordered the puzzled Congressman. The man did as he was told.

Barely thirty seconds later, the phone rang. It was Woods's direct line – not the one his secretary answered. The speaker looked up at Trapp, a tremor rattling his entire body.

"Who is it?"

"I think we both know," Trapp replied, his wraithlike eyes flashing with warning. "Remember. Do as you're told, and I promise I will get you out of this alive. Screw me on this and..."

He shrugged. His hard expression told its own story. If Randall screwed Trapp on this—and by extension the entire country—then his fairytale would not have a happy ending.

With trembling fingers, Woods picked up the phone, pressed the speaker button, and replaced the handset. There was a long silence before a voice spoke on the other end of the line.

"Randy," it said. "A little friend told me that you have been a very naughty boy."

The speaker didn't have to fake the whimper that escaped his lips. "I'm sorry, I –"

"No, Randy. You *will be* sorry. I told you that I was going to make you President. Did you take me for a liar?"

"No, I –"

"Keep him talking, Trapp," Greaves practically yelled with excitement – half-deafening Trapp, but inaudible to the rest of the room. "I've almost got him."

Trapp did as he was told, gesturing at the speaker to extend the conversation. The man looked broken, and as if he would rather do anything else in the world. But eyeing Trapp's expression, he clearly decided that he had to pick a side.

And he chose Trapp's.

"Randy, I'm afraid I will have to punish you for this. You understand that, don't you?"

"Yes..."

"I can't have people working for me who I can't trust. Not even you, Randy. I have big plans for you. But I can always find someone else..."

The voice let the threat hang in the air.

The speaker's voice was hoarse with fear, little more than a whisper. Trapp looked at the man with disgust. Sweat patches had formed beneath his armpits. He was a shell of a human being. "I'm sorry. I promise, I won't do it again. I'll never cross you again."

"Good," the cold, compressed voice replied. "Because you know the consequences if you do. I won't kill you, Randy. I'll let you rot in jail. Maybe release you into genpop, and let the animals deal with you."

The phone line went dead. Trapp slumped back in his chair. Had it been long enough? Or had all of this been for nothing?

"Greaves?"

The scientist took a long time to reply. Long enough for Trapp to start to believe that it was all over – that he had failed. But when Greaves finally spoke, his voice was jubilant.

"Trapp. I have it. I have the location of whoever's operating Birdseye. But you're not going to believe it..."

53

President Nash felt like his presidency was slipping from between his fingers, and there was nothing he could do about it. He hadn't slept in coming on three nights, and the address to Congress was approaching fast – a date with destiny that wouldn't stop dogging his waking thoughts.

His military, intelligence and law enforcement advisors were united in their advice that going through with it was a damn fool idea. On the other hand, his political staff agreed that if he *didn't*, then he might as well kiss his presidency goodbye.

His neck was on the chopping block – damned whether he decided to stick or twist, and Nash hated it.

Since Bloody Monday, he'd been more like a rubber duck than the leader of the free world, bobbing along on currents over which he had no control. His FBI had been exposed as a nest of vipers, the director of the NSA was dead, and there were no suspects in the Bloody Monday investigation. Talking heads were beginning to call for his head, and he'd only been in office for a fortnight.

This meeting was no different. He didn't know where he was headed, for what reason, or when they would arrive at their mysterious destination. His protective detail flanked him in a phalanx of muscle and military hardware, their reflective sunglasses making them look both more than human – and also yet another organization over which he had no real control.

"Where the hell are you taking me, Martinez?" he groused as his Chief of Staff led him through basement access corridors that he imagined many presidents never saw throughout an entire eight-year term.

"I need you to trust me on this, Mr. President," the harried woman replied without turning. "I'll explain, I promise."

She led him to the kitchens of the White House mess. The President's protective detail quickly cleared the room, leaving the two of them alone among the expanse of stainless-steel worktops.

"What are we doing here, Emma?" he asked, pinching the bridge of his nose and closing his exhausted eyes.

A door clicked open at the far end of the long kitchen. Nash flinched – for a second wondering if this was it; if Emma Martinez had sold him out, just like all those FBI agents who had gone rogue. Could this really be the plan – to kill him in the basement of the White House itself?

No.

FBI director Vince Rutger stepped into the kitchen clad in a long black overcoat and matching Oxfords that had been polished until they reflected every glimmer of light in the vast kitchen. He was followed by a woman the president could not quite place. She was of medium height, but extremely fit, glossy black hair pulled back into a severe ponytail.

"That's..."

"Agent Dani Carter," Martinez confirmed. Her voice was tight and clipped, as though she was second-guessing whether she had made the right call. "The agent who almost foiled the bombing at the Hoover building."

"I've seen her before," Nash muttered quietly as the two representatives of the FBI walked toward them, their footsteps loud in the empty kitchen.

"Yes, sir. She attended the briefing in the Situation Room yesterday."

"Well," Nash grouched, "what the hell is she doing here?"

"Perhaps I can answer that, Mr. President," Rutger replied, his voice gruff in the silence. "And I apologize for the cloak and dagger routine. It was necessary."

"I'm not accustomed to being summoned, Director," Nash said.

In truth, he hadn't been president long. The campaign had lasted eighteen long months, and had been a masterclass in being summoned. His time wasn't yet quite as valuable as it would soon become. Still, he was the highest elected representative of the American people, and he wanted to know why the hell he had been dragged into the basement of the White House to speak to a man whose agency was riddled with traitors.

"No, sir," Rutger replied, seeming strangely upbeat for a man whose job prospects were no doubt already in the Congressional firing line. "I'll make this quick."

Nash motioned for him to continue.

"Mr. President, I believe that someone is planning to kill you."

Nash glanced at his chief of staff, wondering if this was all some kind of sick joke. But the woman's expression was grave. He closed his eyes for a second, attempting to process what Rutger had just told him.

"I've got to hand it to you, Vince," Nash replied. "You know how to make an entrance. But you'll forgive me for not taking you at your word. The Bureau isn't exactly riding high in my estimation right now."

Rutger removed his cell phone from inside his coat pocket and held it toward Nash.

"I thought that might be the case, Mr. President," he replied. "So I came prepared. I'd like to play you something."

Despite his reservations, Nash was curious. Though he did not know Rutger well, the FBI director did not strike him as a frivolous man. And despite all the evidence to the contrary, given the Bureau was in chaos, neither did Rutger present the image of a man fighting for his job. He was deadly serious, and the thought sent a trickle of unease up Nash's back.

The President gestured at Rutger to continue. The director peered at the screen of his phone, then tapped it with his finger forcefully. For a few long seconds nothing happened, and Nash's irritation rose. And then the audio file began to play.

The first voice was gruff and rugged. Nash recognized the type of man—if not the voice itself—from his years in the Marines. It was laced with a barely controlled aggression.

"What did he want from you?"

"It's not what he wanted from me. It's what he wanted for me."

"Which was?"

"He said he was going to make me President."

Nash stumbled backward, his eyes widening as he realized who the second voice belonged to. His leather wingtips caught against one of the steel worktops and almost sent him flying. A saucepan fell to the ground, dislodged by the impact, and reverberated around the concrete floor. Instantly, a Secret Service agent entered the kitchen, his weapon half drawn.

"Mr. President?" the man said, eyes darting around the room. "Are you okay?"

Nash regained his footing, his mind spinning. The voice had sounded like – but that wasn't possible. How could this be happening?

"I'm fine," Nash croaked, taking a deep breath to steady himself. "Thank you, agent, but I need the room."

"Yes, Mr. President," the man replied uneasily, holstering his weapon beneath his jacket and stepping out of the kitchen, casting a final curious glance before he left.

Rutger looked at the President with an expression of deep sincerity. "So now you know."

"Humor me, Vince," Nash said, his eyes flickering between the FBI director and the female agent standing at his side, "by explaining exactly what you're driving at."

"Sir," Rutger said. "We have incontrovertible evidence implicating the speaker of the House in a plot to assassinate you. I have a signed copy of his confession in my office safe."

By now, Nash didn't even feel shocked. He was simply drained. The body blows kept raining down, and he was too tired to dodge.

"Have you arrested him?"

Rutger shook his head, looking pained. "No, Mr. President."

"Why the hell not?"

"This isn't exactly the kind of evidence that stands up in court, sir," Rutger replied, looking wary. "And..."

The female agent, Dani Carter, interjected, cutting the director off. "Sir, we believe that Randall Woods's involvement is merely the tip of the iceberg."

Nash raised an eyebrow at the young agent's impertinence, but a combination of a wry smile on Rutger's face and the fierce determination on hers was enough to give him pause. Besides, the unusual nature of this meeting notwithstanding – wasn't this exactly what he had been searching for since Bloody Monday? The inside track – or at least a clue as to what the hell was going on.

The President was sick of feeling around in the dark. He was the commander in chief of the most fearsome military and intelligence services ever assembled by man, and yet none of his advisers seemed to know their ass from their elbow. Until Agent Dani Carter, and her determined emerald eyes. If this was his one shot at getting the truth, he had to take it.

"Okay, Agent Carter," Nash said slowly, "I'll hear you out. But you just told me that Woods is planning to have me go down in history as the first President assassinated since Kennedy. You'll have to go some to trump that."

"Sir, have you heard of the NSA's Birdseye program?"

54

The President needed confirmation that the threat to the Capitol was real before he was even willing to contemplate going ahead with the second part of the operation that Dani Carter had proposed, and Trapp intended to deliver it.

Greaves's limited access to Birdseye had led him to an isolated farmhouse in the country north of Washington DC, near a small town called Clarksville. The address to Congress was scheduled for the very next day, and that meant that they were running out of time. As far as Greaves could make out, the Clarksville farmhouse was the hub for whatever operation the terrorists were planning.

Trapp wished that the NSA scientist would simply turn on the data tap and get the answers they so desperately needed. He was tired of fighting with one hand tied behind his back. But it wasn't that simple, and he knew it.

If Greaves started sucking more intelligence out of the NSA computer program known as Birdseye, then the system would detect the intrusion, and the only advantage they had—slight as it was—would be burned. It was a risk they dared not take. So Trapp was doing what he did best: putting himself into peril in order to gather the information his country so desperately needed.

"Control," Trapp murmured quietly into his throat mic, "I'm moving into position. It'll take me another few minutes."

"Copy, Hangman. We'll be waiting."

Trapp's unequal eyes surveyed the Arctic landscape. They made him resemble a predator more than a man; a Siberian tiger hunting its prey. He was dressed in white winter camouflage and carried a raft of surveillance equipment. Directional microphones and high-resolution digital cameras had competed for space with weapons and ammunition. In the end, the surveillance tools had won out. They needed the intelligence on what was happening at that farmhouse more than they needed Trapp alive.

They knew the when and the where of the attack that was planned on the President. The very next day, during the address to Congress.

They just didn't know *how* the attack would take place. What weapons would be used. How many shooters there would be. Their planned routes of ingress and egress. In short, all the details that would be vital to neuter the assault.

Trapp wasn't ruling anything out. After the airstrike that had nearly killed him at the start of this adventure, and then the cyber attack that had crippled most of the Eastern Seaboard when the Israeli mercenaries assassinated the NSA director, he would not have been entirely surprised if a US submarine emerged from the freezing waters of the Atlantic Ocean in February and fired a nuclear-tipped cruise missile at the Capitol building itself.

Of course, he didn't think it was *likely*, but he wasn't ruling it out.

"I'm in," Trapp radioed as he belly crawled through the snow, clipped a razor wire fence that surrounded the land around the farmhouse, and got eyes on his target. "Setting up the equipment now."

As Trapp worked, he quickly became aware damn cold he was. It couldn't have been more than thirty degrees out, and he was face down in the snow. It brought him back to his time with Delta, training in the Arctic. Trapp had found something to enjoy in pretty much every country he had been sent to over the course of his career.

But not Norway and its frozen North. Right now, memories of hunching over a sniper rifle for days on end were rushing back to him. He'd almost lost a finger on that training op. It still ached in the cold. Now was no exception.

He pushed them aside and concentrated his full attention on the farmhouse that was about a hundred yards before him, at the bottom of a slightly sloping hill. Greaves had discovered that a significant amount of Birdseye's attention was currently focused on this one single address. As such, Trapp knew he had to be careful. A single wrong move, and he might blow the whole plan.

But it was the clue they had needed. Trapp felt in his gut that this was the terrorists' staging area. It was perfect – well connected by road to Washington DC, but isolated enough that the only people who might stumble across it were hunters. And with the weather right now in DC, no one was out hunting.

He attached one of the small cameras to a fencepost at the top of the hill, careful not to show too much of his body as he worked.

"We've got visuals, Hangman. Good job."

Trapp decorated the first surveillance camera with a little bit of snow before inching back and studying his handiwork. If he hadn't known it was there, he probably would not have noticed it. Unless the terrorists had counter-intelligence training—which they had no reason to believe—he doubted it would be noticed.

"Moving to position Bravo," he said.

Trapp didn't stop moving until four separate cameras were installed, covering every inch of the farmhouse's exterior and every entrance in and out. He interspersed the directional mics, knowing that the wind was probably too great for them to pick up anything of use, but figured that since he had lugged them this far, he might as well plant them.

As the last microphone came online, Mitchell's voice buzzed in Trapp's ear. "Okay, Trapp. Get yourself out of there. We got what we needed, and you've got a flight to catch. Good job."

Trapp stayed perfectly still, though the thoughts of tomorrow's mission briefly invaded his mind. He licked his lips hungrily, ready for a change in scenery – and for a more inviting target. Clarksville had been a necessary diversion, but he was ready to hunt bigger game, and finally, after all these months, deliver justice for his fallen friend.

But he couldn't leave, not yet. He needed to see for himself what was happening down there. He knew that Mitchell and Kyle were the best of the best – if anyone could make use of the footage that was now transmitting to the Great Falls safe house, it would be them.

But Trapp was old-fashioned. He preferred the human eyeball. Nothing could beat actually getting close and getting eyes on a target. Cameras missed details, and in Trapp's experience it was those missing details that got you killed. Tomorrow night it wouldn't be his life on the line—not directly, at least— but he had grown fond of Agent Carter in the brief time he'd known her.

"Moving to the extraction point," he radioed.

But he lingered, inching forward to the brow of the hill that looked down on the frozen farmhouse. Light flooded from the bottom of the front door, but the windows were boarded up. Next to the farmhouse was a large barn, probably used for storing tractors and equipment back when this was still a working farm. Now the building was dilapidated, but Trapp thought he saw signs that vehicles had recently entered it. The snowy ground was chewed up and dirty in front of the barn's roller shutter entrance; dark frozen grooves scored the mud. Whatever had driven in there, it was heavy. A tractor, maybe? But that made no sense.

His radio crackled once again. "Hangman, hold your position. We're picking up movement heading toward the farmhouse. Two vehicles."

"Copy."

Trapp did as he was told. He wasn't worried about getting caught. In his white camouflage suit, he was basically invisible from both the sky and the ground. It blocked his heat emissions, making him give off no greater a thermal signature than a small rabbit. And he wanted to see how this played out.

He pulled out a small tactical scope from a pocket on his thigh and brought it to his right eyeball. He listened as the sound of engines growled in the previously silent, crisp February sky. They came closer, and as they did several men spilled out of the farmhouse. Two of them were armed with M-16 rifles, or at least some kind of variant. They held them loosely across their chests – clearly not expecting any danger.

He studied them. If he had to guess, he would have pegged them for ex-convicts. They had that kind of build about them – overly muscular, with a scarcely controlled aggression in their step.

"Are you seeing this, Control?" he whispered. "This is it."

As he watched through his scope, Trapp saw two of the men

drag the barn doors open. Inside, he hit the jackpot. They were parked almost out of sight, likely invisible to the cameras in the gloom, but through his scope he could just make out the white lettering on the sides of the nearest of the two black Ford armored trucks.

It spelled: SECRET SERVICE.

55

Andrew Rawlin sat in the back of a customized Ford F550 truck, his purple birthmark only half-visible behind the balaclava that covered most of his face. The vehicle was an exact replica of the ones used by the Secret Service's Counter-Assault Teams. It was even manufactured by the same company, the Texas Armor Group.

Rawlin did not know it, but TAG was a wholly-owned subsidiary of Atlas Defense Systems. The vehicles were first built over a year before and shipped to a warehouse in Virginia for storage. All evidence of their production had been wiped from TAG's systems.

"I hope you're ready, boys," Rawlin said, speaking into his radio for the benefit of the two trailing, identical trucks. "Because a new America will rise today. And you will be the new founding fathers."

The plan was simple.

The President, along with both the leadership and rank-and-file of both Houses of Congress would be in the same place at the same time in less than an hour. That place was the chamber of the House of Representatives, and except for Area

51, it was currently the most secure location in the continental United States. Every conceivable law enforcement, intelligence and security agency in the country had worked together to create an impenetrable ring of steel.

Plans had been drawn up to simply storm Capitol Hill, to bring every foot soldier trained at Rawlin's camp to the DC area, arm them, and let them loose.

Those plans were discarded.

The United States Secret Service alone had almost two thousand armed agents on site. Field offices from across the nation had been stripped of personnel and shipped back to Washington DC. A frontal assault was considered suicidal.

Overhead, the US Air Force patrolled the skies, and the noise of jet engines was almost constant, like the cracking of thunder. Across the capitol, dogs whimpered with fear as they listened to a terror that seemed like it would never end. Half a dozen F-35 fighter jets roamed the skies, ready to destroy any aerial threat to the President. The idea of hijacking a 747 from the nearby Reagan National Airport and plunging it into the dome of the Capitol Building was similarly crossed off the list.

In addition, several Apache gunships were in the air. Their addition to the security team had been hotly debated. They were more suited to war-torn hellholes where collateral damage simply didn't matter than to the densely populated environment of the District. In the end, their addition was greenlit. Nothing could be allowed to threaten the smooth running of the Joint Address.

Not tonight. Not while half of America cowered in fear, and the other half was ready to invade the Middle East and take its vengeance, even if that meant setting a continent on fire.

No.

To succeed with his mission tonight, Rawlin knew he would have to play the enemy at their own game. But be better.

The only way in was to be invited. To dress like the enemy.

To travel like the enemy. To blend in, to wait, and then finally to choose the moment to strike.

The purpose of the real Secret Service Counter-Assault Team was to buy the President time to escape in the event of an attack. They were armed like special forces, given the same training, and hungered to repel an assault on the President of the United States with overwhelming force.

Every single police officer, FBI or Secret Service agent, along with personnel from almost a dozen other three letter government agencies knew that if the CAT came running, it was time to get the hell out of their way.

That was why Andrew Rawlin, along with five other men, and twelve more in the two vehicles behind his, was dressed in the black battle dress uniform worn by the Counter-Assault Team. That very evening the enemy would invite him in. They wouldn't suspect a thing – in fact, they would welcome him.

And he would pay them back in fire.

"Radio check," Rawlin transmitted.

As his team sounded off, he studied them carefully for any sign of weakness. For any sign that he had allowed his chosen men to be infiltrated by the enemy. Was there right now a wolf among them, wearing sheep's clothing?

Rawlin doubted it.

He had selected each of the men for this mission. They were ready to do their duty. To die in the process. Just as his boys had been back in Houston. That had been a glorious day. Hundreds dead. Rawlin had reveled in the footage on the cable networks.

As the last of his men chimed in, Rawlin smiled. He was pleased. He could survive without the encrypted radios, but it would certainly make things harder.

"Good. You all know what you have to do tonight. Think fast, shoot faster. The President is our primary target. Then

Randall Woods, the speaker of the House. After that, take as many of the rest of the bastards out as you can."

His men roared their approval. Rawlin clenched his fist with pride. If he died in the next few hours, then he would do so beside better men than him.

Each of them was equipped with an SR-16 assault rifle built by the Knight's Armaments Company, and a Sig Sauer P229 pistol strapped to their right thigh. It was precisely the same weaponry used by the real members of the Secret Service's Counter-Assault Team. Everything had to be perfect. There could be no mistakes, nothing that could give them away.

They would only get one chance at this. But God was on their side. They would only need one.

Rawlin thumped his fist on the tinted window to signal the driver of the truck to get moving. It wasn't a long drive to Capitol Hill, but it was imperative that they not be late.

"It's time. Let's move out."

～

THE TEXT MESSAGE WAS UNEXPECTED, and Andrew Rawlin didn't like the unexpected. But he knew it was simply the cost of doing business, when that business was an attempt to alter the course of history.

He glanced down at his phone, which was still buzzing. It was one of the units that his unknown benefactor had sent him some months before. Completely secure. The only person who had access to it was the man who had set all these events in motion. A man who had proved himself to Rawlin a thousand times over.

Every promise he'd made was kept. Everything he said would happen did. So as unwelcome as his message was, Rawlin trusted him implicitly.

Asset inside Capitol captured, the text read. *Complex is in lock-*

down. President being evacuated from secondary location inside Marine One. Teams on site have orders to pull back when you arrive. Good luck.

Rawlin's helmet thudded back against his headrest, its strap biting viciously into his chin. He allowed himself a moment of sheer, unadulterated rage. He'd screwed up with his selection of Cal Cooper. He'd known he was too green, but the kid had convinced him that he could do the job.

Fuck!

All Cal had needed to do was play it cool, and then discharge his weapon when he received the signal that Rawlin himself was to have sent. Cooper's job was to plunge the Capitol into chaos, make the Secret Service harden up on President Nash, and give Rawlin's fake Counter-Assault Team a pretext to storm the building. But the Detroit kid had screwed up. Rawlin's knuckles clenched white, his teeth gritted together, tension rising in every muscle. Curious eyes danced over to him, then at each other as his men wondered what had just happened.

And then the wave of anger subsided. Rawlin forced it to. He had sacrificed too much to fall at this final hurdle. Gibson's face flashed before his eyes, an image of blood against the snow. He had given everything for this. This was merely another test. One he intended to pass.

"Change of plan," he said into his radio, his voice tight with stress. "Divert to the secondary location at the Washington Monument. The Secret Service has set up a landing pad. We will have to take the President the second he exits his motorcade."

One of his men turned to him. The man's face was covered by a black balaclava, so only his eyes showed – a patch of white against the black of his counterfeit Secret Service battle dress uniform. Every few seconds, patches of blue and red reflected off the man's face from the flashing lights which crowned each of the three armored cars.

"What's going on, boss?" he asked. "Why the change of plan? I thought we were supposed to take all of them."

The truth was, Rawlin did not know what had gone wrong. How Cooper had been discovered. He'd selected the man himself. Put his faith in him. The plan had been set in stone for months. Everything he had done, everything his men had trained for, it had all been for this. And now, on the night of the dance, it had changed.

Rawlin saw three more sets of eyes staring at him. He knew that if one had asked, others would be wondering. He was their leader. His job was to know all the answers. And when he didn't, it was to convince his men that he did.

Rawlin grinned, assuming an easy confidence. "Negro or not, Tyson was right. Everyone's got a plan until they get punched in the face. What matters is what you do after you get hit. Are you ready to give up?"

The response was angry. Proud. Immediate. "Hell, no!"

"Good," Rawlin growled back, feeling a surge of pride in his men at their response. So much of his beloved country was falling apart. Polluted by immigrants, and by corruption. But not these boys. The best their country had to offer.

"The Secret Service will bring the President out fast. They will expect their Counter-Assault Team to arrive. But they won't expect us. The second Nash steps out of the Beast, light him up."

56

D ani Carter was on edge.

Emergency lights danced on the Washington Monument itself, an eerie light show, and armed agents dressed in black decorated the marked-out landing zone like specks of ink against the frozen ground. Director Rutger hadn't wanted her down here once the bullets started flying, but she had stood her ground. She wasn't handing this over to another agent. Not now. Not after all she had done.

"Any sign of them?" an agent asked over her radio.

Dani frowned. "All teams, maintain radio silence," she said into her black Motorola encrypted radio. "I repeat, all teams, keep radio discipline. SAC out."

If Dani had any way of finding out which agent had spoken, even on an encrypted channel, she would have chewed them out right then and there. That was the problem with compartmentalizing information. If she had been able to brief every agent on the ground on exactly what she knew, and what she anticipated might go down, then a lapse like that probably wouldn't have happened.

After all, how could the offender have known that they were

up against someone who had access to all the intelligence gathering powers of the United States Government itself?

Unfortunately, Dani still didn't know who she could trust. Trapp had wanted to keep the information circle tight, and she agreed. The more people who knew, the greater the chance the plan got leaked – and if that happened, then the man they suspected of coordinating the whole conspiracy would destroy all evidence of his involvement in the scheme to bring down the President of the United States.

Unfortunately, that meant screw-ups like this were inevitable.

All the agents on the ground knew was that there was a threat to the President. Each was drawn from the FBI's SWAT units – every single one of them an elite sharpshooter. And they were instructed by the director of the FBI himself to follow whatever command she gave. The only departure from ordinary FBI procedure was a big one – every single agent was wearing Secret Service gear.

Dani trembled at the power. Her mouth seemed eternally dry, and she refreshed it for what seemed like the hundredth time from a bottle clipped to her waist. Right now, the lives of dozens of agents rested on her authority. If she screwed up, some of them might die. They would go into the light without even knowing why their lives were sacrificed.

Hell, even if she played her cards completely right, that might still happen. Was she capable of going through with this?

Pull yourself together.

It was too late for thoughts like this. If she was going to chicken out, she should have done it when Rutger tried to talk her out of it. No, Dani had made her bed, now it was time to lie in it.

Dani ran through the operational plan one last time, checking each agent was in their defined position. The helicopter landing zone was demarcated just north of the Washington Monument. It was a breathtaking sight – an enormous marble and granite obelisk, stretching over five hundred feet high. It was lit up with spotlights, making it look like the tourist attraction it normally was, rather than the ambush site it was about to become.

It needed to be, so that the incoming helicopter pilots wouldn't encounter it at the last moment. The pilots flying the Sikorsky VH-3D Sea King helicopters that usually carried the President were equipped with night vision, of course, but as every helicopter pilot knows, any flight that you manage to walk away from successfully is a good one.

Dani's earpiece crackled. "I've got a three-vehicle motorcade traveling east on Constitution Avenue," an agent reported. "Looks like Secret Service."

Dani clenched her fist. This was it, she knew it was. A wave of exhilaration overcame her as adrenaline flooded into her system. Her heart rate spiked, her mouth went dry again, and this time she didn't bother drinking. In just a few minutes, this would all be over, one way or another.

"Copy that. All units, allow the motorcade to proceed to the helicopter extraction point."

Agents all around the perimeter checked in, registering their acknowledgment of her order. They had no idea why Dani Carter had been so insistent that every single vehicle movement, whether friend or foe, was reported directly to her. But it was vital. She couldn't mess this up.

Fewer than thirty seconds later, Dani radioed the perimeter for an update. "This is the SAC. What's the location on that Secret Service convoy?"

The answer came immediately. "They just turned right at the German Friendship Garden. They are heading toward you now."

Dani didn't reply. She needed all her focus on what was about to happen, here now. She turned north and watched the first of the three modified F-550 trucks heading toward her down a path cut through the park. They had red and blue lights on top, flashing, and though she could not yet make out the detail, she knew that the Secret Service's insignia, shaped like the five points of a sheriff's star, would be emblazoned on the sides.

If Dani didn't know that they weren't real, she would have been taken in. Hell, even though she did, she almost was. The three vehicles looked precisely like the real Secret Service rides she had seen in her briefing packs. Someone had planned every detail down to a T.

"Perimeter units," Dani said into radio, "pull back a hundred yards to the border of the park."

The unit in question radioed their acknowledgment, but Dani was only half paying attention. Her eyes were trained on the oncoming vehicles, and the confrontation that was about to come. On a second radio, pulled from inside her windbreaker, she radioed a second source entirely.

"Send in Avalon."

A few seconds later, the first of the suspect vehicle arrived. Almost before it had finished moving, a man jumped out. Like her, he was dressed in Secret Service gear – but while she was wearing just a blue windbreaker with a bulletproof vest underneath, he was kitted out in full battle dress uniform. All black. Bristling with weapons.

"Who's in charge here?" he growled, striding toward her with an excess of confidence. It was amazing. Dani had no doubt that without prewarning she would have been taken in by this charade.

"That would be me," she replied without hesitation.

All of the nerves that had assailed her a few moments ago seemed to have faded away. All that was left was calm. Calm and determination – a fierce resolve to get the job done, to end this. Now.

"Give me a status update," the man said without bothering to introduce himself.

All around Dani, heavily armed men were beginning to exit the three Ford trucks. They set up a perimeter, and she couldn't help but notice that although they were relaxed, their weapons were aimed in the direction of her people.

She knew that this could go very bad, very fast.

"Gaslamp is about three minutes out. Marine One should touch down shortly before he arrives."

Dani could already hear the rotor noise cutting up the DC night sky.

"What the hell happened in there?" the unknown man said, staring directly at her and gesturing at the Capitol Building. Dani's eyes were drawn to the purple blotch that marked his face. She knew his real name—Andrew Rawlin—though she didn't let on.

"In fact, it doesn't matter. Pull your people back. I want my men to have clear fields of fire when the president gets here. If anyone's coming for him, we'll take them down."

Dani noted the conviction in the man's voice. But she knew that it wasn't conviction that he would save the President's life. Whoever he was, he wanted her out of here so that he could kill President Nash.

Still, she couldn't let him have his way so easily. Just in case he suspected something was wrong. Dani shot him a funny look, ignoring the nerves that churned in her stomach. Was she pulling this off? Did he suspect anything?

"That's against protocol."

The armed man masquerading as the lead agent of a Secret Service Counter-Assault Team leaned forward menacingly. Condensation from his breath danced in the cold February air, spiraling in the glow cast by the floodlights.

"Lady, this whole evening has been against protocol. If you don't get the hell out of my way, I'll order my men to open fire. Nothing—nothing—is going to stand in the way of me achieving my mission. I don't care if I end up behind bars over this. The president ain't dying on my watch. You understand?"

Dani threw her hands up in a gesture of peace, knowing she had her man. He was hooked. Now she just had to pull this off without anyone getting hurt.

"Okay, okay, I got it. The President's motorcade will be here in ninety seconds. I'll pull my people back."

The helicopter noise was louder now. That had been Dani's idea. She knew that to have the best chance of this going down without a hitch, everything needed to proceed just as the terrorists would have planned it. They believed that Marine One would be landing to pick up the President, so if they didn't hear the sound of helicopters, they might realize something was off.

Dani glanced up, and even against the light pollution thrown off by DC at night, she could see the black shapes of the aircraft closing on them fast. The end game was upon them.

She spoke into her radio before jerking her head at a nearby agent. "Everyone, pull back and await further orders."

Dani climbed into a marked Secret Service SUV. The second the doors closed and she was hidden behind the dark, tinted windows, she let out a deep sigh. They were so close.

As the driver gunned the engine, kicking flurries of snow up behind the rear wheels, Dani spun around to face Adrian, who was sitting in the back, glued to the bright glow of a laptop screen. Dani was glad she'd read him in. It was good to have someone alongside her she could trust.

"Everything going to plan?"

Adrian nodded seriously. This was one of the FBI's biggest takedown missions since Waco – and everyone knew how that had gone. Back then, the Bureau had been facing a bunch of religious nuts, not hardened domestic terrorists with enough determination and firepower to make today one of the bloodiest days in FBI history.

"Okay, send in the motorcade."

The motorcade was a decoy as well – another step in a delicate ballet. Director Rutger had pulled strings with the Secret Service, and they'd loaned some of their backup vehicles. Because of this, however, there were fewer vehicles than would ordinarily accompany the President. Dani just hoped that this would not be noticed in the chaos.

"It's on its way."

The noise of helicopters beat down overhead, throwing out clouds of snow that danced in the floodlights, painting the whole scene in a thick white fog. They were just seconds out. Out of the corner of her eye, Dani could see the fake presidential motorcade speeding toward the helicopter extraction zone, now marked by smoke grenades. The orange smoke poured out, drifting lazily on a slight northwesterly breeze, but mostly hung low over the snowy ground.

Dani grabbed the driver by his shoulder and told him to pull over. They weren't quite at the border of the park yet, but she needed to watch this. It wasn't like she could do anything to influence the situation now – that was in other people's hands.

But she had to watch.

Her radio crackled. The time for radio silence was over. The takedown was on.

"This is Avalon. We're ten seconds out. Stop the motorcade."

Dani grabbed her radio. "You heard the man. Do it."

She watched as the motorcade speeding down the National Mall obeyed her orders. It screeched to a halt, cutting dark, muddy chunks out of the snow as the vehicles ground to a stop.

The posture of the terrorists instantly changed. Where just a second ago they had been relaxed but determined, now heads began to turn toward the leader.

She could imagine the confusion, then panic that was beginning to overtake them. They didn't have long to figure out what was going on. In an instant, a flight of three Sikorsky VH-3D Sea King helicopters bore down out of the night sky. They had exactly the same profile as those flown by the Marine Corps detachment that handled the President's transport by helicopter.

But these were flown by FBI pilots.

By the time the markings on the side of the aircraft became evident, it was already too late for the terrorists to run. The Sea Kings hovered in a loose formation about twenty feet off the ground. Inside each were eight FBI Hostage Rescue Team commandos – the best trained men the Bureau had.

They were recruited from FBI SWAT teams across the country, along with former US military special forces personnel. They were as comfortable fast-roping from a helicopter in high winds as they were jumping out the plane for a HALO parachute insertion. Each was a perfect shot. And, as two US Army Apache gunship helicopters maneuvered into position around the supposed landing zone, Dani knew there would be no escape for the terrorists. Not on her watch. Not tonight.

"Avalon is overhead. We have them surrounded."

"Understood. Maintain your position and pick your shots. The second one of them makes a move you don't like, take them out. I want them alive, but not at the cost of our guys."

Dani watched as the helicopters maneuvered into perfect firing positions. The men on the ground understood now that their plan had gone off the rails. They were crouched low, sheltering behind their vehicles, aiming up at the helicopters.

Dani trained her eyes on only one of them. Rawlin. He was perfectly still, as though analyzing what was going on. He knew there was no getting out of this.

"Adrian, binoculars," she ordered without looking around.

The agent rummaged for a second, then handed her a pair. She pressed them to her eyes to get a better look.

At this magnification, she could see exactly what was going on. She focused on Rawlin again, watching his every movement. Her heartrate was raised, her adrenal glands forcing an endless stream of nervous energy into her body. With it, her breath was ragged, even though she had performed no physical activity, and the fingers holding the binoculars trembled, causing her vision to blur.

The next few seconds happened in slow motion. Dani watched, powerless to intervene, as the leader raised a radio to his lips. The second he'd spoken, his men rushed into action, several of them firing up at the helicopters hovering overhead, others rushing into the armored vehicles they'd arrived in. Once inside, Dani knew that they would be more or less protected from most of the hardware the Bureau HRT had brought with them. If she didn't act fast, this could end up in a bloody chase through the streets of the District.

That could not happen. These men could not be allowed to escape.

"Take your shots," she said into her own radio. "Take them out, now!"

But the agents in the air overhead didn't need her urging. Well-aimed gunshots cracked down, and Dani watched as the terrorists fell one after another. A few of them made it into their vehicles, gunning the engines and driving in a zigzag fashion.

But they did not make it far.

The Bureau might not have had the firepower to take out the vehicles. But the Army did. For the first time in recorded history, a Hellfire missile was fired in anger on US soil. The distance it had to travel was barely a hundred yards, and before Dani's eyes can even pick up the contrail of smoke in the air, an enormous explosion scarred the ground of the National Mall.

"My God," the driver breathed next to her as a thunderous echo rolled around the Mall. The shockwave compressed Dani's chest, and the SUV rocked from the impact.

The snowy ground had been turned into a war zone. Flames licked what was left of the armored vehicle, and a trail of thick, choking black smoke began to stream into the sky. As debris and shrapnel began to rain down against the ground, the rest of the world seemed to pause. The second armored truck, clearly watching the fate of the first, did not move.

It was as though the shock and awe of the first explosion had stunned them into inaction. Dani knew she had a chance to resolve this without further violence. But she had to act fast.

Dani pressed her radio back to her lips. "Get on the loud-speaker," she ordered. "End this."

Overhead, a speaker mounted underneath one of the Sea King helicopters boomed out.

"Step out of your vehicles. I repeat, step out of your vehicles and put your weapons on the ground."

Nothing happened for a second. Only the beating of the rotors and the snow swirling beneath their downwash. But as the agent began to repeat his message, Dani watched as first one, then two, then all the remaining terrorists exited their vehicles and threw their weapons onto the snowy earth. They walked like beaten dogs, their posture slouched forward, heads down. Snow kicked up into their faces, coating their black fatigues white. They looked like ghosts against the swirling snow.

"Lie flat on the ground. Put your hands behind your head. If you move, you die."

It was over. It was finally over. But as a wave of relief began to sweep through Dani Carter, as her shoulders hunched forward with a release of tension, and exhaustion threatened to overcome her, she knew she had one more task to do.

Dani changed the channel on her radio, cutting out every

agent on the scene. The message she had to give was not for public consumption. If the wider world knew what was about to happen, no matter what she had pulled off tonight, she would either end her days in jail, or in the cold embrace of a lethal injection.

"It's Carter. The President is secure. Tell Hangman his mission is a go."

57

Vice President Robert Jenkins sat in the basement beneath his Texas ranch. In his more grandiose moments, he thought of the basement as his command bunker, although he would never admit it.

Right now, that was certainly what it was. The room from which he would watch the world reborn. A world that would be remade in his image.

The wall of the basement was covered in television screens, with four screens in the center of the display joined together and displaying the same image – a live C-SPAN feed directly from Capitol Hill. The start of the President's address to a Joint Session of both Houses of Congress was only minutes away, and representatives and senators were beginning to file in, alongside security personnel from the Capitol Police, performing last-minute checks.

Jenkins grinned. He swirled a fifty-year-old Scotch in a cut crystal glass held in his fingers. A single mouthful of it cost more than one of those cops made in a month. He didn't really even like the taste.

Soon enough, he wouldn't be forced to hide away in a

cramped little basement in the ass end of nowhere, Texas. In just a matter of hours, maybe even sooner, someone would find him a Bible. He would lay his right palm face down on the sacred book that he didn't give a flying fuck about. He would mouth the words of the oath of office and be sworn in as the forty-seventh President of the United States of America.

Hell, he already knew the words. They had run through his head every night before bed for years. An affirmation he could recite in his sleep. A mantra that had driven him on for so long, which he had spilled so much blood to achieve. And he was so close now. Only a heartbeat away from the office he had desired for so long.

I do solemnly swear that I will faithfully execute the office of the President of the United States, and will to the best of my ability, preserve, protect and defend the Constitution of the United States.

Jenkins loosened his tie and glanced around. The hum of the air-conditioning unit seemed to have stopped. It was hot down here, with all the screens and electrical equipment.

Still, the chamber of the House of Representatives was beginning to fill up now, and Jenkins knew that showtime was only moments away. He could deal with the discomfort for a few moments.

He leaned forward, depressing an intercom button and speaking into it. "Assault team, status check."

Jenkins knew that he didn't have to do this. He had played his cards. The pieces were in motion, and they would fall where they would. But he was a man who hungered for control. The idea that he could simply sit back and let things occur without his direct influence was alien to him.

No answer. A flicker of unease prickled at the back of the vice president's neck. He repeated the message.

"I say again, assault team, status check."

He aped the clipped, professional tones that he had seen special forces teams use in the movies. The vice president had never served in the armed forces. That was for lesser men. No, he saw himself more as a general than a foot soldier. And besides, by the time this night was out, he would be the commander in chief of the entire US armed forces.

"Control," a speaker on the desk in front of him hissed. "This is the assault team. We are in position and waiting for your signal. Over."

Jenkins clenched his fist with satisfaction. Why the hell had he been so worried? His plan was perfect. In a matter of moments, once the President began his speech, several explosive devices would detonate around Capitol Hill. The President's motorcade would be destroyed, along with the backup vehicles held for precisely that reason, and with them the entire Counter-Assault Team.

At the same time, a man wearing the uniform of the Capitol Police would enter the House chamber and fire his weapon. It didn't matter what he hit. It only mattered that he caused chaos. The Secret Service would follow protocol, as they always did. Then they would learn that each of their planned escape routes had been cut off.

Panic would begin to creep in.

The Secret Service radio frequency would be hijacked, and a message broadcast that the heavily armed Hawkeye team, the Counter-Assault Team assigned for the protection of the President himself, was inbound to harden up on the president.

The CAT would enter the chamber, headed directly for the President. They would not be impeded. Hell, Secret Service agents would part like the Red Sea, leaving their boss open.

And then, President Charles Nash would be cut down on live television, in front of a horrified nation. Randall Woods would be next – a loose end not just tied up, but cauterized. With any luck, most of the House and Senate leadership would be taken out as well. But Jenkins knew he had enough dirt on any survivors to bend them to his will regardless of whether they lived or died.

On the screen in front of the vice president, he watched as in unison every man and woman in the House chamber rose to their feet to applaud the entrance of President Nash. Adrenaline surged in Jenkins's veins.

This was it. The culmination of so many years of effort. It was all proceeding exactly as he had planned. In moments, the President would be dead. Jenkins would trigger a computer protocol that would wipe out every piece of evidence in this basement. His own Secret Service detail would rush in, and they would treat him differently.

Because in a couple of minutes, Robert Jenkins would be the President of the United States of America.

The current vice president pressed down on the transmit button in front of him and spoke two words that would go down in history – though no one would ever know. Exactly the way Jenkins wanted it.

"Take him."

58

J ason Trapp kicked the grate that covered the vent of the HVAC system, and it hit the ground with a clatter. His lithe, muscular frame fell after it as he dropped to the ground in a graceful crouch. He had seen enough.

He spoke in a low growl. "With pleasure."

The vice president spun around, leaning his body back and away from Trapp in an instinctive defense reaction. His hand groped underneath the desk in search of the panic button that the Secret Service had installed several months before.

Trapp knew that the Service had screamed bloody murder when Jenkins told them they were not permitted to have an agent stand post in this basement. But the then vice president-elect had held firm. It was underground, with only one entrance, he'd shouted, and they'd installed vibration sensors underneath and around the basement itself to detect any attempt to tunnel in. And besides, he was about to be the vice-president of the United States, and he would God damn well have his way.

The only problem was that now an invader had penetrated Jenkins's sanctuary. That man was holding a pistol that was leveled at Robert Jenkins's forehead. It was a Beretta 9 mm, loaded with hollowpoint rounds that, once fired, would expand inside the target's body, destroying organs and rendering the unlucky subject dead in seconds. And that man was Jason Trapp.

The VP's chickens had most definitely come home to roost.

"Who the hell are you?" Jenkins spat, his fear and fury rendering him almost speechless for the first time in his life.

It was Trapp's turn to smile. "I'm your worst nightmare, Mr. Vice President."

Trapp watched as the man redoubled his attempts to grope for the panic button. His numbed, clumsy fingers finally connected with it, and Jenkins waited with a hint of satisfaction for his Secret Service protective detail to storm into the basement control room.

"I'm afraid, Bobby," Trapp said, "that isn't going to work. Not today. It's just you and me."

Jenkins's mouth bobbed open and closed a couple of times, and his eyes seemed to come in and out of focus, before settling on Trapp with a hint of recognition. He was lost for words. Trapp watched the display with a violent satisfaction. The man in front of him had brought terror to millions of Americans. He didn't deserve to be called the vice president. He was an animal. A psychopath.

And for Trapp, this one was personal.

Jenkins probably didn't even know Ryan Price's name. But he had sent him to die despite that. And now it was time for the man to pay for his crimes.

"What do you want?" Jenkins whimpered, reaching for his Scotch and downing it in one. Whether his eyes watered from the alcoholic burn or from fear, Trapp didn't know.

"I'm here for you, Bobby," Trapp replied, reveling in bringing the man down a peg. "I'm here to make you pay for what you've done."

Jenkins shook his head. "You can't. I'm the vice president, for God's sake."

Trapp bared his teeth. He didn't ordinarily take so much personal pleasure in confronting a target like this. But then they had rarely caused him so much personal pain.

"Correction, Bobby," he chuckled. "You *were* the vice president. Now you're mine."

Trapp watched as the pitiful excuse for an American in front of him searched for a way out. He saw the wheels in Jenkins's slippery politician's mind began to turn. Begin to examine the situation, probe it, looking for a weakness in Trapp's argument. He would not find one.

"What do you want?" Jenkins asked, a fervent light shining behind his eyes. "Money? Power? Whatever you want, it's yours." He turned to the bank of monitors in front of him. "You know what this is?"

Trapp shrugged. "I have an idea."

"It's every secret the NSA has ever collected. From this room I can tap into their files, even the ones they swear to Congress don't exist. I can read transcripts of the last President's evening phone call to his kids. The dirty voicemails he leaves his wife. I can tell you what Senator Whitehead ate for dinner, and how much he paid the whore he screwed for dessert. You can't possibly understand the kind of power that exists from knowing a man's most intimate secrets."

"I don't want your money," Trapp said, flexing his fingers around the pistol. It was still held level, aimed between the sniveling politician's eyes.

"Power, then," Jenkins said, grasping for the next arrow in his quiver. "Whatever you want, it's yours. I can make you a king."

"I told you," Trapp said. "I don't want your blood money, and I don't want your secrets. I want you dead. You took something from me, and it's time I returned the favor."

That shut Jenkins up. He wasn't used to dealing with men did what they did not for money, but for loyalty to their country. It was a desire that a man as venal as Jenkins could never hope to understand.

"What are you talking about?" Jenkins moaned.

Trapp scowled. He thought back to his childhood. Of wrapping his hands around his violent, abusive, rapist father's throat and squeezing until the light went out in that murderer's eyes. Of living on the streets, stealing to survive and drinking to forget. His fingers tightened around the grip of his pistol. The weapon trembled with barely suppressed rage.

And then he thought of Ryan Price. The boy he'd met in basic training, and the man who saved his life. And whose own had been stolen in turn.

"Yemen. Six months ago. You tried to kill me."

Jenkins shook his head.

"Don't lie. You stole something from me. Something I can never get back."

"I didn't," Jenkins whimpered.

Trapp stepped forward, gripping Jenkins's throat with his left hand, squeezing the man's windpipe until his face went blue. He pressed the pistol against Jenkins's forehead and applied all his strength to the point of the barrel. The vice president moaned with pain, his lungs convulsing in a desperate search for oxygen.

Trapp took a calculated step back and lowered his weapon slightly. He bit his lip, aware that he was giving a performance, and he needed to sell this part very carefully. Jenkins sucked in great lungfuls of air, slumped against his seat, legs limp against the ground.

"But," he said. "Your fate is not *entirely* within my power."

"You can't kill me," Jenkins replied, his voice still sounding strangled. "There's no way Nash would greenlight something like that."

Trapp grimaced. This was the worst kind of Washington horse trading. It was reprehensible. The idea that a man like Robert Jenkins could simply get off scot-free for what he had done, when a normal American would go to prison for life for committing even a thousandth of his crimes. But that, sadly, was the way America was going. It was becoming a country where rich men and politicians didn't have to face the same justice as ordinary Americans.

It disgusted Trapp.

"The President sent me to offer you a deal," Trapp said, making his displeasure with the situation abundantly clear. "Believe me, I would rather kill you, but the powers that be have decided that putting a bullet in your head would be too much pain for the country to bear."

Jenkins studied Trapp carefully, massaging his throat in what seemed an attempt to disguise the trembling in his fingers. He nodded once. "I believe you. And a trial would be too embarrassing, I presume?"

Trapp nodded.

"President Nash is prepared to offer you both your life and your freedom," Trapp said, speaking slowly, loading the words with disgust.

"And what does Nash want in return?"

"That's President Nash," Trapp snapped, his weapon shaking with anger. "You piece of shit."

"President Nash, then," Jenkins replied. Now that he knew he wasn't going to die, some of that old arrogance was beginning to return. Trapp could see it in his eyes. "What does he want from me?"

"Names. Your accomplices. Who financed this thing. We know you couldn't have pulled the whole thing off alone. In exchange for telling us everything you know, I promise that I will not put a bullet in your forehead. You will resign your office and live the rest of your life on this ranch."

Trapp paused, studying the impact his words had had on Jenkins's demeanor. The man had recovered most of his cool, which was in a way impressive, given the panic that had consumed him just moments before.

"So," he said, "do we have a deal?"

BY THE TIME Trapp turned the video recorder off, Jenkins had sung like a canary. Trapp had no doubt that the slippery politician had held back certain details and altered other stories to paint himself in a better light. But Trapp was satisfied. He had what he needed. Enough names, dates, locations and computer passwords to keep the dream team of Kyle Partey and Dr. Timothy Greaves occupied for months. Jenkins was the head of the snake, the only one who truly mattered. But there were those—financiers, industrialists—who would have benefited from a Robert Jenkins administration. They would have to pay. And they would.

"So what now?" Jenkins asked.

His legs were crossed in an almost jaunty pose. That old swagger had returned. He was cradling a fresh Scotch, sure that while his plan had failed, he had survived the worst consequences of that failure. He thought himself safe from America's justice.

And he was.

Trapp retrieved a sheet of paper from a folder in his rucksack and slid it in front of the Vice President. Almost as an afterthought, he pulled a pen from his pocket and tossed it onto Jenkins's desk. "You sign this."

Jenkins glanced at the piece of paper. It was already typed up, just waiting for his signature. He came to the eyebrow. "Treason?"

"What else would you call it?" Trapp fired back.

Jenkins shrugged. "Patriotism?"

Trapp retrieved his pistol from the holster in which it currently sat. "Don't make me shoot you, Bob. I don't like to go back on my word. You're about as patriotic as the gum stuck to the sole of my boot. Tell yourself whatever story you want, but don't expect me to listen."

"Have it your way," Jenkins replied. He picked up the pen and removed its cap. The pen hovered in the air for a second, and then Jenkins signed the paper with thick, decisive strokes. "What story are you planning on putting out in the press?"

Trapp walked over to the desk, slid the piece of paper back toward him, and slid it into a plastic bag he pulled from his pocket. Taking another bag, he turned it inside out and picked up the pen and its cap.

"What are you doing?" Jenkins asked, his voice sounding strained. Trapp glanced up and watched the man's eyes following his movements. He took a step back, sealing the bags and placing them in his rucksack.

"I told you I wouldn't shoot you, Bobby," Trapp grinned. "And I held up my end of the bargain. Usually I prefer not to use poison. But you are a special case. Can't have the vice president dying in an airless hole with a bullet wound in his forehead. Would raise too many questions."

"Poison?" Jenkins panted, sweat coating his forehead. "You promised –"

Trapp didn't turn to anger. It wasn't necessary. He had vengeance now, for Ryan Price's death, and for the deaths of so many other Americans. This wasn't just America's justice; it was his own.

"It's Russian," he said as he packed up the last of his equipment. "They really do make the best stuff. We think it was designed in a KGB lab sometime in the '80s. A defector brought it over after the Berlin Wall came down. They called it K2. Stands for some long chemical formula; I'm no expert. The boys back at the Agency coated that pen with it. So I suppose you could say you signed your own death warrant."

"How long?" Jenkins choked.

"A couple of minutes," Trapp replied, turning to leave. He turned his head to look at the paralyzed former vice president. The man's face was red. The nerve agent had severed his fine motor control. He was effectively a vegetable already, he just didn't know it yet.

"It'll look like a heart attack. After the stress of a long campaign, and the last few days..." He shook his head. "So tragic. But people will move on."

"You'll pay for this."

Trapp stepped out of the door to the basement. He didn't bother replying. About twenty seconds later, after he had traversed a long corridor, he nodded at a Secret Service agent with his hands folded across his waist. The man's eyes tracked Trapp the whole way, but he did not move. He had his orders, and he intended to follow them.

Trapp didn't feel so much elated as relieved. It never felt good to kill a man, even one who deserved it as much as Robert Jenkins did. That way lay madness. But he was satisfied with a job well done.

Justice had been served.

59

President Charles Nash looked up as his Chief of Staff Emma Martinez entered the President's Room. The room, as an usher had so proudly told him several hours before, was one of the most ornate in the entire Capitol Building, with fresco paintings by the Italian artist Constantino Brumidi. Whoever Brumidi was.

Though the space was not reserved for the President's sole use—ambitious senators liked to use the room's sumptuous decoration as a background for their press conferences—the President nonetheless used the room before addressing Congress.

The short, Hispanic woman wore an expression of relief that transmitted to her boss before she even opened her mouth.

"Mr. President – it's over."

Nash let his head drop backward, a wave of release draining the tension from his body. This was not how he had wanted his presidency to start. America had been consumed by a wave of fire and blood. He had wanted to rebuild America—that much was true—but not from the effects of guns and bombs and death.

But that wasn't his choice. A president could only respond to the hand he or she was dealt. Nash just hoped that he had risen to the challenge presented him, not shrunk before it. He had been presented with a decision that no president before him had ever faced – a conspiracy to replace him not through politics, not with an election, but by force.

And the person responsible was his own running mate, Robert Jenkins. If the country ever found out, it might tear itself apart. Nash could not allow that to happen. It was a secret that he would take with him to the grave.

The President molded his features into an expression of shocked pleasure. He was a consummate actor—you had to be when running for president. Not to fool people, but because there were days where you really did not want to kiss that baby. But you had to suck it up. Both he and Martinez knew the truth of that evening's events – but the Secret Service agents did not. Could never. Nor could any ordinary American. The psychological scar would be too great to bear.

"What happened?"

"The FBI just took down a cell of domestic terrorists on the National Mall. They had somehow acquired Secret Service vehicles and uniforms and were planning on assaulting the House Chamber during your speech. There was another shooter, too. Disguised as a member of the Capitol Police. Secret Service just apprehended him quietly."

"MY FELLOW AMERICANS. I come before you today with a heavy heart, but also with a message of hope. With my consent, the Federal Bureau of Investigation only moments ago apprehended a cell of domestic terrorists who had intended to attack this very building. I was their target, along with the many brave and hard-working people who keep this place running."

Nash looked out across the House chamber. The represen-tatives, senators, and onlookers were staring up at him with barely disguised horror. They had never thought themselves personally at risk. Danger was for other people. These politi-cians lived in a bubble of wealth and gilded privilege, and the idea that someone had planned to puncture that was almost too difficult for them to believe.

Perhaps that was the message the terrorists were trying to convey – whether they knew it or not. It was the message that Nash had received.

He was going to shake up this town. Not in the way the terrorists intended. And not tonight. But he was going to get America working for her people again, rather than the people working for the benefit of the men and women who inhabited places like this.

Nash gripped the lectern, realizing he had been silent for too long. An uneasy titter ran around the vast chamber.

"I had intended to speak to you today about my program for rebuilding America. But today is not the right time. Today is a time for quiet reflection. A time for remembering those we have lost. A time for deciding how we will repay their sacrifice. I pledge to you, the American people, that I will not rest until this country is once again the greatest in the world. Not just for the rich. Not just for the privileged. But for you.

"Thank you, and God bless these United States of America."

60

According to the American Civil Liberties Union, a body that is deeply opposed to the use of both solitary confinement and capital punishment, the daily cost of incarcerating a prisoner at the Federal Supermax facility ADX Florence is $216.16. That comes out to $78,840 per year.

Andrew Rawlin had been transferred to Florence several days before. He was indicted on over four hundred counts of first-degree murder, as well as charges of treason against the United States of America. He knew that whatever happened he would spend the rest of his life behind bars.

"Step forward," a guard said. Rawlin did so, taking a pace forward and standing on a spot marked with an X just in front of his cell door. It was a routine with which he had already become intimately accustomed.

The guard pointed at the spot. "You don't move until I tell you to, understood?"

"Yes, boss."

The guard leaned forward, pressing his stubbled face against Rawlin's own. "Did I say you could speak?"

But for all of his bravado, all of his protestations to the

contrary, for all these new daily humiliations, it was better than death. It had to be.

Andrew Rawlin feared the eternal darkness that came after this life. When he slept at night—*if he slept,* under the harsh lights that burned twenty-four hours a day in his cell—he heard the gunfire in that Houston church. He saw bodies falling, spattered with blood.

Rawlin was not a good man. This was not guilt, exactly, but the natural rejection of any human mind when faced with a slaughter on that scale. It is not for anything that the Lord commanded, *Thou shalt not kill.* Murder changes a man, like an acid corroding away at the soul.

And that many murders will eat away until there is nothing left. On the outside, if he had remained a free man, Rawlin would probably have found the bottle, just like his parents had. He would have ended his days with his skin yellow and his liver destroyed.

But he was not on the outside. He was currently federal prisoner 753-7821, and he would cost the federal government $78,840 per year until the day he died. Plus inflation. The government would try to speed things along, of course. The evidence against Rawlin was incontrovertible. He had livestreamed himself cutting down hundreds of innocent civilians in a Texas church. He had been found several days later preparing to assassinate the President of the United States himself, caught literally red-handed.

But as Rawlin's lawyer had informed him, the wheels of justice turn slow. There would be a trial. Appeals. Appeals after the appeals. Pleas of insanity. Perhaps they would work, and he would spend the rest of his days in a mental institution.

Still better than death, Rawlin thought. And after all, maybe they would dope him up. Give him a pill that would allow him to sleep through the night. A pill that would block out the sound of gunfire and screams.

Rawlin shook himself out of his reverie. He was still coming to terms with the prospect of spending the rest of his life behind bars. The food was crap. The bed was worse. ADX Florence was the kind of prison the ACLU hated. Its inhabitants never even saw another prisoner – the doors to the cells and the hallways were controlled automatically, and the electronic bracelet each man wore around his ankle would not permit two inmates to inhabit the same space at the same time. At least, Rawlin thought, he was safe. After the things he had done, in any other prison he would have been public enemy number one. General population would be a ticket to hell, but there was no genpop in Florence.

Just solitary.

Rawlin looked left and right at the cell doors that stretched down the white-painted hallway and wondered why the guard had left him alone. It was a bit like the army, he thought. A lot of hurry up and wait. He shrugged. He couldn't do anything about it, and it wasn't worth worrying about. Someone would come and collect him soon enough.

Maybe he had a visitor. His lawyer, maybe. Now wouldn't that be a treat.

Finally, Rawlin's thoughts turned to his best friend, Darren Gibson. He could still feel the cold metal of his pistol grip beneath his fingers, see the look of surprise on his friend's face, and the horror in his eyes as he had raised the weapon.

No loose ends.

Rawlin started with surprise as he realized that that was exactly what he was. A loose end. The rest of his men had known little of the plan. They went where he told them to, did exactly as they were ordered. He had done the same, of course, but at least he had known his benefactor's goals.

To his left, Rawlin heard the buzzing of a cell door. And then another. And a third.

"What the hell?"

His pulse began to thunder, his palms suddenly slick with sweat. This shouldn't be happening. Couldn't be happening. His lawyer had told him, hadn't he? Told him that he would never see another prisoner as long as he was incarcerated at Florence. It was the safest place in the US Federal Penitentiary System, that's what the man had said.

The first cell door swung open. A man stepped out. He was wearing gray sweatpants and a white T-shirt, just like Rawlin himself. But against the man's black skin, the clothes seemed to stand out as if they were freshly bleached.

Terror conquered Rawlin's mind. He knew what was happening. This couldn't be an accident. He tried to take a step back, but his legs would not oblige. They seemed locked to the floor with fright, as though they were held down by immovable chains.

"Please," Rawlin begged. "I'll do whatever you want."

He knew he would do anything to survive. Things that sickened him, things that just weeks before he would never have considered, even in his darkest moments. If these men ordered him to, he would debase himself, and he would do it with pride. Anything to live another day.

But as the man was joined by two fellow prisoners, Rawlin knew that he would not be given the choice. These men were looking for revenge.

"I'm sorry," he whispered.

In the end, the warden's report would mention a critical breakdown in prison procedures. It would not mention the phone call he'd placed shortly after the three prisoners were locked back into their cells, a phone call placed to a secure number that led directly to the Resolute Desk in the Oval Office of the White House.

It would not mention the leniency Rawlin's killers would eventually be given by the Department of Justice, nor the free rein they would be given with any fast food they wanted for the next year. Even a cold beer from time to time.

In fact, after the ACLU registered a formal complaint, the warden would point out that if solitary confinement had worked as it was intended to, Andrew Rawlin would still be alive.

But to no one's great sorrow, he was not.

61

J ason Trapp was wearing a tie, and he didn't like it. Suits he didn't mind. Preferably well-tailored, expensive and Italian. In his experience, a well-cut suit was a good way to impress the ladies. But he was more of an open collar kind of guy. The tie felt like it was cutting off his oxygen supply, but at least it hid the scar around his neck.

There were not very many men for whom Trapp would don a silk noose. Even the men and women on the seventh floor at Langley did not qualify. But the man who had just entered the sub-basement beneath the White House certainly did.

His name was Charles Nash, and he was the President of the United States. Trapp had done everything in his power to ensure that remained the case. And he knew that he would do so again. From everything he'd seen, Nash was a good man. A man with a plan that might actually fix America. And he deserved a chance to at least try.

"You must be Trapp," the President said, a grin stretching across his movie-star handsome face as he reached out his hand. Trapp shook it. "I hear I owe you my life."

Trapp felt an unaccustomed wave of embarrassment

heating his face. He wasn't used to meeting the men and women he saved. That was the whole point in being an under-cover asset. You were a ghost. If you did your job right, the person you saved never even knew they had a guardian angel.

But things worked a little differently when it came to the presidency. There were very few people in the chain of command who had the power to compel Jason Trapp to attend the meeting. Certainly not one with his face uncovered.

President Nash was one of them.

"Yes sir," Trapp replied. He kept his answers short and sweet. He figured that way he had the smallest chance of saying something stupid. "I'm glad I could help. But I didn't do very much." He gestured at the row of people standing next to him. "It was a team effort."

"Ah, yes," Nash said with a smile on his face like a five-year-old meeting a superhero. "Nadine Carter, Mike Mitchell, Kyle Partey, Redneck and Sketch. And of course, the famous Dr. Timothy Greaves."

He counted each name off on his fingers. As he finished, he shook his head, as if with astonishment. "Your country owes you all a great debt. Though I am afraid to say that outside of this room, and a select few others, very few people will ever know your names."

Trapp grinned. He couldn't help himself. "There's a silver lining after all, Mr. President."

Nash returned his smile. "You know, son," he said. "I'd like to think I was like you once, back in the Marines. But I know that would just be flattering myself. Back then, all I thought about was fast cars, beers, and chasing women. Hopefully not all at the same time."

He winked.

"But you, Trapp. You are nothing like me. I read your file. Even the bits the Agency didn't want to send over. If I had done half the things you have, I'd be a shoe-in for re-election in four years' time. You're a real goddamn American hero, you know that?"

Trapp cleared his throat instead of responding. He wished the floor beneath him would swallow him up.

Nash choked back a laugh. "Don't worry, I'll get you out of here soon enough. We just have to deal with the formalities."

Trapp kinked an eyebrow. "Formalities, sir?"

Nash waved his hand airily. "You know, I've been President for less than a month, and I'm already finding out that it's not nearly as fun as I thought it would be."

Trapp didn't know where this was going. But if there was one thing you learned in the military, it was to agree with senior officers. Trapp wasn't in the army anymore, but he figured the President was about as senior as it got.

"Yes, sir."

"You can cut that out, too. Call me Charlie. Least I can do for the man who saved my life."

"Yes, Mr. President. I'll bear that under advisement."

Nash rolled his eyes. "To the formalities then, Mr. Trapp."

He glanced backward at an aide hovering near the door to the basement. The woman walked forward, looking at the lineup of heroes alongside Trapp with open-mouthed amazement. She was carrying a small black leather case. As she reached the President, she clicked open the latch and handed it to him.

"Mr. Mitchell. Mr. Perkins. Mr. Winks. Mr. Partey. You went above and beyond the call of duty over the past few weeks, at great personal risk to not only your careers, but your lives. It is not just your country that owes you a debt of gratitude, but me as well."

Nash paused, opened the leather case, and removed something small.

"I'm afraid that as you men well know, no one will ever learn about your exploits. As far as the general public knows, my dear departed former running mate"—Nash's lips curled with distaste at the mere mention of the man's name—"died of a sudden heart attack at his desk, precipitated by the stress of the preceding few days.

"That is how it must remain. If the country learned how close a man like that had come to the launch codes, I am not sure our country could survive. But I am committed to present you with a small token of my appreciation. Michael, if you could step forward."

The former—and now restored—deputy director of the Central Intelligence Agency's Special Activities Division, Mike Mitchell, did as he was ordered.

"Michael, I am pleased to award you the Distinguished Intelligence Medal."

Trapp knew that it was the second highest award for valor the US intelligence community had at its disposal. And even though he had wanted to kill Mitchell no more than a couple of weeks before, he now realized that it couldn't have gone to a better man.

As the President pinned the decoration onto his suit jacket, Mitchell smiled. "Thank you, sir. It's an honor."

"Believe me, Mike. The honor is all mine."

Trapp believed the words as they escaped the President's mouth, and there were very few politicians he would say that about. He watched as the man awarded three more Intelligence Medals.

He was glad that Nash didn't call his name out, too. The last thing he needed was another trinket. Although at least the CIA's intelligence medals had the advantage that they wouldn't clutter up his possessions – he had no doubt that someone would take the thing off him before he was allowed to leave the room.

Only in Washington could something like that make sense.

"Now, Ms. Carter," Nash said, turning to Dani. "As I understand it, your role in this was pivotal. Great acting in the Situation Room, by the way – I'm not sure I could have contained myself, knowing what you did about Jenkins. You ever think of moving to Hollywood?"

Dani grinned. Trapp couldn't help but think how attractive she was, especially now that the worst of her injuries had healed. A deep scrape across her face had left scar tissue in its place – white against her golden brown complexion. He liked that she wasn't a makeup kind of girl. She hadn't tried to cover it up. But neither was she showing it off. The injury just...

Was.

It was a part of her now. And he liked that. He wasn't sure he was ready for a relationship yet. But maybe someday.

"No, Mr. President," she said. "I'm pretty happy here in Washington."

"You're about the only one," Nash joked. "The director speaks very highly of you. I think you have a very successful career ahead of you indeed. And I heard about your father. How is he?"

"Thank you, sir. He's getting better. Should be out of the hospital any day now."

"That's great," Nash said, with a genuine flash of his million-dollar smile. "If there's anything I can do with the VA to speed up his care, just let me know."

"That means a lot, Mr President. But the old man would hate to get any special treatment. He'll be just fine."

"I bet he will," Nash replied. "I bet he will."

He pivoted, and turned to the next member of their secret unit.

Greaves just looked like he wanted to be anywhere in the world except for this room. He was squashed into a gray suit that might have fit him at his high school graduation, but certainly wasn't sufficient now.

"Dr. Greaves," the President said, "is there anything I can do for you? It seems that you played a vital role in all of this. If you hadn't figured out that backdoor into Jenkins's system, then I would most likely be a dead man right now, along with most of Congress. Although"—his eyes glittered with amusement—"there are those who think that might not be such a bad thing..."

"Honestly, Charlie," Greaves said, before his eyes bulged wide as he realized what he'd said. "Oh, shit, I mean –"

Nash waved the mistake away with a laugh. He shot Trapp a mock-serious look. "At least someone will use my real name. I wouldn't worry about it, Doctor."

"Yes, sir," Greaves replied with relief.

Nash raised an eyebrow. "You were saying?"

Greaves wiped sweaty palms on his jacket. "Mr. President, I just want to get back to work. Someone penetrated my system, and I won't sleep easy at night until I know how they did it, and whether all traces of them are gone."

Nash frowned. "You're saying that Jenkins wasn't working alone?"

"Oh we know he wasn't, sir." Greaves shrugged. "And if you don't mind me saying, every second I'm not behind my keyboard is a one where I'm not finding out where the bastards are."

Nash chuckled. "You don't get out much, do you, Doctor?"

"No, Mr. President."

"Sounds like that's a good thing for our country, at least. Dr. Greaves, you have my word that you will be given every resource you require. Happy hunting."

That, Trapp realized, just left him. He had a sinking feeling in his stomach as the President turned to him, retrieving a final item from the little black case before handing it back to the aide. He realized with sourness that the President knew exactly how uncomfortable he felt and was enjoying every minute of it.

"And last but not least, of course," Nash said, striding up with childlike glee. "That leaves you, Mr. Trapp."

"Sir, if you don't mind, I'd like to get back to –"

"I'm sure you would, Jason." Nash grinned. "But there's this little thing called the chain of command, so if you don't mind?"

Trapp returned the smile. "The thing is, sir, *technically speaking* I am dead. And since dead men don't have to follow orders, maybe we could dispense with this last part?"

Nash shook his head. "I think not. Jason, it is my distinct privilege to award you with the Distinguished Intelligence Cross. What I will *dispense with*, though," he said with a wry smile, "is the speech. We both know what you did. And if there really are more conspirators out there, then I'd rather have you out there hunting them than in here with me. How does that sound?"

Now that was more like it. Trapp replied with gusto this time, as the President pinned the CIA's highest award for bravery onto his suit jacket. "Pretty good to me, Mr. President."

62

Jason Trapp walked into the bar on Prince Street in Boston for a second time. He was exhausted, having stopped on the way to pay one last visit to the former speaker of the House of Representatives. Randall had resigned his office and pledged his entire fortune to victims of the attacks of the previous few weeks. Trapp figured it was the least the conniving weasel could do.

This time, he carried nothing but himself and a faint sense of nervousness in his gut. The door was still open, but the "We're open" sign was reversed, and the lights inside blazing, rather than half dimmed. The bar smelled of male sweat and spilled beer, and still felt warm from the press of bodies that had occupied it not so long before.

"Hey, buddy," someone called out in a lilting Boston accent as the door swung closed behind him. "You can't read? We ain't open."

The voice belonged to Joshua Price, and he was the man Trapp had come to see. Just like last time, Price's height jumped out at Trapp. That, and those piercing blue eyes he remembered so well.

The look of irritation on Price's tired, lined face disappeared as he looked up at the man who had entered his bar. It wasn't replaced with one of recognition, but confusion, as the barman's brain struggled to remember where he had seen this visitor before. Joshua Price was good with names, always had been. It was a trait his brother had shared.

"Do I recognize you?" he asked, squinting up at Trapp.

Trapp shrugged. "I left something with you."

The realization dawned on Joshua's face, and he nodded slowly. "You did. Near enough crapped myself when I opened it."

"What did you do with it?"

Joshua grinned, and jerked his thumb toward the door of a small supply closet behind the long wooden bar. "Put it back there."

"You weren't worried someone might steal it?"

"From here? No chance. People around here know me. They know I ain't got shit to steal."

"You do now."

Joshua Price didn't reply to that comment. The only sign he had heard it at all was a slight flicker at his temple, perhaps a momentary glance at the ground. "Can I get you a beer?"

"That'd be good."

Joshua disappeared behind the bar and returned a moment later with two bottles of Budweiser, just like last time. He handed one to Trapp, and they clinked the glass together. Trapp took a long drag on the bottle, and Joshua did the same. They stood there for a second, neither knowing what to say, but both knowing why the other was there.

Joshua was the first to break the silence. "I wondered if you would show up," he said.

"I took my time."

"I thought I recognized you, you know, the first time. That Monday. Thought I was going crazy, but you looked just like he said. And when you charged off into the gunfire, I knew I was right."

Trapp grinned. "He always did have a big mouth, your brother. Wasn't supposed to say a damn thing about me."

"Ain't that the truth."

Joshua took another long sip of beer. He looked Trapp in the eye, holding his gaze for a long moment. "I don't want your money, man. It's yours. You earned it. Wait right here, and I'll go get it."

Trapp reached over and grabbed the man's forearm. "It's not my money. It was Ryan's. I just did my duty bringing it to you, like he'd have done me." He glanced around the bar and grinned. "And besides, looks like this place could use a bit of an upgrade."

Joshua smiled ruefully. "You could say that. I've been meaning to close for a couple of weeks, get my hands dirty and fix this old bar up, but I couldn't afford to shut the doors, you know?"

Trapp sat there, leaning against the table for a long while, lost in thought. It had been a long time since he'd felt this at peace. He had done a good thing for once. A week from now, or a month, he would need to return to work. Greaves and Mitchell were uncovering more co-conspirators by the day, and each required justice to be delivered. But he had all the time in the world.

"Would you mind if I stayed here awhile?" he asked. "Maybe give you a hand doing this place up. Looks like you could use it, and I could use the company, if you know what I mean."

"I think I do." Joshua nodded slowly. "Ryan was the same, you know. After he came back from wherever you two went. Isn't easy on the man's soul, that kind of work. He never told me your name, you know. Nor what you did. It was like getting blood from a stone."

"Tell me about him," Trapp said, wanting to change the topic, and not, all at once. Maybe they would swing around to it after a time. You work with a man for a week, you'll bare your soul to him. Trapp hadn't had anyone like that since Ryan died. "When he was growing up, I mean."

Joshua stood up and walked a couple of paces toward the bar, then turned back. "Tell you what, let's make a deal. You go lock up, I'll get a couple more beers, and we can trade stories about the dumb grunt till the sun comes up. And," he said, shooting Jason a piercing stare, "maybe we can talk about the money. I can't take all of it, not in good conscience. But if you're really looking to wash your hands of it, I could use a silent partner in the bar..."

Trapp frowned. He'd considered that money burned a long time ago. He had no need for it, and no particular desire to take it back. But he liked Joshua, and the man reminded him of his fallen brother. He couldn't think of a better way to remember his old friend. He reached out his hand, and Joshua Price shook it firmly.

"Sounds about right to me."

ALSO BY JACK SLATER

They say revenge is a dish best served cold.

But Jason Trapp is losing his taste for it. For six months, his personal crusade has taken him around the world, mopping up the last of the Bloody Monday conspirators. There's only one left, and after the crooked financier Emmanuel Alstyne meets his maker, Trapp's debt will be paid in full. He vows he's done with the business of death.

Unfortunately, it isn't done with him.

After a simple kill mission goes sideways in Macau, leaving a CIA spy kidnapped, half a dozen Chinese agents dead, and America's satellites burning in the skies, Trapp is propelled back into the game. Eliza Ikeda was taken on his watch, and he's determined to get her back–no matter the cost. The problem is, he has no idea who took her, why, or what they plan to do next.

Trapp knows he's being played. And with the world's only two superpowers hurtling toward the precipice of war, time is running out...

Retirement will have to wait.

Trapp is back in action. And this time, it's personal.

Head to Amazon to read False Flag, book two in the *Jason Trapp* thriller series.

FOR ALL THE LATEST NEWS

I hope you enjoyed Dark State. If you did, and don't fancy sifting through thousands of books on Amazon and leaving your next great read to chance, then sign up to my mailing list and be the first to hear when I release a new book.

Visit - www.jack-slater.com/updates

And keep reading if you want to learn more about the real-life inspiration that led me to write *Dark State*...

Thanks so much for reading!

Jack.

AUTHOR'S NOTE

If you've read this far, then I hope that means you enjoyed *Dark State*, as opposed to hate-reading just to get to the end!

As this is my first published thriller, I wanted to write a short note to thank you for reading. Pouring several months of one's life into a story is no easy task, mostly because there are hundreds of tasks – ones I'd normally find onerous – that I seem to complete before sitting down in front of the computer to write!

My apartment has never been so clean, so frequently vacuumed, the windows so sparkling or the kitchen so polished as it has been over the course of the past year! It gets me brownie points at home, but definitely doesn't help me get the words down on the page...

It's not the writing part which I find difficult. I'm a bit of a bull in a china shop – I charged forward, with a vague idea of where I wanted to take Jason, along with a raft of other characters, many of whom did not make it into the final draft. It's the second part – editing – that slows me down. Making sure the right words are used at the right time in the right place is significantly more difficult than I could have ever imagined – and I have more respect for the authors I read than ever before.

All that said, writing a novel really is fantastic fun. I get to spend hours every day in a world of my own creation, with people who do exactly as I tell them (mostly), and indulging my imagination in a way that I wouldn't otherwise get to do.

Sometimes that leads me into dark places – there are definitely some scenes in *Dark State* that are very chilling, and the opening chapter to the upcoming sequel, *False Flag* is hard to read, let alone write! Sadly, though, we live in a hard world. My writing is drawn from real-life events, not just (thankfully) at home, but all around the world. Jason Trapp is a product of his unique background and environment, and he's far from perfect. But so is the world he comes from.

I also like to add a healthy sprinkle of both futurism and reality into my writing. I think that's something you'll see to some extent in every book I write. While the NSA's Utah Data Center is a real place, it really is nicknamed the Bumblehive, and it really does have a power station on-site capable of generating enough electricity for sixty-five thousand homes, there is as far as I know no Birdseye program. My inspiration was drawn from the files J Edgar Hoover is said to have kept on America's politicians – dirt he could deploy when and where he chose.

I wonder how Hoover would react today, where every phone call, text message, bank transfer or plane ticket is simply an electronic transmission that passes through one of the NSA's many listening stations. Would he have been able to resist the lure of that information? Can we really believe that our leaders and politicians do so today, or that they will continue to do so in the future?

Maybe.

But then again, maybe not.

At 611 Folsom St., San Francisco, AT&T operates a facility

which carries "backbone traffic" for the entire Internet – basically, much of the Internet data on the West Coast goes through this building. Somewhere in the building is located Room 641a – an otherwise unprepossessing room in a dingy hallway, and no obvious doorknob. The room measures 24' x 48', and contains equipment designed to intercept all traffic that passes through the building. It is believed that facilities like 611 Folsom and Room 641a exist across the country.

The other fascinating area of interest I learned about whilst researching this book was the quickly emerging field of "deepfakes". Let's be honest, we all know that the NSA is listening to everything we say, whether they are *technically* supposed to or not. It might not be 100% legal, but my life is so boring most of the time that they aren't going to discover anything interesting! And since these scaled up data collection activities have been going on for a couple of decades at least, they aren't at the forefront of people's imaginations these days.

Deepfakes, I fear, are about to be. We all know that we can't exactly trust photographs. Photoshop has been around for coming on thirty years, and in an expert's hands, that piece of software can manipulate and merge photos in ways that can fool the human mind. It's not just touching up a model's face before she goes on the cover of Vogue, but inserting people into photos they were were never in, or removing them from history entirely. Very 1984...

A deepfake is along the same lines as a photoshopped image, but done with video footage. Search "Bruce Lee Matrix Deepfake" on YouTube, and you'll see what I mean. It's now possible to almost perfectly superimpose someone else's face onto live video, using highly advanced computer graphics engines. I used this concept in a scene in *Dark State* to great effect, in order to put pressure on Speaker Randall Woods. The technology is about 99% of the way there – it looks amazing, but it's still possible to see that the video has been faked. It also requires a significant database of video footage in order to create the facsimile. But I don't think we are very far away from a future in which video can be manipulated at will, by anyone with a fast laptop.

And that is a very scary future indeed.

So – what can you expect from Jason Trapp?

While writing *Dark State*, I ended up putting pen to paper (or fingers to keyboard) on over a dozen chapters that didn't make it into the final manuscript, along with completely rewriting a dozen more, and making substantial changes to most of the book. In essence, I spent about a month writing chapters that – had I planned better – I would have known didn't make sense for the core story. I might have introduced characters better, and not been forced to go back and rewrite their introductions. I might have done many things better.

That said, it has been a great learning experience, and I wouldn't change it for the world. (Okay, weeks of editing time could probably have been avoided, but still...)

False Flag sees Jason beyond America's borders, fighting a new enemy with apocalyptic intentions, alongside friends as well as a few old ones. It has been a blast to write, and researching it has taken me down some fascinating rabbit holes. Not all of them strictly speaking essential to the plot, but fascinating nonetheless.

It's also extremely action-packed, with twists and turns around every corner, and Trapp in peril from the word go. And the good news is, you can read it right now by searching "False Flag" on the Amazon.

If you enjoyed *Dark State*, it would mean a lot to me if you could leave a review. I read every single one – even the bad ones – and they really do help drive me on when I'm mired in a particularly recalcitrant chapter. Writing is a lonely pursuit, and spending four or five hours a day behind a computer screen on my fiction is sometimes enough to make me forget there's a real world out there. Reviews help remind me that people are actually reading my words!

Of course, if you're thinking about leaving me a one-star, because there was something you really hated, why not email me at Jack@Jack-Slater.com, and let me know directly instead. The beautiful thing about modern-day publishing is that my manuscript is not a chiseled stone tablet. If I made a mistake, I assure you it was one of oversight rather than malice – and it's one that technology thankfully allows me to correct.

In fact, feedback from all sources is always welcome. I personally read every email that comes into my inbox, and everything feeds into my ongoing writing. If you have a "very particular set of skills", to crib from Liam Neeson, I would love to hear from you.

All my best,
Jack Slater

ACKNOWLEDGMENTS

And last but definitely not least, I'd like to express the deepest of thanks to my wonderful editor Kasi, along with the best beta readers anyone could ask for.

Special thanks to:

Julie
Sheri
Jessica
Bianca
Belinda
Rich
Judy
Greg
George
Andrew
Becky
Cheryl
RP
Carl
Angela
Hugh
Steve
Jeff
Chanda

and, drumroll please...
Kathryn!

DARK STATE IS AVAILABLE ON AUDIBLE!

If you're a keen audiobook listener, why not try *Dark State* on Audible? You can scan this QR code on your phone to be taken to the Audible page, or go directly to audible.com.

Printed in Great Britain
by Amazon